ROBIN JARVIS

INTRIGUES OF THE REFLECTED REALM

Deathscent

Collins

An imprint of HarperCollinsPublishers

Check out the official Robin Jarvis website at
www.robinjarvis.com

First published in Great Britain by Collins 2001
Collins is an imprint of HarperCollins*Publishers* Ltd
77-85 Fulham Palace Road, Hammersmith,
London, W6 8JB

The HarperCollins website address is:
www.**fire**and**water**.com

3 5 7 9 8 6 4 2

ISBN 0 00 185702 9

Robin Jarvis asserts the moral right to be identified as
the author and illustrator of the work.

Printed and bound in Great Britain by
Omnia Books Limited, Glasgow

CONTENTS

Two Gentlemen of Physic

redging his oars through the churning water, Natty Pykes grumbled under his breath. The pinching cold no longer pained his fingers; all feeling had long since been swept away by the deluge which hammered from the black heavens. It was a filthy, sousing October night. His cloak afforded little protection from the relentless rain and his hat slopped sadly about his ears. Through the driving downpour he stared at the two figures sitting in the stern of his boat and the storm stung his upturned face. Silently he cursed those gentlemen who had engaged him.

The city was lost far behind them now, its mobbing crowd of chimneys and steeples obliterated by the storm. Through the drenching dark the small craft laboured. Swinging behind, the lanthorn made sparks of the pelting waters, and the surface of the river spat and fizzed like scalding fat.

"'Tis enough to drown the fishes!" he cried, yearning to hear another voice besides that of the endless squall. "Quench the fires infernal, this would. We'll see no other on the river, not in this foulness. Must be an urgent errand to prise you good masters out of doors."

His passengers made no reply. Throughout this drenching journey neither of them had uttered a word, but Natty Pykes had been a waterman for eighteen years and was nobody's fool. As he ferried them ever further up the Thames, his shrewd and nimble mind made many quiet guesses. The large wooden apothecary box they carried was enough to tell him that they were men of physic and, judging by their attire, prosperous ones at that.

Deeper into that awful night they pressed and the hours curdled by. Natty knew only the drag of the oars and the protest of his back; all else he pushed from his thoughts until at last new sounds came to his grateful ears through the rain.

Urgent voices were calling and, turning stiffly, he

glimpsed the landing stage of Hampton jutting out into the river. Lanthorns and guttering torches were held aloft to guide him, and Natty eyed the waiting figures with interest.

Drawing closer, he saw among that restless gathering a man of high rank, whose chain of office glittered in the sputtering torchlight. As his boat pulled alongside the jetty, he knew that the grim expression fixed upon that noble's face was not caused by the storm alone.

Only when one of the palace guards hurried down the river steps to hold the craft steady did the waterman's passengers stir. Binding their cloaks even more tightly about their shoulders, and taking up the apothecary box, they rose. Then, with greater poise and balance than even Natty Pykes could have managed, they alighted. Over the stone stairs the hems of their dark, concealing mantles went sweeping as they ascended to the landing stage.

Natty wiped the rain from his face. "Goodnight to you, Masters," he called, reminding them he had not yet been paid.

The figures halted. One of them turned and a gloved hand appeared from the cloak's heavy folds. Winking bright and yellow, a coin came spinning down to splash in the rainwater which sloshed inside the boat around Natty's boots. The waterman snatched it up.

"A sovereign!" he declared, incredulous. "Black my eyes and call me a stinking Spaniard! A real, whole sovereign!"

Jumping to his feet so that the boat swayed violently

beneath him, he gave a whoop of joy. "Thank you, Masters! Thank you and bless you!"

But the strangers were already striding away, led by the man of rank and the sour-faced guards. Natty watched them march towards the great palace, its vast shape rising black and blind into the pelting night.

Lowering himself into the boat once more, he stared thoughtfully at the golden profile on the coin, now held tight within his callused fingers. His quick mind slotted the pieces of the puzzle together and he began to fathom the strangers' purpose.

"Lord help them this night," he prayed. "May they have the skill to save Her."

Then, putting the sovereign to his lips, Natty kissed it and began the long journey back to London.

Hurriedly, the two strangers were escorted into the palace of Hampton Court where their anxious guide introduced himself as Sir William Cecil, trusted adviser to the Queen. Hastening through the straw-strewn corridors, he rapidly acquainted them with the distressing news.

"Eight days," he announced, herding them past more guards and up a flight of steps. "Eight days *She* has lain abed. There is naught Her own physicians can do."

Their faces still muffled and hidden, the visitors listened but made no reply.

"The German doctor, Burcot," Cecil continued. "He claimed smallpox, but there are no eruptions. She called him a fool and had the impudent fellow thrown out. Yet now a fever has Her and all are sorely afraid. I almost summoned that knave to return till I was minded of you."

Briskly they passed through room after room, where grave-faced courtiers waited and watched, but Sir William and his mysterious guests swept by without acknowledgement.

"Even now the crows are gathering," the lord muttered.

In a grandly furnished bedchamber they halted. There, before a guarded doorway, Lord Cecil turned his grim, grey eyes to the tall newcomers.

"Gentlemen," he said solemnly, "into your care I entrust the hopes of Her subjects. For if you falter, then England will be flung into chaos and war. Above all else, do not fail *Her.*"

With that, he motioned the guards barring the way to stand aside; then, thrusting the door wide, he entered. Behind him the two strangers exchanged a meaningful glance and a violet gleam shone within the deep shadows of their broad-brimmed hats. Into the private bedchamber they stepped.

The room was smaller than the one they had left, but still richly adorned. Fine tapestries covered the panelled walls and sumptuous velvet drapes surrounded the carved oaken bed. But, although fresh rosemary scattered the floor, the air was thick and sickly. Crowding that place, and screening the figure upon the bed, was a crowd of austere-looking officials, each murmuring in despair-ridden, funereal voices.

At the sound of Lord Cecil's entry all heads turned and they stared questioningly at the two figures behind him.

"Fellow councillors," Sir William addressed them with a curt nod, "these are learned Masters of Physic, foreign scholars of whose skill I have heard much excellent report. I have asked them hither to see what may be done."

"Foreign?" repeated a stern-featured man, stepping closer to appraise them. "From whence?"

Cecil raised his hand. "Does it signify, My Lord Sussex?" he asked. "They are healers, let that be enough."

The other man glared at him. "I will not allow it," he hissed. "That German knave was rashness enough. Our enemies have many eager servants. Are you mad, Sir William?"

"Her own physicians are confounded," Cecil answered, glowering back. "What then? Consider carefully, My Lord, She is without issue and as like to die."

Pulling away from him, Sussex returned his hostile gaze to the strangers. "Make yourselves known," he demanded. "Remove your sodden wrappings that we may see what manner of men..."

Before he could finish, a snarling voice rang out within the room. Pushing his way from the bedside strode a young man almost as tall as Cecil's physicians. "Be still!" he cried. "Leave your wrangling outside this place, for I will have none of it here."

Gripping the hilt of his sword, the Queen's favourite, Lord Robert Dudley, cowed Sussex's remaining protests and bade the visitors welcome.

"If you truly have wisdom in this matter then I beg you to spare Her," he said. "Say only what you require and none shall hinder you."

Silently, the physicians moved forward, passing between the troubled councillors until they stood at the foot of the oaken bed.

At last they saw her – a slender woman lying beneath an embroidered coverlet – and their violet eyes glittered brightly.

In the year of Our Lord fifteen hundred and sixty-two, only three years since her coronation, Elizabeth Tudor was dying. She had indeed contracted the smallpox and, although her skin was as yet unblemished by the customary spots, the remainder of her life could be measured in hours. Propped up on the pillows, her oval face was deathly pale and framed by dark rivers of hair, made wet and lank by the sweat which streamed from her high forehead.

At either side of the bed knelt her two most trusted attendants, Lady Mary Sidney, Lord Robert's sister, and Katherine Ashley. The women had been praying for their mistress's immortal soul, but now they looked up at the physicians imploringly.

"The bloom of health is withered from Her face," Dudley mourned. "The fires I have known to blaze copper and golden in the strands of Her hair are extinguished. So it is with Her spirit. Tell me truthfully, Masters, are you come too late?"

Shifting their attention from the stricken figure in the bed, the strangers regarded him steadily.

Finally they spoke. Through the high, muffling collar of his cloak, the physician at Lord Robert's side said, in a strong and forceful whisper, "Death possesses every joint of your Sovereign Prince. If we are to aid Her we must proceed at once."

The Queen's favourite stepped back to give them room, but the strangers shook their heads and in one movement raised their gloved hands as a signal for everyone to leave the bedchamber.

"Permit us to work alone," came the insistent whisper. "The room must be clear and the air purified."

"Impossible!" Sussex objected. "Robert – even you cannot allow this."

Dudley hesitated, but the physicians would not be gainsaid. "Every moment brings Her life closer to its ending," they assured him. "To linger is to destroy what meagre hope remains."

Placing his hand upon Robert Dudley's shoulder, Sir

William gently pulled him away. "We have no business here now," he said. "Come, My Lords, let us yield to their request. The Lady Mary and Mistress Ashley will remain to ensure the proprieties are kept."

Reluctantly, the councillors left the chamber. Lord Robert was the last, his eyes fixed solely upon his beloved Elizabeth. Gently, Lady Mary closed the door after him and looked with apprehension at the cloaked strangers.

"Shall I take your outer garments, My Lords?" she asked.

The apothecary box had been placed upon a table and one of the physicians was busily unfastening the clasps. "Return to your prayers," the other instructed. "Leave us to attend Her Majesty."

The woman obeyed, kneeling beside the bed once more. Yet though she bowed her head, she watched the strangers keenly. From the large black box they had removed a silver incense burner and were already putting a candle flame to a nugget of some black substance taken from one of the drawers.

There was a crackle of tiny sparks as the incense caught light and the gloved hand dropped it into the burner. At once threads of dark, plum-coloured smoke rose to gather in a thick, coiling stream which climbed to the ceiling. Lifting her young face, Lady Mary saw the dense cloud spread ever wider overhead and still the vapour poured upward, fogging the air with a purple fume.

The bedchamber was now filled with swirling smoke.

Roused from her prayers by the sweet, peppery scent, Mistress Ashley glanced around her, then turned to the physicians, now vague and indistinct through the mounting reek.

"Too much!" she cried, placing a hand before her mouth and coughing. "What mischief is this?"

The strangers said nothing. Full of ire and indignance, Katherine Ashley attempted to rise, yet a sudden fatigue cramped her legs and darkness was creeping into her mind. Before she could stand, the woman was sprawled across the floor.

"Mistress Ashley!" Lady Mary called, but she could do nothing to help her. In a moment she too had collapsed, and the last image she saw was that of the two mysterious strangers towering over her.

A moment later the incense burner was stifled and the physicians finally removed their wet garments. Hurriedly they cast the heavy cloaks from their shoulders, threw the broad-brimmed hats aside and tore away their gloves. Whipped by these frantic movements, the livid vapour eddied about their large heads as two inhuman faces turned to the prostrate form upon the bed.

"The Bishop of Rome was more easily garnered," one of them said. "She has proven a most difficult cull."

Stepping over Lady Mary's body, his companion placed long, nailless fingers upon the Queen's throat. "We may yet lose Her," he answered, his protruding brow crinkling with doubt. As he spoke, the jewels which studded a golden circlet he wore around his wide neck sparkled. "Come, Arvel!" he called in concern. "This sickness is worse than I feared."

Taking a small, delicate instrument from the apothecary box, the other hastened to his side and cast a critical glance over Elizabeth's ashen features. "Time enough," he judged, directing his violet eyes to the device in his hands. Holding it up against the candlelight he examined the glass filaments at its centre and pressed his thin grey lips together with satisfaction.

"Detachment," he grunted. "That's what you need, Bosco-Uttwar. Always fretting about them, will they live, will they die? As if it matters after we've called. Oh, look at that embroidery – such intricate workmanship!"

His assistant ignored the frivolous remark. He was agitated and nervous, for the life of the Queen and for their own safety. "But if there is not enough living harvest," he said, "all our endeavours will have been for nothing. What use will the scheme be without Her?"

Arvel took a deep, composing breath; Bosco-Uttwar had never really learned to enjoy himself on these expeditions. "I assure you there is more than enough healthy matter for our great purpose," he declared. With that, his slim frame stooped over the bed and he pressed the tip of the instrument against the dying woman's forehead.

Bosco-Uttwar watched in silence. He had seen the

procedure a thousand times before. A faint glow began to travel along the glass filaments and, when one tiny vessel was full, the device was placed above Elizabeth of England's heart. The pale radiance increased and a second phial began to shine.

Upon her pillows, the Queen stirred in her fever. "Kat?" she mumbled. "Kat, where are you?"

"Lift Her arm from under that beautiful coverlet," Arvel instructed.

Pulling back the embroidered cloth, his assistant saw that the bed linen was drenched with sweat, and the wrist he grasped was clammy and cold.

"Sweet Robert?" the frail woman asked. "Is that you? Where are my own dear Eyes?"

"Delirium," Arvel said, pushing the instrument into her shivering palm.

Holding that fragile hand, Bosco-Uttwar stroked the elegant, tapering fingers of which the Queen had always been so proud. At that moment her eyes blinked open and the dark, wild pupils stared up at the flat-faced creatures bending over her. With her last strength she wrenched her hand away and cried out.

"Lords of Hell!"

But her voice was a cracked gasp and no one outside the room heard her. The exertion had spent her final force and she slumped back on to the pillows, her shallow breaths gradually failing.

"And so she dies," Arvel observed, moving to where Mistress Ashley lay upon the floor. "The attendants as well, I think. We must be thorough. I hope the box is recording everything in sufficient detail – have you seen those miniatures over there? Exquisite. They're so inventive, aren't they? Give the box a tap, would you, just to make certain."

Diligently he commenced the same procedure but, while those glass phials pulsed and shone, Bosco-Uttwar remained at the Queen's side, struggling with his conscience.

"Arvel," he said at last. "I'm going to save Her."

"Ridiculous," came the pert reply. "As soon as I have garnered what we need from the other female we must be gone. We are not charged to deny them death. Garner and record, that's all."

"But it is the simplest of remedies."

Returning Mistress Ashley's hand to her side, Arvel rose and jabbed a long grey finger at his assistant.

"You showed no such compassion for the Spanish ambassador," he snapped. "Nor for any of the others. Why now?"

Bosco-Uttwar strode to the apothecary box and avoided the accusing stare of his superior. "Perhaps I have seen too many of them die," he muttered, removing a small paper packet and returning to the bedside. "This one at least I shall cure."

"I forbid it!" Arvel commanded, the jewels shining at

his throat. "Such healing will be viewed as a miracle here."

Bosco-Uttwar was not listening. From the packet he took a tiny soft disc and pressed it against the skin behind the Queen's ear. "It is done," he said quietly. "Her Majesty will recover."

"You overreach yourself!" Arvel spat in outrage. "Her true life is yet to begin, far from here. That is where Her real destiny lies, that is what matters – not this ephemeral sphere."

The assistant crouched next to Mistress Ashley and fingered another disc.

"No more!" Arvel protested. "You interfere too much."

"She has been exposed to the infection," Bosco-Uttwar said simply. "You had best garner the Lady Sidney before I put the remedy upon her."

Infuriated by his assistant's irresponsible behaviour, Arvel pressed the glass instrument to Lady Mary's brow. But the woman groaned and turned her head away. Again he tried, but she squirmed and pushed the device from her.

"I cannot continue," Arvel declared. "She will awaken if I persist."

With a third small disc ready in his hand, Bosco-Uttwar came forward.

"No time for that," Arvel warned, irritably knocking the cure from his assistant's fingers and snatching the packet away. "She is reviving too soon. We must be gone. Don your outer garments – quickly."

Returning everything to the apothecary box, he swept up his rain-sodden cloak and hat. Unhappily his assistant did the same and presently their outlandish features were concealed once more.

Pulling on his gloves, Arvel glanced back at the bedchamber and moved towards the door. In the grand room beyond, the councillors were bickering in hushed voices. The babble ceased, however, as soon the physicians emerged, wisps of purple smoke still clinging to the folds of their cloaks. Immediately, Robert Dudley dashed across to push by them, but they would not let him enter.

"An hour must pass before the chamber may be disturbed," came Arvel's insistent whisper. "The purgative we have set to smoulder must do its work without interruption. Mistress Ashley and Lady Mary are now versed in what should be done."

Dudley relented. "There is hope then?" he asked.

"As much as we may give," came the cryptic response. "Now we must depart."

"You cannot leave," another voice objected, as Lord Sussex came swaggering forward. "Not whilst there can be any doubt."

From the deep shade his hat afforded, Arvel eyed the man warily. Sussex trusted no one and he searched for ways of placating him. All that mattered now was for Bosco-Uttwar and himself to escape this place with their great harvest.

"There are medicines we must bring before daybreak," he said quickly.

"Does it require the pair of you to fetch them?" asked the suspicious Sussex.

"Indeed it does," Arvel insisted. "There is a great deal of preparation involved. Four hands may barely have sufficient time."

Sussex fingered his neat little beard. His instincts told him that something was amiss but, before he could speak again, Sir William Cecil came to the physicians' defence.

"Let the gentlemen be," the Queen's adviser demanded. "You seek for conspiracy and treason in every corner."

Scowling, Lord Sussex backed away and Cecil escorted the cloaked strangers towards the long gallery which led to the main staircase.

"Till before the dawn then," he said. "Let us hope the new day will bring us glad and hopeful news."

The physicians bowed, but in that instant there came a terrified scream from the Queen's bedchamber.

"Mary!" Lord Robert cried. Forgetting Arvel's false warning, he flung the door open. "God's blood! What is this?"

Rousing from the effects of the incense, Lady Mary Sidney was staggering around the room, shaken and afraid.

Leaping into the chamber, Dudley rushed to the bedside where the Queen appeared as pale and as near to death as ever. With a glance at Mistress Ashley who was still lying upon the floor, Lord Robert flew out of the room, tearing his sword from its sheath. "Hold those men!" he yelled.

Arvel and Bosco-Uttwar were already running down the long gallery, fleeing for their lives. Their cloaks flapping about them and their large, booted feet scattering the rushes, they charged past astonished courtiers, desperate to reach the stairs.

"Assassins!" Lord Robert roared, haring after them, while Sussex and the other nobles fell in behind. "Stop them! Guards! Seize them!"

Battling through the gallery, Arvel thrust blustering officials and shrieking ladies-in-waiting aside, and his assistant did the same. The stairs were not far now, but even if they managed to elude capture long enough to get outside, their lives were surely forfeit.

"It's no use, Arvel!" Bosco-Uttwar cried. "We'll never escape this place. There are too many – they will hunt us down."

His superior said nothing. A stout, florid-faced man suddenly stepped into their path and threw his arms wide to catch them. Not checking his pace, Arvel lashed out and grabbed the front of the man's doublet.

Exhibiting incredible strength, the physician lifted the wailing obstacle off the ground and hurled him high over his head. Up into the ceiling the flailing man went rocketing, cracking the moulded plaster when he struck it with a crash. Then down he fell. Accompanied by a shower of white dust, he went spinning to the floor, just in time for Lord Robert to hurdle over him.

The way to the stairs was clear now and the cloaked strangers went bounding down them, jumping three at a time. Soon they would be out into the grounds, where the dark, drenching night might hide them. With only ten more steps to freedom, their hope was shattered when a company of guards came bursting into the hall. Swords and spears raised, they swarmed up to meet them.

Clutching hold of the banister, Arvel and Bosco-Uttwar slithered to a halt.

"Back!" Arvel shouted, retracing their galloping strides. "Back, up – up!"

Hard on his heels, his assistant was panicking. He had never known such fear before. He understood too well what kind of barbaric punishments these creatures meted out to those they considered their enemies. He had witnessed countless executions and afterwards seen the spikes of London Bridge adorned with the victims' heads and limbs.

Lunging on to the topmost step he whirled wildly around. They were trapped. Dudley and the others were already streaming from the gallery to the right, and the stairs seethed with armed guards.

"Where now?" he gasped.

But Arvel was already hastening down a narrow corridor away to the left. "After me!" he called back. "There may yet be a chance, if we can only reach it!"

Bosco-Uttwar did not wait to be told a second time. Up from the stairs the palace guards came surging to join forces with Lord Robert and, as one fearsome column, they rushed after the terrified physicians.

The corridor was dimly lit by solitary candles, their thin flames wavering in the chill draughts. By this poor illumination Bosco-Uttwar saw several doors lining the passage, but Arvel ignored each of them and hurried on.

Ferocious shouts were trumpeting behind him and, to his horror, the assistant saw that the corridor led nowhere. They were running headlong into a blank wall. It was a dead end and they were cornered by a savage mob. There would be no time to explain, these creatures were too ignorant to believe or comprehend them anyway. He knew that they would both see only the gleam of metal and feel thirsty steel plunging into their flesh. In a frenzy of primitive hate, they would be torn to pieces.

"We have them!" Lord Robert's furious voice bellowed.

Even as the words echoed through the corridor, Arvel threw himself into a doorway which his assistant had not seen. Before Bosco-Uttwar knew what was happening, a gloved hand came reaching out and he was dragged in after.

"Secure the entrance!" Arvel barked, slamming the door and staring frantically around.

The room beyond was small and lit by a single rush light. In that paltry glow he could see a long, low table standing against one wall and he ran to it at once. In a moment the table had been flipped on its end and rammed up against the door.

"There's no way out of here," his assistant blurted. "No window and no other exit. We're trapped!"

The table juddered violently as their pursuers began to kick and heave. "Come out of there! Craven filth!" Lord Sussex demanded.

Holding the table in place, Bosco-Uttwar shook his head in misery. Arvel was still pulling every stick of furniture he could find to fortify the barricade, but it was all in vain.

"Just like one of their rat creatures caught in a hole," the assistant snivelled as the pounding blows increased.

"A musical hole," Arvel noted, for he had discovered a number of instruments in the far corner. But there was no time for him to admire their quality.

Discordant jangling interrupted Bosco-Uttwar's despair as Arvel began dragging a clavichord across the room to prop against the upturned table. From then on, every hammering blow inflicted upon the door was accompanied by a clangorous riot of notes.

The din was unbearable but Arvel merely laughed and ran to pick up the rush light. Bearing the petty flame aloft, he dashed to the fireplace.

"Did I not tell you that it pays to be thorough?" he cried. "For twenty-nine years this has been here, waiting for such an emergency. Behold, Bosco-Uttwar, here is our escape route."

The relief which flooded over his assistant was overwhelming. Beneath the high collar of his cloak, a wide smile spread across his long face when he gazed gladly upon the mirror which hung above the mantel.

In the passageway, Sussex and Dudley had stepped aside to allow the burliest of the guards to throw their weight against the door.

"Break it down!" Lord Robert bawled.

There was a tremendous crash as the table went toppling to the floor in the room beyond, and the clavichord exploded beneath its crushing weight with a jarring finale of twanging scales. A powerful kick sent the door ripping from its hinges, but no one went charging inside. Every vengeful voice was quelled and many crossed themselves in the manner of the old religion.

From that windowless room, brilliant colours were pouring and, for one instant, that dark corner of the palace was ablaze with light. A kaleidoscope of burning images radiated from the splintered entrance like dazzling sunshine streaming through a cathedral window - casting vibrant, fragmented shapes on to the corridor wall.

The vivid glare flashed across Lord Robert's face. Squinting, he saw within that room innumerable visions of the villainous physicians. Over every surface their fractured likenesses flared, but even as he marvelled, the wonder vanished and all was dark once more.

Bewildered, Dudley and Sussex stepped through the

doorway. But the chamber was empty. The strangers were nowhere to be found.

"Where are they?" snapped Sir William, pushing his way through the abashed guards.

Staring into the shadows, Lord Robert could only shake his head. "I know not," he said softly. "It seemed to me I viewed them as if through the heart of a great faceted jewel, and then they were gone."

"Witches and devils!" Lord Sussex growled.

Sir William threw them a disbelieving glance then turned to elbow past the guards once again. "Well," he declared, "if they have flown up the chimney, then there is naught we can do. I'll waste no more time on them this foul night."

"Where are you going?" Lord Sussex asked, hastening after him.

"To summon back that German doctor!" came the stern reply. "If he doesn't save the Queen, then I'll stick a knife in him myself."

Alone in the room, Robert Dudley sheathed his sword and dismissed the gaping guards. In all the years that were left to him he never spoke of that night again, not even to his precious Elizabeth.

PART ONE

CHAPTER 1

Adam o'the Cogs

O ut in the deep darkness, in the one hundred and
seventy-eighth year of Elizabeth Tudor's
prodigious reign, the beatified, uplifted realm of
Britain was reaching the close of another long summer
evening. It was the fifth of June in the Gloriana Kalendar
and in the smallest of the twelve floating lands which made
up the county of Suffolk, the shadows grew deep and rich
about the red-bricked manor of Wutton Old Place.

Malmes-Wutton was not the wealthiest of estates. From

the furthest pasture, through the humble village and across to the outlying wood, the greatest measured distance was scarcely a mile.

The manor had once been a splendid residence. Less than a century before, the Queen had progressed there to admire the quality of the horses, for it was widely believed that there were none in Englandia to match them. During those bygone, shimmering days, the manor's mullion windows blazed with light and a near constant music flowed out over the rose garden.

But the intervening years had changed many things. The fortunes of Wutton Old Place had shifted dramatically. Lord Richard Wutton had fallen from Her Majesty's favour and the monopolies she granted to him had been revoked. Gone was the grandeur which the manor formerly boasted; the large building now looked shabby and was choked with ivy. Every horse had been sold to pay mounting debts and the neighbouring fields barely provided enough to feed those who tilled them. No one of rank ventured near, for who would be seen to frequent such a dilapidated estate?

Yet someone *was* making the journey to this remote and isolated region. Beyond the boundaries of Malmes-Wutton, out in the perpetual void, a night barge was approaching.

Sleek and black, it was an elegant craft but, although gilded scrollwork decorated the prow, it bore no other device or marking. Through the great silence the night barge sailed stealthily, blotting out the unnamed stars as it drew closer. A sable canopy sealed the deck from the airless cold and, beneath that midnight shelter, an austere figure gowned in the darkest Puritan style was staring out across the unending emptiness.

There were few in this new world who wielded such power as Sir Francis Walsingham. This was his private vessel. With his large, impassive eyes, the solemn-faced man gazed intently at the isle of Malmes-Wutton which now filled and dominated his vision.

The impoverished estate was enclosed by a protective firmament. Outside the window of the night barge it scrolled by at a ponderous pace. The opaque colours painted within the curved, leaded panes were beginning to turn transparent and the acres of Wutton Old Place were plainly visible far below.

"Did you ever look upon so sad and squalid a spectacle?" a grave voice asked abruptly.

Not bothering to turn around as a second man emerged from the gloom behind him, Walsingham gave the slightest of shrugs. "Does our business still disquiet you, Doctor?" he asked in his usual arch tone. "I thought you were agreed on this course."

Standing beside him, the white-haired man, cloaked in robes of the deepest red velvet and wearing a black skull cap upon his balding head, stared at the few sheep dotting the pasture now visible through the firmament.

"I understand the necessity," he answered, curling his

33

‡

long beard in his fingers. "It is the method I find not to my liking."

The night barge continued to descend, dipping smoothly below the top of the outlying trees so that the view was obscured.

"I had not imagined the sorry depths to which Richard Wutton had fallen. Did you mark the fields? They were almost deserted; is he really reduced to a handful of sheep?"

Walsingham gave an indifferent sniff and recounted a memorised list. "Nine sheep to be precise; four cattle, a large sow with two piglets, a particularly ferocious boar that no one dares hunt, various poultry, a dog and three pheasants he couldn't give away. The deer, of course, went the route of the horses a long time ago."

The older man regarded him uneasily. "You merit your reputation, My Lord," he admitted. "No wonder so many fear you. Truly, your eyes and ears are everywhere."

"I fear they are not as keen as your own," Walsingham admitted. "Yet they will be the sharper once this affair is concluded."

His voice lowered to a whisper and he added, "I am determined to prove our suspicions, whatever the cost, and where better than out here – away from public notice?"

With that, the night barge dropped beneath the Malmes-Wutton horizon and the great expanse of cragged rock upon which the estate was founded now stretched in front of them.

"Has my secretary prepared everything?" Walsingham asked. "I wish to disembark at the first moment."

The white-haired man gave a slight bow and left the deck to attend to it. Alone, Sir Francis watched the immense, barren rockscape swing slowly by and, with his subtle mind contemplating the coming events, a rare smile crept across his face.

A huge, unlit cavern, roughly hewn to form a tremendous arch, reared up beside the night barge and the craft executed a graceful turn to enter it, disappearing into the absolute blackness within.

"You stupid fat pig!" the young apprentice called, beginning to lose his temper. "Come out of there this instant!"

A bass grunt of protest came wheezing from the sty's low brick entrance and the boy scrunched up his face in irritation.

"Adam!" a voice yelled suddenly from the stables. "Stop idling out there and fetch it in at once!"

Throwing a quick, anxious glance back across the yard, Adam o'the Cogs, or Cog Adam as he was generally known, decided there was only one thing for it. He glowered at the pigsty; that evening there was no time to indulge the old sow's stubborn nature.

"Obstinate old sulker," he grumbled, vaulting over the

piggery fence. "You've done it now. If you won't come out, I'm coming in."

Crouching, he barged into the straw-scented darkness and immediately there came an outraged bellowing.

Old Temperance, the great sow of Wutton Old Place, sent up a snorting uproar as the boy tried to catch her. The two piglets, Suet and Flitch, scudded around her, squealing shrilly.

"Keep still!" Adam cried as she thundered to and fro in the sty, knocking him off balance. "Stay put, you moody old porker."

Tumbling to the ground, he gave the sow a hefty kick and the ensuing baritone bellow almost deafened him in that confined place.

"Adam!" the impatient command came calling from the stables once more.

The boy scrambled to his feet. "I told you there weren't no time for mucking about," he warned. "If you're going to be so block-headed about it, then there's only one thing I can do."

A frantic scuffle broke out as, within the sty, Adam changed tack and tried to catch one of the piglets instead. Their high, piping squeaks lasted several minutes until finally one of them was seized.

"Stop that wriggling!" the apprentice said sharply, tucking the piglet under his arm and crawling from the low entrance. Jiggling and squirming, Suet squealed again but Adam gripped it firmly and hurried back to the piggery fence.

Clambering over, he paused to look up at the darkening sky. At the highest point of the leaded firmament the panes had become completely clear and the first gleaming stars were pricking through.

Adam o'the Cogs spared a moment to consider them. He was a slight youth and the untidy crop of hair that sprouted from his head was almost the same colour as the pieces of straw that now clung to it.

"All them little lights," he declared. "One day I'm going to learn what each is called, even name a few maybe."

A jab in the ribs from one of Suet's trotters returned his thoughts to more immediate matters and he went running on his scrawny legs, over the yard and into the stables.

When she was certain the boy had gone, the ample bulk of Old Temperance came trundling from the pigsty, followed closely by her remaining piglet. Out into the gathering dusk they shuffled. The great sow pushed her snout between the fence's wooden bars to grunt her objections.

Yet the eyes which peered across the yard were lenses of polished glass, set into a roughly carved wooden head, for Old Temperance was not a living creature. In these uplifted lands there were no beasts of flesh and blood except for man himself; every other animal was mechanical. The horses of which Wutton Old Place had once been so renowned were finely tuned automata. Even the ducks which swam in the village pond were engineered with springs and gears that flapped rusting tin feathers.

Old Temperance's concertina-like snout moved rapidly in and out as the set of bellows fixed inside her large, barrelled frame squeezed together, and she gave a long, protracted and miserable snort.

The stables which had once housed the finest mechanical horses of the realm were now reduced to common workshops. Shelves and benches crowded the once grand stalls and from every beam there dripped a hundred gleaming tools.

To bolster his floundering fortunes, Lord Richard Wutton had been compelled to take in the broken and defective animals of neighbouring estates. Here, under the guidance of Master Edwin Dritchly, a man most learned in the study of motive science, Adam and two other apprentices executed repairs. Many of the county's best animals had at some point been inside the stable workshops and even in the great isle of London there were mechanicals which bore the discreetly pasted label 'A Wutton Restoration'.

An endless ark of faulty creatures passed through those stable doors so there was always enough to keep Master Edwin and his lads busy, but today had been the most frantic and trying that he had known in a long while.

Edwin Dritchly had been with Lord Richard for many years and had adapted to this new, uplifted world with greater ease than most. He was a short, round man with a chubby pink, clean-shaven face which broke out in red blotches whenever he became flustered or agitated. Since that morning, when his Lord had sprung the surprise announcement that they were to expect an illustrious visitor from the court, Master Edwin had resembled a very large and overripe raspberry.

Huffing and sweating, he foraged through boxes of odds and ends, muttering to himself.

"Fourteen year it's been," he grumbled under his breath. "Fourteen year without so much as a hafternoon revel on the green, and now all of the sudden I'm hexpected to put those old gleemen back together and make them fit to be heard. Well, I haren't no conjuror and what I doesn't have can't be grabbed out of the hempty hair."

Thrusting the box to one side, he pushed past the other two apprentices and began searching beneath one of the benches.

The last of Lord Richard Wutton's finest mechanicals, the only ones which had never been sold for revenue, were two life-size mannequins: a lutanist and a recorder player. These musicians had not been used for many years, and when Master Edwin was commanded to fetch them out and prepare them for a performance that evening, his plump face had fallen and immediately blotched up.

From their dusty corner in the stable loft the mannequins were brought down and Master Edwin groaned loudly. For too long these marvellous mechanicals had been used as the repositories of excellent spares and so when they were laid upon the workbenches he saw that they were in a truly dreadful, ransacked condition. Most of the internal works were either corroded or missing, pipes had perished and brass joints had been stripped away.

"May the celestial orbs fall upon me!" he warbled. "I fear Lord Richard will look like an impoverished fool this night."

The apprentices, however, were not so easily dismayed and were certain they could manage to lash something together. They were rarely allowed to work on any automata as intricate as the musicians and were eager to show off their skills. For the whole of the afternoon they toiled unceasingly to replace plundered cogs and levers. Gears were removed from several sheep, and the legs of chickens and geese were robbed of their springs. Master Dritchly's wife took time away from the kitchen, where a feast was being prepared, to whisk the faded velvet costumes from the mannequins. She then set to work beating the dust out of them and sewing up the holes.

Eventually, as the day wore on, their confidence that the task would be completed on time increased.

Inspecting the labour, Master Edwin had congratulated his apprentices. But when he opened the head of the recorder player to check that the breath pipe was still in place, he made an awful discovery and buried his face in his hands. "The cordials are gone!" he had wailed.

Inside every mechanical, from the most crudely fashioned tin fighting cockerel, to the Queen's own Ladies of the Privy Chamber, were glass phials containing a fluid named *ichor*. The sophisticated models possessed four vessels of these different coloured 'humours', each one governing separate aspects of function.

The basic fluid was the green which maintained balance and motion. Vulgarly called 'phlegm', it was present in even the most rudimentary creature. Amber ichor, also known as 'yellow bile', controlled intent and obedience; a skilled master of motive science would ensure that this was in harmony with 'temper', the red fluid which instilled character. Last and most precious of all was 'black bile', a rare elixir to be found in large quantities only within the servitors of the richest households. This costly liquid imparted elementary thought to a mechanical and was valued many times higher than gold.

At some point during the years of repairing the 'livestock' of other estates, the ichors of the musicians had been removed and never replaced. Without them, they could neither move nor play a single note.

In the little time that remained before the important guest's arrival, Master Edwin and the apprentices tried to refill the empty phials. Every cow had been rounded up and their dismantled pieces lay in corners alongside overturned or half-open sheep. Heads of all sizes stared up from the floor, the glass lenses of their eyes gazing sightlessly at the three boys feverishly topping up the musician's vessels with scavenged cordials. But there was still not quite enough of the amber for the recorder player.

Only a few drops more were needed and so Adam o'the Cogs had been sent out to the piggery to fetch in Old Temperance. The great sow had yellow bile in abundance.

"Where is that clotpole of a boy?" Master Edwin called again. "Hum hum, how long does it take to haul the old pig in here?" Even as he spoke Adam came running in with the piglet under his arm.

"I couldn't get Old Temperance out of the sty," he explained hurriedly. "So I brought Suet instead; there ought to be just enough in him."

Master Edwin waved a podgy hand at the main workbench. "Set it down and hopen it up," he instructed. "Hardly any time left – we won't have a chance to rehearse these gleemen."

Taking the piglet from under his arm, Adam placed it upon the wide workbench. The wooden creature gave a shrill squeal and went scooting from the boy's grasp. Through a heap of small brass wheels and miniature pulleys it bolted, sending them rolling to the floor. Over a sheep's hind leg the piglet leaped, darting this way and that as it hunted for an escape.

"Catch it!" Master Edwin roared.

Henry Wattle, a curly-haired apprentice who was the same age as Adam, could not help laughing as the small creature scudded across the bench. Suet looked so comical, dodging and swerving on its small trotters, that Henry was of no assistance at all. Still squealing, the piglet darted to the end of the workbench where the recorder player sat awaiting the remaining drops of amber ichor.

Master Edwin's stout arms came reaching across to grab it but Suet was too nimble. Nipping aside, it ran straight into the musician's velvet-covered back.

A high squawk sounded as the piglet's nose squashed flat. To everyone's dismay, the figure was knocked from the bench and went lurching to the ground.

"Save it!" Master Edwin cried.

Henry Wattle, who had not stopped laughing, slithered across just in time to break the mechanical's fall.

Pushing its nose out again, Suet hopped a brief victory jig. Then it jumped from the bench, landed upon the musician's back, sprang on to Henry's astonished head and leaped the remaining distance to the floor.

With a triumphant shake of its stiff, leathery ears, the piglet rocketed for the stable door. Haring under Adam's legs it set off, pelting between the disassembled sheep and cattle which lay between it and freedom. But, even as the yard came into view, a pair of strong hands seized its stumpy body and Suet was plucked from the ground.

Jack Flye lifted the small creature high into the air until it was level with his own lean face and stared into the tiny eyeholes cut into the animal's carved head.

"Now then," he said firmly, "we'll have no more of that. You can go back to Old Temperance tomorrow."

Before Suet could begin to squeak a protest, it was whirled around and the oldest of the apprentices pressed the Wutton crest which was chiselled upon its back. In that instant the piglet's struggles ceased, the small trotters juddered to a stop and dangled limply from their axles as the concertina snout extended to its full length with a sad whine of escaping air.

"Thank you, Jack," Master Edwin sighed, mopping his forehead with his cuff. "Hum hum, take hout the cordial and we can lug the gleemen across to the manor house."

Suspending the inert piglet from a wire by the hook of its tail, Jack unfastened the clip that held the creature together and the wooden keg of its body swung in half. Deftly, the apprentice reached inside and removed a small glass phial which he carried to where Adam was helping Henry lift the fallen musician back on to the bench. Master Edwin fanned his glowing face with his hat while overseeing this final adjustment.

At seventeen years of age, Jack Flye was the most experienced of his apprentices. He was a serious young man, determined in his ambition to possess his own workshop one day. Adam and Henry both looked up to him;

they watched in respectful silence as the youth brushed the dark hair from his eyes and measured several drops of Suet's ichor into a larger glass vessel already swilling with yellow bile.

"There," he breathed, placing the second phial into the mannequin's polished brass head. "The level is amended, the amber cordial is in perfect accord with the red. This fellow is ready to toot until his bellows bust."

Nodding in satisfaction, Master Dritchly closed the musician's face and fastened it shut.

"Well done, lads," he said, a great grin splitting his own features. "I never thought has how we'd do it – I never did, most honest I never. Hum hum."

Jack sucked his teeth thoughtfully as he gazed at the renovated mechanicals. Arrayed in their repaired finery, the figures looked quite presentable. The recorder player was dressed in a peascod paunch doublet of popinjay green, embellished with gold brocade with matching slops. Not an inch of the internal frame could be seen, and that was just as well for one of the arms was undoubtedly a modified cow's leg with chicken-claw fingers. Hidden from view by sleeve and glove, nobody would be able to guess – especially at a distance and in candlelight, which was the plan.

The lutanist was dressed in much the same manner, except that the velvet was Coventry blue, pinked with silver tinsel. Yet the colours had faded from both costumes, the trimmings were tarnished and, despite Mistress

Dritchly's best efforts, she had been unable to eradicate the worst patches of mildew.

"Let's just hope they'll play in tune after all these years," Jack murmured.

"Hum hum, may God and the heavenly spheres permit it," Master Edwin said, "for there's no time to test them."

Bidding Henry and Adam to follow them with the actual instruments, Master Edwin and Jack hoisted the musicians over their shoulders and marched from the workshop.

Cog Adam glanced around at the wreckage of animals and birds that littered the stables. "Look at the state of this mess. It'll take three days at least to put everything back the way it was," he muttered. "We won't be able to find half of what's needed, there'll be bits missing and most of the sheep will end up limping."

Henry Wattle picked up the detached head of a tin goose and blew through its neck as though it were a trumpet. The head wagged and a loud "HONK" blasted throughout the workshop. "Duck!" he shouted, throwing it at Adam and cackling at the bad joke.

Adam scowled at him, then clambered up to the hay loft where the instruments had been stored. He reappeared a moment later carrying a large recorder and a very dusty lute.

"One of the strings is broken," he said, passing the unusual, bowl-shaped object to Henry. "Do you think it matters? Will anyone notice?"

The boy shook his curly head and snorted rather like Old Temperance. "Listen, Coggy," he laughed, "the less strings there are the better. Less racket, see? Do you really think them mechanicals are going to be able to play? I'll be amazed if they can hold the instruments, never mind a tune."

"Master Edwin knows what he's doing," Adam insisted. "There's no one better at motive science than him. If he thinks they'll work that's good enough for me!"

Henry wiped a hand across his already dirty face and succeeded in making it worse. "Hog's breath!" he said scornfully. "If Hummy Hum, Dull as Ditch Water Dritchly was really any good he wouldn't be stuck in this dung pile. He'd be out there on some rich estate making heaps of money. That's what I'm going to do, soon as I'm able. Sir Henry Wattle, that's who I'll be one day. Work for the Queen Herself, maybe, and have pots and pots of gold coin."

"Well, you'll just have to make do with that lute for now," Adam told him as he went into the yard. "Bring it to the house."

Alone in the workshops, Henry Wattle spat on the floor, then kicked an upended, headless sheep, forcing air through its internal pipes. A hoarse "Baaaaaaa" echoed from the circular neck hole.

"I *will* be rich," he said defiantly, "I *will* live in a great house of my own – I know it."

Leaving the stables, Henry was surprised to see Adam still in the yard. It was quite dark now and the fair-haired boy was staring out along the dusty road that led to the village.

"What you doing?" Henry asked.

Adam pointed with the recorder. "They're here," he murmured. "Lord Richard's guests."

Then Henry heard the faint sound of cantering hooves and saw indistinct shapes riding through the shadows.

"Five of them," Adam counted. "No, there are five horses but only four riders. I wonder who they are."

The message that Lord Richard Wutton received that morning had not divulged the identity of the important guest who would be visiting his estate. The desire to know the answer to that mystery burned in the hearts of both apprentices. Their errand momentarily forgotten, they stood rooted to the spot as the riders drew closer.

"What if it's the Queen Herself?" Adam whispered.

"You loony," Henry scoffed. "Why would Her Majesty come to this muddy backwater? Nowt in this muck hole to interest the likes of Her."

"She came here once," Adam answered. "Supposed to have been good friends with Lord Richard in the old days, when he were rich and important."

Henry clicked his tongue. "Well he ain't neither no more," he said flatly. "I'll wager this'll be a big wash out. Won't be no one worth mentioning at all and our hard slog today will have been wasted. Prob'ly one of the court cooks come to maunder the secret of Mistress Dritchly's pear tart."

"Cooks don't get to ride on steeds like that," Adam murmured.

The riders were very near now and even in the gloom the boys could see that their horses were infinitely superior to anything they had ever seen.

Then into the yard they came, reining their mounts to a stamping halt.

The horses were magnificent. Fashioned from black steel, they were elegant and powerful and the boys gawped at them. Never had they imagined that any mechanical could be so beautiful as these incredible creatures. Every sinew of the original beast was hammered into the flowing panels and their proud heads tossed and strained at the reins in a most natural and convincing manner.

Yet among those horses there was one even greater than the rest. It was a whole hand taller, the mane and tail were of the finest silken fibres and it was shod with bronze. In the obsidian globes of its eyes there gleamed a fierce intelligence, and both Henry and Adam guessed that somewhere within that fabulous steed there was undoubtedly a quantity of black ichor.

"You, boy!" a clipped, commanding voice called down from its rider whose face was concealed in shadow. "Where is Richard Wutton? Why is he not here to greet us?"

Not certain which of them the stranger was addressing, both apprentices bowed and began gabbling at once in apology.

"I'm sure he don't know of your arrival yet, sir," Adam said.

"I'll go fetch Lord Richard out," Henry spoke over him.

An impatient, disdainful sniff was the only reply. Then another of the riders said in a conciliatory voice, "Look, Sir Francis, he is here!"

The large oak door of Wutton Old Place was creaking open and a wedge of yellow candlelight flooded the yard. Adam and Henry backed away, for at last they saw just how forbidding and important the strangers appeared. Framed in the entrance, Lord Richard Wutton looked on the grave countenances of the horsemen and the ready smile failed on his lips.

Richard Wutton was a jovial man, much respected by his few tenants. Their remaining with him throughout his years of banishment from court was a testament to the loyalty he inspired. His exile and the subsequent loss of fortunes had, however, grizzled and greyed his temples and he was more fond of the bottle than he ought to have been.

Standing there upon the threshold of his run-down manor, he stared at the faces of his guests and wished he had quaffed a cup of wine before meeting them.

There, upon that splendid horse, was Sir Francis Walsingham, stiff and intractable in his stark black garments, his mirthless face ringed by the white circle of his ruff. Lord Richard's heart quailed inside his ribs. What could that calculating old spider want here?

Hurriedly he glanced at the others. He did not recognise two of them but guessed that the one closest to Sir Francis was undoubtedly his personal secretary while the other, a sullen-faced man dressed in russets and already dismounting, was his groom. The fourth man Lord Richard knew very well and his mind began to race as it sought for the reason which had brought the old, white-bearded scholar back to Malmes-Wutton after all these years.

"Welcome, My Lord Walsingham," he called, leaving the doorway and walking towards them. "I am deeply honoured by this visit."

Like a huge raven unfurling its wings, Sir Francis threw back his black riding cloak and jumped from the saddle. His dark eyes glinted at Lord Richard but he said nothing and his host fidgeted uneasily under their glare.

"I'm afraid the message I received made no mention of whom I was to expect," the man mumbled to cover the silence.

"That is because I did not want you to know," came the bleak and disconcerting answer.

"I trust you'll find the meal and entertainment adequate..." Lord Richard said, his voice falling to a wretched whisper as Sir Francis Walsingham strode rudely away and entered the manor house.

"A most tiring journey," the secretary broke in. "You must pardon My Lord's abrupt manner. What a pleasant isle this is; quite the smallest I have seen, but such plaudits I have heard concerning the work that is done here. Most interesting, all your merry apprentices tinkering away with broken cattle."

Lord Richard was hardly paying attention. Walsingham frightened him and he turned to the other man he had recognised.

"And you, Doctor?" he began. "Why are you here? Have you ceased casting horoscopes and conversing with angels?"

Doctor John Dee met his questioning glance for an instant, then had the grace to look away. "I should have called upon you earlier, Richard," he said regretfully. "I am most sorry for that. Fourteen years is too long."

There was an awkward pause and, watching from nearby, Adam saw that the embers of an old argument lay between these two men.

"Come!" the secretary cried, clapping his hands together. "Let us not tarry without when light and merriment awaits us. Let all quarrels be put aside this night."

Lord Richard remembered his duties as host and, clearing his very dry throat, guided the men to the doorway, leaving the groom behind.

Adam o'the Cogs watched them enter the manor but, on

the topmost step, the white-bearded man known as Doctor Dee paused and stared back at him. The boy shuddered under the intense scrutiny, before the elderly stranger followed Lord Richard inside.

"I wouldn't sleep easy this night if I were you, boy!" the groom chuckled unpleasantly. "Don't you know who that were?"

Adam shook his head. The name "Doctor Dee" had meant nothing to him.

Holding the reins of all five horses, the groom gave him a leering smile. "Astrologer to the Queen, that's who," he said, affecting a hollow, sepulchral voice. "Invented the new Kalendar, he did, and more besides if rumours be true. Decent folk are scared of him, more so than they are of my master."

"Why?" Henry demanded.

The groom's eyes slid quickly from side to side as if afraid of the surrounding shadows. "They say he digs up corpses," he hissed. "Grubs up the churchyard dirt and, by his wicked arts, speaks with the dead bodies."

Henry snapped his fingers in disbelief. "Donkey warts!" he said.

"Is it?" the man murmured. "Jenks here thinks not. An imp from Hell does his bidding, that's no lie – there's plenty enough who've seen it. A crafty, clever man is Doctor Dee, but also a mighty dangerous one. You'd best watch out, lad, if he takes notice of you – no knowing what might come for you in the night to cart you off."

Adopting Henry's sceptical stance, Adam managed a feeble laugh but he did not like the look of the groom. The man had a suspicious face and, when he saw that his attempts to frighten them had failed, his mouth twisted into an arrogant sneer.

"Now then," he began, his sly glance darting around the yard, "where are my master's steeds to be housed?"

Adam returned the hostile stare. "There's the barn yonder," he answered with an impudent tone which set the man's lip curling again. "Over there, behind the piggery."

"The barn!" came the insulted response. "Do you know how costly these beasts are? Have you no proper stable?"

The boys shook their heads. "We don't have horses here no more," Henry said. "But when we did, I reckon they'd have been even better than your fancy one with the bronze shoes. Even Old Dritchly could cobble up something like that if he had a mind to."

Strolling forward for a better view of the creature, he asked, "What are the innards like? How many pendulums do it have and how big are the cordial vessels?"

"Don't you even think of coming no closer," the groom growled. "That's far enough. These ain't none of your peasanty clankers, specially not Belladonna here. If anyone touches these fine beasts, Jenks'll cut their throats for them, you understand?"

Leaving the threat hanging in the air, he led the

mechanical horses over to the barn and the boys stared after him, mouthing insults to his back.

"Who wants to see the workings of your old nags anyway?" Henry grumbled.

"What do you think the extra horse was for?" Adam asked.

"To carry the baggage," Henry suggested. "Had a dirty great chest strapped to it."

Adam was not so certain. "No," he said, "there's something weird and secret happening here. Lord Richard didn't like it and nor do I."

As he spoke he tapped the mouthpiece of the recorder against his lips until he suddenly realised what he was doing and gave a horrified yelp.

"The instruments!" he cried. "We should have took them inside ages ago."

And so the two apprentices raced into the manor house and the tragic events that were to occur that fateful evening were set in motion.

CHAPTER 2

O Mistress Mine

Within the banqueting hall, Sir Francis Walsingham brusquely appropriated the place of honour at the table. Anxiously, Lord Richard sat beside him. The secretary and Doctor Dee assumed their seats and their host eyed the food spread before them with considerable relief. At least here there was nothing to be ashamed of or which might cause offence.

Mistress Dritchly had worked miracles in the kitchen and the board was covered with a respectable variety of dishes. There was fine white manchet bread, miniature pastries filled with spiced chicken, generous cuts of boiled mutton, a large onion tart, a sallat and a cheese pie with herbs. It might not have equalled feasts at court but few of the country gentry in the neighbouring isles dined upon grander fare than this.

The best plates had all been sold, so the guests were obliged to eat off wooden trenchers and drink from earthenware cups. There were only two jugs of wine, but it was the best Lord Richard's depleted cellar could provide and when that ran out there was always the strong October ale.

"Pray commence and help yourselves," he encouraged. "Mistress Dritchly is a fine cook, as you are about to learn."

Leaning forward to take some slices of mutton, the secretary, who had readily introduced himself as Arnold Tewkes, smiled ingratiatingly. "I am always eager to partake of such lessons," he said. "A more willing student would be difficult to find."

As he was a small, thin-boned man whose head jerked about like a bird with faulty neck springs, that statement was rather difficult to believe, but he attacked the food with surprising zeal.

Doctor Dee busied himself with one of the pastries and a slice of cheese pie, but Lord Richard observed that Walsingham partook of nothing and wore such a stony expression that his own appetite withered within him.

Several difficult minutes passed during which not a word was uttered by anyone and Lord Richard swigged his first cup of the evening.

The banqueting hall of Wutton Old Place was panelled with oak and the ceiling mouldings were painted bright colours. Four large iron candlesticks, each bearing ten candles, gave a warm illumination to the room and at the far end, upon a little stage, Master Edwin and Jack Flye were busily placing the mechanical musicians in position.

Sitting stiffly in his chair, Walsingham regarded the activity with significantly more interest than he bestowed upon the food.

"A little entertainment for later," Lord Richard explained, "to accompany the compotes and marchpane. I find music aids the digestion."

Sir Francis made no reply and continued to stare in that unsettling way. Like a hawk viewing some remote and unsuspecting morsel, Lord Richard thought unhappily.

"Most excellent onion tart," Master Tewkes declared, trying to soothe the tension. "It would appear that I am graduating the Dritchly College with honours. The mutton also was very flavoursome and cunningly done. You are very lucky in your cook, My Lord."

"I'm glad to hear it," Richard Wutton answered. "My Lady Fortune has been noticeably absent from these estates of late. I thought she had abandoned me."

Brushing pie crumbs from his beard, Doctor Dee commented, "If a man slams the door in the face of sound advice and refuses to listen to all good sense, then what else is she to do but depart?"

His host opened his mouth to respond, then caught sight of Walsingham still sitting like a forbidding gargoyle and thought better of it, settling for another draught of wine instead. Old arguments and resentments could wait but, try as he might, Lord Richard could not guess the errand that had brought these important visitors here. He grew more and more concerned as wild suspicions frothed up in his mind.

"If Your Lordship wishes," he began again, desperate to glean anything at all from Her Majesty's spymaster, "on the morrow you could go hunting in the outlying woods. There is a wild boar which is in dire need of a-catching. A real terror it is."

"Sounds a most fearsome beast," Master Tewkes clucked in between mouthfuls. "What a thrill that would be."

Walsingham stirred and diverted his gaze from the far end of the hall. "I think not," he said in a voice of ice, with a purposeful glitter in his eyes as his features hardened all the more. "My quarry never has more than two legs."

A faint, strangled noise gurgled in Lord Richard's throat and he drowned it hastily in yet more wine.

Just then, Adam and Henry came running in with the

instruments and they hurried over to where Master Edwin was waiting.

"Tell me," Master Tewkes began, leafing through the sallat as though it were a set of disarranged accounts, "what has been the most outlandish creature to pass through your workshops? Has the new fashion for imaginary animals penetrated this corner of Englandia yet? I've seen such fanciful constructions of late – why, there was a cockatrice in particular which I admired at Nonsuch..."

"I know a place," Lord Richard mumbled guardedly. "A place where such fabulous beasts were in abundance. Dragons and gryphons, basilisks and lake monsters – all were there and might be still, for all I know."

"And where is that?" asked the secretary, unaware that the ashes of the old argument were being disturbed and stoked once more.

Without warning, Sir Francis rapped the table sharply. "Go no further with this!" he snapped. "Do not even think to mention that forbidden isle or that traitor's name! Not even in your own house. Will you never learn, Lord Richard? Look around you, see where that misguided loyalty has brought you. Be thankful you lost only your revenues and not your head – that could still be arranged, if you persist."

Richard Wutton returned his attention to the cup which was trembling in his hand. Finally he said, "Tell me. Why are you here? Have I done something new to offend Her

Majesty? Does she suspect me of another crime?"

"Are your musicians never to play us anything?" Walsingham asked blithely, ignoring him.

Baffled at this interest in his mechanicals, Lord Richard signalled to Edwin Dritchly at the end of the hall. The raspberry-faced man bowed in return and whispered quickly to his apprentices. "This is it, lads," he said. "Hum hum – you ready, Jack?"

The eldest youth nodded; the recorder and the lute had been thrust into the mannequins' gloved hands. Now they would see if their efforts had been in vain.

Master Edwin's podgy fingers ran over the lutanist's velvet-covered shoulder until he found the raised carving of the Wutton crest beneath. "Now," he told Jack as he pressed firmly.

The crest gave a click and immediately the figure jerked into life. Within its brass head the ichors began to bubble, and a pendulum suspended in its chest swung steadily to and fro.

A disharmony of notes sailed up to the painted ceiling as the mechanical's fingers strummed the long neglected lute and it paused for a moment to pluck the empty air where the missing string should have been. The blank brass face turned to Master Dritchly, tilting to one side as if in puzzlement.

"You'll have to make do," the man instructed.

The musician shook its head slowly in mock disgust, and

Master Dritchly was glad that it was not able to talk.

Meanwhile, Jack had pushed down the Wutton crest of the recorder player, but that figure was finding its newly repaired arm intensely fascinating. Flexing and fluttering the chicken-claw fingers, it waved and waggled the hand, then tried to remove the glove for a better inspection.

"Leave it," Jack ordered. "Just play your rotten recorder!"

The mannequin turned its polished face to him and blew two blasts of air through the opening of its mouth which sounded vaguely insulting. Then it lifted the recorder and assumed the correct pose.

By now the lutanist had tuned the remaining strings and it too was waiting to begin. They had not been used for so long that Master Dritchly had forgotten they needed to be told which melodies to play and he said the first one that came into his head.

"*O Mistress Mine*," he whispered. It was also his favourite.

The lute strings played and a bellows-blown breath blew the opening notes on the recorder. The hall of Wutton Old Place rang with music once more.

"A fine pair of musicians," Walsingham declared. "They keep the refrain well."

Lord Richard was still perplexed. Sir Francis was too sour and serious a man to indulge in such trivial frivolities. There was obviously something more behind his interest, but he could not comprehend what that might be.

"Indeed," he replied uncertainly. "Edwin Dritchly is exceeding proficient in matters mechanical. He is the most able and adept craftsman in all of the Suffolk islands."

Walsingham's eyebrows knitted into a single dark line. "How gratifying to hear that," he commented. Then, resting his elbows upon the table and pressing his fingertips together, he finally related the purpose of his visit. "You may rest easy. I am not here to accuse you of anything."

Lord Richard breathed his thanks but knew enough about the Queen's counsellor not to relax completely.

"Fourteen years is a long period to be absent from court," Walsingham continued. "Here, at the extreme rim of society, you are no doubt ignorant of current policy and state affairs."

"I know only what the winds of rumour bring," Lord Richard admitted.

Swallowing a morsel of bread with a gulp, Master Tewkes eagerly brought him up to date.

"Never have diplomatic relations with the Catholic powers been so strained," he rattled. "France and Spain – alas it's become quite impossible. The Queen refuses to grant an audience with either ambassador and will not even permit them at court. A crisis is approaching. Those despicable Spaniards are plotting some vile outrage. Is that not so, Doctor?"

Doctor Dee nodded. "You enquired earlier about my

angelic messages, Richard," he said. "Those Enochian studies have confirmed to me that a terrible conflict lies ahead. There is much in the future which bodes ill for Englandia. The new stars tell me so."

"Our fears are not based solely upon horoscopes," Walsingham was quick to point out. "My spies in Europe report the same. France and Spain are preparing for war. Even now they are mustering their forces; it would be a fatal mistake if we were found lacking."

Master Tewkes banged a bony fist upon the table, making his knife and trencher jump and clatter. "Those whey-faced idolaters!" he cried passionately. "May they all burn on a pyre of their own incense!"

Lord Richard pushed his half empty cup away. "Assuredly," he began, "this is a most frightening intelligence, and yet why does it bring you to Malmes-Wutton?"

The dangerous light gleamed in Walsingham's eyes once more, and he looked across the hall to where the musicians were playing.

"One hundred and seventy-five years," he said. "That is how long we have been in this uplifted realm, out here in the deep darkness. During that time there have been no major wars – who then can say what manner of contest such strife would be? I cannot. This is a new world, filled with marvels undreamed of. If we are to win through, then we must be ready."

As he spoke, the music ceased. The tune had ended but the lutanist played no more for there came a creak of metal from within and, with a judder, the mechanical stopped moving. Master Dritchly attended to it at once. In the mean time the other musician was waiting for a new melody. When no fresh instruction came, it recommenced *O Mistress Mine*.

"There appears to be some problem," Walsingham observed.

"Edwin Dritchly can remedy it," Lord Richard assured him.

"Her Majesty has need of such skilled men," came the ominous reply. "In the approaching battle their talents will be in great demand. For many months, under cover of secrecy, I have been recruiting masters of motive science to create engines of destruction fit for the impending war."

Lord Richard's heart sank as he perceived where this was leading.

"Seventeen men I gathered from all across the realm," Walsingham continued. "Yet it has been proven that agents of foreign powers are at work in this land, for nearly all of those learned masters have met with accidents and misfortunes whilst making the journey to London."

"Waylaid and murdered!" the secretary interjected. "The finest talents of sweet Englandia, butchered by Philip of Spain's heinous envoys."

Walsingham raised a hand for silence and Master

Tewkes reluctantly drew a great breath to stifle his fizzing outrage.

"Henceforth," Sir Francis continued, "I shall ensure the safety of such craftsmen by escorting them personally to the isle of London."

Lord Richard had listened to this discourse in mounting dismay. "You are going to take Edwin Dritchly away from Malmes-Wutton?" he murmured.

"It is by Royal decree," Walsingham answered with a cold finality in his voice. "We shall depart at first light."

"If you had the slightest notion of the approaching conflict," Doctor Dee put in, "you would not demur."

Richard Wutton looked to the stage where Master Edwin was still making adjustments to the lutanist. Without his expertise the sole income of Malmes-Wutton would disappear, but that was not the impoverished Lord's first thought.

"What of his wife?" he asked. "Will she be permitted to accompany him?"

"If he wishes."

Lord Richard drained his cup. "Edwin was never one for the city," he said. "Nor is Mistress Dritchly, but if it is commanded then there is naught I can do to halt their going."

"Nothing whatsoever," Walsingham stated.

"Forgive me," Master Tewkes broke in with a blank expression upon his sharp features. "But is this not the

"*Assassins!*" Lord Robert roared, haring after them, while Sussex and the other nobles fell in behind. "Stop them! Guards! Seize them!"

Battling through the gallery, Arvel thrust blustering officials and shrieking ladies-in-waiting aside, and his assistant did the same. The stairs were not far now, but even if they managed to elude capture long enough to get outside, their lives were surely forfeit.

"It's no use, Arvel!" Bosco-Uttwar cried. "We'll never escape this place. There are too many – they will hunt us down."

fourth time we have heard *O Mistress Mine?* Can your minstrels play no other music?"

Unaware that his future was being discussed at the table, Master Dritchly had completed his repairs to the lutanist and urged Jack Flye to still the recorder player. The seventeen-year-old obeyed and the ensuing silence was a welcome relief to everyone.

"I hate that stinky tune," Henry muttered to Adam.

"Hum hum," Master Dritchly puffed, mopping his face with his hat. "Let us start them both up again."

The crests of both musicians were pressed and the mechanicals lifted their brass heads to await instruction.

"*The Honiesuckle*," Master Dritchly commanded.

The two mannequins began to play. The sound, however, was horrible to hear, for although the lutanist was performing the desired melody, the recorder player had launched into *O Mistress Mine* for the fifth time.

"Stop it!" Master Dritchly growled, but the mechanicals ignored him and the ear-jarring discord continued.

Jack reached up to press the Wutton crest on the recorder player's shoulder, but the device was jammed and would not budge beneath his fingers. The terrible noise persisted and Master Dritchly threw a worried glance at the table. A distressing grimness was etched into every face, even on that of his own Lord, and his blotches deepened to a rich plum colour.

To extinguish this awful din, he gave the lutanist a sound slap and the instrument fell from the abruptly frozen fingers as the mannequin became like a statue. With a reverberating bump, the lute dropped to the floor but there was no time to attend to that. Jumping on to the stage, Master Edwin raised his fat fist and brought it down on the other musician's shoulder.

O Mistress Mine piped on regardless.

"Be still!" Master Edwin ordered, hammering blow after blow upon the immovable crest. "I insist."

Watching from the side, Henry Wattle bit into his lip as he tried to keep from laughing, while Adam stared across to Lord Richard and his guests. "That Walsingham's got a face to curdle cream," he told the other apprentice.

A sixth rendition of *O Mistress Mine* started and Richard Wutton refilled his cup. "Most unfortunate," he announced, although secretly he was almost enjoying the embarrassing situation. If the ridiculous scene continued, Sir Francis might have second thoughts about removing Edwin Dritchly to London.

"Can this foolery be all a part of the entertainment?" Master Tewkes suggested brightly. "Most novel of you, Lord Richard."

"Assuredly not," his host informed him. "I really cannot think what Master Dritchly imagines he is doing."

Suddenly the music stopped for, in desperation, Master Edwin wrenched the recorder away, leaving the mechanical to blow only upon its twitching fingers. "Let that learn you!" the man hissed.

The brass head turned to him and, to his astonishment, emitted a low "Moo". Master Dritchly blinked in bewilderment and the musician snatched the recorder back from him. The all too familiar tune piped up again, louder and more shrill this time.

Catching sight of Walsingham's thunderous expression, Lord Richard feigned disappointment. "Perhaps his reputation is a trifle exaggerated," he ventured.

By this time Master Dritchly had lost all composure. "Be quiet!" he bawled at the obstinate mannequin. Then, discarding the final shreds of his dignity, he grabbed it by the throat and dragged the minstrel from the stage. The velvet-clad arms flailed wildly and the raucous notes squealed to a stop when the instrument was jolted from its grasp by Edwin's violent shaking.

"Back to the workshops!" he cried.

Adam had never seen Master Dritchly look so furious, but the sight was too much for Henry. Clutching his stomach, the boy leaned against the wall, sobbing with laughter.

The mechanical's brass head was swinging from side to side in protest, but Master Dritchly had been pushed too far. "It's the hammer for you," he swore.

Unfortunately, the man had forgotten that directly behind him the lute was still lying on the floor. Striding backwards, holding the recorder player aloft, his boot came crashing down through the wooden instrument. It slid along the ground and Edwin went tumbling through the air, with the musician crashing on top of him.

Henry Wattle's shriek of exploding glee could be heard throughout the manor house.

"Get it off!" Master Dritchly yelled, wrestling with the thrashing mechanical. "It's completely deranged."

Jack and Adam dashed forward to help, but the musician was stronger than all of them. Pounding its gloved fists against Edwin's chest in revenge for its earlier rough handling, it shoved the apprentices away and began bleating like a sheep.

Leaping to the stage, Jack Flye picked up the empty chair and smashed it against the mannequin's side. The figure toppled from Master Dritchly's stomach and Jack stamped on its back before it could recover.

At once Adam sprang in, sitting on the shuddering shoulders as the musician attempted to rise. The determined mechanical was so powerful that Jack was pitched off balance, but Adam clung on and, taking hold of the brass head, unfastened the clasp.

There was a dainty clang as half of the face fell to the ground and, before the chicken-claw fingers could come reaching for him, the boy delved inside and removed the ichors. With a droning moan, the figure slumped down - inert and motionless.

"Good... good work, Cog Adam," Master Dritchly huffed breathlessly while rubbing his bruised chest. "Hum hum... help Jack take it to the stables, and give young Wattle a kick to halt his hooting."

In disgusted silence, Walsingham watched the musicians being carried from the hall. Master Dritchly gave the table a shame-faced glance, then he too departed.

"A highly unusual diversion," Master Tewkes offered, not knowing what else to say.

Doctor Dee turned to Sir Francis. "I propose we take the boy with us instead," he stated wryly. "At least the lad knew how to put a stop to that absurd spectacle."

"I agree!" Lord Richard said quickly. "Adam could be a great help, I'm certain. Why, he's called Adam o'the Cogs because that's all he's interested in. Always got his nose buried in some faulty clanker. Born to it, he was."

"The learned Doctor was speaking in jest," Master Tewkes told him.

Walsingham rose from his chair. "I have witnessed enough disgraceful nonsense this night," he declared. "See that Edwin Dritchly knows of our plan. We leave at dawn."

His secretary followed him from the hall but, before Doctor Dee accompanied them, he looked long at Lord Richard. "Can you forgive me?" he asked.

Richard Wutton turned to stare at the empty stage. "For this final privation?" he said. "I daresay the apprentices will struggle through. Jack Flye is quite proficient and the two youngsters are capable in their own fashion. Somehow we will manage."

"I did not mean what happened this evening," the astrologer murmured. "This is all Walsingham's doing, I wanted no part of it."

An embittered smile appeared on Lord Richard's face. "And you had not the courage to gainsay him," he said. "How familiar that sounds to me. No, John, go back to the horoscopes and mathematical formulae you cherish more than your fellow man. I do not forgive you and never shall."

There was nothing more to be said. Doctor Dee wrapped his robe about him and swept from the hall.

Alone, Richard Wutton contemplated the task ahead. Telling Edwin that he was to leave for London the next morning was not going to be pleasant. Slowly he emptied his guests' unfinished wine into his own cup and drank.

An hour later the deed was done. Master Dritchly had received the news unhappily but without objection. He knew it would be futile to refuse but he was certain that his wife would not be so calm.

She was not.

A great deal of wailing and cursing had come from the kitchens but eventually the commotion had subsided and now the couple were discussing what was to be done.

Mistress Dritchly loved her husband dearly but she could not bear to think of leaving Lord Richard's service at such short notice. Between them it was decided that she would remain at the manor until a replacement could be found, then she would follow her husband to London.

After speaking with his wife, Master Dritchly had gone to tell his apprentices. The boys sat at their benches in stunned disbelief and dejected silence pervaded the stables.

Half-heartedly they started to dismantle the musicians to see what had gone wrong, but they were too preoccupied to concentrate on the task. After a while they climbed up to the loft where they threw themselves on to their beds.

"S'pose you'll be boss of us now," Henry said to Jack.

The older boy was chewing a piece of straw and merely grunted in response.

"Reckon you can do it?" Henry persisted. "Can you tackle the tricky bits of work what come in?"

Jack spat the straw from his mouth. "I can tackle you and that's all you need bother about," he said.

"Eyes is always difficult," Henry went on. "Old Dritchly might be a sweaty pink slug but he were clever with them eyes. Lining them up's awkward; when I've had a go the lousy mechanicals end up with a squint and can't walk in a straight line."

"Hush up, can't you?" Jack groaned from the darkness. "We got to see the old boy off at dawn."

The hay loft fell quiet. It was a warm, airless night.

Outside a morose snorting came drifting across the yard and Henry turned over restlessly. "Can't sleep with that filthy row," he grumbled.

Adam had been lying on his back, staring up into the blackness which crammed the rafters. He could not sleep either but it was nothing to do with Old Temperance. The boy disliked change and he could not imagine what the workshop would be like without Master Dritchly to guide them along.

Out in the piggery the great sow's snuffling continued.

"Foul, rumbling swine!" Henry seethed.

"She's missing the piglet," Adam said softly. "Funny how they get attached to one another. I'll go give him back to her."

Down the ladder he clambered. Then, taking up a lantern, he unhooked Suet and set about refilling a small glass phial with amber ichor taken from the recorder player. Fastening the two halves of the wooden creature together, Adam strolled out into the yard.

Old Temperance's large shadowy bulk was pressed against the piggery fence. The moment the sow saw him, the snorting grew louder and the glass lenses of her eyes glimmered in the dark.

"Here you are," Adam said, lifting Suet over the railing and pressing the Wutton crest on its back.

Immediately the piglet jiggled into life, squirming in the boy's grasp until he placed it upon the ground.

"Glad to see someone happy," Adam observed as Suet
went scuttling for cover beneath its 'mother's' barrel of a
stomach.

The mechanicals greeted one another with almost
genuine affection and when Flitch, the other piglet, came
scooting from the sty, the three of them went tearing about
the piggery, squealing and squeaking as loud as their
internals would permit.

"Shut up or I'll come down there and hack you all into
kindling!" Henry's voice shrieked from inside the stables.

Adam managed a faint grin and, leaning on the fence,
looked across to the manor. Several windows were still
aglow with candlelight. In the topmost room, Mistress
Dritchly was busily helping her husband to pack, and two
of the guest bedchambers were similarly illuminated. A
light downstairs showed that Lord Richard had not yet
gone to bed. Adam guessed correctly that he had started on
the October ale.

"We're going to have to work mighty hard once Master
Edwin's gone," he told himself.

Behind him, the wooden pigs had calmed themselves and
Adam turned towards the stables.

Hearing the boy leave, Suet came trotting to the fence
where it rested its chin on the lowest rail and pushed out its
snuffling nose. Then, very softly, it began to grunt and the
sound brought Adam to a standstill. Slowly he turned
around and gazed at the piglet in amazement. The little

wooden mechanical was grunting to the tune of *O Mistress Mine*.

"Suet?" he breathed. "How on...?"

Before he could say any more, a frantic yell suddenly erupted from the barn and Jenks, Walsingham's groom, came lunging out.

"Fetch Dritchly!" the man called, running up to Adam and seizing him by the shoulders. "The horse! Belladonna! There's something wrong! Quick, boy – quick!"

All traces of the groom's former sneering arrogance were gone and, glancing past him to the barn, Adam could see why. Through the wide, open doors he saw the magnificent steed of Sir Francis Walsingham staggering backwards and forwards, juddering alarmingly.

"Shaking sickness!" Adam gasped.

Jenks pushed him aside. "It cannot be!" he snapped fiercely. "No beast in my charge has ever succumbed to that. Go fetch your master!"

Adam nodded and raced to the manor house. He understood why the groom had denied the suggestion with such vehemence. Shaking sickness was a rare, unexplained condition which affected very few mechanicals. Yet once they fell victim to it, there was absolutely no hope of redemption. Every piece of internal working had to be completely scrapped and melted down. Even the ichors were ruined and had to be destroyed in case they infected another creation. If Walsingham's grand horse did have the shaking sickness, then it was now only a four-legged lump of worthless metal.

Hurrying into the manor house, Adam called for Master Dritchly. The groom dashed back to the barn and stared in horror at the plight of one of the most expensive horses in Englandia.

The beast was shuddering all over. Each segment of black steel was scraping and grinding against the next and horrible screeches issued from the delicately crafted mechanisms. The proud head shook furiously and the obsidian eyes rolled in their sockets. Bronze hooves bruised the air and the silken tail cracked like a whip as the great hind legs kicked out at the barn walls.

Fearfully, the groom held up his hands. "Belladonna!" he cried, trying to get within striking distance of the horse's neck, where Walsingham's crest was emblazoned. "Be at peace. Let me help you."

But the creature shied away. A grotesque, screeching neigh shrieked from its trembling mouth and Jenks saw threads of dark smoke escaping from the quivering joints.

Roused by the clamour, Jack and Henry came racing across the yard. They stared at the scene, afraid and stupefied. "Where's that other boy with Dritchly?" Jenks shouted in desperation.

At that moment Adam came running from the manor, with Master Edwin huffing along behind, dressed in a nightshirt and pulling on his boots.

Within the barn Belladonna lurched to one side, crashing into one of the other horses, denting it severely. Then back it came, its mighty legs shivering and stumbling beneath it. Throwing back the fabulous head, it gave a ghastly scream and the apprentices knew there was nothing anyone could do.

"Heavens pickle and keep us!" Edwin Dritchly exclaimed, pushing past the gawping boys. "Hum hum, never in all my—"

Before he could finish, Jenks whirled around and dragged him through the barn doors.

"Save her!" he demanded. "Dritchly, you must!"

Suddenly the horse screamed worse than ever and, with a clash of gears and whining metal, it bolted forward. No power in this uplifted world could stop it. Like the devil's own infernal steed the mechanical came thundering, smoke steaming from its nostrils.

Blundering back, Master Dritchly cried out, but the nightmare raged straight for him. High it reared – up into the dark, smashing its steel head into the lintel of the door. The oak beam splintered and Belladonna brought her bronze hooves plunging down.

"No!" Adam yelled.

A rioting blur of destruction filled the boy's cringing eyes as those massive legs stamped and kicked, and Master Dritchly was caught beneath them. Battered to the floor, the man crumpled like a bundle of linen. Belladonna trounced and pounded, tossing her buckled head and flicking her tail in a frenzied, murderous dance.

Across the length of Malmes-Wutton the grisly tattoo went drumming. The demented horse's shrill, insane whinnies echoed beneath the vaulted firmament, penetrating the outlying woods where even Old Scratch, the wild boar, withdrew into the deepest shadows.

Jenks was hurled across the yard and the horrific crunching slaughter continued. Each of the apprentices turned away in revulsion. The entire household was roused now and everyone came streaming towards the barn bearing candles and lanterns.

Rivers of deep blue vapour were flooding from the horse's mouth, and within its mad, prancing frame, bright flashes of fire crackled as brilliant sparks spat from its joints. Abruptly, the wild capering halted. With its steel legs splashed scarlet, the bronze hooves steeped in Master Dritchly's blood, the horse reeled away from the man's crushed and broken body, then keeled over and fell to the ground with a tremendous crash.

CHAPTER 3

Lantern Illuminates

The interior of the barn bounced with light as sharp tongues of flame lapped around the fallen beast. Still quaking and trembling, the mechanical lay upon the floor, plumes of blue smoke rising from every warped and gaping crevice.

At the threshold, all eyes gazed on Master Edwin's stricken corpse but not many could bear to look at him for long. The most learned master of motive science in Suffolk was dead, and for several moments the only sound was the harsh clicking and grinding of his mechanical destroyer. The people gathered around were too distressed and aghast to utter a word.

Sir Francis Walsingham's calm, cold features betrayed nothing but, beside him, his secretary was almost wilting, covering his face with jittery hands. Sorrow and compassion were graven in Doctor Dee's solemn, white-bearded countenance, yet when he shifted his glance to the collapsed horse, fierce curiosity assumed their place.

Met with the sobering sight of his dead servant, Lord Richard Wutton searched for Mistress Dritchly in the crowd.

Master Edwin's widow was not among the assembled faces and, looking back at the house, he saw the plump, prim-looking woman, with her greying hair tied up in curling papers, come bustling towards them.

"Jack," Lord Richard said hastily. "Go to her – she must not see her husband thus. Take her back indoors."

Dragging himself away from the stunned group, the apprentice nodded and hurried to obey.

Henry Wattle's eyes were bulging from his head. "Squashed and stamped on!" he breathed. "You could slide the bits under a door."

"Don't," Adam balked.

"Fetch a cloak to cover him," Lord Richard commanded, and Henry scampered away. Then, with a face as grim as the appalling scene before him, the master of

Malmes-Wutton glared at his distinguished guests and strode to confront them.

Sir Francis Walsingham and Doctor Dee had already stepped over the dead man's crushed body. Remaining at a safe distance, their black and red figures peered at the quivering mechanical horse through the billowing blue reek which bled from every opening.

Into this fog Lord Richard went wading. "A man is dead!" he roared. "Yet all you care about is your vile charger! What manner of ice-blooded creature are you?"

Walsingham waved a silencing hand which only served to enrage his host all the more. "This tragedy would never have happened if it were not for you," he cried.

Sir Francis ignored him and gave a signal to his secretary. With a handkerchief of Holland cloth clamped over his mouth and averting his eyes from the gruesome spectacle, Master Tewkes tiptoed into the barn.

"Lord Richard," he began, spluttering in the smoke and the sharp stench of scorched metal. "Do you not see? Yet another skilled craftsman has met with an unlikely accident. This is not the work of unhappy chance – it was purpose meant and blackly done. Your man has been murdered."

For an instant Richard Wutton's anger was quelled as he struggled with this awful revelation. The secretary seized this opportunity to expound.

"Verily!" he declared. "Here again do we see the

malevolent ministries of the hated Catholic powers. This is assassin's work! May the Lord visit his vengeance upon their evil heads!"

"Tewkes!" Walsingham scolded. "If you can curb the damning of our enemies for a moment, make yourself of use and send that melancholy audience away."

Tucking the handkerchief into his sleeve, the secretary turned to face the gathered members of Lord Richard's household. "Be off with your morbid goggling," he told them. "There is naught you can do for Master Dritchly now. We shall attend to what must be done."

The servants shifted uncomfortably but made no move until Lord Richard added, "Go - pray for Edwin's soul, my friends."

Slowly the group drifted back to the manor, but Adam o'the Cogs was reluctant to leave and lingered at the threshold.

Nursing a badly grazed arm and hobbling upon an injured foot, the groom returned to the barn and Master Tewkes eyed him with undisguised hostility.

By now the choking vapour had thinned to a haze and Doctor Dee edged closer to the fallen horse. Faint tremors still shivered across Belladonna's battered form, but the flames were dying and the astrologer stooped over her to prise one of the contorted sections free. A fresh cloud of smoke rose from inside and he held his whiskery face clear until it dispersed.

"Now," he said, bending over the hole he had made, "let us see how this wickedness was achieved."

"Permit me, My Lord," Jenks said, limping towards him. "I know the workings better than any."

Master Tewkes thrust out his hand to prevent the man from going any further. "You remain where you are!" he objected, his voice loaded with reproach and accusation. "You have engineered enough this night."

Startled by the charge, Jenks backed away in fright. "You cannot think I was responsible for this," he gasped. "My hands are clean of any blame."

"Was it Spanish gold or French which bought your base treason?" Tewkes persisted. "A quartering is too merciful a punishment for you!"

The groom turned pale and he stared imploringly at Sir Francis. "It is not true!" he denied. "On my life it is not!"

Peering over Doctor Dee's shoulder, Walsingham did not even look up at him. "I will listen to neither plea nor indictment till we have determined what truly happened here this night," he said. "What have you learned from this wreckage, Doctor?"

The astrologer raised his head and drummed his slender fingers irritably upon one of the steel flanks.

"Alas!" he confessed. "My limited knowledge of the new stars is greater than my understanding of this once noble charger's internals. 'Tis a grievous pity that the one man who could aid us was the beast's victim."

Covering Master Dritchly's body with the cloak that Henry had just brought, Lord Richard snorted with contempt at the scholar's apparent lack of concern. "Grievous indeed!" he said.

Hearing the talk, Adam plucked up his nerve and stepped into the barn. "Beg pardon, My Lords," he began, "but I may be able to assist."

Everyone stared at him and in the accompanying silence the boy wished he had not volunteered but had waited instead for the return of Jack. Lingering by the door, Henry watched in admiring fascination. He would never have dared approach those nobles and he suspected that his friend had just earned himself a whipping.

"You?" the secretary snapped in amused disbelief. "What can a cog urchin possibly...?"

"I know how to put a cow together, make it walk and eat so its bags fill with milk," Adam retorted impulsively. "Which is more than you do."

Master Tewkes gave a shout of indignation and raised his hand to strike the insolent boy.

"Wait!" Lord Richard intervened. "The lad's mine to deal with – not thine, Master Secretary. If any discipline is needed, it'll not be measured by your hand."

Tewkes' nostrils flared in outrage and his bird-like head darted aside, looking to Sir Francis for support. "Let the boy approach," came Walsingham's astonishing response.

Leaving the secretary fuming behind him, Adam crossed

to where the great mechanical lay upon the ground and knelt before it. The metal was still hot. His face tingled in the baking airs and his fair hair rippled as he leaned over the opening that the astrologer had made.

"Bum boils," he murmured, unconsciously using a favourite phrase of Henry's. Never in his life had he seen such a mangled confusion of workings. Within the stricken creature all was twisted and blackened. Strands of stinking smoke curled up from the inaccessible recesses where occasional sparks still spat and sizzled, but there was no more danger and Adam lowered his head inside for a more thorough inspection.

Along the horse's length, a few brass wheels were still spinning, but others were fused and welded to their spindles. Springs were stretched and distorted, the teeth of every cog had been worn smooth, levers were bent and broken, and the four pendulums which Belladonna boasted had actually been melted out of shape.

"This was no shaking sickness," he declared. "Master Dritchly never told of this happening."

An indulgent smile lifted the corners of Doctor Dee's white beard. "What then?" he asked. "Enlighten us."

Gingerly reaching his hand up inside the neck, the apprentice felt along the bellows pipe and winced when his fingers burned on a fragment of smouldering metal. Cursing under his breath, he proceeded until his stinging fingertips found what he was seeking.

"The ichors are there," he said, "but the vessels are all cracked and broken. The cordials have leaked out and boiled away."

A puzzled frown scrunched the boy's brow.

"What is it?" the astrologer asked.

"Not sure. There seems to be something else here... if I can only..."

Master Tewkes folded his arms and tutted peevishly. "What use is this?" he complained. "The young idiot is making geese of us all."

"Here!" the boy exclaimed, extracting a small glass phial from the horse's insides. "It was attached to one of the ichor pipes – definitely doesn't belong there."

Taking it from him, Doctor Dee walked over to where a lantern hung on the wall and examined the vessel in detail. The bottle was spherical in shape, with a tapering neck tipped with a barbed, silver needle which appeared capable of piercing the toughest leather. Inside the phial were the dregs of a dark, indigo-coloured liquid and the old man sniffed them tentatively.

Thoughtful and silent, he passed it to Walsingham and the Queen's spymaster received the object with great solemnity.

"Is it as we feared?" he asked.

Doctor Dee inclined his head. "It is," he answered. "The enemies of Englandia have contrived a way of distilling a new and deadly ichor."

"Then the intelligence furnished by my agents in Europe was correct," Walsingham reflected. "With this mordant liquid those hostile powers can transform any mechanical into a killing engine."

The old astrologer looked questioningly at Adam. "In your opinion," he began, "how long would the effects of this loathsome venom take to work its evil within such a creation as that horse?"

"Can't tell you that, Sir," the boy replied, taken aback to be treated with such respect from so important a figure. "I never seen nothing like it before."

"Your finest guess then?"

Adam looked in at the extreme damage once more and shrugged. "Not long I don't reckon," he said finally. "To pump round all the feeder veins wouldn't take no more than a quarter hour."

"Remarkable boy," the Doctor observed.

Weighing the glass vessel in his palm, Sir Francis brought his piercing glance to bear upon the groom and the man struggled to proclaim his innocence.

"No other has been near the horses this night!" Walsingham said, his assured, level voice more daunting than any shouted threat. "Who else could have done this?"

"As God is m–my witness..." Jenks stammered.

"Search him and his belongings," Walsingham commanded.

Eager to obey, Master Tewkes snatched a leather purse

from where it hung at the groom's waist and emptied the contents into his eager hand. "Ha!" he proclaimed, casting groats and pennies to the ground but brandishing a small object with a jubilant flourish. "Behold – the knave's guilt is proved beyond further doubt."

Held between the secretary's fingers was a second phial of glass, identical to the one Adam had discovered – yet this one was full.

"Who can say for whom this was meant!" Master Tewkes cried, shaking the blue fluid within. "One of Her Majesty's own steeds perhaps?"

Jenks stared at the bottle with a look of horror etched into his face. But, before he could voice any protestation, Doctor Dee prowled forward, his keen eyes sparkling.

"Your next words may condemn you," he warned. "So choose them with wisdom. Tell me truthfully, what happened here this night?"

Jenks blinked and nodded at the other mechanical horses which were still standing at the darkened end of the barn.

"I saw to the beasts," he said. "Unloaded them, polished the dust away, brushed the manes and tails then sat and ate the bit of supper the kitchen girl brought out to me."

"Is that all?"

The groom nodded. "It was then that Belladonna started. A frightful noise she made."

"No, no, no," the astrologer remarked with a disappointed air. "That will never do. Like many puzzles this is merely a question of mathematics. You have left out the most significant factor in your account."

Jenks shrank against the wall, looking like a cornered animal of the old world about to be delivered to the wolves. "It's true I tell you!" he cried wretchedly. "Every word."

Master Tewkes spat at him. "The rack will teach you the meaning of truth," he promised.

"Hold!" Doctor Dee's voice rang sharply. "I had not finished, hear me out." He waited until he had their complete attention, then continued. "Observe the groom's appearance," he said. "Does it not speak of more than he has related?"

"I always thought he looked like a surly gypsy!" the secretary put in, unable to stop himself.

A warning glance from Walsingham caused Master Tewkes to bite his own tongue and say no more.

"Note the particles of straw in this man's hair," Doctor Dee resumed. "There is also a quantity upon his back; is that not suggestive? Look also to the great heaps piled yonder – mark you that singular depression?"

He indicated the hills of straw kept at the back of the barn. Upon the lower slopes there was a curiously deep hollow.

"The fact you omitted to tell us," he said, returning his attention to the groom, "is that you fell asleep. Replete with Mistress Dritchly's victuals, you sat at your ease and were awakened only when Belladonna began making those horrible sounds. No doubt there were preliminary whirrs and other signs of distress, but you missed them entirely until they were loud enough to rouse you from slumber. Perhaps in all the confusion you did not realise you had even closed your eyes, but it is the only hope of salvation you have for the moment."

Walsingham pursed his lips and considered what the astrologer had said. "Then some other party may have stolen into this place and tampered with the horse," he said. "It is possible."

"Fanciful nonsense!" Master Tewkes blurted. "The groom had the other phial in his keeping. Of course he is the one! He was the only person here this night and he is responsible!"

To everyone's surprise, the Doctor gave a slight chuckle. "Oh no," he corrected. "There you are mistaken. As I have said, the solution to this enigma is mathematical in nature. I shall demonstrate how, in this instance, one plus one can equal three. Jenks was not alone in the barn – there was another."

Stepping aside he lifted his lined face and called out, "Lantern!"

Still kneeling by the ruined wreck of Belladonna, Adam picked up the light that was nearby and offered it to him. Doctor Dee declined with an amused smile and pointed to the shadow-filled corner of the barn, beyond the remaining horses.

"The illumination I seek," he said, "is of another sort."

Everyone stared. Standing by the entrance, Henry peered around the door and held his breath.

From the gloom he heard a rustling. There, in the dun murk, one of the straw mounds was moving. It shook and wobbled for a moment, then a dark shape clambered free and Jenks choked in fright.

"The imp from Hell!" he breathed.

Both Henry and Adam recalled what the groom had told them about Doctor Dee. Over there in the unlit corner, a small, dwarf-like figure was brushing the dust and hay from its shoulders, then through the shadows it came.

"Gentlemen," the old astrologer announced, "permit me to introduce my own personal secretary – Lantern."

The squat shape ambled towards them, the discs of its eyes glowing with a pale green radiance. Adam gazed at the stranger in wonder. It was a mechanical, but the most peculiar one that he had ever seen.

Fashioned in the shape of a short, round man, Doctor Dee's secretary was wrought almost entirely from copper. The head was a gleaming globe and, apart from the large circular eyes, the only other feature was a hinged hatch in place of the nose.

The body was also hammered out of the flame-coloured metal, forming a tubby doublet with rivets for buttons, and a high collar with a crimped and corrugated edge. Scarlet velvet covered the arms and legs, and the hands were protected by white gauntlets. A conical hat, almost as tall as the rest of him, sat on top of the domed head and Adam was intrigued to see that a grilled window was cut into the front. It was too dark to see what, if anything, was within.

Standing before the astrologer, the outlandish creation executed a low, courteous bow and three copper feathers affixed to a riveted band about the hat scraped over the floor.

"Good evening, Lantern," Doctor Dee greeted as warmly as if addressing a real person. "I trust your journey here in the travelling chest was not too disagreeable?"

Not even the most expensive mechanicals had the power of speech. Lantern's burnished head slid from side to side, then the secretary bowed once more.

"Tell me," the astrologer said, "have you witnessed all that occurred this night?"

Lantern nodded and the trio of feathers jiggled up and down.

Doctor Dee indicated the fearful groom. "Did Jenks commit this dastard crime?" he asked.

The mechanical gave a forceful shake of its head, and the groom sank against the wall, sobbing his gratitude.

"I was convinced as much," the old man muttered. "What, then, were the circumstances of this tragedy?"

Executing another bow, Lantern trotted over to the four remaining horses and began to mime the events he had seen. Reaching as high as his diminutive stature allowed, he pretended to polish their flanks and brush the tangles from their tails.

It was rather embarrassing for Jenks because the mechanical repeated everything he had observed in accurate detail. He was adept at mimicking the groom's mannerisms and copied the arrogant jaunty swagger perfectly. It was soon proved, however, that Jenks adored the horses in his care, for Lantern kept throwing his arms about them in a fashion which appeared quite absurd and comical.

Then, with a nimble hop, he sat cross-legged on the ground and shovelled imaginary food into his non-existent mouth, wagging his head and rubbing his copper stomach as if enjoying it heartily.

"The supper was to your liking I see," the Doctor remarked to the groom.

Jenks managed a weak smile; the provisions had been tastier than anything he was accustomed to.

Lantern stretched up his arms as though fatigued, then rose, inspected the horses again, and wandered over to the straw where he eased himself down and lay in precisely the same hollow that Jenks had created earlier.

Walsingham shot the Doctor an impatient glance. "A very pretty mummery," he said. "But what happened then?"

The mechanical bobbed up again and shook off the persona of the groom. Striding to the entrance he assumed a new role and came sneaking into the barn, looking this way and that and advancing with nervous, jerky movements.

"Now we have it," Doctor Dee declared. "The third player in this lethal equation."

Lantern stole over to the empty impression in the straw, rubbing his gauntleted hands together as he had seen the malefactor do before. Taking pains not to make any sound, he performed the planting of the incriminating bottle in the sleeping groom's purse, then turned to where Belladonna had stood.

Holding out his small hands to appease and calm the high-spirited steed, he stalked towards the now empty spot, his copper shoulders shaking as if with mirth. Deftly, his palms travelled across unseen contours until, with an expert twist which had obviously popped one of the steel plates free, he reached up, holding something carefully between his fingers.

"Enough," Walsingham rapped. "The rest is plain. Who, then, is responsible?"

The burlesque over, Lantern took a side step to cast off the villainous character. Returning to his master, his round head revolved slowly in order to survey everyone present.

From the door, where Henry was still standing, those green lenses panned through the barn. Over Master Tewkes they roamed, then Jenks, Lord Richard, Adam and the remains of Belladonna, until at last they rested upon Sir Francis Walsingham.

"Is the rogue present?" the Queen's advisor demanded.

Lantern bowed then walked purposefully towards the entrance. Watching him approach, Henry Wattle began to splutter, but there was no need to be alarmed, for the copper figure veered aside and pointed an accusing finger at Master Arnold Tewkes.

"What game is this?" the man exclaimed in an injured voice. "Get away from me, you walking kettle!"

The mechanical stood his ground.

"Tewkes," Walsingham hissed. "What have you to say?"

"Only that I find no jest in this. Remove this clunking hobgoblin at once, before I lose my temper."

Lantern continued to point. Master Tewkes snorted angrily and lashed out with a vicious kick which sent his denouncer staggering back.

"Explain yourself!" Walsingham growled.

Master Tewkes drew himself up. "Surely, My Lord," he objected, "you are not serious in this? I have served you faithfully for many years, yet you are ready to accept this silent clowning as evidence against me. I am dismayed and affronted."

"Lantern is never mistaken," Doctor Dee said firmly. "His vision is often deeper and clearer than mine own."

"He is at fault, I tell you!" Tewkes denied hotly.

The mechanical shook its head and again the finger pointed. Incensed, the furious man sprang forward, pushing Lantern off balance then leaping on top of him. In an instant he had wrenched the copper breastplate away and spat upon the exposed, delicate workings.

The little figure flailed beneath him as Master Tewkes raised his fist to smash the glass vessels of the controlling ichors. "You'll accuse no more!" he ranted. "A pan for stewing cabbages is all you'll be fit for when I'm done."

Before the threat could be carried out, Doctor Dee and the groom dragged him clear, and Jenks pinned him against the wall. Master Tewkes struggled and demanded to be set free; then he caught sight of Walsingham's grim face and his efforts ceased. A wintry light was glinting in Sir Francis' dark eyes.

"You knew," he breathed, bewildered. "You have suspected me all along."

"Not all along," Walsingham confessed. "Your singular condemnation of all Popery did kindle my initial suspicions, for they were such ardent damnings that they left a bitter tang upon even my Puritan palate. Yet gradually I learned of your treachery and collated as much intelligence pertaining to it as was possible."

"How much?"

Walsingham's eyebrows bunched together. "You are in the employ of Spain," he stated. "You were indiscreet enough to be observed at a clandestine meeting with the ambassador, the Count de Feria, on two occasions during the past five years. Yet I have further proofs than that and expect many more still."

Master Tewkes turned pale. "There is no need for torture," he said quickly. "I will tell you everything."

"Oh, I know, but it's tidier this way, don't you think? You were always such a zealous clerk that I am certain you understand. A tickle of torture to give veracity to your statements, and then..."

"Then?"

Sir Francis permitted himself a grave smile. "The Tower," he snarled.

"No!" Master Tewkes yelled in terror. "Not there! I beseech you, My Lord! I would rather die a hundred deaths."

"One will suffice," Walsingham said coldly. "The Tower it is."

"Never!" the man cried in panic, and with a shriek he stamped violently upon Jenks' injured foot. The groom recoiled, and in that brief moment of liberty, Master Tewkes snapped the neck of the bottle containing the indigo ichor and poured the liquid down his own throat.

A wild, dangerous look clouded his face as the fatal juice trickled into his stomach, and his stained lips blistered immediately. "I'll not go to that doom!" he cried, his voice rising to a high, mad laugh. "Though you, My Lord, may shortly be consigned there. The time of Elizabeth, the misbegotten usurper, is over! The crown of Englandia will be cast from Her head. Philip will reign here. This uplifted world is for the true Catholic faith – not your filthy heresy. It must be cleansed of your infection, as God plainly wills..."

The secretary shuddered as an agonising spasm seized him and he gripped his stomach feverishly. The venomous ichor was scorching his insides and he dropped to his knees, convulsing in torment.

Lord Richard hastened over to him but Master Tewkes was beyond rescue. Dark blue vapour trailed from his nose and mouth and, emitting a last gurgling cry, the traitor fell on his face and expired.

Richard Wutton knelt beside the dead man, whose features had assumed a hideous, chalk-like pallor. The master of Malmes-Wutton looked across to the crushed corpse of Edwin Dritchly lying by the barn entrance. It had been a night of horrors and countless emotions broiled inside him.

"I did not expect that," Walsingham said dryly. "There was much he could have told us – what a squandered opportunity."

Doctor Dee agreed. "I did not foresee what other purpose the malignant ichor might be used for," he murmured. "We must be doubly vigilant. 'Twould seem our enemies have been most busily occupied."

"They are massing their strength, constantly devising new weapons of destruction. My spies in the Spanish court have recently despatched reports of mechanical torture masters, diabolic instruments which only a Catholic mind could envisage. I would dearly like to obtain a copy of the plans."

Lord Richard could endure it no longer and his simmering rage finally burst forth. "Listen to you!" he snapped. "You chatter and squawk whilst two men lie dead, and pick over their carcasses like carrion birds. This ridiculous visit was orchestrated solely for the purpose of unmasking your secretary. The blood of Edwin Dritchly besmears you both."

Walsingham regarded him with faint surprise. "I regret the death of your craftsman," he drawled in his usual composed and maddeningly detached manner. "But it was necessary to capture Tewkes as far away from court as possible. You still do not realise the perilous state of affairs. There was simply no other way."

Lord Richard could not bear to look at him. "I want you gone," he ordered. "Now that your odious mission is complete, you are to leave my lands. Get from this place, you are no longer welcome."

Sir Francis was already striding for the entrance. "You were always an emotional fool, Richard," he reflected. "To buy the safety of Her Majesty and ensure the welfare of Her blessed realm I would gladly sacrifice any number of lives."

"Then I pity your conscience," Lord Richard murmured and he turned his back on him.

Walsingham's tall black figure departed, but Doctor Dee remained. "I told you this was not of my doing," he said.

"Spare me your hypocrisy, John," Lord Richard retorted. "May another fourteen years go by before we see one another again. You spend the lives of my friends too freely."

The astrologer fell silent and motioned to Lantern to follow him. Still sitting upon the floor, occupied in the task of replacing his own breastplate, the little figure rose to his feet. Only then did they realise the damage caused by Master Tewkes' savage kick.

The mechanical's right leg was buckled and bent backwards. Peering down, Lantern gave the disfigured limb an experimental shake and the green light dimmed in his eyes when there came a tinkling rattle of fragments that clattered down into his boot. Abruptly the leg gave way beneath him and, with a clang, the copper man sat down again.

"My dear fellow," Doctor Dee exclaimed, offering him a hand. "Can you not walk?"

His leg twitching pitifully, Lantern gave him a forlorn look then hung his head.

"Take it to the workshop," Lord Richard said with some reluctance. "I'll send Jack Flye to deal with it."

The colour rose in the astrologer's face and he thanked his host for this last kindness.

Richard Wutton went stomping from the barn. "I go now to speak with Mistress Dritchly," he said tersely. "When that painful interview is over I will expect to find that you and Walsingham have gone."

A short while later, Jenks had readied the remaining horses. The body of Master Tewkes had been slung over the beast that had carried him to Malmes-Wutton and Sir Francis Walsingham was impatient to be away. Master Dritchly's remains had been respectfully removed into the manor.

Within the stables, Lantern was sitting upon Jack Flye's workbench, keenly watching the boy repair his leg.

"Nasty bit of harm done here," the seventeen-year-old declared. "Don't think it can be mended back to what it was before. Need a whole new limb, this will."

Casting an interested eye over the impressive array of tools gathered in the workshop, Doctor Dee tutted into his long white beard. "How inconvenient," he muttered. "Such skilled work requires time. I rely upon my secretary a great deal. His assistance is invaluable to me, as is his steadfast companionship."

Jack scowled. "Master Dritchly might have been able to do it," he said with undisguised reproach. He resented having to work on anything belonging to those who had caused Edwin's death and he was tired after so long and bitter a day.

The other apprentices were leaning on the bench, watching. Although the hour was late and they were both drained after the night's awful events, they were also eager to see the inside workings of this wonderful creation. Never had they seen such cunning devices; there was a delightful harmony of swinging weights and clicking levers. Wheels spun smooth and silent, while brass chains slipped gracefully across their gears. It was all ingenious and engrossing, but the most fantastic element, which drew a long, low whistle from Henry, was the quantity of ichor.

The three usual humours were there in long glass cylinders, but next to them was an even larger vessel containing the black cordial – the most expensive of all.

"This mannikin must be smarter than all of us put together," Henry marvelled.

"Imbeciles," the Doctor commented, "whether human or not, are tiresome society."

As the minutes passed, Henry began to nod, but Adam was becoming concerned at Jack's treatment of Lantern. He was being inordinately rough and ham-fisted. Where gentle, persuasive tappings with a small hammer were required, the older boy bashed and bullied the damaged metal as though venting his anger and frustration.

Despite being brutalised in this way, Lantern remained quietly tolerant and suffered every fresh attack with remarkable forbearance. He even assisted Jack by passing him the tools he needed and at last Adam saw what was kept inside the tall, conical hat.

It was a stout candle and, now that it was lit, tiny punctures were revealed over the whole copper surface from which the warm light pricked and twinkled, casting a field of fiery stars across the wall.

"Is that where he gets his name from?" Adam asked.

Doctor Dee said that it was not, but he explained no further for he was also beginning to realise that Jack was applying more force than was entirely necessary. Sternly, he drummed his fingers on the bench until the boy moderated his technique.

"That's the best I can manage," Jack said at last. "If I carry on it'll be doing more harm than good."

Lantern was lifted from the bench and set on the floor. But when he tried to walk, he limped so badly that Jack actually looked guilty and embarrassed. The small mechanical hobbled gamely about the workshop, tottering unsteadily between the disassembled sheep and cows which still littered the place. When eventually he halted before his master, he shook his head in such a dejected fashion that Adam felt sorry for him.

"It'll need proper attention when you get to London," Jack said.

The Queen's astrologer gave a curt nod and led the faltering Lantern to the door.

"You did that on purpose," Adam hissed at Jack.

The older boy smirked and began climbing the ladder to

the hay loft. Adam watched the little mechanical struggle to the yard then ran after both him and his master.

"Stay a moment," he pleaded. "I believe I can be of service. The injury may not be as serious as we thought. If you could spare a little while longer."

Sir Francis Walsingham was shaking his head, anxious to leave, but Doctor Dee assented and so back to the stables they went. Adam worked quickly. Sitting Lantern upon his own bench he was appalled at the sloppy workmanship of the older apprentice, but made no comment. Carefully, he put new steel pins into the knee joint and tapped out the remaining dents.

"You are very skilled," the Doctor complimented. "Previously, in the barn, you excelled with Belladonna where I could not. You know your trade well – I foresee a prosperous future for you."

Adam laughed. "Tell that to Henry!" he said indicating the boy who was now lying fast asleep across two sheep in the corner. "He's the one who wants to be rich."

"And you do not share that ambition?"

"I don't want to leave Malmes-Wutton. I like it here. This is where they found me and this is where I belong. Lord Richard's been more than kind – even lets me read the books in his library. The ones he didn't have to sell, of course."

The Doctor was impressed. "A scholar, in addition to your practical accomplishments."

Again Adam laughed. "I just like to know things, that's all."

"Knowledge *is* all," came the compelling reply.

Pausing in his work, the boy looked at the old man's lined face. The pale hazel eyes were ageless, and wisdom more ancient than his august years was written across those brows. Almost without realising what he was saying, Adam asked, "Do you really dig up bodies and speak to the dead?"

The impertinent question did not irritate the Doctor in the least. "I use whatever means I can to further my understanding," he said warmly. "I have studied necromancy, alchemy, I am a cabalist, hermeticist, mathematician and much more besides. I alone have cast the Queen's horoscope without fear of losing my head, for it was at Her own bidding, you see – I luxuriate in the indulgence of Her Majesty."

"Is She really as beautiful as talk would have Her?"

Doctor Dee's features took on a solemn aspect and in a low, almost reverent voice said, "She is Gloriana. In the old world that is gone, She ruled us with honeyed words and a lion's heart. Flattery deified Her then, but now She is indeed a Goddess. Though we ordinary folk endure our extended years more ably than before, hardly a mark of age blemishes Her countenance. Where we weather one year, a single day passes for Her. Yes, She is beautiful, but then what is beauty? The sea may be deemed a ravishing sight, and yet ships are lost and men drowned."

At that moment, a stern voice called from the yard. Walsingham would wait no longer.

"I think that's as much as can be done anyway," Adam said. "I've strengthened the joint and fixed a few bits that Jack overlooked." Covering the mechanisms, he helped Lantern from the bench and the copper secretary took a couple of hesitant steps.

Adam had proven better than his word for the leg was stronger than ever. The limp was gone completely and, as his confidence returned, Lantern gave a dance for joy and bowed repeatedly to the apprentice.

"We are grateful," Doctor Dee announced. Then, giving the scrawny boy a long, appraising look, said, "This is not the end of our acquaintance, young Adam o'the Cogs. We are destined to encounter one another again. Perhaps you will even inspect my library at Mortlake; it is considered to be the greatest in all Englandia. I look forward to that day."

Wrapping his dark red robe about him, he left the stables and Lantern went skipping after.

At the entrance, however, the mechanical paused. His round head swivelled about and the green eyes shone back at Adam, the gentle light flickering uncertainly. Retracing his steps he stood before him once more and opened a small door set into his side.

"What are you doing?" the boy asked, puzzled. "They're waiting for you."

Taking an empty bottle from the workbench, Lantern proceeded to syphon a small quantity of black ichor from his own internals and handed it to Adam with yet another low bow. It was the most precious thing he had to give and the only way of expressing his gratitude.

Deeply touched by the startling, unexpected gift, Adam was not sure what to say, but Lantern was already bustling from the barn.

In the yard, Walsingham, Doctor Dee and the groom were seated upon their horses when the secretary came pattering out. The astrologer hoisted the mechanical up behind him and they were ready.

Surveying the darkened manor of Wutton Old Place, Sir Francis commended himself upon the highly favourable outcome of his plan. The traitor had been dealt with, and in such an unimportant, benighted place that only minor ripples would ever reach the court. Confident that he had served his sovereign well that evening, and regretting only the loss of a most valuable steed, he spurred his inferior horse into action.

Emerging from the stables, Adam watched them depart. Along the road which led through the village, the four horses went galloping, merging with the black shapes of the night. Only the candle which still burned within Lantern's hat disclosed their progress, but more than once the boy imagined he saw two circles of green light glow beneath it.

When even that receded into the distance and passed out

of sight, and the only sounds to be heard were remote mechanical hoof falls, Adam wandered across to the piggery and sat upon the fence.

In the manor house a solitary light bobbed behind the windows as Lord Richard ascended to his bedchamber. He had observed the nobles' departure and earnestly prayed to God Almighty that he might never have to deal with any from court again. A grim silence settled over the estate, broken only by a faint bellowing which echoed from the outlying woods.

"Even Old Scratch has been disturbed and upset," he muttered dismally. "None of us can get any rest this evil night." And he tramped to his room, a candle in one hand, a jug of ale in the other.

With his back against the pigsty, Adam listened to the distant trumpeting of the wild boar which terrorised the woodland. His mind was churning over everything that had happened. The horrendous events of the night were only just beginning to sink in. He had never encountered death before and it frightened him. In this uplifted world people aged much more slowly and only lost their lives through sickness or misadventure. This loathsome murder was the first death to have blighted Malmes-Wutton since before he was born.

Edwin Dritchly would never praise nor criticise his work any more and tears streaked down Adam's face when he realised he would not hear that familiar "Hum hum" again. Bowing his fair head, the boy wept quietly.

Presently he became aware of a soft snuffling noise at his feet and, swivelling around on the railing, he saw that Suet had come toddling from the sty and was gazing up at him.

"Hello," Adam said, wiping his eyes. "Is Old Scratch's booming bothering you too?"

The piglet's nose puffed in and out, and *O Mistress Mine* rose up composed of grunts and snorts.

A sad smile spread across Adam's face at the sound of Master Dritchly's favourite tune. Then, on impulse, he took from his pocket the phial of black ichor which Lantern had given to him and eyed Suet critically.

Next moment he was running back to the workshop with the little wooden piglet wriggling in his arms.

CHAPTER 4

The Scorched and Drunken Bee

Edwin Dritchly was buried two days later in the neglected churchyard of Malmes-Wutton. In the one hundred and seventy-five years since the Beatification only four people had been interred in the overgrown cemetery and Master Blackwill, the parson, had been forced to refresh his memory of the order of service.

It was a warm June morning. The twenty-three inhabitants of the estate gathered to pay their respects to a man they had all liked, and Mistress Dritchly murmured gentle words of thanks to each. Watching the coffin being lowered down into the grave, Adam thought that it was really too beautiful a day for anything so sad as a funeral to take place. It seemed so unreal.

Henry thought so too, and that, coupled with a peculiar, giddy nervousness, compelled Master Wattle to hang his head lower than anyone else in an effort to hide the silly grins which flashed without warning across his face. Mistress Dritchly was not so consumed with mourning that she was incapable of administering a sharp smack.

The man's death had cast a dismal pall over Malmes-Wutton and a dejected languor crept into everyone. In the workshop, Jack Flye was finding it difficult to concentrate on repairing the animals and was daunted by the extra responsibility of Master Dritchly's duties. Henry and Adam did their best to help, but as the only work they had was reassembling all those sheep, cows and poultry, their minds wandered and the dreary task took three days longer than it ought to have done.

Finally, when all the mechanicals were back out in the fields, swimming on the village pond or scratching around the yard, Jack was at a loss what to do next. No fresh consignment of faulties was due to arrive until the thirteenth of the month and so, as was the custom in the stables of Wutton Old Place, the apprentices were free to do as they pleased.

During these infrequent intervals, it was usual for them

to work on their own pet projects, which they constructed from whatever scraps they could scavenge. Jack Flye had spent every spare moment of the past fifteen months building a bear from large wooden barrels. In the bear pits of nearby islands such beasts were much in demand, for the mechanicals baited there were always of a very poor quality. Jack was determined to make the finest that the gamblers of Suffolk had ever wagered upon. Originally it had begun as a way of earning enough money to set himself up in business elsewhere, but now he had succeeded Master Dritchly, his heart was no longer in that dream and he decided to let the others complete what he had started.

Adam and Henry were delighted. At that moment, however, they were both too busy with their own little schemes to take on Jack's unfinished bear. They were adding the last touches to a pair of tin hawks which they believed were finally ready for a first trial flight. Standing at the edge of the manor's wide lawn, they made last-minute adjustments and cast professional glances over each other's creations.

Adam's was a faithful representation of a goshawk, with neat talons forged from steel and a deadly-looking hooked bill. The tin feathers had been painstakingly coloured in grey and black, according to the drawings in Master Dritchly's bestiary. But Henry's was hopeless. He had painted it a garish blue on the top, while underneath it was a striking red with yellow stripes.

"I'm calling her Quicksilver," Henry announced.

Adam resisted the temptation to point out that in all of the ludicrous colouring, there wasn't a patch of silver anywhere. Instead he said, "The wings are too large – she'll be too strong. If she were any bigger she'd be an eagle. You didn't follow the plans properly, did you?"

Sporting a shapeless straw hat to shield his eyes from the sunlight which blazed through the painted panes of the firmament, Henry lifted the brim so that his friend could observe the rude face he was making. "Privy slop!" he scoffed. "You're starting to sound like Hummy Hum hisself."

"The diagrams are there to keep animals in proportion," Adam insisted.

"Who cares any more? I don't see why the birds or beasts I make can't be stronger and brighter than the real things were. Neither you nor me ever saw the genuine articles so I don't see why you get so priggy about it."

"You might as well make giant mice then," Adam retorted.

Henry hastily pulled the hat back down over his face and hid the knowing smirk which had suddenly appeared. "Least I got the eyes right this time," was all he said.

Sitting at Adam's feet, Suet the piglet looked up at him. Since that night when the boy had added Lantern's gift of black ichor to its internals, the little creature had idolised him and, whenever possible, followed him about like an adoring puppy. Every time Adam went for a walk, Suet squealed in the piggery to be let out, then trotted happily at his heels.

Donning thick leather gauntlets, the boys laid the inert hawks on the backs of their hands and carefully pressed the small Wutton crests they had set on top of the birds' heads. There was a rattle of tin feathers as the creatures clicked into life, the tiny ichor vessels bubbling inside each one. Strong claws gripped the leather-clad wrists as they scrabbled upright, spread their metal wings for balance and jerked their heads about.

Seeing the hawks shake into being, Suet sprang up and started running in circles about Adam, snorting with excitement. The boy raised his hand, then flung the hawk high into the air.

Furiously, the mechanical wings flapped and up the goshawk flew, soaring over the lawn. The piglet bolted along beneath until Adam called him back.

"Look at that!" the boy breathed, greatly pleased with himself. "She flies perfectly. The best set of wings I ever made."

Screwing up his face to watch the bird's progress against the scant-rendered clouds, Henry gave an impish snigger and let his own creation loose.

The garish Quicksilver shot away, flying swifter than even Henry had anticipated or hoped for, and he went rolling back in the grass, hooting with pleasure.

"How's that, Coggy?" he crowed. "She'll outstrip yours in no time."

Up and up the gaudy bird ascended, cutting through the air like an arrow. Within moments it reached Adam's goshawk and the boys heard a chime of metal as the tips of their wings brushed together. Briefly, the two mechanicals flew side by side, heading out over the woodland, skimming the tops of the trees. Then Quicksilver sped onwards, dashing faster and higher, rising in an arching curve to match the underside of the buttressed firmament above.

"If she'd a fork of lightning up her tail she couldn't go better," Henry called, clapping his hat over his heart. "Oh, Coggy, don't it make you green? Yours flaps like a roast goose next to mine."

Adam had to confess that he was impressed. Quicksilver's speed and agility were incredible. Viewing his own goshawk wheel almost lazily above the trees, he wondered if adhering to the principles laid down in the diagrams was such a good idea after all. Henry's brilliantly coloured bird was exhilarating to watch. It catapulted itself from one side of the estate to the other, then suddenly down it swooped – plunging with frightening velocity.

"Henry!" Adam shouted. "She's falling like a stone."

Ramming the hat back on his head, the other boy stared at the blur that was Quicksilver, rushing unerringly towards the outlying woods. "What's the matter with her?" he groaned. "She'll dash herself to bits."

Through the tin feathers of his hawk's wings the wind went rattling as down she plummeted. Then at the last instant, just before she disappeared below the topmost branches, Quicksilver gave a piercing cry and rocketed over the trees, straight and level – the momentum propelling her faster than ever.

"She's headed right for my goshawk!" Adam murmured. "She's going to attack!"

Her talons outstretched, ripping up the tips of leaves in her bolting progress, Quicksilver went racing after her chosen prey. She would share the confined space beneath the firmament with no other and for Adam's bird there was no escape. There was a crunch of colliding metal as Quicksilver cannoned into her target, knocking it from the sky.

The goshawk spiralled down, but Henry's aggressor snatched it up, and even as she flew over the wood her savage bill went rending and ripping. The cruel talons slashed at those wings which were so much smaller than her own, shredding the delicate creation into ragged strips.

Adam could not believe what was happening, but Henry was jubilant and jumped up and down, punching the air.

"Good girl!" he cheered. "Go on – slice that skinny sparrow to ribbons. Oh yes, Coggy, that is what I call a hawk. Snot and glory – I'm a genius!"

Torn tin scraps rained down upon the trees, the bright splinters glittering in the sunlight and Quicksilver shrieked her victory as vainly as her creator as she circled above the woodland.

Furious, Adam turned on the other boy and thumped him in the chest. Henry stumbled and Adam hit him again until he fell over.

"You did all that on purpose!" Adam yelled. "You put too much red ichor in that monster of a bird, didn't you? Just so it would attack mine."

Henry could not help giggling. It had been a marvellous stunt. "Toe cheese!" he snickered. "She's a beauty and your piddly squawker wasn't worth keeping."

"My hawk was accurate – yours is a flying devil. We've already got one horror skulking in Malmes-Wutton – now you go make another." Adam was so annoyed that Suet brushed up against him, then toddled forward and grunted threateningly at the other boy.

Henry laughed all the more.

"It's not funny," Adam told him. "You go too far – I can't even go retrieve all the pieces because Old Scratch is in that wood."

Propping himself up on one elbow, Henry threw his hat at Adam. "Cease your puling!" he said.

That was too much for Suet. Thinking that his master was being assailed, the piglet lunged at the boy and gave his arm a sharp nip. Henry howled and sprang to his feet, while Suet leaped up at him. The small mechanical clacked his lower jaw against his snout, trying to pinch the apprentice again.

"Call this deranged swine off me!" Henry demanded, hopping across the lawn with the piglet in pursuit. "If you don't, I'll whistle Quicksilver over and get her to carry it off."

Enjoying the spectacle for a little while longer, Adam hesitated before clapping his hands. Obediently, Suet forsook his victim and came trundling to heel.

Henry kicked at the lawn and glared at the pair of them. Then he craned his head back to see where his hawk had got to.

After destroying Adam's bird, Quicksilver had flown steadily higher, surging upwards until at last she could go no further. At the absolute apex of the protective firmament, Henry's creature was angrily battering her metal wings against the leaded panes.

Far below the boys could hear the insistent clattering, but however loudly Henry called, Quicksilver took no notice and remained up there, floundering hopelessly beneath the glass.

"She'll never come down now," Adam said. "I told you she was too strong. A bird like that needs a bigger isle than this to fly in. All that temper you put in didn't help either."

"But she's so high," Henry declared. "You're only jealous, you with your pet pig."

Adam shook his head and threw a stick for Suet to fetch. "That hawk of yours will be stuck up there until the tin rusts or she bumps her crest on the glass and stills herself.

I'll warrant that before either of those happen, we're all going to be heartily sick of her incessant, clacking din."

This had not occurred to Henry and he gave a gloomy sigh. He was a dreadfully light sleeper and detested any form of noise at night. Lord Richard would not like it, and nor would anyone else on the estate.

"Fish wigs!" he droned.

For the rest of that day the inhabitants of Malmes-Wutton tried to grow accustomed to the annoying clatter with little success. Everyone was angry with Henry. Lord Richard reprimanded him, Mistress Dritchly scolded and threatened him with mouldy bread and maggot soup for a month. Folk in the fields grumbled and shook their fists at the nuisance bird, and when the boy's father heard who was responsible, he came marching from the village to administer a belated beating.

When evening came and the hawk still tapped and rattled against the glass, Henry climbed into the darkened loft and eased himself on to his bed, grimacing from the bequeathed bruises. "What with them and that row," he griped miserably, "I won't get no sleep at all. No one wants me round here. Don't know why I stay."

Lying close by, Jack heard Henry's grumbles and tried to console him. Thus far he was the only person in all of the estate not to have made any complaint. "Don't get maudlin," the older boy said. "We've all made mistakes in our time. Look what I did when I was your age – the first job Dritchly entrusted me with and I went and put too much temper into Old Scratch. Terrible devil that thing is and it's all my fault. Learned from it, though; always measured the cordials exactly ever since."

Pulling more hay beneath him, Henry sighed. "Least that boar hides in the wood and don't make a clackety clackety riot all day and night."

In the yard, Adam was lifting a reluctant Suet over the piggery fence. "Go back in there," he ordered. "I've got to go to sleep and you don't want to come with me into the loft, do you?"

The piglet danced excitedly so that the boy knew there was nothing the wooden mechanical wanted more.

"All right," he submitted. "If I don't say yes then you'll only start squealing. To think, it wasn't a week ago when you didn't even like me picking you up." Snorting with bliss, Suet jumped into his arms, the little snout pumping furiously.

Before crossing the yard, Adam raised his eyes to the distant shape of the hawk flying far above. A crooked smile played across his face. Poor Henry – he really had a flair for getting himself into trouble.

Beyond the hawk's fervent fluttering, through the clear panes of the firmament, the bright stars shone cold and fierce. It was a spectacle that Adam never tired of seeing. Above the horizon, the nearest floating isle was a remote black crag. Saxmundham was many times larger than

Malmes-Wutton but there was such a gulf between the two uplifted lands that it appeared small enough to fit snugly inside his pocket.

Viewing it through half closed eyes, Adam held up Suet and played games with the beguiling perspective.

"Suet the Great!" he pronounced, lining the piglet up with the faraway island. "Monstrous enemy from the Outer Darkness, come to trample and destroy. All Englandia quakes at his approach. Spare us, oh colossal fiend!"

The mechanical snuffled gently while paddling the empty air with its trotters.

Adam laughed. "Come on, you terror," he said, "time to sleep. But don't start grunting *O Mistress Mine* or Henry will go berserk."

Suet made no sound. He was still looking up at the glittering heavens. The little snout stopped moving and the lower jaw dropped open slowly.

"What's the matter?" Adam asked.

The piglet gave a fearful grunt.

Adam glanced up once more. Something was moving. Out there in the eternal void, one of the celestial lights was travelling across the sky with astonishing speed.

"A night boat?" the boy murmured doubtfully.

It was still too distant to be certain, but he had never known anything move so rapidly, nor make an approach from that desolate direction. A vague recollection of Master Dritchly telling him of how, in the old world, stars would fall from the sky surfaced in the back of his mind, but since the Uplifting of the lands no one had ever witnessed such an occurrence.

"Besides," he breathed, "that thing's whirligigging about like a scorched and drunken bee."

Across the stark heavens the mysterious object came blazing, swerving and spinning in all directions, growing larger with every passing moment. Intense flashes of light flared and spangled around its surface, scribing a bright, wavering path through the darkness. Haloes of dazzling colour rippled in its twisting wake and, watching this wondrous display, the apprentice began to grow fearful. "It's headed this way," he spluttered.

Though it tumbled erratically, the object was plunging directly towards the isle of Malmes-Wutton.

Suet hid his wooden face, but Adam could not wrench his eyes from the awful vision. The silence of the surrounding night made the spectacle even more sinister and vivid. An anxious knot tightened in his stomach, yet he was powerless to do anything other than witness the fireball speeding faster, careering ever more wildly.

The bursts of light were blinding now and Wutton Old Place leaped beneath their bleaching glare. There was no time for panic, no time to raise an alarm. All Adam could do was blink in the crackling light and hold grimly on to Suet.

Then it hit.

The island of Malmes-Wutton shuddered hideously as
the fiery missile cannoned into the firmament and Adam
was hurled off his feet.

At once there was an explosion of glass and sound.
Shattered panes bombarded the outlying trees and the estate
was flooded with flame as immense sheets came whooshing
in. Fiery torrents boiled above the woodland and the noise
screamed and roared in the boy's ears.

A violent gale whipped into existence and the breath
was snatched from Adam's mouth. The inferno which
seethed around the ruptured sky was sucked out into the
cold night, its lurid fires immediately quenched in the void.

All debris was snatched up by the clawing squall. Soil,
straw, leaves, the raging wind seized everything and, at the
top of the vaulted firmament, Henry's garish hawk was torn
from the air.

Thrashing her painted tin wings, Quicksilver was swept
away on the filthy whirlwind and dragged down to where
the horrendous collision had occurred. Through the broken
leads of the sky the bird was expelled, flung into the Outer
Darkness upon a fount of rubble and dirt. Wheeling
helplessly yet still flailing madly, Quicksilver shot into the
great cold.

Within the steeple of the village church the bell began
a desultory tolling as the windstorm increased in might.
Every door and window of the manor slammed and in the
stable workshops, the lighter tools and pieces of equipment

were caught up in the tempest as howling forces blasted through the entrance.

Scrambling from the loft, Henry and Jack stumbled out into the swirling chaos which thundered through the yard. Adam was crouched by the piggery fence, battling to breathe while flying grit and stones stung and cut his face. Fighting their way through the maelstrom, the other apprentices strove to reach him. It was impossible to see anything; the thin air was choked with surging dust, but they blundered on, guided only by Suet's piercing squeals.

And then, abruptly, the shrill tumult died as suddenly as it began. A hail of gravel and muck rattled down and, with aching lungs, the boys dared to lift their faces.

There was not enough air to speak so Adam pointed across the dirt-covered lawn to the woods.

Jack and Henry could not believe it.

In the starlit dark, suspended ten foot above the trees, a great shape, twice the size of a house had smashed through the firmament. There it was, a huge, incongruous enigma jutting from the vaulted heavens – irrevocably gripped in the new panes which had slotted in around it to seal the sudden breach.

Frightened shouts accompanied by frantic hammering reluctantly drew the apprentices' attention away from the weird object now wedged and set into their sky. Lord Richard and his household were desperately trying to leave the manor house but the doors would not budge.

Gasping in the sparse atmosphere, Adam and the others hurried to the main entrance but before they could reach it there came a deep rumbling from the red-bricked building's foundations, followed by a tremendous hiss high above. Out of the manor's tall chimneys there steamed a funnel of white vapour which rushed swiftly upwards, dispersing in a vast cloud as it hit the underside of the firmament.

A cool draught fanned the apprentices' grubby faces when waves of sweet, fresh air swept over them and they gulped it down gladly.

With a bang, the large oak door of the manor unexpectedly swung open and Lord Richard fell out, startled and spluttering.

"What in Hades' name has befallen us?" he demanded, staring at the debris which carpeted everything around him. "I was shaken clear out of my bed. What manner of evil visitation is this? Where has this foul rubbidge come from?"

Still panting and filling their lungs, the boys looked at one another, then in one movement turned and pointed at the unknown thing that had smashed into their sky.

Lord Richard choked back a yelp of shock and staggered forward.

"By the beard of Harry the Eight!" he exclaimed. "What can it be? How came that fearful, giant device there?"

"I reckon its a secret Spanish war engine," Henry

declared darkly. "Or a French one. It's a wonder it didn't blast us to pieces – must be packed to busting with exploding powder."

Concerned murmurs went rippling through the household but Lord Richard did not give the boy's dire suspicions any credence and told everybody to remain calm. Henry pouted indignantly; now that the irritation of Quicksilver's clattering had been removed and forgotten, he was quite his former self again.

"We must investigate this perplexing riddle," Lord Richard announced. "Fetch torches and lanterns – we shall go at once."

"I'm not going into them woods to look up at that nasty great thing," Mistress Dritchly protested. "Not whilst that boar's still skulking there."

Lord Richard assured her that she could stay behind.

"Well I'm going!" said Anne Sowerby, the usually lazy kitchen maid.

"I do not think we have aught to fear from Old Scratch this night," Richard Wutton added. "Besides, here come folk from the village. A formidable band such as we shall form will not be pestered by one mad pig."

Along the road, the troop of worried villagers came hurrying. Several homes had been damaged by the shuddering impact and the ensuing wind had ripped many thatches from their roofs. All were agog to know what had caused this calamity, and after several minutes of intense discussion, Lord Richard led a large group towards the outlying woods.

The apprentices went with them, with Suet happily tagging along behind his master.

Neither Henry nor Adam had ventured into the trees which bordered the estate since they were eight years old and were both brimming with excitement at this midnight excursion.

"If that big boar comes charging," Henry blustered, "I'll give him such a wallop, then beat his snout with a burning torch. That'd tame the brute."

Adam laughed at his friend's vainglorious pledge but was too fascinated by their goal to make any answer.

Stomping through the mantle of dirt which had obliterated the lawn, the group had drawn close to the edge of the wood and the mysterious object loomed ever nearer. Holding every torch and lantern aloft in order to see the thing more clearly, the inhabitants of Malmes-Wutton progressed through the dense bracken which flourished beneath the oaks, their eyes trained upwards. Clashing emotions vied within them, hope and fear bubbling side by side. Just what was this foreign device and where did it come from?

Everyone was muttering in wishful whispers; each one had their own idea and was eager to give it an airing. Rumours and opinions leaped down the trail until one theory in particular began to be accepted by most of them.

"'Tis a signal from the Almighty," they told themselves. "Now we'll know why He raised the lands and brought us closer to Him."

The remaining distance was covered very quickly, for the desire to know such answers consumed them all and presently they were hastening through the wood, the flames of their torches streaming after.

"Keep together!" Lord Richard called, growing concerned that some of the more elderly members of the party were falling behind. "Jack, Henry, Adam – go back and ensure they come to no mischief."

The boys obeyed, but Henry was impatient to stand beneath that amazing sight and scolded the stragglers rudely. "Knees up, Mister Panyard!" he yelled. "Come on, your rusty nanny goat can do better."

The two hundred and thirty-two-year-old Thomas Panyard shook a bony fist at the impudent boy but quickened his pace all the same.

Barging through the tangled undergrowth, Suet squeaked with delight. This was an excellent new game and, keeping close to Adam's heels, the piglet revelled in this lush and unfamiliar environment.

"Put some effort into it," Henry shouted, spurring on the last villager. "If you knew your leg was playing up, why did you bother coming at all, you hobble merchant? Keeping us waiting, you are."

When they were finally herded in front of them, the

boys heard cries of astonishment and wonder issuing from those ahead.

"No slacking!" Henry cried to the old folk in front. "If you don't use that stick any faster, Mister Dumblewick, I'll grab it off you and hit you with it!"

And then, suddenly, they caught up with the others and for several minutes no one could find any words to express what their eyes beheld.

"Go lick a witch..." was all Henry could whisper to himself.

They had reached the far rim of the wood. A little distance away, the immense stone buttresses of the firmament plunged down into the rock upon which the estate was founded. Here the leaded glass that formed the sky arched over the trees in a shallow curve, before sweeping up to the highest point directly above the manor house. The torchlight shone up into the branching gloom and every pair of eyes was wide with overwhelming disbelief.

There it was, hanging above the tallest oak, a huge, impossible outline which glowed in the warm glare of the flames. Its shape was that of an enormous blunt cone with curling trenches cut into its lustrous surface. Only a third of it had crashed through the glass panes; the vast remainder projected out beyond the protecting sky and into the empty night. A dense wreath of new leads marked the juncture, and so it was caught, locked completely in the vaulted ceiling like an insect snared in a metal web.

Lord Richard was one of the first to find his voice.

"From what is it made?" he murmured. "See how richly it throws back our lights! Is it polished steel, or a pearl from the most monstrous oyster of the deeps?"

"Can it be a missile?" Jack asked uncertainly, harking back to Henry's ominous suggestion.

"I know not what it is," Lord Richard answered, "but consider the terrifying size of the cannon needed to fire such gargantuan shot. No no, we must construct a scaffold so that we may ascend to it for a closer examining."

"Whatever it is," Adam put in, "it's beautiful."

Sitting down in order to angle his head back sufficiently, Suet gazed at the extraordinary thing above, but his ichor-fuelled intelligence could not comprehend what he saw. Leaning against Adam, the piglet snuffled with bafflement and listened to what everyone was saying.

Speculation spouted from their lips. The initial wonderment had ebbed and although no one knew what the device was, the majority felt there was no doubt about whence it came. "Heaven!" they asserted, prompted by encouraging nods from the parson. "'Tis a token. On my oath, it can have travelled from no other place."

"Aye, its origins can only be divine."

At that moment the chatter ended, for a loud crack split the air like the firing of a musket. Above them, something was happening.

Fearfully, the people of Malmes-Wutton backed away into the surrounding trees as, in the side of that huge, unusual shape, a large opening suddenly slid into existence. Immediately a shower of crackling sparks came spilling out into the dark, raining down on to the trees below, fizzing and blazing through the branches.

"It *is* a weapon!" someone bawled. "It's going to explode!"

Lord Richard tried to quell the rising panic but the terror was short-lived for, in that same instant, Adam cried out, "Look! Inside! Look!"

Through that new opening they could see a fiery interior. Whatever the object might prove to be it was burning furiously. Black smoke, lit lurid, coiled into the air.

A terrible bang blew a ball of angry flame against the leaded glass, but there, lumbering into view within that infernal entrance, a figure came lurching.

Silhouetted against the fires, with golden sparks gushing around it, the man-like form hesitated a moment as if stunned, then clutched at its arm.

"He's injured," Jack exclaimed.

Before the words were out of his mouth the legs of the stranger collapsed beneath him and he tumbled from the burning opening. Down he fell, snapping the oak's branches and bouncing off the greater boughs. Like a stilled mechanical, his long limbs flopped about him as he crashed and splintered his way to the ground. Then, with a hideous thud, he hit the earth amid an avalanche of broken twigs and sputtering sparks.

The hearts of the onlooking crowd beat many times before the first of them was stirred into action. It was Adam who rushed forward, with Suet close behind.

Beneath the oak tree, the crumpled body lay motionless as the fiery specks dripped down on to his flesh, smouldering into his skin.

"Help me!" the boy called to the others.

At once they hurried forward and the strongest of them dragged the stranger away from the scorching rain.

"Easy now," Lord Richard declared. "Let's have a look at him."

Raising their torches, the villagers stared down at the battered and bleeding figure now lying prostrate at their feet. Astonished cries escaped from each of them.

The person they had rescued was not human.

PART TWO

The Best Panacea

❋

Richard Wutton stared at the unusual face. Although marred with burns and gashes, it was unlike anything he had ever seen.

"Is it a Spaniard?" asked Anne Sowerby. "Plum ugly fellers, aren't they?"

Crouching over the body, Jack Flye held a small circle of polished brass over the unsightly mess where he assumed the nose might be and waited. The faintest film of condensation misted the metal and he looked urgently at

‡

Lord Richard. "There is life!" he exclaimed.

The Lord of Malmes-Wutton needed no further prompting. "Bring two sturdy branches," he commanded. "We must make a litter to bear the stranger to the house."

Several of his tenants wavered before doing as he instructed. "But what is it?" they asked in fearful wonder.

"A creature in pain," their Lord answered tersely, "and that is all we need know for the time being. Our Christian duty is clearly to give what comfort we can to this poor soul. Now, do as I bid – or must I cut down the boughs myself?"

Abashed by his words, the wary villagers hastened to obey and it was not long before a rough stretcher was prepared. The motionless figure was lifted on to it with every gentleness. Taking a corner each, four robust men lifted the creature off the woodland floor and began the journey back to the manor house.

The other villagers filed in behind but Jack hung back and stared dubiously up at the great object suspended overhead. The fires were still burning within and, beneath the seventeen-year-old's fringe, his forehead furrowed with concern.

"What if there are more of those creatures in there?" he murmured. "They shall be consumed by the heats."

Henry and Adam had lingered with him.

"You can't hope to reach that opening," Adam said. "Even if you climbed to the top of the oak, it'd still be too high."

Henry nodded briskly. "Too late anyhow," he proclaimed. "You could melt iron in that furnace. I can feel the heat belting out from here and the leaves are all withered and smokin'. Whoever else was in there is well and truly cooked now. Grease sliding down the walls, that's all they are."

Keeping well away from the falling sparks, Suet snuffled about the ground. He could sense the tension which charged the atmosphere and he toddled back to Adam, staying close to his ankles. A powerful emotion thrummed like a pulse through the woodland - a violent hatred which lurked just beyond the encircling trees - and the piglet squeaked miserably.

Out there, in the leafy darkness, a hostile force was moving through the bracken, glaring at those who had presumed to invade its domain. Brooding malevolence rustled in the unlit gloom and Jack gave a shudder as he too felt the wrathful presence draw near.

"Time we caught up with the main group," he told Adam and Henry. "Yon pig's nervous and so am I. This is Old Scratch's territory and we've trespassed long. That old devil is out there watching us."

The other boys made no jest, for they too were feeling uneasy, and all three ran from there, with the wooden piglet scooting along behind.

As soon as they had departed, a large black shadow thrust its way to the base of the oak where the stranger had fallen, and the blood-drenched ground was gored and trampled with horrific savagery. A bellowing roar of challenge went echoing across Malmes-Wutton, as Old Scratch reclaimed his kingdom.

Keeping a vigil from one of the manor windows, Mistress Dritchly saw the large group come striding from the woodland and clucked with concern when she beheld the stretcher.

"Some poor wretch has been hurt," she cried, bustling to the door and hurrying over the yard to meet them. "Done a misfortune unto himself trying to get at that unnatural thing, no doubt. Why are men like children? Any excuse to shin up a tree or play tomfool games and tricks."

Hers was as plump an outline as her husband's had been; they had formed a perfect pair. Mistress Dritchly's face was round and pink, and her small grey eyes resembled two thumb pricks in a mound of freshly kneaded dough. Just as surely as Edwin had overseen the work in the stables, so his widow ruled the kitchen. Never one to sit idle, she possessed the energy of a tireless spinning top. When her fleshy arms were not elbow deep in pastry, she was broiling over steaming pots, organising the dairy, breezing through the herb garden or scolding the maid. Her tongue might have been sharp but her chastisements were always deserved – even Henry Wattle grudgingly admitted that.

With a white linen cap pulled over her greying hair and still dressed in her nightgown, she hastened to the wounded stranger. Unlike everyone else, she showed no outward reaction to the inhuman visage. Her terrible grief was still too recent to permit any revulsion; here was a job of work to be done and that was enough. A life had to be saved and Mistress Dritchly seized absolute control.

"Carry him into the house," she called, emphasising her words with a clap of her hands. "The rest of you, go back to your homes. There's no more you can do here – be off now."

The tenants did not want to return to the village when there were so many questions unanswered. But it required doughtier men than they to resist the will of Mistress Dritchly and she shooed them away like flies from the dairy.

Even Adam, Jack and Henry were dismissed back to the stables and for many hours they lay awake in the loft, debating the night's events. Nestling in the warm, dry hay, Suet lay next to Adam and grunted his very quietest.

Meanwhile, in the manor house, the singular patient was placed in a four poster while Mistress Dritchly attended to his horrific injuries. A wooden chest had been dragged to the foot of the bed, for her charge was so tall that his feet dangled over the end and she insisted that he be as comfortable as she could possibly make him.

The only other person she permitted in the bedchamber

was Lord Richard and now that a semblance of calm had descended, the master of the estate studied the stranger thoughtfully.

"Uncommon fish we catch hereabouts," he said, considering the figure's extraordinary attire.

Mistress Dritchly had bound her patient's deepest wounds and was starting to cautiously dab at the others with a cloth that she continually rinsed in a large dish of water.

"Such a lake of blood he's lost," she declared.

Glancing at the liquid which she wrung from her cloth, Lord Richard took a deep, steadying breath. The creature's blood was the colour of a mouldering orange or putrid apricot. "Is there a hope of survival?" he ventured.

The woman squeezed the cloth yet again and, pattering on to the landing, called out to the lazy Anne for clean water.

"If he lives the night through it'll be the Lord's doing not mine," she said upon her return. "Such dreadful mutilations – I don't know how his spirit cleaves to him, I really don't."

She had mopped up most of the blood, but when she scrutinised that unearthly face she gave a sorry shake of the head and threw up her hands in resignation.

"There's such a quantity of openings and slashes," she sighed. "But bless me Jesus if some of them aren't meant."

Lord Richard rose from his chair. "What are you saying?" he asked.

"Look on this pitiable beast," she replied. "Can you puzzle out our visitor's natural aspect? If so then tell it to me, for I cannot."

Bringing a candle dangerously within the curtained confines of the bed, Richard Wutton regarded his outlandish guest with renewed interest. Mistress Dritchly's tender ministrations had made the features more apparent but they were no less exceptional. The hue of the stranger's skin was a pale, greyish yellow, yet around the bulging eyes the flesh was pigmented with a dark red, flame-like pattern.

"Mark the high forehead, My Lord," she said. "See you the large slit in the centre of the brow? I have seen no blood flow from there. Now, note the knot of flesh which can only be the nose – count the number of holes therein."

Scrutinising that battlefield of a countenance, Lord Richard nodded. "A breed apart from we all," he agreed. "But concerning that left eye – surely it is beyond aid and healing?"

The woman folded her arms over her bosom and tutted with all the sympathy her great heart could offer. "I can only dress the burns and bind the cuts as best I can," she admitted. "There can be no surer remedies but time and patience."

"Then we shall see of what stuff our visitor is made," Lord Richard commented. "Now, I advise you to get some rest of your own, Mistress."

Edwin's widow was scandalised by the idea. "Gracious

no!" she puffed. "I must be on hand in case of crisis. You sleep if you wish, My Lord, I will remain with my charge."

Richard Wutton understood. Her beloved husband had been taken from her; now this woman would do everything in her power to try and save this unknown creature. "No one could want for a better nurse," he told her in mild amusement as he left the bedchamber and went in search of some ale before retiring.

Mistress Dritchly closed the door behind him, then went to the window and shut that, for a summer rain had started to fall, sprinkling down from the carved bosses fixed up in the firmament.

Settling herself into a comfortable chair next to the bed, she took up a psalter and whiled away several hours reading psalms by the feeble candlelight. Throughout the night she listened to her patient's frail breathing, expecting the weak gasps to falter and cease at any moment. Twice she changed the bandaged wrappings, and cleansed the wounds each time. But when the dawn inched into the sky outside, she was fast asleep, a bloodstained cloth still clutched in her hand.

A clear, dry day was waking. The rain that had fallen during the night had washed most of the blanketing dirt away and only muddy puddles remained. Slowly, the sunlight slanted into the room, glittering over the floating dust and stealing across the panelled walls, then over the heavy bed curtains. By seven o'clock it had nudged its way down on to the pillows and was shining full into the injured stranger's face.

A hesitant quivering began to pulse through the inhuman nose as the chamber's musty air was tested and explored. A myriad unfamiliar smells clustered the room; there was the scent of the rushes which strewed the floor, a cloying aroma of warm candle grease and Mistress Dritchly's personal odour of slightly stale biscuits mingled with a remote waft of freshly sliced onions. Yet there were a host of others which were too exotic and unknown to his questing senses. The tang of his own blood in the basin, however, infused everything.

Beneath the lid of the undamaged right eye there was a trembling movement. Very gingerly, the fine, translucent skin slid open – revealing a lemon-coloured orb in which a green, horseshoe-shaped iris flicked about the room.

Blurred shapes and colours swam in vague, disordered swirls and the eye watered until, abruptly, the bedchamber swung into focus and a choked cry sprang from the creature's thin lips.

That dismal sound jolted Mistress Dritchly awake and she sat upright in the chair, blinking in drowsy delight at the sight of her conscious patient.

"Praise to Him who raised the righteous," she cried, leaning forward to pat the bandaged hand which lay upon the coverlet.

The horseshoe eye fixed upon her and the stranger

shrank against the pillows, his long hair falling across his face and his many nostrils flaring wide and snorting with fear.

"Hush now," the woman soothed. "No need to be afraid – you've made it through the darkness, my fine foreign fellow. All threats and fears are past, the danger is over."

A faint gurgle bubbled in the patient's throat, then the eye closed and he slipped back into the deathlike sleep.

Mistress Dritchly nodded to herself.

"That's the way of it," she cooed. "Sleep is the best panacea. Just you take your time."

Looking benignly at the unfortunate beast lying in the bed, Mistress Dritchly rubbed the end of her own, unremarkable nose. If he did endure then he would be hideously scarred.

Now that her worst anxieties were over, she whisked herself off to the kitchen where Anne Sowerby had not even began making the breakfasts.

The day that unfolded was a busy one. Those few villagers who were not busy repairing their roofs and mending other damage caused by the previous night's gale, betook themselves to the manor to enquire after the stranger. Then they ventured to the edge of the wood to stare up at the huge projectile which had brought him.

As soon as they had shaken the sleep from their heads, Adam and the others hurried across the lawns and added their voices to the cries of wonderment. In the daylight the weird object was just as mysterious as the night before but appeared even more remarkable. Jutting from the sky, it was a lovely, pearlescent blue, yet other colours seemed to lap its gracefully contoured surface. Depending on how he tilted his head, Adam saw pink and gold sheens wink across the smooth ridges, then watched bronze shadows play within the deeply curving hollows.

Gambolling about the dewy lawn, Suet took no interest in the unexplained marvel but was overjoyed at the amount of puddles that the rain had left behind. He went splashing through each one, squealing with unbounded happiness.

"Got to be a night boat of some sort," Jack Flye remarked after long consideration.

Henry was not certain. "It don't have no sails or no deck," he said. "There aren't even any windows."

"Maybe that's why it foundered," the older boy replied with a smile.

At that hour there were not sufficient onlookers to form a large enough party to venture into the woodland and so closer inspection was denied the boys. When they had observed all they could at this distance, the trio made their way to the manor to see if there was anything they might do and hopefully get a peep at the stranger.

Mistress Dritchly formed a great pink barricade at the door and, with a wooden spoon wagging threateningly in her hand, told them to leave her patient in peace and be about their business.

Adam and the others returned to the workshop where they tidied up the scattered tools. They were kept occupied for the rest of the day by a steady stream of callers bringing in mechanicals which had been damaged in the storm.

Within the manor, Lord Richard and Mistress Dritchly took turns to sit in the sickroom to await developments, but the visitor made no other movement that day or the next.

On the third morning, Edwin's widow thought that her patient appeared a little better, although she was concerned that he not eaten a morsel since his arrival. Applying clean bandages, she was satisfied, however, that the wounds were beginning to heal and decided that it was time for the bed linen to be changed, for it was stained and spoiled by the dried blood. She enlisted Lord Richard and Jack's assistance, and she even donated one of her late husband's nightshirts for the stranger to wear as his own peculiar apparel was ripped and scorched beyond further use.

"Time I set some folk to work erecting a scaffold beneath our friend's property," Richard Wutton said when all this was done. "No one has yet inspected the wreckage; there may be a great deal to be learned in there."

"I thought it might be a night boat," Jack suggested.

Lord Richard shrugged. "If it is then I have never seen its like," he admitted. "But maybe you are right; there's a good deal of sense in that head of yours, Master Flye."

That afternoon a band of villagers strode into the

woodland equipped with axes, saws, hammers and lengths of rope. Adam and Jack were among them but Henry had elected to remain in the stables to work on the unfinished mechanical bear – at least, that was what he told them. In truth he was aching to get on with a secret project of his own which he believed would cause everyone a great deal of merriment, not least himself. He had been working on it for several weeks in private and another day's refinement would see it completed. Cackling mischievously to himself, Henry took a sack from its hiding place and emptied the contents on to his workbench.

Following Adam into the woodland, Suet's little keg-shaped body gave a violent shudder when they reached the place where Old Scratch had torn up the earth and he squeaked unhappily.

Adam o'the Cogs looked down at the ravaged ground then directed his gaze upward. Through the branches of the oak he stared at the wondrous object transfixed above and pondered on what secrets it might contain.

The first thing to do was to chop down great branches from surrounding trees and shape them into usable poles. It was a stifling day. Hours of toil sweated by and the structure made slow progress in the sweltering summer heat. Working together, Adam and Jack were an efficient team, and Suet helped by fetching tools and carrying away sawn-off twigs in his small mouth.

The distant sun continued to blaze through the azure-coloured panes of the firmament. Adam's fair skin began to burn, the freckles on his reddening forearms clustered ever more thickly and glints of copper shone in his hair.

Eventually, the baking afternoon waned and the delicious cool airs of evening drifted through the trees. Up against the oak the scaffold reared, and when the first shadows of dusk began to creep out from the undergrowth and bedim the woodland, the boys stood back and viewed what they had all achieved.

"See what we've built this day," Jack said proudly. "And you, little Cog Adam, you've worked hard as any. Dritchly would've been mighty pleased with your labours and so am I."

Regarding the towering framework which now rose over all their heads, the young apprentice grinned. Both he and Henry admired Jack Flye and it delighted Adam to receive his praise.

The structure had climbed almost to the top of the tree – a little more and the visitor's night boat would be reached. Yet, to the boy's disappointment, no one wished to continue working into the evening, for fear of Old Scratch. Throughout the day they had heard nothing from the wild boar, but as the darkness pooled beneath the trees, everyone grew uneasy.

"It must wait till the morrow!" Josiah Panyard called and all agreed with him.

Hurriedly collecting their tools together, they started to trail through the woodland and their thoughts turned towards their suppers. Following Jack at the rear of the company, Adam wheeled about to give the scaffold one last look. "A goodly bit of work indeed," he complimented himself. Then the smile faded from his features and he halted in his backwards trampling. "What can that be?" he murmured.

The shades of night had swollen within the oak's tangled branches but, high in the midst of that inky dark, he saw a circle of metal upon which a small, sapphire-coloured light was blinking.

"That's a strange will-o-the-wisp," the boy said to Suet who was waiting impatiently beside him. "It must have fallen from the stranger's night boat. Been too bright all day to see it. What do you reckon it is? A weapon maybe? Some magic device? Just look at the way yonder blue flame winks and pulses. 'Tis regular as a pendulum. I cannot account for it."

A wooden trotter pawed at him. The piglet's little nose was pumping fast and fretful.

"You have more wisdom than I do," Adam said, glancing nervously around at the night-swamped woodland. "Whatever that thing is, it'll still be up there tomorrow."

To the mechanical's relief, the boy hurried after the others and, when they had left the dangers of the outlying wood behind, Suet gave a glad grunt of contentment. From the piggery, Temperance's bass voice droned in answer and the piglet bounded forward to snuffle a greeting between the fence posts.

On reaching the yard, Jack whistled through his teeth. The area in front of the stables was crowded with many large crates and iron-bound chests.

"A consignment's arrived," he said in an irked tone. "Ain't one due for another few days yet."

Suddenly, from the workshop, a loud raspberry came blasting, followed by Henry's unmistakable hooting. Pushing the doors wide, the Wattle boy came staggering out, laughing helplessly. "Listen!" he gasped when he saw that the others had returned. "It sounds just like a great big buttock buster! Ah – there it goes again!"

Another trumpeting raspberry ripped through the air and Henry fell to his knees, clutching his aching stomach.

"Can't wait to see Widow Dritchly's face when she hears that!" he honked. "Let's not repair it, not for weeks and weeks – 'tis such a glorious marvel. I love each glisty spindle and every costly spring."

Adam and Jack stared at him until a third ripe report blistered from the stables and they went to investigate. Inside the workshop they discovered even more crates and boxes and there, strutting disdainfully among these deliveries, was a beautiful, gilded peacock.

It was a magnificent and expensive mechanical, an extravagant, exquisite creation. Set upon a tapering, snake-like neck was a small regal head which jerked about to glare at them, while the tiny golden bells fixed within its crown tinkled sweetly.

Shuffling into the stables, Suet gave a snort of astonishment and hid behind his master. The peacock trained a glittering, haughty eye upon the piglet and lifted one of its elegant feet off the ground as if in disgust. Then it spread its ravishing plumage in a wide fan, which swept tools and instruments from the surrounding benches, and opened its prim and disapproving beak.

Yet, instead of the expected imperious cry, a ridiculous fruity parping gusted from the bird. Jack gave a curt nod of understanding. "Sound pipe's perished," he said, reaching out to hit the creature's crest.

At once the bird became still and Jack examined the design with interest. "From the manor at Dunwich," he said with surprise. "What they sending their faulties to us for? This sort of fancy work usually goes all the way to London."

"There's more like that in them boxes over there," Henry interrupted, his voice still quivering with abating mirth as he came sloping in. "Been busier here this afternoon than I've ever known it. Hardly got a scrap of mine own work done. Three night barges there were, laden with repairs."

"We must have most of the broken mechanicals in the whole of Suffolk here!" Adam exclaimed. "Why?"

Jack's eyes gleamed beneath his curtaining fringe. "The visitor," he guessed. "Rumour's got around already. Folk want to see him and these repairs are just an excuse to come to Malmes-Wutton."

"That's just how it is," Henry declared. "Them crates arrived with a steward who went to see Lord Richard. Went to the sickroom he did, only Widow Dritchly wouldn't let him in. So did another who brung a chest of twenty goldfish what only need a good polishing. Came to steal a glimpse at our 'heavenly messenger', that's what they really journeyed here for."

Jack flicked the hair from his face. "Is that what they're calling him in the neighbouring isles?" he muttered in irritation. "I don't like that, and nor will Lord Richard."

"Why not?" Henry asked.

The older boy fixed him with a reproachful stare. "Because them at court will get to hear of it," he said. "How long do you reckon it'll take the Queen's ministers to get back here, when they find out?"

It was an unpleasant prospect and Henry fell silent. Adam looked around at the cluttered workshop and knew that Jack was right. He could not imagine how many nobles would descend upon Wutton Old Place this time. Yet, even as he despised the notion, he could not help thinking that it would be agreeable to see Doctor Dee and Lantern once more.

The softly snorting strains of *O Mistress Mine* came floating up from the piglet at his feet and they were all sharply reminded just how perilous a visit from the Queen's ministers could be.

"We'll say nothing to anyone outside Malmes-

Wutton," Jack decided. "When the owners of these mechanicals return to collect them, and whoever else brings more, we don't so much as mention the stranger to them."

The others agreed. "Won't do no good though," Henry mumbled. "They can see that whopping great thing stuck in our sky plain enough."

At that moment they heard the sound of heavy footsteps running across the yard and Anne Sowerby, the idle kitchen maid, came lumbering into the workshop.

"Jack!" she cried, her eyes bulging as she leaned heavily against the wall and panted for breath. "Lord Richard tells you – oh my, I weren't made for dashing about – I feels awful ill and gaspy and my foot's a-throbbin'."

Jack Flye hurried to the entrance. "What's happened?" he demanded.

Still wheezing, Anne looked at him blankly. At fifteen years of age, she was a shiftless girl who sought and found as many reasons to shirk and delay her chores as often as she could. Lately her favourite excuse was that of a black-headed wart which festered on her foot and which she called an abscess. When she remembered, she even contrived to limp. With a ruddy complexion scarred by a bout of meezles, and dull green eyes which showed no flicker of shame when she lied, Anne was one of the main pokers which stoked the flames of Mistress Dritchly's anger.

Recently she had taken a shine to Master Flye and,

looking at him now, pushed a broad smile across her face, revealing her small, gappy teeth. "How you caught the sun on your neck today," she cooed admiringly. "Like a real gypsy with your dark hair and burned skin."

Ignorant of her secret yearning, Jack thought the girl was being more stupid than usual. "What of the message from Lord Richard?" he snapped.

"Oh that!" Anne shrugged with indifference. "He calls for you to go to the sickroom as he might have need of you there. Without delay, he said, but they always say that, don't they? Makes no matter when a task's done so long as you gets around to it in the end, that's what I says."

But she was speaking to herself for Jack had sprinted towards the manor house and she pouted sulkily.

"What's he wanted there for?" Henry asked.

Fiddling with her lank brown hair, the girl answered with a disinterested moan. "That Spaniard feller they're nursin'," she drawled. "Seems like he's wakin' up at last."

Within the sickroom, Richard Wutton and Mistress Dritchly stared at the figure in the bed, excited and anxious. Every opening in that unnatural face was trembling – quivering and dilating like the tiny mouths of stranded fish.

"Merciful Lord in Heaven," Mistress Dritchly whispered as, suddenly, the many nostrils flared and took a deep, savouring breath.

"There can be no doubt," Lord Richard murmured. "The swoon is lifting."

Even as he spoke, Jack came leaping up the stairs and bolted along the landing to the bedchamber. Lord Richard beckoned him into the room but signalled for quiet. "I sent for you as a precaution only," he said softly. "Our guest may not prove as friendly as we could wish and we might require your strength, Master Flye."

Jack nodded and tensed himself as a plaintive groan issued from the creature's thin lips. Mistress Dritchly clasped her round face in her hands.

"He wakes," she murmured.

A curving slice of bright yellow appeared beneath the bandaged brow as the patient stirred from unconsciousness and, very slowly, the eyelid eased open. Mistress Dritchly had seen the remarkable horseshoe-shaped iris before but the others had not, and they muttered under their breath in astonishment.

An instant later, a rapid clumping up the stairs announced the arrival of Adam and Henry. They were determined not to miss the excitement and they stumbled over one another in the doorway, gaping and amazed.

"Bum boils!" Henry hissed. "Just look at that!"

Mistress Dritchly's practised hand flashed out to deliver an admonishing smack to his head, yet she was far too absorbed in her charge's awakening to bundle the intruding boys out of the chamber. Every attention was glued upon the stirring figure and the atmosphere within the sickroom crackled with fearful anticipation.

Adam held his breath as he gazed into the emerald crescent of the stranger's yellow eye. He could not begin to imagine what would happen next – what if the rumours and hopeful suspicions were true? Could this long-limbed creature really be a messenger of the Almighty? Were they about to hear an angel's voice? Mistress Dritchly obviously thought as much, judging by the rapture written clear across her doughy face.

Slowly, the livid eye began to roam about the chamber, starting with the plaster ceiling then dropping to take in the panelled walls. At last it flicked between each of those persons present. This time there was no fear, only a wary curiosity, combined with the wincing awareness of the pain from his wounds.

With his nostrils tasting the air, the patient registered the faces of those who had cared for him and, with a clearing mind, was finally able to link sight and scent. Close by was the pink and careworn form of Mistress Dritchly, the one whose floury presence he had perceived before. He was vaguely aware that she had been almost constantly by his side, the stale echoes of her company lingered in every corner of the room and the knowledge comforted him.

Another familiar scent was that of Lord Richard. Here was the owner of that pleasant fermenting fragrance, which had seeped into the oblivion of his long sleep and brought with it remote visions of ripening grain and spoiling fruit.

Jack Flye's appearance struck only a distant note of recognition, but the day's exertions had clothed the youth in loud degrees of grime, sweat and sunburned skin. Adam was similarly wrapped, but Henry was different; no hard toil clung to his form. The sharpness of filed metal covered his fingers, but olive-coloured vapours swirled about the seat of his breeches.

When he had drunk in each of the onlookers, the stranger's thin lips parted and he struggled to speak.

Mistress Dritchly clasped her round face in her hands but Lord Richard bowed courteously and said, "Good evening, Sirrah. It eases our hearts to see you awake at last."

The flame-pigmented skin around the bright lemon eye crinkled as the creature frowned.

"He don't understand English," Jack murmured.

"I could try him with a little Latin," Lord Richard suggested. "Although I doubt if even then..."

Before he could begin, the patient raised his head off the pillows, cringing at the pain caused by the movement. Then he opened his mouth, and suddenly the bedchamber rang to one of the most beautiful sounds any of them had ever heard.

It was a language which had never before been uttered in that uplifted world. More like a song than mere words, yet nearer to music than singing, and the very atmosphere of the bedchamber seemed to lighten. "Heavenly," Mistress Dritchly declared, enchanted.

"Old John Dee's Enochian researches," Lord Richard marvelled. "Those angelic voices of his..."

Compared to the sublime sound of their visitor, their own speech was harsh and brutal, but Adam's mouth fell open in wonder when he heard them.

"Then... then it's true!" he stammered. "This fellow really is... is a messenger of the Almighty!"

"Pope's armpits!" blurted Henry.

The captivating music came to a halt and Richard Wutton hastily tried to retract what he had let slip.

"Dear me, no," he cried. "I was only pondering foolhardy thoughts aloud. Don't you go repeating my rash words in the village – there's rumour enough already."

"They won't," Jack promised. "We spoke of this afore."

Upon the bed, the stranger was gingerly touching his bandaged eye, then viewed the burns which marred the back of his hand. He shuddered. The entrancing music began once more and he fumbled at his throat as though searching for something.

"Don't excite yourself," Mistress Dritchly told him. "'Tis food you'll be wanting after all these days. I'll get Anne to heat up a bit of broth for you." She paused then tutted to herself. "No, I'll see to it myself or 'twould be suppertime before that snail-child puts a pot to heat."

Beaming with pride at the successful outcome of her

nursing, and eager to feed her charge, she fled the room and pounded down the stairs.

Adam and Henry had rushed so swiftly into the manor that Suet had been left in the stables, but the little mechanical had followed them and was even now attempting to negotiate the stairway.

Mistress Dritchly's voluminous bulk went sailing by and the piglet scooted close to the banister for safety from her whirling skirts. Then he resumed his clambering journey. It was not easy, for his trotters were short and each step demanded much concentration and effort. Puffing out his snout, Suet doggedly scaled the stairs.

In the sickroom, Lord Richard scratched his head in frustration. It was maddening not being able to make himself understood, and there were so many questions he longed to ask.

His singular guest was similarly confounded. A crooked smile lifted the corners of his mouth as he regarded them.

"We're as much a mystery to him as he is to us," Adam said.

"I don't think there is much in any of the beatified isles with which he would be familiar," Richard Wutton agreed, observing the stranger stare in perplexity at the lighted candles. "It appears that even the simplest and most commonplace items are new and beyond his experience."

"P'raps he's used to better," Henry suggested.

Lord Richard sank into a chair and began to chuckle

with amusement. "I think young Wattle has the measure of him," he said. "I truly believe that our injured friend here believes he is amongst barbarians. Who are we to gainsay him, even if we spoke the same tongue? Hello, what's this?"

A dainty clattering sounded unexpectedly upon the landing, accompanied by a triumphant snort. Suet came gambolling into the bedchamber, capering joyfully through the rushes and leaping up against his master's legs, highly pleased with his achievement.

"Cog Adam!" Lord Richard said sternly. "A pig has no business in a sickroom – remove it before Mistress Dritchly returns."

Reluctantly lifting the mechanical off the ground and tucking it under his arm, the boy turned to leave.

"Wait!" Lord Richard cried. "Behold our guest!"

The moment Suet had entered, the stranger had leaned forward in the bed and his injured face was a picture of disbelief as he stared at the wooden piglet. Signalling Adam to draw closer, his melodic voice babbled forth and he ran his bandaged hand over Suet's wooden sides, trying to peer between the joins at the internals.

The piglet grunted happily at being the centre of attention and Lord Richard nodded to himself as he viewed the stranger's astonishment.

"'Twould appear that we are not as primitive as he first thought," he said wryly.

Musical sighs of wonder issued from the patient's lips

as he examined Suet and it was plain that there was much he wished to ask. Growing agitated, he glanced about the room then tugged at the nightshirt that Mistress Dritchly had provided for him.

"He's asking for his own attire!" Adam declared. "There must be something he wants from it."

Lord Richard opened the chest which stood at the end of the bed and hauled out the stranger's torn and scorched costume. At once the clothing was snatched from his hands but, whatever the mysterious visitor needed, it was not there and a moment later the apparel was flung across the room.

"He's tapping his throat again," Henry said. "Maybe he's swallowed a moth."

Lord Richard's face rumpled with thought. "Something which he wears about his neck," he pondered. "A chain of office perhaps? A miniature portrait? A costly jewel?"

The stranger was staring at him intently, as though willing him to comprehend, but Lord Richard shook his head and his guest slumped back against the pillows.

"Here's a lovely bit of broth, my angel," Mistress Dritchly called as she bustled back into the room with a steaming bowl. "Oh, Cog Adam! Get away with that foul pig – be off with the pair of you. You also, Henry Wattle – get gone. You've both seen enough this night, so be thankful and depart."

Henry grumbled mutinously. There was no love lost

between himself and Edwin Dritchly's widow and he was forever seeking new ways to bring little rain clouds of annoyance into her life. There was no arguing with her, however, and both boys were briskly herded from the bedchamber. "Just wait till my new project's ready," he vowed at the door which closed in his face. "If it don't make her shriek her kitchen down then I'll kiss Anne Sowerby's abscess. What say you to that, Coggy?"

But Adam was not listening. All expression had drained from his face and he gazed at Henry with glittering eyes.

"I know what the stranger wants," he breathed. "I've seen it."

Normally Henry would have scoffed at his friend, but Adam was so sure and the lights which danced in his eyes disconcerted him.

"I'm going to go fetch it now," Adam cried, taking the stairs two at a time. "Come on!"

Haring after him, Henry asked, "But where is it?"

"Out there," Adam called back. "In the dark - in the wood."

"But Old Scratch is there!" Henry yelled. "Adam, come back - Adam!"

CHAPTER 2

A Shiny Blue Acorn

"This is madness!" Henry protested. He had caught up with Adam in the stables where the boy was arming himself with a strong stick and a hammer.

"Stay behind if you're afraid," Adam told him, deliberately nettling the other apprentice's pride. "Suet and me will go on our own."

Henry glanced down at the piglet sitting at Adam's feet. "What use will that be?" he cried.

"He's an excellent alarm," Adam replied. "Whilst I climb the tree he can keep watch. There'll be naught to fret about though."

"Oh no," Henry added sarcastically. "You don't mind being gored by long brass tusks?"

"Old Scratch has never actually hurt anyone, has he?" Adam said.

"Only because no one's been lunatic enough to go wandering into his realm at night! He'll get you for certain, he's a killer!"

But Adam's mind was made up and, brandishing his simple weapons, he marched from the workshop.

Cursing, Henry ran after him.

"What devil's got into you, Coggy?" he asked. "This ain't like you."

But there was no dissuading the boy and Henry felt compelled to go with him. Of the apprentices, Henry was the one with a reputation for recklessness and a fearless disregard for rules. He could not bear the thought of Cog Adam stealing that prestige away from him. The prospect of journeying into the woods at night, however, was more than daunting and he marvelled that his friend could even contemplate the idea.

"If we do meet that monster," Henry promised as they crossed the lawn, "you'd best gallop as fast as you're able, I'll not tarry for you. I'll race out of there so quick you'd think my hindquarters were aflame."

"We shan't be there long," Adam assured him. "I know the exact spot to make for. All three of us can be back at the manor before Old Scratch even knows we've been trespassing."

Henry was not convinced. They had now reached the edge of the woodland and the dark trees thrust high before them in huge mountainous waves of shadow.

"Pox buckets!" Henry hissed. "I'm not venturing in there. Even if Old Scratch don't get us, then goblins and sprites will. My dad used to tell stories of wild folk in the wood, of witches and things unnatural."

Adam stifled a laugh. "Don't be so daft," he whispered. "The worst that'll happen is you'll trip over a root in the dark. Still, maybe that'd knock a morsel of sense into that wooden head of yours. No, not you, Suet."

Henry was still unsure, until Adam goaded him a little further, explaining how courageous Jack would think the pair of them. That settled it; winning the good opinion of Jack Flye was worth a frightening journey in the dark.

"What you waiting for then, Coggy?" he murmured. "Last one there has to tell Widow Dritchly she's fat as Old Temperance but thrice as ugly."

"I thought you'd already done that," Adam chuckled and, with the piglet plodding after them, the two boys proceeded into the wood. Neither of them knew what to expect. They had hardly grown used to the woodland in the daytime, but at night it appeared to be a different country entirely.

Adam attempted to keep to the track which he and the others had used earlier but quickly found that an impossible task. No moon sailed above the uplifted isles; only the starlight pricked through the firmament and that was not bright enough to guide him. Beneath the leaf-laden trees all was pitch and silent, like a forgotten realm placed beneath an enchanted slumber. The boys' cautious trudging briefly broke the spell but it was swift to close in behind them once they had passed.

It was so quiet that Henry imagined he could hear his heart beating and for the first time he wished that his hawk was still clattering high overhead. He had never felt so vulnerable in his life. The tormented nightmare which dwelt in this woodland could not fail to hear their intrusion – they might as well have brought lanterns and shouted their presence at the top of their voices. An icy dread began to creep up his spine and his fearful glances around them became ever more frequent.

The intense black forms of the surrounding trees were alarmingly sinister and in every new patch of gloom he pictured hollow caves where a tusked terror might make its lair. With Suet shuffling dejectedly between them, they pressed towards the far edge of the wood, near to where the stranger's night boat was wedged in the buttressed heavens.

"We almost there?" Henry croaked.

"A little way more," Adam replied. "'Tis not easy in this..."

Without warning he halted and the piglet bumped into him, a surprised squeak escaping from the abruptly compressed snout.

"Look," Adam whispered. "Up there."

Through a break in the dense leaf canopy, Henry saw the stark outline of a scaffold rise up against the familiar oak. Within that great tree, there beat a small point of blue light.

"God's spit!" Henry exclaimed, speaking louder than he had intended. "Did you ever see such a shiny blue acorn? What can it be?"

"The thing that the stranger desires," Adam said, stepping forward again.

A moment later they were standing at the base of the oak, the chill light flashing down on to their raised faces.

"Well, here we are," Henry remarked, puffing out his chest and slapping the trunk. "Told you there weren't nothing to be scared of, Coggy."

Adam let that pass and knelt beside Suet, laying his weapons down and fondly stroking the piglet's face. "Now, you remain here," he instructed. "You're a sentry tonight, so keep alert and listen out for you know who. If you hear him approach, then squeal your loudest. Good boy."

The mechanical wiggled the back portion of his keg-shaped body. If his tail had been real and not simply a hook it would have wagged furiously. Holding his carved head as high as he was able, Suet watched the two apprentices scramble up the oak and disappear into the leaves.

Then, with a jerk which flipped one leathery ear over his face, making him look as fierce as possible, the piglet began to patrol around the tree. His master had given him a command and he performed the guard duty with devoted obedience, no matter how afraid he might be.

As the apprentices swarmed up the oak, lured by the unusual winking light, another presence travelled the darkened woodland.

In the deep mirk, a great shape was moving, treading down the bracken and shouldering aside the low, outstretched branches. A rumbling growl trembled the air and the trampled undergrowth suffered even more as something dragged in its wake.

All day long he had sheltered from the searing heat in a cool green tunnel ripped into the dense ferns which grew close to the village. No one suspected how nigh this monster drew to their homes, but the woodland was no longer large enough to contain him. Now, rested and strong, Old Scratch swaggered through his realm, his sharp glass eyes gleaming cruelly in the shadows. The rage which constantly blazed within his misshapen body was bubbling, streaming through the feeder pipes to forever fuel his unquenchable wrath.

Circling the oak, Suet paused for an instant and tottered smartly about. He had heard a noise. Faint at first, he mistook it for a breath of air threading through the trees.

Dismissively scraping the earth with his trotters, he resumed his watch.

Far above, Henry had ascended higher than Adam. The source of the peculiar, pulsing light would soon be within his reach and his expectant features flickered beneath that spectral sapphire glare.

So engrossed were both boys in the climb that neither of them noticed the noise which made Suet halt a second time. The sound was growing louder and the wooden piglet stood stock still as his nose pumped rapidly in and out.

Dry twigs were snapping on the woodland floor and the mechanical began to shake with fright. Old Scratch was coming. The hostile waves which Suet had sensed that first night were flowing through the woodland, heralding the nightmare beast's arrival. A loud, questing grunt resounded in the distance – the horror would soon be aware of their presence. Suet's back legs folded beneath him and he stared up as far as his neck would allow, but the angle was not acute enough. He could not see his master and he squeaked desolately, longing for him to return.

Suddenly, a fierce shriek blasted through the woodland and the piglet knew Old Scratch sensed that his realm had again been invaded. At once Suet's internal bellows squeezed together and he let out a shrill squeal which soared up into the branches. The ground beneath him began to quiver as steel hooves stampeded through the darkness, but still the little piglet squealed the alarm.

High in the branches, Adam heard the signal and turned a stricken face to Henry. "Scratch is coming!" he yelled, beginning the scramble down. "We have to go!"

But Henry Wattle's fingertips were even then stretching out to where a circlet of metal was caught in the uppermost twigs. Set in the rim of that ornate band, the ghostly light enticed him on, splashing coldly across his grubby features. Nothing could make him turn back now.

"Henry!" Adam cried. "Leave it!"

"Just a sneeze away," the other boy muttered as he inched further along a perilously thin branch and reached out as far as he could.

Jumping the remaining distance to the ground, Adam was horrified to see that his friend had not yet started down. Suet rushed over to him and whimpered wretchedly. To the right of them the night-crowded trees were filled with a crashing uproar as the wild boar came thundering and panic surged through Adam's veins.

"Henry!" he shouted. "Hurry!"

At the top of the oak, Henry's fingers grazed against cool metal. "A whisker more," the boy said, leaning as far forward as he dared. "There!"

With a whoop of joy he snatched the circlet from the snaring twigs and grasped it firmly in his hand. Yet there was no time to even look at what he had retrieved for at that moment Old Scratch burst from the undergrowth, shrieking like a demon.

"Satan's monkey!" Henry wailed, seeing the hideous shape tear across the ground below.

Seizing his hammer and stick from the ground, Adam stood against the trunk and, with quailing nerves, beheld the grotesque creature erupt from the foliage. Suet let out a petrified yowl.

The wild boar was a horrendous spectacle. Carved from rosewood, it had once been a handsome creation, but the feral years had wrought a monstrous change. Adam had never seen anything so evil and malignant. The face was an unholy image of savage fury and the boy's legs turned to water at the sight of it.

Old Scratch had been built as mechanical game, a beast to be hunted on horseback, and so possessed every cunning necessary to evade his pursuers, combined with devices to make the chase more satisfying and dangerously real. At some point during his ferocious exile, Old Scratch's snout had smashed in two, leaving splintered jags which were far more vicious than the original design had ever intended. Flanking this merciless maw were two solid brass tusks. They were tarnished now but their tips were still sharp and bitter. What the ragged snout ignored they gladly ripped and gouged.

Crimson fires raged behind the slanting glass eyes and spearing from the boar's broad, humped back were long rows of deadly steel bristles. Yet what made this harrowing vision even more grotesque was a tattered train of tough, stale proudflesh – the stuffings which had burst from the beast's internal moulds, splitting and squeezing through the rotten rosewood casing.

Dragging and flapping behind the charging monster, the shredded grey mantle was like a filthy, moth-eaten veil. Resembling a squat, demonic bride, Old Scratch came ravening, roaring and snorting terrifying shrieks of challenge.

The stick fell from Adam's grasp. Such a weapon was useless against so powerful and dreadful a creature; all he could do was try to escape. His first thought was to climb the tree once more, but there was no way he could accomplish that with Suet and he could not leave the piglet down here to confront the wild boar's savage wrath alone.

There was only one course of action left to him. With Old Scratch bearing down on them, the boy grabbed Suet from the ground, flung the hammer with all the force that was left in his trembling arm and fled.

Spinning through the darkness, the hammer struck the boar above one eye and bounced off. The blow made a slight dent in the carved wood but that was the only effect it had. Without checking his speed, Old Scratch stormed on and, sprinting as fast as he could, Adam raced away.

Hastening down the oak, Henry clambered on to the bottommost branch and saw the nightmare go galloping after. Cog Adam had no chance. The wild boar was gaining on him – a minute more and the apprentice would be hurled to the ground as brass tusks drove into his scrawny legs.

"The devil's dinner," Henry murmured. "That's what Coggy'll be."

A brief instant of indecision tormented Henry Wattle. If he remained quiet while Adam kept the monster busy, he might be able to sneak off and run to safety. Yet his conscience rebelled at the craven idea and he was sickened to have even thought it.

From the branch he leaped and, holding the coldly flashing circlet over his head, the boy yelled. "Hey! Offal brains – over here! Ho – bacon breath! Call yourself a wild boar? I've seen scarier sheep. You look like a hunchback granny in her shift."

Faltering in his pursuit of Adam, Old Scratch veered around and glared at the insolent child standing beneath the oak tree. Henry shouted more insults and the malevolent beast's temper boiled as never before. Snorting like an enraged bull, he stamped upon the ground and bolted straight for the apprentice.

"Witch juice!" Henry wailed. "You've done it now, Wattle!"

Dodging around the trunk and pelting past the scaffold, the boy ran. Old Scratch's ferocious shrieks reverberated through the woodland, tearing into the darkness and echoing beneath the firmament. The crimson ichor seethed within him and the flames of his fury shone from his eyes. Only death would placate this fiery rage, to let his beautiful, curved tusks slash and rend, to roll across the fallen quarry for his bristling steel to do its shredding work, then to trounce and push his splintered maw into what remained. That was what Old Scratch lusted for and he shot over the ground as if fired from a musket.

Not looking over his shoulder, Henry did not know how quickly the boar was gaining but, a little distance ahead, he saw that Adam had stopped running and was staring in despair.

"Don't stand there gawking!" Henry bawled. "Fly, you idiot!"

Hesitating uncertainly, Adam did not know what to do.

"Save yourself!" Henry yelled.

Whisking around, Adam went crashing through the trees with Suet juddering under his arm. An instant later Henry came dashing after them. Yet Old Scratch plunged in at his heels and the boy screamed as he felt hot vapour pumping from the broken snout come blasting around him.

"You're dead, Wattle," he told himself.

But before a thrust of tarnished brass gored his thigh, there came a strangled shriek and the wild boar was hurled off his hooves.

Daring to glance behind. Henry saw what had happened and a rush of relief flooded over him.

Old Scratch's train of rancid proudflesh had caught on a low, thick branch and yanked the infuriated mechanical off balance. Yet even now the boar was fighting with the tough fibres, hacking and chewing to free himself. Swiftly, the dirty grey growth was torn asunder and, with the remaining tatters flowing behind him in ribbons, the hideous creature resumed the chase.

Haring through the remaining trees, Adam and Henry's spirits soared when they saw the lights of Wutton Old Place shine beyond the lawns, but there was no time for resting, not yet.

As they hastened toward the yard, they heard the awful blaring roar of the horror behind them and their hopes perished when they realised Old Scratch had crossed the boundary of his realm and was berserking across the grass after them.

"Not far!" Adam cried. "If we can only make the stables!"

The apprentices' chests were aching as their hearts pounded and their lungs wheezed for breath. Over the lawn they sped, their ears ringing to the murderous trumpeting.

Suddenly their feet crunched on to gravel and, jumping over the assembled crates and boxes, they hurtled for the workshop. As one the boys threw the door open and slammed it behind them. Leaning against the stout barrier, they gasped and panted while outside they heard Old Temperance's deep voice call in fear.

Suet gave a forlorn whimper, Adam and Henry listened to the thunderous crash of Old Scratch's hooves approach.

The wild boar was tearing across the yard and they stared at each other in fear.

"He's never left the wood before," Henry whispered. "What have we done?"

Before Adam could reply, the door gave a violent bang as the incensed mechanical smashed his head against it. The boy dropped Suet in shock. The frightened piglet scuttled beneath the nearest workbench as a second battering blow slammed into the door.

Horrified, the apprentices heaved their shoulders against the juddering wood and another jarring collision shook their bones. Again and again Old Scratch smote the door and Adam feared that the timbers would shatter.

Abruptly, however, the violence stopped and they heard a frustrated snorting pull away from the entrance.

"He's had enough," Henry breathed thankfully. "He's going."

Still pressed against the door, the boys listened intently to the receding grunts only to jump in alarm when an almighty din exploded in the yard as Old Scratch vented his rage on the crates of faulty mechanicals.

"Sounds like a battle out there," Adam said. "Hope he leaves Old Temperance alone."

Feeling a little more secure, the terror had subsided from Henry and his eyes were shining with excitement. "Oh yes!" he whistled. "I hope they dash each other into kindling."

A mournful whine came from beneath the workbench but Henry ignored it and revelled in the pig combat he was imagining.

"Better than bear-baiting," he said. "No one's had hog duels before. Think of it, Coggy, two angry porkers making chops of each other. Earn me a fortune, that would. I could go from sty to style."

In the yard the violence ended. Old Scratch let out a tremendous, defiant shriek which fired Henry's fear once more and he said no more about his absurd idea. Bracing himself against the door in dread-filled expectation, he waited, but no further attack was launched against the stables.

"It's over," Adam said at length. "He's returning to the wood."

"Frog hair!" Henry disputed. "Its a trick. He's still out there – soon as we peep out, he'll ram us again."

A remote bellowing proved that Adam was correct but Henry still clung to his doubts. "He might be throwing his voice," he suggested.

His friend laughed, yet when he opened the door it was with every caution.

The wild boar had definitely departed, but the scene which met Adam's eyes filled him with horror. The yard was a wreck. Every crate and chest had been smashed open, and the contents destroyed and mangled. Pieces of broken mechanicals lay strewn about the gravel like fallen soldiers after a bloody combat and Adam gazed at them guiltily. Old Scratch had thrown all his malignant savagery against them and they were beyond repairing.

"I'm to blame," Adam berated himself. "I led him here. What am I going to tell Lord Richard?"

Emerging from the stables, Suet picked his way through the destruction and hastened to the piggery where he pressed his snout through the fence and squeaked piteously.

From the brick sty a low voice answered, accompanied by a similar squeal. Old Temperance came lumbering out, joined by Flitch. Suet hopped up and down with glee and the great sow ambled over to him, their noses meeting through the wooden rails.

Seeing them united, Adam smiled in spite of the devastation around him and gently lifted the piglet over the fence to place him with his family. Suet pressed lovingly against Old Temperance's large bulk then ran joyful rings around Flitch.

"Glad that devil didn't get the pair of you," Adam said affectionately, then added with a pang of envy, "Must be nice to have a family."

Leaving the mechanical pigs to their greetings, the boy returned to the workshop.

Henry had not bothered to look at the damage Old Scratch had inflicted in the yard and when Adam entered, he was sitting at his bench beneath two lanterns. The thing he had rescued from the oak tree was in his hands and he was examining it under the light. Staring over his shoulder, Adam uttered a gasp of wonder.

It was a beautiful necklace or collar, fashioned in a band of yellowish metal which was neither brass nor gold. Intricate designs snaked and writhed over its surface and many coloured stones were set about the rim, the largest of which was a polished blue gem the size of a blackbird's egg. It was this smooth jewel that had first attracted Adam's attention in the oak trees, for in its depths a bleak light was pulsing steadily. Neither boy had ever before seen its like and they stared at it in silence for several minutes.

"It's lovely," was all Adam murmured eventually.

Henry ran his fingers over the gleaming metal and touched the glimmering stone. "Must be worth a tidy sum," he declared.

Adam agreed. "Pity it isn't ours," he said.

"Who says it isn't?" Henry asked. "We found it. In truth, it was me who fetched it from the branches. I have a valid claim to it."

Adam frowned at him. "You can't have it!" he cried. "It belongs to the stranger."

"Not no more. It's mine and I'm keeping it. Earn me a few sovereigns, this will."

But before he could bear the glittering thing to his secret hiding place, Henry was pushed off his stool. While he sprawled upon the floor, the collar was grabbed from his hand.

"Adam!" he bawled as the other boy ran from the workshop. "Come back, you thieving orphan! I hate you!"

Mistress Dritchly's raw pastry features rumpled into a thoughtful expression. Her patient had shied away from the broth she had so wanted to give him and she was considering what other dish she could prepare.

The stranger regarded the three onlookers sadly. Apart from pointing and shaking his head, there was nothing else he could do to make them understand.

"My Lord," Jack Flye began hesitantly, "could he not be one of the special ambassadors that I have heard tales of?"

Mistress Dritchly brightened at the remembrance. "Oh, I recollect them exceeding well," she clucked. "Time was when they were always a-visiting, when the lands were first uplifted."

Lord Richard leaned back in his chair. "Nay," he said. "Those noble folk were not as our friend here."

"True enough," Mistress Dritchly agreed with an emphatic nod that sent her greying curls bobbing. "I ought to know, for did not my Edwin himself become great friends with one? It were they who taught the first masters of motive science. Learned a barn full of cog lore, Edwin did, from that gentleman."

Lord Richard fingered his neat pointed beard. "For the

first thirty or so years after the Beatification," he said, "they guided and reassured all those of us who were fearful. Kindly mentors, they were."

"What would we have done without them?" the woman sighed. "Showed us how to glean the proudflesh, and how to work the rind of the hide trees until it's as supple as the best Spanish leather.

Chewing the end of a lock of hair which had strayed across his cheek, Jack eventually asked, "So where did they come from? What happened to them? No one ever really speaks of it."

Mistress Dritchly tutted and, with a wobble of her plump pink cheeks, told him, "They would never say from whence they came, yet I and most others knew that they were doing Our Lord's bidding. How they delighted in everything they did. Alas for the day which saw them depart. As abruptly as they appeared amongst us, they left. No word of farewell or explanation, they merely stopped a-visiting."

She paused and dabbed at her eye. "Edwin missed his merry, clever friend. Bless me, but he conjured some fanciful notions. Reckoned that wherever those noble people hailed from, danger and trouble was brewing there. I told him that was a wicked thing to say, for how could there be any manner of strife in the divine province of Heaven?"

"You're swift to populate every corner of the

Almighty's kingdom," Lord Richard teased gently. "First the special ambassadors, now this fellow – a crowded place it must be."

Jack let the hair fall from his mouth. "So they never returned? Not one?"

"None that I ever heard of," Richard Wutton answered. "But they were a people apart from our guest, their features as unlike his as his are to our own."

"Faces flat as smoothing irons," Mistress Dritchly put in. "And foreheads like a proving loaf, but such lovely manners."

She was prevented from saying any more by a sudden rush of footsteps as Adam came rushing into the house, hotly pursued by Henry.

"Give it back!" Henry demanded, but Adam raced up the stairs and came tumbling into the sickroom.

"What's this?" Mistress Dritchly squalled in outrage. "I told you to be gone! Were you the cause of the din we heard afore outside? Impudent child! No supper shall you receive this night – you must learn and your belly groan."

Under her barrage of complaint, the boy could not squeeze a word out, but Lord Richard observed the serious gleam in his eye and called the widow to silence.

"What is it, Cog Adam?" he asked.

The apprentice stepped forward and held out the gleaming object, even as Henry barged crossly into the room behind him.

"This, My Lord," he said. "I believe it belongs to the stranger."

There was no time for anyone to proclaim its beauty. As soon as the wounded figure saw what Adam grasped in his hand, he called out in a beguiling cry. It was so insistent that the boy did not wait for instruction from his master but hastened to the bedside and surrendered the collar immediately.

With his bandaged hands, the patient clumsily clasped the thing around his slender neck and touched the lesser stones in sequence. At once a sizzling noise came crackling from the blue gem and its glow flared, banishing the shadows and dimming the candle flames. Yet the glare lasted only a moment and, when it had dwindled, the stranger opened his thin mouth.

"My thanks to you," a rich, melodious voice chimed from the heart of the flickering jewel. "I am called Brindle and I owe you my life."

CHAPTER 3

The Balm Trader

The stunned silence which followed was swiftly swept aside by an eruption of spluttered words and exclaiming cries. Mistress Dritchly made a noise very like the bass squeals of Old Temperance, while Adam and Jack whooped with delight and Lord Richard gave a hearty cheer. Only Henry remained silent but none of the others noticed.

The patient regarded them with an amused glitter in the green horseshoe of his eye, until Lord Richard called for silence.

"At last," he breathed, turning to his guest, "there can be understanding betwixt us."

A smile formed in that scarred face. "The torc permits us to share a common speech," the answer came. "I am thankful for its retrieval, yet I sense that this young pair have been at some pains to fetch it. Fear, freshly dispelled, clings to them still."

The others looked at the two apprentices and Henry squirmed uncomfortably. Brindle stared at him most keenly until the boy felt sure that somehow the stranger knew what he had intended. Blushing, Henry looked at the floor.

"Now I may discover something of this interesting land and those who have saved me," Brindle said.

Lord Richard introduced the visitor to each of them in turn then went on to describe what happened on the night they found him. Brindle listened gravely and, although he wished to know more of this place, he could see that his host was barely containing his own curiosity.

"Again I perceive how deeply I am within your debt," he began. "A worthy people you are. There is so much you would ask of me and yet you forebear to perform the courtesies. Ask then, and I shall answer."

Before Lord Richard could speak, Henry had overcome his awkwardness and piped up, "You really come from Heaven?"

"I am from the sphere of Iribia," Brindle replied, much to Mistress Dritchly's disappointment. "Are you unaware of its... fame? 'Tis a world renowned for its great beauty and fragrance. As a garden is my world, for it does boast the greatest species of plant and flower, more than anywhere I have ever visited."

"Well it certainly sounds like paradise," Mistress Dritchly said, her faith restored. "Now, my angel, you must eat a little. Not a crumb has passed your lips these three days gone."

Brindle held up his hand and shook his head. "Do not think me unmindful of your good intention," he assured her, "but I have received enough nourishment this day."

"When?" the woman cried. "Has that lumpen Anne been feeding you when my back was turned?"

Her patient grinned. "Nay," he vowed, indicating the jug of flowers at the bedside. "'Tis the way of my kind to find sustenance of a different sort. The blooms you have daily sweetened this chamber with have more than maintained my strength. I marvel at them for they are all new unto me."

"You don't eat at all?" she murmured in dejection. "Not even a morsel of marchpane?"

"Let him be, Mistress," Lord Richard told her. "I should like to know how our friend came to be here and why his conveyance crashed into our firmament."

The yellow eye narrowed and a pain that was not borne of his injuries etched into Brindle's face.

"I am lost," he said simply. "I am a balm merchant by

trade, exchanging the rare perfumes of my home with other provinces. Returning thither, my night boat suffered a misadventure and the instruments of navigation were destroyed. For six weeks or more I have journeyed blind and without hope of aid."

He paused and stared down at the coverlet. "Never have I known such a darkness in my life. A horror was with me always, for any moment might have spelled the end. I knew not where the vessel rushed me but collision was certain. Hourly, Death tapped at my shoulder and in my bleakest moments I came near to embracing Him."

"Don't speak of it," Lord Richard said kindly.

"The good Lord delivered you to us," Mistress Dritchly declared. "He has a way of caring for His own."

"'Twould seem a power greater than chance watched over me," Brindle agreed. "To have brought me safe to this unknown region and into such friendly hands."

His voice trailed into silence and it was clear that fatigue was creeping over him. Mistress Dritchly decided that it was time for them all to leave. Her charge needed his rest and even Lord Richard dared not refuse her.

"God's peace be upon you," she whispered, closing the door behind her.

Wearily lowering himself back on to the pillows, Brindle reflected that he liked this unusual race. Not certain what to do with the candle flame, he left it burning and closed his eye. The scents of the room closed over him and, breathing deeply, the Iribian surrendered himself to them.

The next day dawned early for the apprentices. The wreckage that Old Scratch had left behind had to be cleared up and, surveying the damaged mechanicals, Lord Richard knew that the cost of replacing them would fall to him. He worried how he could possibly begin to afford it, as there was nothing left in Malmes-Wutton worth selling.

"That wild boar is becoming expensive," he told himself, "not to mention hazardous. It should have been attended to years ago. It must be captured and stilled as soon as possible."

He was in the yard, helping Adam and the others remove the last traces of Old Scratch's violence, when a cart arrived bearing a fresh consignment of repair work. This time it was three broken ponies in desperate need of an overhaul, and a horse whose head was jammed upside down. The esquire who brought them was eager to look on the heavenly messenger, but Lord Richard politely refused the request, then hurried indoors to deny the man an opportunity to ask a second time.

In the sickroom Brindle awoke feeling much stronger. Mistress Dritchly removed several of his bandages and decided that it was time for the air to do its healing work upon his lesser wounds. The left eye, however, was still too inflamed and this she bound firmly with clean dressings.

Staring in fascination out of the window, Brindle shocked her by announcing his intention to rise from the bed and learn something of this unfamiliar land. Against her better judgement and with many shakes of her head, Mistress Dritchly brought him a jerkin and breeches of homespun.

Brindle accepted them thoughtfully, his nostrils quivering. "The nightshirt I wear," he said. "It too belongs to the owner of these garments. An image of a large-hearted, blustering man adheres to them. His presence is close about you also... and yet."

Mistress Dritchly gasped and her small eyes blinked the unexpected tears away. "My Edwin," she breathed, glancing expectantly about the room. "You... you can see him? Here in this chamber?"

The Iribian hastily tried to explain.

"I see but an impression of him. A memory if you will. My perception is keener than yours and does not rely on sight alone. Were both my eyes blinded in the crash I would not consider myself impaired. An Iribian lives by scent; all other senses are but complements to it."

"But how did'st you know what my Edwin looked like?" she asked in disbelief.

Holding up the jerkin, Brindle's nostrils dilated. "Clothing remembers its wearer," he answered. "How could it be otherwise? The traces of his moods seep into the weave. It recalls no anger, but agitation in abundance. The fermented juice which His Lordship drinks was not unknown to him, but he partook of it seldom. This man worked with his hands; metal, oil and timber – all passed through his fingers. Such is the testimony of his raiment. There is a deal more should you wish to hear it."

Breaking off, he turned to Mistress Dritchly who was gazing sadly at the clothes with glistening eyes.

"The hues of his essence shade your being also. You were bonded with him, though the colours I discern are old and unrefreshed. Where is this man? Why has he been absent these many days?"

"Edwin was my husband," she murmured thickly. "He has been dead nigh on two weeks now. God love him."

Brindle returned the jerkin. "Then you must not cast his signature scent away," he told her. "You are overly generous."

The woman rubbed her nose. "No," she insisted. "I keep his memory alive and bright in my heart; I don't need his clothes to remind me of the years we had. You have them, my angel. Wear them with my blessing and Edwin's also."

The Iribian bowed. Then, gingerly, he pulled the unaccustomed apparel over his bruised and aching limbs. The arms of the jerkin were a little too short and the legs of the breeches did not reach his ankles, but around the waist there was plenty of cloth to spare. A tight belt gathered the excess and held it in place, while a pair of leather boots donated by Lord Richard completed the attire.

Peering into a small steel mirror hung on the wall, he saw for the first time the extent of the injuries to his face and looked away quickly.

"Don't you trouble yourself over that," his nurse said firmly. "Folk hereabouts have gazed on much worse of late. If they do stop and gawk at you, send them on to me and I'll give them an aspect to match."

Brindle moved away from the mirror and, standing by the window, set his eye roaming over the peculiar landscape outside. "What miracle is this place?" he asked, staring up at the arching buttresses of the leaded firmament. "This is no ordinary sphere."

"Indeed it is not," she replied proudly. "These are the uplifted isles. We were brought here by the grace of the Almighty and given understanding enough to dwell in His new and great design."

The Iribian's brow creased in confusion. "This is not the world of your birth?" he asked.

"Mercy, no!" Mistress Dritchly exclaimed. "That was a wicked place, brimming over with sin. We were saved from that by the Beatification and set here instead."

Brindle was still bewildered but Lord Richard had entered and, hearing Mistress Dritchly's words, rolled his eyes to the ceiling. "The character of Man has not changed a whit since that time," he interrupted. "We are just as corrupt and iniquitous as before."

Edwin's widow opened her mouth to argue the matter, then remembered the number of tasks she had to accomplish that day. With a last simmering glance at Lord Richard, she removed herself to the kitchen.

"So," the master of Malmes-Wutton addressed his guest, "you wish to explore this modest estate. Permit me to guide you, then I must attend to the scaffold building. Your night boat will be within reach by noon if you wish to return and see what may be salvaged."

Brindle nodded. The scents which wafted into the room from the open window were setting his mind aflame with brilliant colours and he was itching to investigate further.

With his good eye gleaming, the Iribian left the bedchamber and descended the stairs in slow, careful steps. A hundred perfumes greeted him: the heavy musk of beeswax which permeated the furniture, a musty, resinous odour that flowed from the crackled varnish of the wall panels and the cool barren dryness of the stone flags in the hall below. Reaching one of the few unsold tapestries, he halted to admire the workmanship, then savoured the many different fragrances which poured from its fibres. Each woollen thread possessed its own unique scent, heightened by the countless vegetable dyes, and a pleasing harmony of images paraded through his mind.

"This way," Lord Richard prompted, leading him down into the hall.

Thus escorted, and with new discoveries waiting around every corner, Brindle spent a most agreeable hour. He was constantly amazed and intrigued by the slightest thing. The Wutton family portraits perplexed him utterly, for his kind had no need of such flat likenesses and he found the two-dimensional expanse of pigmented oils difficult to interpret.

The library of Wutton Old Place enchanted him completely. For many minutes he was content to stand in the centre of the room simply breathing in the collected aroma of the bound volumes.

"The knowledge of many years lies upon these shelves," he said, running his fingers along a row of books. Selecting one of the largest, he leafed through the pages, gazing at the jumble of signs and squiggles which marked the paper.

"Would that I could learn your written tongue," he sighed.

Standing a little shyly to one side, Lord Richard gave him an encouraging grin. "In time you will master it," he promised. "Cog Adam might help you there. He's often in here with his nose buried in some dusty page or other."

"Where are the children?" Brindle asked.

"In the stables. They repair broken mechanicals there."

"Ah yes, the small wooden creature that burst in upon us last night. Why do you keep such devices?"

"Oh, many reasons. Food being one of them."

The familiar confused expression crossed Brindle's face

and Lord Richard chuckled. "Allow me to show you the workshops," he said. "That might furnish you with the answers you seek." Returning to the hall, he opened the main door and a warm June breeze wafted inside.

Brindle drew a sharp breath. The summer air was laden with delicious fragrances and he stepped out into the sunlight, trembling with excitement.

The scents of Malmes-Wutton were overwhelming. From the stretching lawn a sweet, heady vapour rose and beyond that the outlying woodland seethed with rich green flavours. There was much here to savour and enjoy, and the Iribian's palate watered. Yet there was one perfume lacing the air which ignited brilliant sparks in his thoughts and he longed to trace its source.

There was no chance to hunt for it, however, for Lord Richard was already crossing the gravel yard and heading for the stables. Gazing about him, with his many nostrils flaring, Brindle followed.

"How goes the labour?" Richard Wutton called as he approached the workshop.

Jack Flye and the other apprentices looked up from their benches where the ponies and the horse that had arrived that morning were in various dismantled states.

"Well enough, My Lord," Jack answered. "There is naught here to present any problem."

Lord Richard said that he was glad to hear it, then bid them keep Brindle company for a short while. "I must see how the scaffold fares," he told his guest. "There were few keen to venture into the wood this morning after hearing what Old Scratch was up to last night."

"You're not going alone?" Jack asked.

"How else am I to get there?"

Jack Flye placed the steel horse's head he had been rectifying to one side. "I'll go with you, My Lord," he said. "That devil is more deadly than ever."

Lord Richard assented and, with a farewell flourish of his hand, they crossed the lawns to the trees. Standing in the stable entrance, Brindle stared at his night boat fixed in the sky and uttered a soft murmur of fascination that the blue stone in his torc could not render into English.

"The skill and ingenuity of this fabricated land impresses me mightily," he said at last. "Behind the outward simplicity there lies an incredible science. You are a formidable people to own such wisdom."

"Bog beetles," Henry snorted. "We didn't make the firmament, nor raise the lands."

Brindle turned his attention from the leaded sky to the work that the apprentices were doing. Adam had completed the repairs to one of the ponies; it had only needed its gears adjusting and the boy was already replacing the jointed wooden panels which formed the animal's body.

As usual Suet was sitting upon his bench, watching him work and snuffling gently.

"A bit of a clunker, this one," Adam said, fixing the

last section in position. "They're not the best we've had in here."

Brindle looked at the surrounding mechanicals with great interest. Stooping beneath the hanging tools and dangling spares which stretched across the beams, he peered into the open casings and his bright eye sparkled. "There is something here..." he murmured, almost to himself, "...that I seem to recognise."

The moment Jack had left with Lord Richard, Henry had stopped working and was now watching the Iribian closely. "You have mechanicals where you come from?" he demanded.

Brindle gave a shake of his head. "Nay," he said, examining the internals of the now disassembled peacock. "Yet the fundamental principles of these automata appear familiar to me. Except for these liquids – for what purpose are they?"

"They're the ichors," Adam told him. "Without them nothing would work."

"A stupendous achievement," the Iribian breathed. "To have dissolved and suspended complex control procedures into an emulsion so that they flux and flow through a dynamic system. How is it accomplished?"

"Gibble-gabble!" Henry scoffed. "What manner of talk is that? Ichors is ichors. Phlegm, yellow bile and temper, that's what the cordials are – and black bile if your purse can stretch to it."

Brindle fumbled for comprehension. "But surely, they are fabricated somewhere?" he said.

"No," Adam replied. "The ichors, or humours, were already here at the time of the Beatification, together with the first mechanicals."

Contemplating the three glass vessels within the peacock, Brindle's scarred face crinkled in puzzlement. "A staggering advancement purposely masquerading in simple guise," he muttered. "Yet why should this deceiving science strike chords of recognition within me? Where could I have seen its like before?"

The Iribian searched his memory for an answer. It eluded him and he shrugged, dismissing the thought from his mind for the time being.

"Were you the only one on your night boat?" Henry asked abruptly. "Or will there be burned bodies to find in there?"

Adam threw him a hateful look. There had been a strained tension between the pair of them that morning. Although Henry was glad that he had not kept the torc, the other boy had not forgiven him for the hurtful things he had said.

"I was alone," Brindle assured them. "Yet I had the signature scents of my children by me. Those precious tokens preserved my desperate wits. Alas, I fear that the ampoules will not have survived the heats of the collision."

"How many you got?" Henry interrogated.

"Five boys and two girls," came the proud reply. "The youngest, Nidor, I would reckon to be of an age with yourself."

"Does he look like you? Is his nose as big?"

"Henry!" Adam snapped.

But Brindle was laughing. "Nidor takes after his mother," he said. "Although I trust his nose will grow to be as mine. In my world it is a feature of much esteem. I cannot conceive how your race exists with its scant lack. Impoverished and pitied would you be amongst us."

Adam completed fitting the pony together and decided that he should take Brindle away from Henry's impertinent questions. "Have you visited the gardens yet?" he asked. "There are some lovely smells there this time of year."

The Iribian allowed himself to be led away and, to Adam's surprise, Henry made no attempt to follow them. He claimed he had far too much work still to do, but Adam did not believe a word of it.

Trying to guess what the Wattle boy was up to, Adam o'the Cogs lifted Suet from the workbench and strolled with Brindle from the stables. Past the piggery and the barn they went, skirting around the manor's red-bricked walls to where the ground rose and a thick hedge of box screened the garden which lay beyond. "There are some steps leading into it over there," Adam said, pointing to a shallow rise of mossy stone treads cut into the rising sward. "The flower beds are rather neglected. They still bloom, but with many a weed for company."

Brindle made no answer. His keen senses thrilled to the enticing scent he had experienced earlier and already his refined vision beheld blazing lights shine and scintillate over the dense hedge.

Grunting gladly, Suet scooted ahead of them. He loved this part of the estate, for the kitchen garden grew within the enclosure and there was always something scrumptious sprouting. Snorting greedily, he avoided the difficult steps and scurried up the grassy bank.

Adam and Brindle followed him in and at once the Iribian let out a strangled cry. The sapphire gem at his throat burned fiercely as he began to sob with emotion.

The apprentice stared at him, astonished, and cast about for what could have wrung this terrible reaction from the wounded visitor. All he could see was an ill-tended, circular flower bed.

Every nostril on Brindle's pale face was shivering, and tears began to roll from his undamaged eye as he staggered forward.

"From the barbarous... empty dark..." the torc said, faltering, "to perfection sublime... a treasure beyond rejoicing!"

Halting before the thorny bushes, he raised a quaking hand and cupped the nearest bloom in nervous fingers.

‡

To him, it was as if he held a ball of brilliant flame whose raging scent chimed and echoed through his head. Vibrant colours snaked through the air and the garden was thick with a shimmering fog that wreathed intoxicatingly about him. Conquered completely, Brindle's legs buckled and he fell to his knees, a shower of crimson petals scattering about his shoulders.

Adam watched with increasing alarm. He thought that the Iribian had suffered a deadly attack and the boy stumbled backwards, ready to race into the manor and summon help.

"Sirrah?" he called in a wavering voice. "Fear not – I shall fetch Mistress Dritchly."

Suddenly Brindle flung himself on to his back and threw his long arms wide, gulping the air into his lungs. Then an elated yell blared from the torc.

"Stay, child!" he cried as he started to shake with laughter. "I am in no pain. How could there be anguish in the midst of such undreamed beauty?" Rolling on to his front, he fixed the emerald horseshoe of his eye upon Adam. "Pray tell me the name of those wonders!" he begged. "I must put a label to this glorious sensation."

The Iribian's delight was infectious and Adam began to giggle as he looked across at the tangled plants and said, "'Tain't nothing remarkable – 'tis naught but a rose."

"A rose," Brindle repeated. "Oh, the title is fitting. Verily I say unto you, that my kind have seldom endured a bliss so aching as your rose. Though I have traded a prodigious tally of musks and fragrance, this would be the glittering jewel of my wares. You are blessed beyond your understanding, my young friend."

Returning to his feet, he paced about the circular bed, enthralled at the different varieties which strove against the weeds. "I cannot recall when last I felt so light of heart," he laughed. "'Tis though all grief and care have been stripped from me. I feel young again!"

His words became lost amid the outpouring of his joy and Adam chuckled with him, swept along on a burbling tide until the pair of them could only shake their heads at each other, helpless casualties of their own merriment. As the hot summer sun beat down upon the garden and bees droned in and out of the flowers, Adam o'the Cogs hoped he would remember this moment for the rest of his days. After the death of Edwin Dritchly, life at the manor had been mournful and solemn but, since the Iribian's arrival, that had all changed. A purpose had returned to their blighted existence; even the dead man's widow had discovered a new role for herself. Perhaps Brindle was a heavenly messenger after all, in spite of what he said.

Recovering a little, his chest heaving with abating mirth, the boy gazed at the roses as if viewing them for the first time. "I wish I could smell them in the same way as you," he sighed. "Can you describe what it's like?"

Brindle's eye glittered over him. "It is the breath of

innocence," he answered gently. "When I dip into this beguilement, the burden of my tormenting guilt is lifted. Oh, I could live my life in this garden and never once yearn for home or kin. Yea, even remembrance of my wife and children would not move me nor have any place in the chambers of my heart. Such is the virtue of these blooms. They seek out the child within and I... I am happy."

The boy smiled at him. It was exciting experiencing commonplace things with an outsider.

"That's a damask," he said when Brindle paused to gaze upon a particular pink rose. "Mistress Dritchly uses it to make medicines. There's a syrup to be had from the petals which she says will keep your bowels open, but I've never had cause to try it. She made Henry take it once though and I don't think he's ever forgotten."

"And this white specimen?" the Iribian asked, moving to another.

"Eglantine," Adam informed him. "'Tis said to denote purity."

"Purity, aye that is the word. No blemish, no memory of wrong, no damnation, all screams are stifled and quieted. Never did I think to find absolution, yet here it is in five white petals. Purity and absolution – amen to that."

Adam did not know what he was speaking of. A remote look had glazed the Iribian's eye and the boy mumbled on. "The Queen Herself favours it, so they say, for that very reason."

The faraway look vanished and Brindle's head reared above the flowers. "This little land is ruled by a monarch?" he asked doubtfully. "I did think your Lord Richard was master here."

"Malmes-Wutton isn't the only part of Englandia," Adam laughed. "There are many floating isles like this, only far larger in size. Then there are the realms of Europe."

"I must have journeyed far indeed," Brindle said. "Else I would have surely heard of these places. To which forgotten corner of the Outer Darkness did my night boat thrust me?"

Adam could not answer him and, while the visitor pondered, the boy realised that he had not seen Suet since they had entered the garden. "Where's he got to?" he voiced the thought aloud.

Leaving Brindle to the captivating roses, the boy went in search of the wooden piglet. The hunt was not a prolonged one. Rounding a plot filled with the flowering purples of sage, rosemary and lavender, he saw a trail of broken stems leading to the cultivated patch where Mistress Dritchly grew vegetables.

"Suet!" he cried crossly. "Get out of there!"

Standing trotter deep in freshly dredged soil, the piglet turned a dirt-covered face to Adam and snorted happily as his lower jaw chomped and chewed. Over half a row of turnips had been gobbled up, the ragged fragments of their top shoots littering the plundered trench behind him.

"I said get out," the boy insisted. "Mistress Dritchly will have apoplexy when she sees this."

The mechanical tilted his head quizzically, not understanding why Adam was so angry. Quick to obey, but still crunching the last mouthful, Suet waddled over and prepared to grunt *O Mistress Mine* to placate his master.

"No you don't!" the apprentice scolded, plucking the piglet from the ground, then shaking the soil from his carved legs and wiping the snout to remove the evidence. "You can't get round me that way."

Stomping back to the rose bed, he found Brindle still lost in admiration, but he glanced up when Adam returned and looked with surprise at the munching creature under his arm.

"The device is eating!" he exclaimed.

"'Course he is," Adam answered. "He's a pig – that's what he does best."

"But, 'tis only a lifeless mechanism."

"You tell that to the turnips he's just devoured," the boy replied, regaining his good humour.

"Do all automatons eat in this strange country?"

Adam grinned. "Only if they're to be eaten themselves," he said.

The confusion appeared once more on Brindle's face and the boy promised to show him the kitchen where all would be explained.

"Very well," the Iribian assented. "Lead me there. Though my heart grieves to depart this garden."

"Have you really never seen a rose before?" Adam asked.

Taking one last breath of the eglantine, Brindle said, "Were I to return to my sphere with but a single bloom, wealth unending would be mine – so rare is its sweet perfume. The blossoms of Iribia will be as colourless and drear as clay in comparison. My people are afflicted with much sorrow, young Adam. Our spirits are heavy laden but, in this hallowed fragrance, we could find pardon and perhaps forgive ourselves at last."

Adam scratched his head in mild amusement. "If this poorly tended garden holds the finest smell you've ever known," he began, "you'd best not venture to any house grander than Wutton Old Place for fear of bursting apart with joy. Why even at Saxmundham I've heard..."

His words faltered, for the enchantment had dissolved from Brindle's face. The merchant's features had clouded and were set into a frightening grimness.

"Nay," he whispered in a hushed tone not intended to be overheard yet nevertheless proclaimed by the torc. "I did not say it was the finest..."

The clear voice which spoke from the jewel broke his solemn reverie and Brindle looked up uneasily.

There was something furtive about that hasty glance. Adam had the disturbing feeling that he had caught an unguarded glimpse into a side of the Iribian which he was not meant to have seen. The notion unsettled him and he found himself struggling to know what to say.

It was Brindle who dispelled the awkward silence. Sampling the warm air with a shallow breath, he announced, "The child named Henry approaches."

A moment later there came a rattling clatter and Henry Wattle bounded into the garden, a sack slung over one shoulder and a mischievous smirk stretched across his face.

"You still dawdling out here?" he called.

"We... we were just going to the kitchen," Adam stammered.

Henry cackled and gave his sack a purposeful shake. "So am I," he uttered in a tone brimming with impish intent. Then, addressing the Iribian, he said, "I always find the kitchen the best place for heavenly whiffs, but this morning, 'tis my turn to give Widow Dritchly the vapours."

And, sniggering like a lesser demon, the boy strode determinedly towards the manor house.

CHAPTER 4

Rats and Ashes

The kitchen of Wutton Old Place was far too large for Lord Richard's present needs and with only Anne Sowerby to help her, Mistress Dritchly found it a great deal of hard work to maintain.

She was alone when Brindle and the apprentices entered, her ample form stooping over the great wide table which dominated the room and her back turned to the huge fireplace.

"There you are, my angel," she cried, glancing up from

a mound of freshly chopped carrots. "I pray these two rogues aren't tiring you on your first day out of bed."

His nostrils closing sharply, Brindle shrank back from a wall of smoke he had wandered into as the hearth spat and sputtered.

"A curse on that Anne!" the woman grumbled. "Damp wood on the fire; is she completely addled or does she do it to plague me?"

An appreciative grin lit Henry's face and she glared at him reproachfully. "You're no better, Master Wattle!" her caustic tongue lashed. "I abide Anne because she's a lack wit – you're just plain knavery seeking to torment."

Brindle looked around him. Wedges of sunlight beamed through large windows at one end of the kitchen, bathing the long table in the glare of the summer's day. A host of earthenware jars and pots thronged the shelves, gleaming in their glazes, and bowls of dwindling size were stacked in precarious towers. From the ceiling beams an aromatic assortment of herbs was drying and, suspended over the table, an iron chandelier was home to many sprigs of elder which lured flies away from the dishes being prepared beneath.

Henry was quite right – this place housed many tempting smells. Beneath the stringent reek of the fire there was an attractive, tingling fragrance emanating from an oak cupboard where Lord Richard kept costly spices under lock and key, and many diverse odours flowed thickly from the shelves. The unctuous scent of black treacle was oozing from an imperfectly sealed jar, and a bowl of vinegar, to which crushed mint leaves had been added, brought goose pimples to Brindle's pallid skin. Upon a trestle, next to the cooling brick oven, the yeasty fumes effusing from five warm loaves drew a smile on his thin lips and painted comforting shades across his spirit.

Yet nothing here could compare to the rapture he had known outside and even now he was anxious to return to the garden and relive that joy anew.

"Where is that idle Anne?" Mistress Dritchly demanded. "She's using that black-headed wart to pardon her idleness again. A sharp knife and a nimble hand would soon cure her of that affliction – though the idleness would remain."

The unmistakable grunting of Old Temperance heralded the kitchen maid's return, for she had been bidden to the piggery to fetch the great sow. It was time for her to be gleaned and Brindle was intrigued to discover what this cryptic phrase signified.

Moving aside to give the large pig room to enter, he watched it lumber into the kitchen with Anne Sowerby slowly shuffling in behind. Suet darted out from Adam's feet where he had been sitting and the two mechanicals exchanged snorting salutations.

"You took a dollop of time, my girl!" Mistress Dritchly berated.

Anne's mouth twisted to one side, the way it always did when Mistress Dritchly admonished her, but her eyes were fixed upon Brindle's tall frame and grew wider with every second that passed.

"Ooh, what a noribble face to cart round all the time," she said with much sympathy. "Don't that great nubbly nose give you pain? Like a big wormy tumour, that is."

Her rude observations were quickly curtailed when an onion struck the side of her head. Yelping, she hurried to the far corner and pretended to be busy. Dropping a second onion back into its basket, Mistress Dritchly rubbed her hands together and turned to her patient.

"Wool for brains," she explained, cocking her head towards the sulking Anne. "Anyone would think she's a court beauty the way she goes on."

Breezing around the table, the woman halted before Old Temperance and smartly struck the Wutton crest carved into the animal's expansive side. At once the sow was stilled, the concertina snout slid to a stop and all movement ceased.

A faint whine of distress issued from Suet and the piglet pushed against his mother, trying to get her to move again. Adam saw him and knelt down, giving his small wooden body a reassuring pat. "You've seen this before," he said. "Nothing to get upset about. "

Mistress Dritchly held out her arms and bent her knees, seizing the sow's vast bulk and taking the strain.

"Nay, Mistress," Brindle stopped her. "Permit me."

The woman tried to prevent him but the Iribian would not hear of it and, before she could cluck in protest, his strong arms had lifted Old Temperance off the ground.

"Oh, you shouldn't!" she fussed. "Not in your delicate state. You'll undo all the good healing. Oh well, put the pig on here, there's a dear angel."

Brindle obeyed and in a trice the mechanical sow was standing incongruously upon the kitchen table.

"Quite a weight, isn't she?" Mistress Dritchly remarked. "Well beyond time for a thorough gleaning."

Deftly, her podgy fingers unclasped the fastenings that held a section of the mechanical's side in place and took up a knife.

"Should have been attended to over a week ago," she stated. "But a body's only one pair of hands and they're usually needed elsewhere with Anne to watch out for. I pray the proudflesh hasn't gotten tough and chewy – Lord Richard hates that."

To Brindle's astonishment he saw that packed inside Old Temperance's barrel-shaped casing was a thick layer of a cream-coloured, spongy substance which smelled musty and damp.

"Oh, couldn't be more perfect!" Mistress Dritchly trilled, setting to with her blade and trimming the dense matter from the sow's interior. "Just ripe and ready as the good Lord intended."

Hearing the knife go slicing in, Suet trundled away from Adam and hid his face behind the flour sack which was propped against the wall.

"There!" the woman declared when the mechanical was thoroughly cleaned out and a great pile of the floppy proudflesh had been heaped upon the table. Brindle stared at it, bemused, looking to the apprentices for enlightenment.

"Pork, bacon and ham!" Henry said unhelpfully.

"It's the proudflesh," Adam put in, seeing the Iribian's difficulty. "It forms within the mechanicals and in the hands of a skilled cook is delicious – tasty as the real thing."

"Bat's toenails!" Henry scoffed. "You wouldn't know and nor would I. There's nobody had real meat these past hundred and seventy-five years. Could be a world of difference and we're none the wiser."

"You'll not be wanting any of this for your supper tonight then?" Mistress Dritchly remarked. "I'll give you naught but the cold pottage of yester, Master Wattle, and you'd best be thankful or you'll get nothing tomorrow neither."

The boy grumbled to himself and retreated to the furthest corner out of her vision, carefully setting his sack upon the floor and crouching over it.

"Now for the offal," Mistress Dritchly announced, reaching inside Old Temperance and detaching odd, pewter shapes from their pipes.

"Kidneys, liver, lungs, tripe and heart," Adam explained as more proudflesh was popped out of these moulds.

"Folk like to see a shape they're familiar with, on their trencher or in their pie," the woman added. "Lord Richard does."

With her consent, Brindle picked up one of the squashy kidneys and studied it with interest.

"A form of fungus," he pronounced at length. "So that is why the devices need to eat – the decaying matter nourishes the spores within."

"Better than any mushroom I ever cooked," his nurse said, sliding a large jar from the shelf and wiping the inside of the heart mould with the dark brown liquid it contained.

"For flavour as it grows," Adam told him. "The proudflesh takes on whatever taste you coat the insides with."

Mistress Dritchly fitted the pewter shape back into the sow then took up another jar and began daubing the contents into the kidney patterns.

"But that's venison!" Adam said, reading what was written on the glaze.

Mistress Dritchly wagged her head in distraction. "I know, I know," she retorted. "But his lordship has run out of the kidney essence and, as he don't own any deer no more, there was a tidy lot of this left. I'm not one for wasting – you know that, Cog Adam."

"Lord Richard is not a wealthy man?" Brindle interrupted.

"Bless us, no," she lamented. "He was once but not no more. Loyalty fills no pockets it seems, not even in this uplifted world."

A slow smile spread across the Iribian's injured face. A way to reward his host had surfaced in his mind, but now was not the time to mention it. He would have to investigate the interior of his night boat before he could tell them and raise their hopes.

When the pewter moulds had been returned to Old Temperance's insides, Mistress Dritchly closed the great pig up again and Brindle gallantly lifted the mechanical back to the floor.

"There," the woman grunted with satisfaction at the heap of proudflesh upon the table. "Another four months before she'll be ready for another gleaning. Anne, take the bacon layers and slice them into rashers whilst I dress the hams for curing."

Dragging her feet across the floor, the kitchen maid trudged over and collected the rubbery pieces on to a large dish.

"Remove the sow to the piggery," Mistress Dritchly told Adam, "or it'll be under my feet for the rest of the day."

Whistling for Suet, the boy pressed Old Temperance's crest and the bass voice started up as the sow jerked into motion, sprightly and alert. Suet let out a gleeful squeak and scampered from behind the sack to nuzzle against his mother once more.

"Come on," Adam said, nudging Old Temperance with his knee. "Back to the sty for you."

The mechanical wheeled vigorously about, but at that moment the kitchen exploded in chaos.

Anne Sowerby was traipsing back to her usual place, bearing the dish of proudflesh when, suddenly, she encountered one of the things Henry had released from his sack. Shrieking, the girl threw down the dish. It smashed upon the stone floor, and the gleaned cuts went bouncing under the table and across the room.

A dark shape shot across her feet, snatching up the smallest piece of proudflesh and darted off with it into the shadows.

Anne shrieked again and danced backwards, flapping her arms wildly. "Orrible!" she bawled. "It were orrible!"

No one else had seen what had frightened her and they stared at the girl.

"Nasty, dirty thing!" she continued to wail. "Oh, what were it?"

Seizing hold of her flailing arms, Mistress Dritchly shook her sternly. "What ails you, girl?" she demanded. "You just pick all that up again before you get a hiding—"

The woman would have said more but then she too saw what had frightened the kitchen maid.

Running along one of the shelves was a tin rat.

It was hideously life-like, with a long, leathery tail that thrashed between the jars, slapping their sides, sweeping through the air and dangling over the edge. Woolly fur had been painstakingly gummed to the jointed body then slicked down for added effect while, from the sharply pointed head, long whiskers came spiking. Jagged metal teeth chattered under a trembling sprung nose but, most repulsive of all, were the two black beads which made the eyes. A consuming desire to pillage and terrorise glittered in them, and they swivelled from side to side, coveting everything they saw.

Mistress Dritchly roared in outrage and for a second she and the creature glared at one another until she hurled an onion at the loathsome thing.

The rat was too quick. With a crack of its tail, it dived from the shelf. The onion struck only the jar of treacle which toppled over and hit the ground with a tremendous crack, followed by the sticky squelching of the dark contents as they spread slowly across the floor.

Anne Sowerby screamed afresh, but her mistress grabbed an iron ladle from a pot by the fire and hunted for the creature, waving the weapon above her head.

Adam and Brindle watched in startled amusement. Then a second rat leapt on to the table, stole a slice of carrot and rushed off again.

"There's a third!" Adam cried, pointing to where

another of the metal vermin was ripping the flour sack apart with tin claws and causing a blizzard in the process.

Over the floor the first rat bolted and the ladle came clanging after, bashing a desperate rhythm on the stone flags. "Catch them!" Mistress Dritchly yelled as the creature snaked away.

Adam lunged at the one on the flour but the small mechanical jumped clear and the boy fell against the sack, splitting it completely and choking the kitchen with a swirling whiteness.

The three rats seemed everywhere. They swarmed into baskets, upset pots, spilled jugs, broke bottles and scattered grain. One of them bounded into a bowl of dried apricots and began to fling them at whoever came near, before dashing away again.

Whirling about her kitchen, Mistress Dritchly swung the ladle murderously, forcing everyone to duck and dodge out of her path.

Then Suet decided to enter the fray. When one of the ugly creations scooted past him, the piglet set off in pursuit, squealing loudly.

His face caked with flour, Adam could only watch as Suet scampered after the tin rat and, to his dismay, the boy realised that Old Temperance was about to join in too.

"Halt!" he yelled, lurching for the sow's Wutton crest – but it was too late. With a maternal bellow, Old Temperance charged after her piglet who was galloping under the table, still chasing the rat. With a crunching splinter of timbers, the great sow thundered beneath the buckling table, dragging it across the room until the wood shattered and collapsed in three pieces.

Over the wreckage two rats went capering, the joints of their jaws squeaking in mockery, while the third doubled back on itself and joined them in a renewed assault upon the shelves.

Suet swerved aside but Old Temperance was not built for agility and her carved trotters skidded upon the scattered proudflesh. Blaring a woeful squeal, the sow skated forward, crashing into the trestle where all five loaves were catapulted through the air. One of them hit Anne Sowerby on the back of her head and, believing it to be a rat, the girl fled the kitchen, howling and tearing at her hair.

Protecting his nostrils from the billowing clouds of flour, Brindle stumbled after her and behind him the riot continued to rage.

Bent double, Henry Wattle crawled over the kitchen threshold, gagging on his laughter. He had been working on the rats in secret for several months but he had never dared to hope that they would prove so successful. Clutching his cramping stomach, he staggered over to the Iribian and threw himself upon the ground, spluttering with awful relish.

"I did it!" he crowed. "No kissing Anne's abscess for me

– hark at that din. Widow Hummy Hum's nigh to having kittens in there. Oh, Wattle, you're amazing."

Brindle looked at him in bewilderment, then as more pots and dishes went crashing to the ground within the kitchen, he threw back his head and laughed.

A little after midday Henry Wattle was not so jubilant. Lord Richard had returned to the manor to find it in uproar. A full hour after their release, only one of the mechanical rats had been captured. The other two had escaped into the main part of the house and would prove to be a constant nuisance in Wutton Old Place for as long as the building remained standing.

When it was clear that there was nothing more to be done and the one cornered specimen had been well and truly flattened under the ladle, Mistress Dritchly took to her bed and lay there with her apron over her face for most of the afternoon. Anne Sowerby was burdened with the task of clearing up the kitchen and she stood gaping at the devastation, not knowing where to commence.

It was obvious who was to blame and, though he lamely tried to protest his innocence, Henry was marched to the village where his father gave him the soundest thrashing he had ever received. Now he stood in the workshop, unable to sit down, feeling sore and sorry for himself and with only the memory of his prank for company.

The stables were empty. The scaffold was completed at last and everyone had gone to the woodland to inspect Brindle's night boat. As punishment, Henry had to remain behind and finish the repairs to the horse and ponies. Muttering mutiny to himself, the boy worked grudgingly, aware that if he did not get the task done, then he would be in for another beating. "They were brilliant rats though," he breathed wistfully.

In the woodland Brindle and the others stood within the clearing that had been made around the oak tree and the newly constructed scaffold. The lustrous contours of his strange vessel loomed high overhead and cast a deep shadow over the bare ground.

"Are you ready?" Lord Richard asked. "If you do not feel strong enough to climb, it could wait till the morrow or the following day. None shall enter your night boat meantime. They have been bidden with the strictest command, although I truly believe they are a little afraid of it."

The Iribian averted his gaze from the peculiar shape above and, looking Lord Richard steadily in the eye, said, "I will ascend."

And so, accompanied by Jack Flye and Adam o'the Cogs, Brindle began scaling the scaffold.

Feeling it to be his duty, apart from being intensely curious, Richard Wutton followed, but he was not as spry as he used to be and huffed and puffed more than the others.

Up past the branches of the oak they clambered until eventually the topmost leaves were left behind and the keel of the night boat was within reach.

At the top of the scaffold a wide platform butted against the side of the Iribian vessel, close to the opening from which Brindle had originally fallen. Heaving himself on to this ledge, Adam accidentally caught a glimpse of the ground far below.

He had never been this high before and, throughout the climb, had concentrated on the way up rather than looking down. Now he saw for the first time just how far they had risen. Suet was a small speck, pacing about the poles beneath and the apprentice's stomach turned over.

"I pray they built this thing stout and well," he murmured.

Jack Flye and Brindle were standing on the platform, heedless of the dizzy height. Jack was running his hands over the hull of the Iribian's night boat, marvelling at the perfectly smooth metal and aching to explore inside. Brindle, however, was waiting for Lord Richard to join them before entering and was presently absorbed in the inspection of the firmament.

The panes of the curving sky leaned low over the scaffold's summit and the Iribian studied the sections of opaque azure glass with shrewd and critical observations.

"Again the deceptive simplicity," he said, tapping the adamantine material. "This people have not the knowledge to forge such a shield, yet it masks itself in a manner fitting to their perception."

Bringing his face close to the coloured panes he could almost see through to the faint glimmer of stars beyond, but their configuration was unfamiliar and again he wondered how far he had journeyed.

Gazing across at his vessel, the Iribian's mind reeled at the advanced science which had trapped it. The thick webs of lead that now gripped the craft ensured that it could never be released; even if the night boat were undamaged, it was imprisoned in the Malmes-Wutton sky forever more.

"What a spectacle!" Lord Richard's voice exclaimed as he finally pulled himself on to the platform. "'Tis larger than my barn."

Staring in awe at the blunt, cone-shaped prow of Brindle's night boat he spluttered and cooed his admiration. "To think that yet more of this projects outside the firmament," he marvelled. "Such a size, for a single mariner."

Brindle smiled at him. "I have need of the capacity," he said. "As a merchant there must be somewhere to store my wares."

"Of course," Lord Richard nodded. "Shall we enter?"

The Iribian bowed. "Indulge a want of manners if I proceed," he began. "'Twould be safest if I lead the way."

No one demurred at that, so Brindle moved to the opening which gaped in the side of his vessel and disappeared within. Lord Richard followed and then, with an excited wink back at Adam, Jack went after. Exhilaration flooded through Adam's veins and, taking a sobering breath, he stepped from the planks of the scaffold and into the mysterious craft from a distant sphere.

Soot and cinders crunched underfoot when he crossed to the night boat and an oily film coated every surface. The inferno that had raged had left a bitter tang in the air and Adam wondered what Brindle's fine senses made of it.

Down a narrow corridor with featureless, curving walls Brindle led them. But, away from the entrance, the interior became dark and Lord Richard called a halt.

"We cannot stumble about in this blind night," he declared, his voice echoing along the passage. "Is there no lantern to be had?"

The jewel at Brindle's throat crackled with its soft sapphire glare as he apologised. "Forgive me," he said, the ghostly light shining up into his scarred face. "I had forgot you are so reliant upon your eyes. I fear that we have no choice; the heats have destroyed everything and there can be no gleam to guide you."

Lord Richard muttered gruffly. "Should have foreseen this," he upbraided himself. "Well there's nothing for it, one of us will have to go back and fetch lamps."

"No need," Jack answered, highly pleased with his own resourcefulness. "I have pockets filled with candles."

Lord Richard applauded the lad's sharp wits and a

moment's labour with his tinder box kindled a bright flame from which three candles were lit. Jack passed them around and Adam received his eagerly. The darkness was pushed aside and they ventured deeper into the passage until Adam wondered if they were still in the confines of Malmes-Wutton or if they were now standing in that portion of the vessel which extended out into the cold darkness. It was a strange sensation but there was no time to dwell on it for, without warning, the corridor opened out into a spacious chamber and they all stared about them.

A pall of acrid smoke still lingered here, obscuring the upper reaches, but the flickering glow of the candles revealed arching walls, ribbed with graceful ridges. They were made of a translucent, chestnut-coloured substance, shot through with branching threads of amber and cinnamon. Yet the fires had scorched and blackened it, and in many places the material had melted completely, disclosing knots of tangled wire beneath. Dribbled stalactites of the stuff speared down from the unseen ceiling and, when Adam touched them, he was astonished to find them as strong and firm as iron.

The burned-out remains of peculiar counters and desks, shaped like the growths which sprout from rotting trees, jutted from these ruined walls. Bringing the candle flame closer to them, he saw that they contained a jumble of furnace-cracked lenses and bizarrely fashioned tubes.

To the front of the room the roasted wrecks of three

large chairs stood before a huge oval frame, but the picture within was utterly destroyed. Adam wondered why it had been backed by a mesh of peculiar looking wafers of criss-crossed metal.

One large desk curved halfway around the chairs and, though it too had been incinerated, there were still tokens of its former usage. Tall levers protruded from the sagging, carbonised mass and gourd-like pods filled with shattered glass were fixed upon articulated stalks. More unusual shapes were suspended from above, many bearing rows of coin-sized discs which depressed when touched, rather like a mechanical's stilling crest.

It was unlike anything Adam or the others had ever seen.

Examining this bleak interior, Brindle shook his head then strode purposefully to the rear wall which was riddled with deep, recessed shelves.

"This is the wheel house?" Lord Richard asked, holding his candle aloft.

Brindle made no answer – he was too occupied searching among the sooty debris which littered the irregular-shaped niches. Finally he let out a glad cry as he found what he was looking for and tore it from the ashes.

With every flame raised to him, they all saw that he held a small box which might once have been silver. Struggling with the clasp, he wrenched it open and looked anxiously inside. There was a tense silence, then the Iribian choked back a grieving sob and let the box fall from his hands.

The glitter of broken glass shone in the candlelight and Adam knew what it was Brindle had found and why his despair was so passionate and profound.

"Your children?" the boy asked.

Brindle turned away. "The ampoules of their signature scents were damaged by the fire," he uttered. "There was a cargo of fluvial lotion and bendren oils on board. They burn most fiercely."

His words failed and he squeezed his eye shut, forbidding the pain of loss to overwhelm him. "No matter," he said, mastering his anguish. "The joy of our reunion will be all the greater."

Stiffening, he moved quickly to the curving desk and took one of the hanging pods in his hands. His long fingers moved rapidly over the metal discs, then he leaned across to where a circular grille was still visible in the melted mess of the counter and inspected it closely. After several minutes he pulled back. The glint of hope had perished in his eye and the dejection was wretched to see.

"All is dead," he whispered.

"What were you trying to do?" Lord Richard asked. "This night boat will never set sail again."

Brindle ran his fingers through his long hair, wondering how he could explain. "My people have a method of communing," he began, "in which speech can travel as fast as thought across great distances. If the heats had not wrought so much destruction I could have contacted them."

"Impossible," Jack said. "'Tis the fancy of wizards."

Lord Richard hushed him. "Continue, friend," he prompted.

"What use is there?" Brindle answered. "It is all beyond repair, even if..."

The blue stone fizzed and flared as a sudden idea gripped him. The Iribian rushed to the far wall again, where he dropped to his knees and hunted in another of the recessed compartments. Swiftly he fished out two circlets, identical to the one he was wearing, but Adam could see that they were both blackened and burned, their gems fractured.

"The flames have done their worst," Brindle groaned in defeat as he threw them down. "The torcs are spoiled – what evil influence dogs me?"

Stooping, Lord Richard picked the collars from the ground. "What did you hope to gain from them?" he asked. "What virtue would there be in three such devices?"

"Two is all I plead for," Brindle replied. "With elements taken from both I could have set up a beacon for my kind to follow. But no, providence would not allow it; no mercy for one so shunned. This torc alone is not enough. I am marooned in this land of strangers, isolated and alone – never will I see my family again."

Richard Wutton put his hand upon his shoulder. "I know what it is to lose those dearest to your heart," he said gently. "I am sorry, my friend."

Brindle hung his head and a bitter laugh rang from the stone at his throat.

"We have double cause to lament," he cried. "It was in my power to restore the fortunes of your estate a thousand-fold. My race would have paid the highest prices to revel in the fragrance of your rose garden. I could have been the sole merchant for this benighted territory and you would have had the monopoly. I regret that now I am unable to repay your many kindnesses to me, My Lord. I wished it most dearly."

Richard Wutton gripped his arm. "Never let avarice or greed govern your soul," he told him. "We have our lives and the good opinion of our friends – what more is there?"

"Would that my people had heeded such advice in the long years past," Brindle murmured. "We are all accursed and deserve whatever sour fate awaits us."

There did not seem much point in exploring any more of the vessel. Brindle was too despondent to continue and his first day out of bed was beginning to take its toll.

Jack was keen to press on but Lord Richard would not hear of it. "It can wait," came the firm instruction. "This craft will be here for many years yet, Master Flye. You shall have ample opportunity to tire of it in the time to come."

It was a disheartened group that descended the scaffold, although Suet's glad welcome did much to revive Adam's spirits. They and the rest of the villagers set off out of the woodland. No one had seen anything of Old Scratch all day and for that they were all grateful.

"Mistress Dritchly has recovered," Adam said suddenly, seeing the woman's large outline standing at the entrance of the manor.

A look of displeasure darkened Lord Richard's face. "There's fresh mischief been done," he uttered.

"If it's more of Henry's..." Jack began.

Brindle interrupted him. "That boy is innocent in this," he said, diverting his thoughts from his private distress. "There are foreign scents in the air. A mechanical not of this estate stands in the barn, and in the house a man awaits. The odours that envelop him are like no other I have experienced in this land."

Lord Richard's features became even more severe and he strode the remaining distance in stern silence. Mistress Dritchly rushed across the yard to meet them. It did not need the refined senses of an Iribian to notice how distressed and anxious she was. "Oh, My Lord!" she cried, wringing her hands. "Whilst you were out, a messenger came."

Before she could say any more, Lord Richard and the others saw that a man in fine clothes had left the house and was standing upon the step, overblown with self-importance.

"Sir Richard Wutton?" he called, his voice barely concealing his disdain for one so out of favour.

The master of the estate nodded. "I am he," he answered, marching over to him. "And you, Sirrah?"

"Thomas Herrick, bidden with an errand from the isle of London, My Lord."

"London, is it?"

The man bowed in honour of that great city. "Aye, from the palace of Whitehall, from Gloriana herself, Her Majesty, Elizabeth of Englandia – the Queen."

Richard Wutton took a step back and Adam was shocked to see that the colour had all but drained from him. Mistress Dritchly stifled a gasp of dismay.

The boy studied the newcomer more closely. He had a youthful face, but it was not a pleasant one. Although Thomas Herrick might mislead many in thinking him handsome, that day nobody was deceived. The blond, swallow-tailed beard was overly mannered for one so young and the pale blue eyes were hard and selfish. There was too much ambition simmering beneath the surface for any pleasing impression to be sustained without constant effort. Needless to say, he made no attempt to hide his boredom and irritation from the inhabitants of this mean estate and his mouth curled with disparagement.

Adam guessed he was annoyed at being away from court for, judging by his clothes, that was certainly where he believed he belonged. He wore a velvet cap with a bag crown of the Italian style that was so fashionable in London and done in the new pale green colour known as willow. It sat at a jaunty angle upon his head and was embellished with an orange plume. His clothes were of the same bright shade and positively Venetian in pattern, with the bottom corner of the short cloak draped affectedly over the opposite shoulder. In the presence of other aspiring nobles he undoubtedly cut a striking figure, but Adam o'the Cogs was ignorant of such trends and thought the man looked a complete fool, dressed up to resemble a spring lettuce.

"What does the Queen desire?" Lord Richard muttered in a flat, leaden tone.

The envoy looked squarely at Brindle and, with a want of courtesy, addressed his remarks to him. "She has heard rumour that a celestial visitor did fall into this land. My errand was to see the truth of it and that I clearly do."

"What else?" Lord Richard demanded, irritated by the man's insolence. "For more there most surely will be."

"You are requested at court, My Lord – you and your singular guest. The Queen does wish to view him for Herself."

"Requested?" Lord Richard's voice rapped sharply.

Thomas Herrick gave a simpering smile. "Commanded then," he said coldly.

CHAPTER 5

Hunting the Devil

It was useless for Lord Richard to offer any protest –
defying a royal command was treason. The journey
to London would take two days and Thomas Herrick
told him that the Queen was expecting them no later than
the evening of the seventeenth.

"But we shall have to leave at first light on the morrow!"
Lord Richard cried.

"Not at all," came the haughty response. "You have
until an hour before noon till we must depart. More than

sufficient time to organise the affairs of this modest estate. There is room for two more of your household should you wish to bring them. I shall await you on board the night barge within your Stygian boat house."

With that, the ridiculously overdressed man led his mechanical horse out of the barn and rode from the yard.

"No later than eleven of the clock!" he called over his shoulder. "Or you shall earn not only the Queen's enmity but Her steel also."

Lord Richard and the others watched him canter through the village. Then, with the air of a man who has an appointment with the axe, the master of Malmes-Wutton went silently into the manor house to begin the necessary preparations. Mistress Dritchly drew a hand over her moistening eyes as she regarded his retreating figure. "I cannot bear to see him so," she sniffed. "His back all bent and bowed. Has he not paid penance enough?"

Brindle moved to go after him. "This is my doing," he said. "If it were not for my presence this would not have occurred. Your Lord's kindness to me has earned him naught but trouble."

"Oh, bless you – stay!" the woman called him back. "Let him be awhile, till the black mood leaves him. In no way are you to blame. This is the doing of a stony heart – I thought it then and say it now. Whilst She reigns there can be no peace for him. This is vengeance and spite for a devotion done these fourteen years past."

No one understood the widow's words and she dabbed at her eyes with the corners of her apron. It was Adam who finally dared ask what he had always wanted to know.

"Why was Lord Richard banished?"

But Mistress Dritchly refused to answer, and bit her lip as she shook her head, fighting to staunch the tears which were now streaming down her flushed face.

Brindle put his hand upon her arm to comfort her and, looking up at his ravaged features, a fierce glint shone in the woman's watery eyes. "Why not?" she cried. "Why should you not be told? It's hushed I've been these many years but not any longer, 'specially not in front of you, my angel. If you're to face that woman you'd best be warned what manner of cold-blooded creature She is."

"Mistress!" Jack Flye objected, appalled to hear her utter such sedition.

"Tush!" she retorted. "You were too young to know the truth of it, so think not to silence me."

Glaring at the road which Thomas Herrick had taken, the widow of Edwin Dritchly peeled away the years in her mind.

"Before the Beatification," she began, half closing her small grey eyes to remember how it was before the sky was scored with strips of lead and arched buttresses of chiselled masonry, "Lord Richard was a great friend of Robert Dudley, the Queen's favourite. There, I've said the name aloud at last. Oh, never has a man been as close to Her as he.

They were children together and, in the time of Catholic Mary, were both confined in the Old Tower that was. When Elizabeth became Queen they were a scandal spoken across Europe. They were inseparable, always riding and dancing with no time for any other."

Mistress Dritchly lowered her gaze as the confining firmament impressed itself upon her once more.

"After the Uplifting," she continued, "they became even closer. She made him Earl of Leicester and they played at lovers – there were some who gossiped that they did more than play. It could not continue. Lord Richard foresaw it and privily warned Robert Dudley, but he would heed no counsel. He believed that the Queen and he would marry – vain fool."

There was a pause as she sucked the air through her teeth and folded her arms, doubting if she should proceed. The memories were more painful than she had anticipated.

"What happened?" Adam goaded. "How did this bring about Lord Richard's banishment? Did he say something wrong to the Queen?"

Mistress Dritchly bristled in defence of her master. "Him? Do aught incorrect? You do not know him if you think that, Cog Adam!" she said hotly. "To be steadfast and true, that's why he was punished."

"How?"

"Between Her Majesty and Robert Dudley some quarrel occurred – I know not what, but the Earl of

Leicester fell from favour more swiftly than a stone. There had been stormy upsets before but none to match this and all at court were petrified to intervene. To the Tower She sent him, that place more feared than its namesake in the old world. His property and wealth were seized, and the isle of Kenilworth, in which he built a castle for the Queen's delight, was locked and is still a place forbidden."

"An entire island locked?" Adam breathed in amazement.

"Bless me, yes! Barred and sealed and the linking chains severed. The Queen had never been in such a foul, blue-faced temper before. So terrible was Her anger that Robert Dudley's name was not even to be mentioned and no one dared defy Her or support him."

Turning her head, the woman looked with pride at the manor house. "None except a single brave soul, Dudley's loyal friend – Sir Richard Wutton. He was the only one who spoke out and was bold enough to defend him to Her face, appealing on his behalf. But it was too late. None ever return from the Tower and Her heart was hardened. Dudley was never seen again and Malmes-Wutton was stripped of its incomes."

Hearing this, Adam and Jack finally understood why their master had no love for the court or those who made their life there. Respect and devotion swelled in their hearts and they longed to make him proud of them.

A sharp blast ricocheted across the yard. Anne Sowerby

had been listening to all that had been said and, overcome by the tale, was blowing her nose on her sleeve.

Brindle stared at the girl, aghast at the uncouth action, but it reminded Mistress Dritchly that there were pressing matters which had to be dealt with.

"I must attend to Lord Richard's wardrobe," she declared. "I would not have him appear shabby before the Queen and you, my angel – you must have fitting garments also. I shall see what I can amend of Edwin's. I'll not have Her looking down Her nose at either of you."

Sweeping the snivelling Anne Sowerby before her, Mistress Dritchly sailed into the manor and launched herself into an afternoon of frenzied activity.

Brindle hung back, feeling awkward and, in spite of what she had said, very much to blame.

"I have no desire to meet with your Sovereign," he murmured. "Look at the misery this summons has caused."

Jack shrugged. "I think Lord Richard reckoned this would happen," he said. "He's been dreading this from the moment you came amongst us."

"What shall I do?"

"Whatever you can to restore him to favour, if that be a thing at all possible. Succeed – and I'll really believe you're an angel." Laughing, the seventeen-year-old turned to his apprentice. "Come on, Cog Adam," he said. "Let's see how Henry has fared with them faulties."

Adam gave Brindle a grin then trailed after Jack, and

Suet in his turn waddled after him. Alone in the yard, the Iribian was filled with doubt. Stranded among this strange people, who did not belong in this desolate region any more than he did himself and who did not understand the superior science which surrounded them, he felt wretched and vulnerable.

Grinding the gravel under his heel, he spun around and wearily headed for the rose garden.

Henry Wattle had slaved all morning on the wooden ponies. When Jack and Adam entered the workshop, they found that the remaining two were finished and the boy hard at work on the stallion.

"Enough," Jack said warmly. "You have laboured long. I shall complete the repairs."

A relieved Henry thanked him, then fired a volley of questions at both of them.

"What was the night boat like inside?" he demanded. "Who was on that horse that rode by before? What's happening?" The boy was so anxious for news and so bereft of his usual irreverent cheerfulness that Adam forgave him his jibes of the previous night. Between him and Jack they told Master Wattle everything that had passed in the Iribian's vessel and all about Thomas Herrick.

"Going to London!" Henry cried as soon as he heard. "Bum boils! Who else is Lord Richard taking?"

This was something neither of them had considered and Jack's face lit up at the prospect. "I'd like to look on that great isle," he confessed. "To view the splendour of that big city and its river – just the once."

Henry sighed dreamily. "Only the grandly rich dwell there," he pined. "I'd dearly wish to live in a palace with golden roofs and have the finest mechanicals attend me."

Jack scoffed at the notion and busied himself with mending the horse's head.

"You're sure to be picked," Henry muttered jealously. "If I begged Lord Richard do you suppose...?"

Jack's laughter obliterated the question and Henry slumped on to his stool, sullen and miserable.

"Well I wouldn't like to go," Adam said. "Sounds a frightening place, that isle does – brimming with villainy and every vice, so Mistress Dritchly says. Look what happened when the nobles came here. Nay, I'll adhere to Malmes-Wutton and be content."

"You're plain stupid," Henry commented.

A short while later, Jack Flye was discreetly gumming the usual 'A Wutton Restoration' label inside the horse's head and reattaching it to the truncated neck.

It appeared to be a serviceable beast – nothing elaborate or unduly expensive – and he was curious to see how the repair would hold. The esquire who brought it had told him that the mechanical had formed a habit of tossing its head at an awkward angle and that was how it jammed. Jack thought it prudent to check whether this tendency had been tamed in the mending and pressed the crest set into the stallion's shoulder.

At once the creature flicked its braided tail, and the shudder which denoted many of the lesser automata shook it into life. Bronze hooves stamped upon the workshop floor and the glass orbs of its eyes rolled in the polished metal head. Throwing a saddle over its back, Jack secured the fastenings then led the stallion into the yard, listening to the whirrs and clicks that accompanied its movement.

"Bring the ponies," he told the others. "Let us ride these uncomely beasts and see how well we have corrected their flaws."

Three more crests were pushed and a moment later the wooden ponies came plodding from the stables.

"I don't think I can ride," Henry grumbled, ruefully rubbing the seat of his breeches. "My dad's got heavy hands and I'm still tingling."

Fetching another saddle from the workshop, Jack thrust it into the boy's hands. "It'll take your mind off it," he said.

"Not my mind I'm worried about," Henry replied.

As the apprentices began buckling the saddles to two of the wooden mounts, Lord Richard emerged from the manor, his face still troubled. He called Jack over to him.

"Master Flye!" he began. "I have decided that you will accompany friend Brindle and myself on this unpleasant journey. I trust you will lay objection aside and consent."

Somehow Jack managed to hide the smile which
threatened to leap upon his face and nodded solemnly. "Oh
yes, My Lord," he uttered. "If you will it so."

"My thanks," Richard Wutton said, his breath
betraying the mug of ale he had downed to settle his shaken
nerves. "There is one more place to be filled. Mistress
Dritchly must remain in charge here, so perhaps a fellow
from the village? I was thinking Josiah Panyard. What say
you?"

Jack sucked the inside of his cheek. "A mite too fond of
harking to his own counsel with little regard to that of
others," he finally answered.

"Like as not," Lord Richard agreed reluctantly. "And
friend Brindle will need to be at ease for his encounter with
the Queen. Who am I to choose?"

Brushing the hair from his face, Jack looked across at the
two boys standing by the ponies. "What of Cog Adam?" he
ventured. "The stranger likes him well enough."

"No, no," Lord Richard said hastily. "Not him, but
what of the other – the Wattle lad?"

"Henry?" Jack spluttered.

"Aye. He might prove a match for Her Majesty's sharp
tongue. A pity his tin vermin are not captured – I should
have dearly liked to set them capering about the royal
palaces. So be it, I have decided. Henry Wattle it is. Tell
him the news and both make ready for departing on the
morrow."

Shaking his head in disbelief, Jack went to inform Henry of his unwarranted good fortune but was instantly called back by Lord Richard.

"You are readying those steeds to be ridden?" he asked as if noticing the mechanicals for the first time.

"Yes, My Lord."

Richard Wutton rubbed his bearded chin thoughtfully. "Send one of the lads to bring Brindle here," he said. "The Queen's passion is Her horses. It would stand him in good stead if he could learn something of the art before we leave."

And so, as Henry's whooping shrieks of delight rang beneath the firmament, Adam was dispatched to fetch the Iribian, with Suet scampering in his shadow. The boy knew precisely where to find him and walked briskly to the rear of the manor house, much to the piglet's greedy glee.

There in the garden, Brindle was sitting cross-legged before the roses, his head dropped to his chest, fast asleep in their cleansing scent.

Adam did not like to wake him but could not disobey his master's commands. Gently he nudged the Iribian's shoulder and Brindle stirred, the blue stone of the torc pronouncing the words he mumbled drowsily.

They were the names of his children and Adam felt like an intruder, breaking in upon his dreams. Guiltily, the apprentice stood back as Mistress Dritchly's angel came blinking from sleep, refreshed and willing to participate in this unusual practice of riding a four-legged device.

As soon as they had retrieved Suet from the vegetable plot once more, they strode back to the yard and Brindle was assigned the stallion as it was the only mount capable of accommodating his height. Sitting tall in the saddle, the Iribian appeared uncomfortable, uncertain what to do with the reins and stirrups. Lord Richard tried to explain, then decided that experience was the best tutor and set the horse pacing about the yard.

Confounded by the jolting movements of the beast beneath him, Brindle almost leaped clear but was quickly assured that it was perfectly safe.

Seated upon the ponies, Jack and the apprentices drew alongside to prove that there was nothing to fear. The three of them had ridden many times before; there were always horses passing through the workshop to be repaired and it had become second nature to them. Almost immediately, however, Adam was forced to dismount because Suet kept running between the pony's hooves and the boy was worried that he might accidentally be trampled.

"You stay in here for now," Adam instructed, lifting the piglet over the piggery fence and setting him down by Old Temperance and Flitch. "Don't whine like that – it's for your own good."

Pushing his snout between the rails, Suet glumly watched Adam climb back on to the pony, then sat on the ground – dejected.

"That's better," Lord Richard commented, noting Brindle's growing confidence. "You're beginning to handle it less like a timid goose. There, you learn swiftly."

Round and around the yard Brindle walked the steel horse and, to his own astonishment, actually started to enjoy the sensation. A kick of his heels against the sensitive plates upon either flank spurred the mechanical to a trot and his scarred face creased with smiles.

"An amusing pastime!" he called to Lord Richard. "There is naught like this upon Iribia."

Jack and the others impelled their ponies to keep up with him and the wooden creatures went rattling and clunking over the gravel, shaking their riders and bringing a pained expression to Henry's face.

Everyone was surprised at how quickly Brindle overcame his awkwardness. In no time he had the measure and mastery of the steel charger and it was clear to Lord Richard that he was no longer content to circle the yard.

"How swift may these devices travel?" Brindle called.

"'Tis for you to discover!" his host answered.

Brindle flashed a grin at him then gave the plates an urgent kick. Throwing back its head, the metal horse let out a shrill whinny then bolted off across the lawn. Standing in the stirrups, the Iribian yelled with exultation, steering the beast on to the road which led through the village.

"Well don't let him leave you like statues," Lord Richard cried in mock outrage. "Go race him."

With one shout, Jack and the apprentices went clattering from the yard and the master of the estate almost forgot the heaviness that lay on his spirit.

Through the small village Brindle galloped his horse, his yellowish grey face bent over the steed's steel neck and his long hair streaming out behind. The warm air carried a hundred scents and they mingled with the excitement of this new experience, making him light-headed, and he laughed loudly.

Startled faces appeared at the small windows of the cottages and people in the street leaped out of his way. Past the church and over the green he sped, where the calm surface of the pond erupted with fleeing brass ducks.

When the three ponies came cantering after, their riders saw that he had already reached the fork in the track where the left-hand path led to the jetty beneath the ground.

"It's incredible how fast he picked it up," Jack remarked. "He's a better horseman now than any I've seen."

"He's returning," Adam said. "Just watch him fly over the grass. I couldn't get such motion from that steed."

Henry raised himself off the saddle and delicately re-arranged the folds in his breeches. "Suck a custard!" he scorned. "Of course he's rode before. What dupes you are. Anyone can tell he was play-acting at not being able. I tell you, Coggy, there's more to your flower seller than he lets on."

There was no chance to argue for Brindle was almost

upon them. Skirting around the church, he drove his horse splashing through the edge of the pond and raised a hand in greeting. "First back to the manor!" he challenged.

Jack and the others needed no further incitement and wheeled their wooden ponies about, tearing back through the village.

The cloud of dust which filled the street from the three sets of hooves was doubled moments later by Brindle's stallion as he shot between the cottages, provoking angry but admiring cries from the inhabitants. The clamour of the race thundered beneath the firmament and, leaning against the piggery fence, Lord Richard watched the last stretch.

Jack was leading, followed by Adam and Henry who were level with each other, yet Brindle was swiftly gaining on them. In the bright June sunshine, the steel horse glinted and gleamed over the road, like a flash of light skimming across a river.

Just as Henry started to pull away from Adam, the Iribian passed them both and was catching up to Jack. An instant later and they were neck and neck. Then the horse shot ahead and, before Lord Richard could open his mouth to cheer, was suddenly crunching over the gravel of the yard. "Astonishing!" he cried as Brindle brought the steed to a stamping halt and welcomed the others home.

"Did you see it, My Lord?" Jack exclaimed. "We had a full half furlong gain on him and still he romped by us."

"I had the fortune of the better steed," Brindle said modestly.

In the piggery Suet jumped up and down as Adam came cantering into the yard behind Henry, and both boys praised Brindle's skill.

"The Queen will be rightly pleased," Lord Richard applauded. "She will surely command you to ride with Her and it is good that you will impress. Few men ever become so proficient. She may even invite you on a hunt."

Brindle looked at him blankly.

"Another favourite recreation of Hers," Lord Richard explained. "She revels in the sport, hunting the mechanical game, whether it be stag or..."

"Wild boar!" Jack interrupted. "My Lord, is this not a perfect time to rid the estate of Old Scratch's menace? If we could still him once and for all, my conscience would be greatly relieved. His cordials could then be put in balance and never again would the woodland be a place of fear."

Lord Richard considered the suggestion. Four mounts certainly constituted enough of a force with which to combat the terrible boar, so he gladly gave his permission.

"My hunting days are long spent," he excused himself, "but go, you four, and teach that devil his manners."

Henry could hardly remain in his saddle with excitement – to participate on a real hunt was an incredible treat.

They would each need a stilling pole and so Adam

dismounted to fetch them from the manor where they were kept. Returning to the yard he spared a moment for Suet, telling the agitated piglet to settle down. Then, when everyone had a long staff of steel-tipped yew in his hands, he was back on his pony and eager to be away.

"Don't tarry beyond dusk," Lord Richard warned them. "That demon is danger enough in broad daylight."

With brave yells and shouts, the party set off and were soon galloping across the lawn to the edge of the woodland.

"Rejoice whilst you may," Lord Richard murmured. "For there'll be little enough joy at court if I know Her Majesty."

Peering through the piggery fence, Suet had watched his master ride to the outlying wood, remembering all too well the terror which dwelt there. Letting out a woeful whine he marched restlessly behind the rails and nothing Lord Richard could say would soothe or quieten him.

Slowing to a trot, the horse and ponies entered the trees and Brindle took the opportunity to ask Jack what the stilling poles were for. The seventeen-year-old chuckled; he had forgotten that Brindle knew nothing of this and was quick to explain.

"Unlike ordinary mechanicals," he began, "those intended as game possess many stilling crests. On every boar or stag there are two on each side of the beast's body and a fifth in the centre of its head."

Brindle thought he understood. "Then we have only to strike one of those points and the device is rendered insensible, like the great pig mother in the kitchen?"

"Too easy!" Jack answered. "What sport would there be in that? No, there must be three blows to still the creature, the first will inflame its fury, the second will slow it and the final one send it crashing to the ground. I hope your aim is as good as your horsemanship."

Brindle merely smiled in reply, then gave his attention to the surrounding woodland. The pungent smell of lush green growth pervaded everywhere and to him it was like riding through veils of glimmering, emerald mist. The lingering late blossoms laced the air with a dusty sweetness while the verdant carpet of fern and nettles underscored it with deep, shadowy odours. Leaf mould added earthy, seasoned layers, but permeating this agreeable scentscape was a repellent rankness which set his nose crinkling.

"Where we going to find Old Scratch?" Adam's voice broke into his thoughts.

"Have to discover his lair," Jack said sagely. "Flush him out, then..."

"Witch spit!" Henry cried. "That horror might have lots of dens. There's a quicker way to find him than poking into every hole from here to the other side of the estate."

"And what may that be?" the older boy asked.

Henry spurred his pony past them and pointed a little way ahead to where a cloud of flies was buzzing about the low branches.

"This is the same track Coggy and me used to escape from Old Scratch last night," he told them. "And yon bluebottle dinner is the devil's proudflesh that got caught."

Jack regarded the tattered grey mass, none the wiser. "How can that aid us?" he asked.

"If we had a bratchet from the old world you'd know what to do," the apprentice groaned in exasperation. "Well, we don't have one of them hounds, we got better – we have our Lord Brindle."

Then Jack understood and was irked he had not thought of it before Henry Wattle. Turning to the Iribian, he asked, "Can you do it? Can you track our demon?"

Brindle's yellow eye was already gleaming and he forced himself to inhale the loathsome stink which hummed from the rancid shreds of proudflesh.

Almost balking, he saw more clearly a noisome trail of the same filthy reek weaving an ugly skein through the emerald mists. "This way!" he declared, setting his stallion upon the malodorous course.

While they were pushing deeper into the wood, Suet was fretting inside the piggery. Lord Richard had been unable to comfort him and the piglet's plaintive squeaks were beginning to unsettle his nerves.

"Hush now," he said. "Your Cog Adam will be

perfectly safe. He has Jack Flye with him and will return before evening falls."

But Suet would not be placated and pawed at the fence post with his trotter.

"Oh, you obstinate animal," Lord Richard grumbled. "I thought you were supposed to be more intelligent now. Why will you not listen to me?"

Staring at the distant woodland, the piglet continued to bleat, then gave a determined grunt. Pulling back from the fence, it glared at the barrier and rushed forward. A gentle shudder travelled through the railings as the little mechanical slammed into the post.

"Ho there!" Lord Richard cried. "Desist from that. Your tiny skull is no match for this stout stake."

Suet ignored him and rammed into the post a second time.

"You will crack yourself to splinters," Richard Wutton said crossly. "Stop at once."

But the owner of the estate was not Suet's master and so a third and a fourth blow rained against the fence, with the piglet taking a longer run up to it each time. After a fifth attempt had produced only the faintest wobble, Suet snorted belligerently then scooted into the brick sty.

"You just stay in there till Cog Adam returns," Lord Richard called after him. But an instant later the piglet was scampering out again, followed by Flitch and Old Temperance.

Lord Richard hurriedly backed away as the large sow lowered her head and lumbered towards the fence as fast as her carved legs would allow. There was a tremendous snapping of wood as the post buckled before her thundering weight and the fence collapsed with a clatter of rails.

Old Temperance gave a superior sounding grunt, then sauntered back into the piggery with a self-satisfied air. Her piglets squealed proudly. Suet gave her a grateful nudge with his snout then, before Lord Richard could stop him, darted out and hared across the lawn in search of his master.

The sow's deep voice rose in farewell but Suet had already vanished into the trees.

Through the undergrowth the bronze hooves went pounding as the hunting party sought the scourge of Malmes-Wutton. They had ridden to the fringes of the woodland, where the trees grew in a gradually thinning margin behind the village. They were close to him now. The stench of rotting proudflesh hung thick about the dense bracken and concealing ferns. Jack and the apprentices no longer needed to rely upon Brindle's keen senses; the evidence was plain for all to smell.

A gloomy expanse of scrubland stretched between the sparse trees and the nearest cottage. Tangles of briar formed prickly dunes which rose darkly above the waving grasses and flowering nettles. It was a cheerless, bleak place, the perfect domain for the rage-fuelled mechanical and Adam began to wish he had remained behind.

"I never reckoned on him lurking so close to the village," he murmured.

"Scratchy's getting too bold," Jack said firmly. "The sooner he's dealt with, the better."

Gripping their stilling poles in readiness, they rode into the high grass, following the course of the boar's heavy trampling until one of the larger hillocks of thistle and bramble reared in front of them. They looked in disgust at the fog of flies which swarmed above it.

"Never did understand why the Almighty had to inflict them on us," Jack muttered. "Why couldn't they have been left in the old world, with snakes and frogs?"

Brindle's eye was watering. The stench was unbearable for him but he made his horse wade towards the sprawling clump of briar, tensing the muscles in his arm. The others came after. Within that mound of knotted barbs, several rough holes and caves had been made and they suspected that inside one, hostile eyes were glowering and spying upon their every move.

"How do we flush him out?" Adam asked, his voice not rising above a whisper.

"Easy!" Henry suddenly yelled. "We shriek and beat the bushes till he can't bear it no more!"

Plunging his pony forward, the boy shouted and bawled,

thrusting the steel tip of his pole deep into the thorns. "Awake, you hunchbacked devil!" he cried. "Give us some sport before we pull you apart."

Jack joined in, thrashing the staff through the spiky boughs and calling fierce threats.

Watching them torment the great clump of thorns, Adam drew his pony to a standstill and held back. Something was wrong. He glanced quickly at Brindle to see why he was not taking part.

But the Iribian was not even looking at the others – he was facing away to the left, towards an overgrown pile of lopped branches.

"Your demon has more than one refuge," he said.

At once a fearsome roar boomed from within the mound of mossy logs and the frightening bulk of Old Scratch came tearing from its hollow interior. Jack and Henry brought their ponies up sharply as the wild boar came charging into the middle of the hunting party, eyes blazing with fury.

Brindle stared at the creation in revulsion. He had not imagined anything so hideous. In the revealing light of day, Old Scratch was even more grotesque than Adam or Henry remembered. After catching its mantle of proudflesh the previous night, the boar had bitten and torn it clear. Now that discarded, sweaty grey mass lay in the brambles and that was what the flies were feasting upon.

Free of that ragged veil, the rows of steel bristles

spearing from the mechanical's back appeared longer and more savage. The wild boar no longer resembled a deformed bride – he was a spectacle of pure terror and everyone abandoned the initial plan to still him and return the ichors to their correct balance. Old Scratch had exceeded that point long ago; for him there could be no redemption.

Snarling and rattling with hatred, the fiend faced each of them in turn, his cloven hooves tapping the ground menacingly as if considering which to attack first.

Then, inexplicably, the boar gave a defiant shriek, whipped about and stampeded into the trees behind.

In an instant Jack Flye took command of himself. Old Scratch's nightmare condition was entirely his fault and, with a yell of challenge bawling from his lips, he spurred his pony after the monster he had created. Brindle and the apprentices looked briefly at one another, then the chase began.

Holding grimly to the reins with one hand and the pole with the other, Jack galloped in pursuit as Old Scratch zigzagged between the trees. The hunt was no longer a game to him. How could he be a master of motive science while that abomination still terrorised the estate? This hour would be the mechanical's last and the seventeen-year-old had already vowed to smash the cordial vessels himself.

Then Brindle was at his side, his face intent upon the darting, horrendous form ahead. United, the pair of them drove the wild boar to the very edge of Malmes-Wutton.

Within Old Scratch's ruptured rosewood body, the large bellows pumped fast and furious, and the crimson temper gushed through the feeder pipes as every gear and toothed wheel worked tirelessly. It had been a long time since any had been reckless enough to seek him out, but the low cunning that had always been in him knew how to deal with such audacity.

At the extreme perimeter of the estate, a wall of solid, hewn rock crowned the entire island. It was this enormous barrier that the leaded firmament curved down into and from which the stone buttresses rose. With that immense wall at his back, Old Scratch could pick off the riders one by one as they fought their way through the bowed trees which grew there.

Leaping the remaining distance, the wild boar spun around and his cruel, slanting eyes watched Jack and Brindle come battling through the thickets of twisted elms that reared crippled and bent beneath the low arch of the glass sky. Henry and Adam were not far behind and Old Scratch snorted in evil anticipation at the carnage that would be his.

"I do not like this!" Brindle called to Jack. "There will not be room to raise our staffs. How are we to strike?"

"I'll manage," Jack answered. "No game beast is going to outwit me. If I have to punch them stilling crests with my fists, I'll have him!"

Brindle was the first to see Old Scratch at bay. Above

the wall the leaded panes blazed a fierce blue and the bright glare glittered over a pair of brass tusks as the devilish creation turned towards him.

The Iribian tried to lift his pole but it struck the low glass overhead as he had feared. He edged his horse back into the trees as Jack's pony came pushing through.

"Leave it!" Brindle shouted. "It's impossible here."

But Jack was determined. "Three hits and he's gone forever," he cried and to the Iribian's surprise, the lad struck his staff against the nearest tree and snapped it in two.

The wild boar shook its repugnant head. Then, with a trumpeting scream, launched itself at Jack's pony.

A tremendous crack shivered up the device's foreleg as Old Scratch's jagged snout rammed violently into it and Jack was nearly thrown from the saddle. The wild boar sprang back and prepared for another savage attack. Seeing this, Brindle drove between them, splintering his own staff in half with his bare hands and bringing the steel tip whistling through the air to strike a resounding blow against the beast's side.

But Old Scratch shifted and the pole missed the intended target by inches.

Suddenly Henry and Adam came bursting from the buckled trees. "Brain him!" Henry yelled.

Jack pushed his pony forward and swung his arm back to deliver a punishing hit, but the boar leapt up and the vicious tusks wrenched the staff from the lad's fist, almost dragging him to the ground.

Bringing its ghastly head about, Old Scratch lunged and raked his tusks into the pony's leg and Jack's steed staggered backwards, juddering under the ferocity of the beast's assault.

In that cramped, low space, hemmed in by the tortured trees, there was no room for Henry and Adam to lunge into the fray. With Brindle already there they could do nothing but stare at the scene in horror.

"Get back – get away from it!" Adam called to Jack.

Jack Flye's pony was shuddering wildly. It would not respond to any command and reeled to and fro as the demon of Malmes-Wutton lashed and gouged, shredding the device's leg until only a splintered stalk remained.

A hideous splintering of wood signalled the end and the pony collapsed, falling sideways on to the ground. Old Scratch let loose a triumphant bellow. Jack called out in fear as his mount went crashing down.

Then Brindle's strong hand came reaching across to seize him under the arm and before he knew what had occurred, Jack Flye found himself seated behind him. Swiftly the Iribian leaned over the stallion's neck and whispered into its metal ears. The steel horse bucked beneath them and gave an almighty kick with both hind legs.

Bronze hooves cannoned into Old Scratch's side. The

wild boar screamed horribly and was hurled into the air - away from the wall. Against the trunk of a gnarled tree the malignant demon went crashing and every leaf rustled upon the quaking boughs. The monster fell, close to where Adam and Henry sat upon their ponies, landing on his back, his steel spikes knifing into the ground.

"Now!" Brindle shouted to the apprentices while Old Scratch struggled to right himself. "Still the beast!"

Adam was the nearest. Lifting his pole, he aimed at one of the Wutton crests.

"Three times!" Henry yelled at him.

The boy stabbed downward and the crest pushed into Old Scratch's malformed casing. The creature bellowed more fiercely than ever, his trotters flailing madly as he jerked and jolted in his desperate efforts to rip up his spikes and escape.

Again Adam raised the steel-tipped pole but, even as he plunged it down, a high squealing filled the woodland and the blow went wide.

"You missed!" Henry scolded.

Adam o'the Cogs turned in his saddle and stared back through the trees. The shrill squeals were almost upon them, and then Suet came rushing from the undergrowth.

"Adam!" Jack bawled at him. "Do it quickly!"

Flustered, the boy tried to ignore the piglet which was capering around the thrashing wild boar, yapping angrily. But when he lifted the pole again, it was too late.

Snorting with rage, Old Scratch wrenched himself free, sprang upright and went raging into the wood.

"Coggy!" Henry growled. "You let him go. You had him – two more hits and it'd be over."

Adam stammered an apology but no one would listen. A fearful look was graven into Brindle's face. "We must pursue that creature," the Iribian declared grimly. "He is now more deadly than ever. Did you not say that the first blow would inflame his fury?"

Jack nodded slowly. "Aye," he uttered in a dread-filled whisper as the awful realisation sank in. "The crimson ichor will begin to froth and foam. Old Scratch is as near a true demon now as ever he could be. If he reaches the village..."

They had already wasted too much time. Without another word, Brindle spurred the stallion into action. Still bearing them both, the metal horse sprang into the trees.

Giving Adam a despairing look, Henry chased after.

Suet ran around the legs of Adam's pony, imploring to be picked up. "See what you've done!" the boy shouted down at him.

The piglet yelped as though hit and sucked his snout in sharply.

"You just stay there!" Adam cried. "You're naught but a nuisance! I wish I'd never given you that black bile! Stay away from me!" With that he dug his heels into the pony's flanks and charged after the others.

Suet grunted unhappily to himself, not understanding why his master was so cross. His little snout slid sorrowfully out as he gazed after the boy disappearing into the woodland. Then the sound of hooves faded and the only noise to be heard was the anguished wheezing of Jack's fallen pony.

Suet shambled over to where the mechanical was still twitching and shuddering. The splintered stump waggled uselessly and the pony's glass eyes were swivelling in confusion.

Snuffling soothingly, Suet clambered on to its quivering neck and made his way to the stilling crest. With a comforting grunt that seemed to ease the pony's tremors, the piglet pressed down. Jack's mount became inert and Suet hopped to the ground, tilting his head to the trees.

Muffled shouts were echoing through the woodland. A remote rumbling bellow blared in the piglet's ears and his snout began to pump rapidly. More shouts came shrieking, the human voices mingling with the high screams of a horse and ponies.

Suet froze. His master had ridden into peril and he must do what he could to save him. Disobeying Adam's last command, the piglet gave a war-like grunt as every mechanism whirred within him and, with a determined flick of his trotters, bolted off into the wood.

CHAPTER 6

Angel Versus Demon

Pushing the stallion to its limits until it clattered and jarred beneath them, Brindle and Jack had ridden like a hurricane and finally caught up with Old Scratch in the clearing beneath the Iribian's night boat. There, against the newly built scaffold, the wild boar made his stand and whirled a horrendous head towards them.

From the slanting eyes and the mutilated maw, scarlet froth was spitting as the temper inside him boiled to a new degree. Sitting behind Brindle, Jack Flye looked on that infernal beast and knew that from this place only one of them could walk away. "Give me the pole," he demanded urgently. "Get in as close as you can and I'll strike. One direct blow will slow him, then I'll finish it."

Brindle pressed the broken staff into his hand and spurred the horse nearer. Yet, at that crucial moment, the metal steed tossed its head and the mechanisms locked, jamming it completely. Nothing the Iribian did could free it, the horse floundered blindly before the scaffold and Old Scratch seized his chance.

With a roar, he flew forward, slamming his mighty shoulders into the steel legs which dented and crumpled like tin. Another punching blow brought the stallion to its buckled knees and Brindle and Jack leapt from its back. The brass tusks went ripping inside, crashing deep into the horse's chest.

A hideous crunching of metal filled the woodland and the stallion toppled motionless to the ground. Old Scratch pulled away. Mangled copper pipes twisted about his tusks and a victorious gargle bubbled from his scarlet foaming jaws. Then, malevolently, he turned to glare at Jack and Brindle.

The Iribian was helping Jack to his feet, while casting around for the stilling staff. "Make for the scaffold!" he ordered.

Jack leaped on to the first rung, swinging his legs high and out of reach. The Iribian remained on the ground, pacing a wide circle away from the scaffold, keeping Old Scratch busy while Jack ran to safety.

The cloven hooves scraped the ground and, with a barbarous shriek, Old Scratch charged. Brindle darted aside but the mechanical mirrored his movements and the tip of one brass tusk went tearing through a leg of the homespun breeches, gouging into the flesh beneath.

Clinging to the scaffold, Jack watched helplessly as Brindle faltered, grasping his leg while the dark orange blood welled between his fingers. The boar's bellowing rang beneath the firmament and he lunged in for the kill.

Suddenly there came a thundering of hooves and Henry Wattle galloped into the clearing, wielding his staff like a lance and hollering terrible cries.

"Begone!" he bawled, rushing straight for the murderous beast and hitting him squarely in the side with the steel tip. "Prince Henry, destroyer of dragons and killer of giants, is here to make sawdust sausages of you!"

Knocked aside by the stilling pole, Old Scratch snarled. Henry doubled back for a second attack while Brindle hurried to the scaffold. "This time I'll not miss your crest!" Henry yelled, charging his pony towards the ferocious boar. But the tyrant of the woods would be nobody's target and rampaged to meet him.

A deafening collision shook the surrounding trees. Henry Wattle dropped the staff and grappled with the reins as his pony reared on its hind legs, for those at the front had been smashed. A twisted tusk and a broken ear were the only damage inflicted upon Old Scratch. The boar stalked before the crippled beast, waiting for it to tumble in ruin, bringing its rider with it.

"Steady, you shoddy clunker!" Henry cried in panic. If he could only keep the pony staggering backwards, he might reach the scaffold – But the mechanical was already teetering and set to fall.

Into this hopeless scene Adam o'the Cogs came barging and saw Henry's plight at once. Standing in the stirrups, he spurred his own pony onward and reached out to grab the other boy's hand.

But Henry's mount spun madly around. As Adam came bolting to the rescue it wheeled about, its hooves slithering beneath it. Down the creature plunged, whinnying hideously, and its crushing weight came toppling on to Adam's pony.

Both boys shrieked as they were flung from their saddles and the two steeds fell together. In a thumping confusion of trouncing hooves and splitting casings they crashed to the floor, their combined screams terrible to hear.

Henry had been thrown close to the scaffold but the wind had been knocked from his lungs and he rolled on the ground gasping for breath. Further away, Adam lay face down in the dirt, dazed and groggy – with a bright cut on his temple.

Prowling into the shadow of Brindle's night boat, Old Scratch skulked menacingly towards him. Jack jumped from the scaffold and dragged Henry to safety.

"Adam!" Jack yelled. "Get up – run!"

Wincing, the boy lifted his head. With bleary vision he saw the fearful bulk of the wild boar advancing, a crimson lather dripping from his jaws.

"He's done for," Jack breathed.

Choking the air down, Henry turned away. "Coggy!" he rasped.

Even though there was no chance of rescuing the beleaguered boy, Jack could not simply watch him die. Leaving the sanctuary of the scaffold, he turned to Brindle for assistance – but the Iribian was not there.

Incredulous, Jack stared upward and saw that Mistress Dritchly's angel was climbing the ladder as fast as his wounded leg could take him.

"Brindle!" Jack yelled. "Come back!"

Henry's face scrunched in misery. "He's left us," he wailed. "The craven beggar's left us!"

Not once did the Iribian glance down, and Jack spat in contempt before whisking around to do what he could for Adam, alone.

Old Scratch's jagged snout came slavering ever closer to the stricken boy. Adam could see a hellish light burn behind the small slanting eyes and he closed his own.

Shaking his wonderful spikes and ploughing his tusks

through the soil, the demon charged, straight for Adam's head. Feeling sick, the boy heard the cloven hooves gallop towards him.

Then a brutal thump punched him in the back as a familiar shape went squealing over his ears. From the undergrowth Suet had come scooting, rocketing into the clearing with a flurry of leaves whirling in his wake. Direct to his master the piglet darted, not even pausing when his little eyes beheld the nightmare that was bearing down upon the fallen apprentice.

Bravely, Suet bounded on to Adam's back and launched himself through the air, flying right into Old Scratch's horrendous face. There was a clattering clonk as the piglet smacked against the wild boar's snout and Suet instantly clamped his small jaws about the ragged rosewood shards. The monster bellowed in thwarted rage. He skidded to a halt and shook his head violently. Biting hard, Suet refused to let go, his eyes staring defiantly into the diabolic fires of the enemy.

Racing across to Adam, Jack hauled him to his feet, dragging him to the scaffold. "Get up there," he urged, lifting him on to the first supporting pole.

Weakly, Adam heaved himself up, then turned to see Old Scratch spinning in an infuriated circle, with Suet still biting hard on his snout, refusing to let go. It was like a mouse battling a tiger and Henry Wattle gave a whooping cheer to see the valiant piglet so confound and incense that foul beast.

The wild boar trumpeted in wrath. With an almighty, jolting jerk of his head, he finally loosened the piglet's jaws and Suet was catapulted clear. Trotters paddling madly, the keg-shaped mechanical sailed through the air and went bouncing over the ground. Old Scratch turned his baneful attention to the scaffold and lowered his head as he rampaged towards it.

"Climb higher!" Jack told the apprentices. "Hold as tight as you can – here he comes!"

A dreadful shudder travelled the scaffold as the boar rammed the supporting poles, which quaked alarmingly.

"Get gone!" Henry squawked down at him. "You can't touch us now."

His arms wrapped about one of the shivering struts, Adam had been shaken from his daze and when his mind cleared, he uttered a cry of dismay.

"Suet!" he called, scanning the awful spectacle around him. "Where are you?"

The two ponies were still thrashing upon the ground, but beyond them, lying on his side in the flattened grass, was the small piglet. When Adam saw him he choked with anguish. Snuffling forlornly, Suet was attempting to right himself. One of his trotters was hanging loose on its axle and as soon as he stood, it fell off completely.

"Get away from there," Adam hissed under his breath. "Oh, don't let that devil see him."

Almost as if he had read the boy's desperate thoughts,

Old Scratch turned and his glaring glance fell upon the broken piglet. A spray of bloody froth spattered from his unholy jaws and the wild boar stormed away.

"No!" Adam yelled, beginning to clamber from the scaffold. "You leave him be – you hellswine! Come on – catch me instead, you stupid lump of dung."

Jack yanked him back again. "Are you mad?" he snapped. "Stay here, you fool!"

"But Suet!" Adam pleaded.

"It's only a mechanical!" Jack told him.

Suet tried to limp to a hiding place but promptly fell on his chin. Trembling, the piglet saw Old Scratch come hurtling towards him and every cog whined and clicked inside as he tried to stand once more.

Then the wild boar had him. Raging insanely, the fiend scooped Suet up in his evil tusks and the piglet was rushed back across the clearing, over to the oak tree next to the scaffold. The last thing Suet saw was the great trunk racing up to him. In a rupturing explosion of wood and bark, the little piglet was dashed to pieces. Springs and wheels flew everywhere and shattered splinters rained about the oak tree's roots.

"SUET!" Adam screeched.

Ripping his tusks from the trunk, the wild boar turned to stare at the figures upon the scaffold, taunting them with a gloating grunt. "Oh, Coggy," Henry murmured, knowing how much the piglet had meant to him.

Adam said nothing, but he covered his ears when Old Scratch purposely stamped upon a tiny set of bellows and Suet's unmistakable squeal was heard one last time.

But the danger was far from over.

With fragments of Suet's body dangling from his tusks, the wild boar charged at the scaffold, ramming his head again and again into the supporting posts.

"We'll not get out of here," Henry howled, rocking back as another brutal blow set the structure quivering.

"Don't move," Jack warned them. "Just hold on and pray."

"*Pray?*" Henry wailed.

At that moment a clear, commanding voice called down from high above.

"Fear not!" it boomed. "I am here!"

As the scaffold jolted again, everyone peered up through the network of supports and saw Brindle clambering down from his night boat.

"I thought he abandoned us!" Jack exclaimed.

Adam shook his head. "He's got something with him!" he cried.

"It had better be a mechanical elephant," Henry whimpered.

Old Scratch butted the scaffold once more and one of the main poles smashed in two. Shrieking, the boar crashed further inward than he had expected and another great post came thudding down, striking him behind the shoulders and wedging him firmly in. Pounding his hooves on the floor, he roared and jostled but could not break free.

"He's stuck!" Jack crowed. "The demon's stuck! We have him!"

Old Scratch wrenched and tugged, but the posts held and Jack Flye began clambering down.

Above them, Brindle was descending as swiftly as he could. "Do nothing!" he shouted. "Wait till I reach you. I will deal with this."

Jack jumped to the ground. "I think not," he laughed. "Scratchy's mine now."

"Master Flye!" Brindle called.

"Jack!" Adam joined in. "Listen to him."

The lad ignored them both and ran to where the rear of the wild boar was sticking from the scaffold, twisting and stomping in furious frustration.

"Ho, you foulness," he proclaimed, striding to the malformed casing and looking on it with revulsion. "Five long years you've haunted and plagued me. Well, now 'tis time to mend my mistake. Goodbye, you despised villain. You'll not be mourned."

With that he hit out at one of the Wutton crests – but, to his consternation, the thing would not budge. Too many years had gone by and it was cemented in position by an encrusting of ancient proudflesh.

Fuming, Jack tried the crest on the other side, but that too was glued fast. "Which one did Cog Adam strike before? One of them must be of use."

But the other three stilling points were situated on Old Scratch's shoulders and in the middle of his skull, out of reach. Frantically, Jack battered his fist on the hind crests and the wild boar snorted threateningly behind the posts, mocking his efforts.

"I *will* stop you!" Jack swore, his voice rising with rage.

Again and again he punched and pummelled, then in desperation he stood back and gave the great bulk a tremendous kick. The wild boar staggered under the violent attack, but Jack's frenzied pounding had loosened the post that trapped him. Without warning, Old Scratch tore from the scaffold and Master Flye realised he was done for.

"JACK!" Adam shrieked.

Henry Wattle threw his hands over his eyes and, above them, Brindle heard Jack's scream. Heedless of the gash in his leg, the Iribian leapt the remaining distance to the ground. His scarred face contorted into a mask of aggression and the torc around his neck flared with a dazzling light as he called to the wild boar.

"Leave him! A battle is what you crave - so be it. I shall not run. You and I - to the finish."

Old Scratch lifted his harrowing head from Jack's wounded body. Blood stained his tusks and it mingled with his own foaming ichor.

Slipping a hand down to his hip, Brindle took from its large scabbard the thing he had brought from his night boat and flourished it before him. The summer sun flashed and sparked over its surface. It was a weapon unlike any ever seen in the uplifted world. Two spearing blades – one jagged, the other like a razor – projected either side of his fist, while a tapering shaft reached up to his elbow where a third, hooked barb glittered lethally.

The reflected sun burned full into the wild boar's face, blinding and tormenting him. He bellowed with rage.

Still clinging to the scaffold, Adam and Henry looked across to where Jack lay.

"Is he hurt bad?" Henry whispered.

"I can't tell," Adam murmured.

The wild boar had gored Jack and thrown him to the ground, but there were still feeble movements.

Henry stared at Brindle and sobbed with despair. "A fancy knife," the boy wept hopelessly. "Against that devil! He won't last an instant."

Purposefully, Brindle had stepped away from the scaffold and was advancing towards Old Scratch.

Flinching from the bouncing glare, the wild boar grunted angrily then tossed his head and, in a spray of crimson, came stampeding to kill. Adam and Henry caught their breath and the terrible conflict began.

Like a tempest Old Scratch raged, thrusting his tusks and ripping with the cruel jags of his snout. Yet every lunge Brindle avoided, dodging deftly aside, then swinging his blades down as the mechanical charged past.

It was a savage, brutal engagement. The wild boar

harried and butted him, spinning suddenly around so that his steel bristles could snag and rend. But always Brindle was too nimble. Like a dancer he leaped clear, then the strange knives would go jabbing in retaliation.

Chips of rosewood started to fly as the Iribian hacked and chopped, whirling expertly around and pushing the hooked barb in with his elbow. Old Scratch bellowed and screeched. After five long years of undisputed supremacy, he had finally met his match.

Henry's mouth fell open and he gazed on Brindle with spiralling admiration. "He's doing it!" he breathed.

Adam nodded slowly. "Why doesn't he just still him?" he muttered. "He's had plenty of chances."

The Iribian's eye was gleaming and his nostrils were flared wide. Seeing this, Adam suddenly realised that Brindle was enjoying himself.

Exultant, he continued to hew and slash, moving with fluid speed to cut through the wild boar's casing. Old Scratch could not evade him but countered with vicious shoves. Then at last his tusks caught Brindle's jerkin and in that moment the Iribian stumbled.

Greedily, the mechanical's awful head butted into his stomach and Brindle was hurled against the oak. He cried out, then slumped to his knees and the wild boar swerved aside. Perched in the scaffold, Adam and Henry called for Brindle to move out of the way. Old Scratch was stalking backwards, preparing a long run up. His head was lowered, ready to smash right through his stricken adversary and impale him to the tree.

Kneeling at the roots, the Iribian did not budge. The wild boar gave a final, victorious bellow then shot towards him. His tusks poised for a magnificent kill, Old Scratch pounded over the ground. At the last possible instant, Brindle jumped up like an uncoiling spring. Dropping his blade, his large hands lashed out and seized hold of the curved brass tusks.

Using the mechanical's own momentum, the Iribian snatched him into the air, swung him around and flung him with all his strength. Roaring, Old Scratch went crashing into the scaffold, splitting posts and struts. A quivering groan snapped up the towering framework and it came crashing down. Through the upper branches of the trees it fell, shearing off outstretched boughs, shattering and disintegrating in its ruin.

An eruption of earth hailed into the clearing as the foundations were torn from the soil, and Adam and Henry were thrown sprawling under a tempest of dirt and collapsing poles.

In the midst of the wreckage and upheaval, Old Scratch stumbled to his hooves, but Brindle had already picked up his large glittering knife and was running towards him. The wild boar bayed in defiance and the two clashed for the last time.

Into the tough casing the bitter blades ripped, carving a

ragged hole in the mechanical's side. Even as Old Scratch screeched in protest, Brindle held him firm and the twin knives went gouging inside, scything through the tarnished gears and spindles as though they were made of paper.

Fiery sparks gushed from the wild boar's evil snout and a horrendous whine of agonised metal vibrated within him. The frothing ichor ceased squirting from his narrow eyes and gradually his frantic movements slowed until only the jaw twitched and flapped. A burbling rattle bubbled up through the severed internal tubes before spilling out of the throat in a surprised snort.

Then it was over and Old Scratch fell inert at Brindle's feet. The Iribian stared at the monstrous creation coldly, then returned his weapon to its scabbard.

Glancing quickly at the destruction, he saw with relief that Adam and Henry were unharmed. Then he leaped over to where Jack was lying upon the ground and knelt at his side. One brief look was enough to tell him Jack was close to death – Old Scratch's tusks had done their foul work well and the lad knew it.

"Master Flye," Brindle said gently. "The danger is over."

Jack's eyes were gazing fixedly above but they blinked slowly when he heard those words and flickered across the Iribian's blurring form. "Scratchy's ended?" he asked in a failing voice.

Brindle nodded.

"Good," Jack murmured. "Master Edwin always said you have to pay for your mistakes, sooner or..." A spasm of pain twisted the lad's face and, gritting his teeth, he reached for Brindle's hand and grasped it tightly.

"I'm... I'm sorry," he stuttered.

"There is naught to be ashamed of," the Iribian answered. "If you were one of my sons, I should be proud indeed."

"I thought you'd deserted us – I... I was wrong..."

Jack coughed then stared up at the stranger. A darkness was creeping into his vision, forming a ring of light about the dim outline of Brindle's head and a faint chuckle drifted from his lips.

"I believe it now," he laughed feebly. "'Tis well that you're here, My Lord. No longer do I fear the end – I have an angel to send me hence." And with that, Jack Flye's last breath sighed from his body.

Bruised and aching, Henry and Adam clambered from the destruction and hurried over to where Brindle was kneeling. Henry paused to stare with round eyes at the sight of Old Scratch's motionless carcass and gave the wooden husk a vengeful kick. "A lovely bonfire we'll have with you!" he promised.

Approaching the Iribian, Adam saw his wide shoulders sag and his head droop. Adam halted. "Brindle?" he asked. "Is... is Jack...?"

The Iribian made no answer. He rose and walked a few, faltering steps away from him and the boy understood.

"God have mercy," he said in a cracked whisper.

"How is he faring?" Henry called, stilling the broken ponies. "There's much to do this night." When he received no reply, Henry hurried across and stared aghast at Jack's body. "Stop this!" he cried. "Jack! We must away and pack – we're to London on the morrow. Jack?"

Adam looked into the other boy's stricken face. "He's gone," he said simply.

A strangled cry blurted from Henry's mouth and he dropped to the ground.

Adam o'the Cogs turned to Brindle. The Iribian still had his back to them but the boy could sense that he had been greatly affected by Jack's death. He was holding his fist to his forehead and had unclasped the torc from his throat so as to keep his sounds of grief private and unproclaimed.

The same sense of unreality which had followed Edwin Dritchly's passing spared Adam's feelings now. The lowering sun had dipped behind the trees and the depthless shadow that swallowed the clearing made everything appear flat and false.

Adam suddenly felt chill and he made his way to Brindle. "Are you well?" he asked, for the Iribian had not moved since stumbling to his feet and shuffling those few steps.

Drawing closer, he put out his hand, then withdrew it sharply and blinked. For an instant he thought he had caught a glimpse of something strange. An ethereal, almost luminous sheen was moving under the skin of the Iribian's face and the long slit in his forehead was pulsing.

Looking again, Adam shook himself. He had imagined it, a trick of the failing light. "Brindle?" he said, putting his hand on his arm.

The balm merchant flinched at the touch, then stared at Adam with his one lemon-coloured eye and its green, horseshoe centre. It was an empty, vacant stare, almost as though he were viewing the boy for the very first time.

Slowly he returned the torc to his throat and in a croaking voice said. "Forgive me – I am fatigued."

Regarding him, Adam thought he looked anything but tired. In an odd way he actually appeared younger.

"Some of your scars have healed," he observed in surprise. "Your face – 'tis smoother and less seamed than..."

The Iribian moved away quickly. "We must bear Master Flye back to the manor," he announced.

Stooping over Jack's body, he lifted him in his arms with infinite gentleness and strode solemnly from the clearing.

Adam hurried to the oak where Suet had been smashed. Hunting quickly through the splintered bits and pieces of wood and brass, he collected all the fragments that he could find. Then he threw them down again.

The broken ichor bottles twinkled dully. Suet's perky personality had already seeped into the soil. Like Jack, the piglet was beyond repair.

‡

Abruptly, a pounding uproar blasted into his sorrow and he turned to see Henry feverishly battering Old Scratch's casing, pulling it apart with his bare hands. Adam decided it was best to leave him to it. Departing from the oak, something sparkled in the corner of his eye and, when he investigated, the boy discovered a small phial lying by the tree's roots.

By some miracle, the glass vessel was still intact. It contained Suet's black ichor and Adam pocketed it morosely as a token of the friendship and devotion the piglet had bestowed upon him.

Following Brindle's trail, his thoughts were a turbulent wreck. Even so, he kept returning to the vague and disturbing suspicion that once again he had chanced upon a secret that the Iribian did not wish to be revealed.

Behind him Henry Wattle fell, exhausted, on to the wild boar's ruins.

Never in his darkest dreams could Adam have guessed what Brindle's terrible secret might be, or why his people were so reviled and hated.

PART THREE

CHAPTER 1

To the Copper Cow

*T*he estate of Malmes-Wutton awoke to one of the bleakest days it had ever witnessed. An unbearable night had preceded in which grief and anger reigned, and the God who had raised the lands was cursed by many voices. Now a raw emptiness had taken possession and, almost as if they too were mechanicals, the inhabitants roused themselves and prepared for the grievous day ahead.

The royal summons still had to be obeyed. Lord Richard knew the Queen too well to suppose she would excuse him

285

‡

because a servant had been killed. But he refused to embark on Thomas Herrick's night barge until Jack had been laid to rest in the churchyard.

Mistress Dritchly had toiled through the night, mending clothes and ensuring her late husband's best would fit Brindle. By first light, everything was packed and ready for the journey. Now, dressed in the sober black of Edwin Dritchly's Puritan best, his long hair groomed and tied neatly in a ponytail, Brindle was a striking presence. Studying his face, the woman was pleased to note that it had healed beyond her expectations – now only the left eye remained bound with a bandage. Silently, she praised the Almighty but also privately preened herself for her own nursing skill.

It had been decided the company should depart as soon as the interment was over. Lord Richard deemed it would be plain cruelty to leave Cog Adam behind and alone in the workshop. The boy needed companionship and perhaps the spectacle of London's great isle would help ease his grief.

The last farewells were said. Richard Wutton voiced final words of condolence to Jack's mother and father while Henry's parents warned their boy to behave himself.

Adam o'the Cogs had no one to wish him goodbye, except Mistress Dritchly who hugged him tightly before returning her attention to Brindle.

"Only the second day out of the sick bed," she declared in a wobbling tone. "Here you are going off to visit Her

Majesty. Well you just remember this, my angel: She's no dominion over you nor where you're from. Don't be intimidated; you'll be attending Her in the capacity of ambassador and She must show you the proper courtesies, though you're already worth a hundred of any at court – aye, even Her."

For the first time since the previous afternoon, Brindle managed a smile. A salty tang flavoured the woman's floury scent that morning, as tears brimmed in her eyes.

"I have much to thank you for," he told her. "I pray one day I can repay your kindness."

"Seeing you hale and well is the only reward I seek. Just come you back to us."

The Iribian could not answer and slung the pack he had been given on to his shoulder. At his hip he still wore the weapon he had taken from his night boat, safely sheathed in the oddly shaped scabbard.

"The hour is nudging past eleven," Lord Richard announced. "We must away. I shall return as soon as the Queen permits. Farewell."

The calls of his tenants and friends sped him and the others along the road which soon began to slope downward, cutting a deepening valley into the ground. At the end of this green channel, spanning across the gulf, there stood a large, red-bricked wall.

Roofed with grass, a pair of large double doors, carved with the Wutton arms, were set into the centre. Adam and

Henry had seen it many times but had never ventured beyond the entrance. As they approached, the doors were pushed outward.

Two surly-looking men wearing the apparel common among seafarers, being Monmouth caps and the baggy breeches known as gallygaskins, held the wooden barriers open. Then, from the gloomy, lantern-lit interior, the finely dressed figure of Thomas Herrick sauntered into the bright day.

That morning he was decked out in the shades of red, violet and purple which he termed gingerline, lustie gallant, murrey and zinzolin. He watched Lord Richard's group approach, his face twitching with impatience while blinking from the brilliant sunshine.

"Hardly punctual, Sirrah," he declared. "'Tis now less than an hour before noon. Do you flout the Queen's command?"

Lord Richard met his haughty stare and replied in a gruff tone which set Thomas Herrick's eyebrows lifting. "Did you not hear the passing bell rung with speed last night? There has been a death in this estate. We have lost one dear to us. I delayed only to see him lowered in the ground."

The Queen's messenger waved the excuse aside. "I did think the church bell was rejoicing in your departure," he said lightly before turning his attention to Brindle. "Let us tarry no longer on this dismal shore. If we are to arrive at the steps of Whitehall tomorrow evening we must be gone at once to catch the tidal breath. Her Majesty is most eager to make your acquaintance, Excellency."

With a sweep of his murrey-coloured cloak he strode back through the entrance. Lord Richard gave Brindle an apologetic and exasperated look.

"There are many more of his kind at court," he whispered, "so you'd best get accustomed. Arrogant young fellows hungry for advancement and desperate to attract the Queen's attention. I wonder what Master Herrick's reward will be for conveying you thither?"

Brindle was too wrapped in thought to make an answer. It was Henry who quipped, "P'raps a new suit of clothes, for he looks like a beetroot's twin in that garb."

"He was a lettuce yesterday," Adam remarked.

"Then he is a sallat," Henry said. And with that they passed under the red-bricked archway and the bright day of Malmes-Wutton was left behind.

A deep thudding of oak proclaimed the closing of the doors behind and everyone except Brindle paused a moment to adjust to the sudden dark.

The Iribian glanced around him. They were in a wide, arching tunnel that smelled richly of stale, green water, damp earth and wet sand. Mingling among the dun, dank odours were the lingering scents of the food which had formed the cold breakfast of Herrick and his servants, interspersed with the stale memory of the previous night's supper and the chill ashes over which that had been cooked.

They were standing upon a sandy path that led down to a long, tar-seasoned jetty which stretched out over the surface of a great subterranean pool, where two wildly different vessels were moored.

The first and most humble was the Wutton night boat, used to return or collect broken mechanicals. It was a modest and unremarkable craft but vital in trading with the neighbouring Suffolk islands.

The second vessel could not have been more different. Low at the bows and high at the stern, it was more like a ship than a simple night barge, with small leaded windows set into the fore and aftcastles. In spite of its size there were no masts but a row of eight oars, withdrawn upon either side, and a crew of twenty standing stiffly upon the deck, awaiting the order to man their posts.

"That's no night barge!" Lord Richard muttered. "'Tis almost a brigantine."

The Iribian gazed at both vessels in disbelief, wondering how such primitive constructions could possibly sail out into the emptiness of the Outer Dark.

Henry and Adam were also staring at the pompous night barge. Its timbers were painted a gaudy scarlet, embellished with gilded flounces and showily festooned with flickering amber lanterns. It obviously belonged to Thomas Herrick.

"My own little craft is honoured to bear you to our beloved Gloriana, Excellency," the Queen's envoy told

Brindle. "Alas that its comforts are rudimentary, but we shall overcome any want and look forward to the bounty of Her presence on the morrow."

Down the slope to the jetty he took them and the apprentices marvelled at the sound of their footfalls echoing over the boards. Into the high, cavernous gloom the noise went soaring, only to bounce back a thousandfold until it sounded like an army was marching behind them.

A wide plank served as the gangway and, one by one, they crossed it to step aboard Thomas Herrick's ostentatious night barge. At once the crew ran below decks to take the oars. The two men who had pushed open the boat house doors hurried over the plank behind then pulled it in and dashed to their stations.

"We shall be hard pressed to reach Whitehall in time," Herrick said. "Although this vessel is faster than most."

Setting his heavy pack on the deck, Richard Wutton looked at the night barge with a studious scowl. "But this craft could arrive at London before dawn," he retorted.

Herrick assumed a pained expression. "My men cannot row all night," he said. "We shall see what progress we make this day then put in at some hospitable place. I have spent one night in my cabin and will not endure another."

Slowly, the night barge was pushed away from the wooden quayside. Gracefully the oars slid out, dipped into the water below and the craft glided through the darkness. The lanterns that lit the jetty began to recede and Adam and Henry leaned over the side to watch them dwindle into the distance.

"We're off, Coggy," Henry breathed, unable to quell his excitement.

Adam peered down at the black water. Churned by the rhythmic motion of the oars it sparkled and glittered in the light of the barge's ornamental lamps. It was as if they had already left the island behind them and were sailing the airless void.

"Stand clear there," Thomas Herrick scolded. "The canopy is about to close and you'll forfeit your fingers."

The boys stood back as one of the men cranked an iron handle and two halves of a canvas-covered framework were hoisted above the deck, unfolding with a rattle of chains over pulleys.

Brindle observed the operation with interest. The canopy closed overhead to the sound of a muffled clang and, when the join was made secure and the mechanism locked, the deck was totally encased and sealed.

From the enclosing canvas a chemical vapour came pouring which only his delicate senses detected and a murmur of recognition left his lips. "So, it is true," he said.

Everyone looked at him.

"Excellency?" Thomas Herrick asked. "What is this truth?"

"The canopy," Brindle explained. "I have seen its like before. I am familiar with the mordant in which the canvas is steeped. Matters are now much clearer to me – that is all."

Herrick gave a bemused grin. "Such knowledge is for shipwrights and labourers, surely?" he laughed. "Come, view our departure – we are approaching the mouth."

Stepping on to the forecastle, he beckoned Brindle to follow. The Iribian complied, and so did Adam and Henry.

Across to the far side of the raven black pool the night barge skimmed, to where the surface foamed and bubbled before a cliff of rock that reared up into the darkness. Yet high in that craggy wall there gaped an immense opening.

"Raise the oars," Herrick instructed as the vessel entered the seething waters.

As every oar pointed upward, the night barge gave a gentle lurch, then began to rise from the boiling pool, causing a teeming rain to pour from its elevating keel.

Their faces pressed against a window, Adam and Henry stared in amazement at the unfolding scene. Lit by the soft glare of the amber lamps, the shadowy expanse of sheer rock rolled by, gradually giving way to the rim of that enormous, arch-shaped opening – the gateway of Malmes-Wutton.

"Duck's plums!" Henry exclaimed. "You could drive three galleons abreast through there and still have room either side."

"Hold her steady," Thomas Herrick commanded the helmsman. "The current will catch us any moment."

Drifting towards that great hole in the rock, the

apprentices beheld the eternal, star-pricked night beyond and knew that soon they would be out there, setting a course between the uplifted lands.

The night barge gave a sudden jolt and the timbers trembled as a howling wind began to whirl outside, and the craft was dragged into a funnelling squall which battered the canopy, buffeting and whooshing against the canvas.

"The tide has us," Herrick called calmly. "Keep her on course."

Standing back from the window, Brindle looked questioningly at Lord Richard.

"We are riding the breath of the Almighty," Richard Wutton told him. "It gales continuously about the entrance but twice daily allows passage through to the Outer Dark.

Ploughing deeper into the twisting strait, the night barge sailed under the vast arch and Brindle stared searchingly out of the window. Through the spiralling gloom, set into the towering sides, he saw what appeared to be roughly hewn designs gouged into the rock.

"Once more the consummate science concealed behind crude imagery," he said softly. "I did not suspect the special ambassadors of such artifice. What pleasure they must have drawn from their hidden playground."

"Who do you mean?" Adam asked.

"Stand by," Thomas Herrick called before the Iribian could answer.

With a final rush of swirling air, the night barge was through, shooting out into the empty void. The bagging canvas was given a last pummelling and an eerie calm descended. They were outside the isle of Malmes-Wutton.

Henry and Adam dashed to the stern where a smaller window showed them a spectacle they had often dreamed of but never witnessed.

Their home.

Up from the rocky archway the night boat floated and the rugged crags sank behind it until, abruptly, the encircling wall in which the firmament was set finally came into view.

The leaded panes were of the deepest blue and, although no glimpse of the estate could be seen through them, it was a ravishing sight. Thousands of refracted facets gleamed and dazzled in the harsh, unfiltered sunlight. To the apprentices, it was as if they were gazing upon the most monstrous jewel ever quarried from the mines of God.

At the western edge of the island, the links of a gargantuan chain were plainly visible reaching out into the distance, joining with the neighbouring land of Saxmundham. Every corner of Elizabeth's uplifted realm was connected in this way, anchoring and uniting each manor and county. Adam had heard that the same was true for the isles of Europe but he gave no thought to them; for the moment this was enough.

Even Henry had no phrase to describe it and they

continued to gawp out of the window. The covered island dropped below them until they could see the place where Brindle's craft had shipwrecked and was wedged permanently in position.

Then the oars of the night barge were lowered and Herrick's men began their back-wrenching work. Away from the island they pulled and the apprentices watched its gradual retreat in thoughtful silence. Out into the immeasurable regions of the night the scarlet vessel journeyed, its merry decoration of amber lamps glimmering through the endless cold.

Brindle looked out at the brightly burning stars but failed to recognise any of them.

"Excellency," Thomas Herrick began, leaving the forecastle and nodding towards a small door at the stern. "This modest craft does boast one comfort. I have a cabin yonder where we may speak privily. I would talk of the Queen with you; She is greatly interested to know from whence you came and many other matters of intrigue and import."

The Iribian's reply clearly showed his irritation with the man. "I am a merchant only," he said. "I trade in perfume and balms and see no reason why your sovereign would wish to see me. I am stranded amongst you without hope of returning to my own sphere, and with nothing of worth to exchange or reward Lord Richard's great kindness unto me."

"Hardly nothing of worth," Herrick remarked with a nervous laugh. "Your gracious society alone is above price. Then there is your noble wit and wisdom. But come, let us remove to my cabin where we may discuss this more freely and away from vulgar hearing."

"Is there room there for Lord Richard also?"

"Why, no – of course not."

"Then I shall remain here."

Herrick gave a slight cough, then excused himself and snarlingly took his vexation out on the helmsman.

"Have a care how you deal with him," Lord Richard advised Brindle with a warning whisper. "I have no doubt that the real reason we are to stall our journey this evening is to give him the opportunity to despatch some tattling letter to the Queen. It would be best not to earn Her anger before you have met Her."

The Iribian stared out at the empty darkness. "The man is sore in need of a lesson in humility," he said. "I like not his manner with you."

"I've been scorned by better than he," Lord Richard answered. "Old scars feel no fresh hurt."

Following the line of the great linking chain, within an hour the night barge had drawn near to the much larger isle of Saxmundham. Beyond that the other ten islands of Suffolk loomed large and glittering.

Eventually, Adam and Henry wearied of looking upon the passing estates; the fierce glare of the firmaments strained their eyes and so they sat quietly upon the deck. Adam tried to marshal his thoughts. The loss of Jack was too raw and recent a wound to touch upon. Besides, Henry refused to talk about it. So Adam fished in his pack for the phial of black ichor he had brought with him and mourned for Suet instead.

It was strange not having the wooden piglet grunting at his heels. When he had returned to the manor the previous night he had gone to the piggery and knelt before Old Temperance. The great sow had stared into his eyes and the boy wondered if she knew what had happened. Without a sound, she had moved away from him and entered the brick sty from where, a short while later, her deep voice lowed and Flitch squealed desolately.

"Praise be for that dumpy widow!" Henry cried and Adam was yanked back to the present. Henry had been rifling in his travel bag and was thrilled to discover the food Mistress Dritchly had packed for him.

"Mutton pasties and apple tart!" he exclaimed, shovelling a bite of each into his mouth and relishing the mingled flavours.

Smoothly the night barge voyaged on. Above and below the uplifted lands it made its way in silence, leaving Suffolk behind and passing over the first of the six isles of Essex.

By the time the afternoon had slipped into evening, Adam and Henry were restless and had grown to resent the cramped deck with its canvas canopy. They longed to stretch their legs over solid ground and one glance at Brindle told them that he too rebelled at this confining journey. The atmosphere had grown stale and stifling and everyone yearned for the day to be over.

Thomas Herrick had removed himself to his cabin where, as Lord Richard so rightly guessed, he was engaged in the writing of a report to the Queen, detailing the little he had learned from the celestial visitor thus far.

"What were you talking of before?" Adam asked the Iribian. "When you spoke of a hidden playground, who did you mean?"

Brindle seemed to find the question uncomfortable and stared up at the canopy. "I am not the first stranger to come amongst your people," he said. "There have been others. Every sign points to their presence. The wisdom hidden in the functioning of this vessel alone is testament to them. You are a fine people but know nothing of the force conversion now taking place below decks and propelling you through the darkness. Yes, others have certainly been amongst you."

Adam considered for a moment. "There have only ever been the special ambassadors."

Brindle's flame-patterned brows arched at that but the boy could not tell whether it was from amusement, surprise or dismay.

"Did you know them?" he continued. "Lord Richard

says that they were kind and helpful to us after the Beatification."

The Iribian stared down at his hands. "I knew them," he answered. "Yes, I knew them. I cannot count the number of times I have cursed the day my people encountered them."

An abrupt groan from Henry interrupted any further conversation and Brindle appeared relieved.

"I don't feel well," Henry uttered. "My guts squirm like serpents."

"An overstuffed stomach and the motion of this craft do not a happy combination make," Lord Richard declared, descending from the forecastle where he had been sitting in meditative thought. "You had best lie down, Master Wattle."

For another two hours they travelled, during which Adam had no further opportunity of speech with Brindle. Then, at last, as the leaded panes cleared to let in the surrounding night they sailed by, Thomas Herrick was called from his cabin by the helmsman.

"Havering lies ahead of us!" the Queen's envoy announced to his passengers. "That is where we shall put in for the night. Thither is a wayside inn which is not too disagreeable."

Leaving Henry to moan and clutch his stomach, Adam stared through the window and saw an island four times the size of Malmes-Wutton stretching before them. Through the transparent panes of its gigantic sky, the apprentice beheld darkened fields and huddled, clustering villages, their small windows tiny flecks of orange light.

Over the expansive firmament the night barge moved, descending in a sweeping arc down to the horizon where the rough stone of the island formed a desolation of deep crevices and jagged ridges. Past this bare wilderness the oarsmen pulled until at last a cavern, far greater than the gateway of Malmes-Wutton, gaped dark and black beside them.

Two large windows were chiselled into the side of the opening, each the height of a man and, behind the topmost, a lantern burned, glowing through the green glass, signalling to travellers that the way was open.

"Take us in," Thomas Herrick instructed. "I have a thirst in me which can only be slaked by good wine."

Rolling slightly, the night barge swung around and the oars were raised. Into the great entrance the vessel went coursing until the tidal breath seized its timbers and the canopy began to billow and thump once more as the cyclone spun all around.

Minutes later, the scarlet craft was sailing serenely through becalmed waters, the canopy was opened and everyone breathed deep lungfuls of the fresher air.

Adam and Henry looked about them.

The boat house of Havering was unlike the one they had left behind. This was no cheerless, dank cavern beneath the ground. Here, many vessels were moored to a stone quayside. Lanterns shone everywhere and dwellings had been cut into the surrounding rock.

When the gangway had been stretched across the gap, Thomas Herrick had a word with one of his men then stepped ashore and bade Brindle to follow him.

"A night in Honey Lane will revive us," he said.

The Iribian hesitated. "What of Lord Richard and my young friends?" he asked.

"Can they not remain on board?" Herrick inquired. "My purse is not without its bottom and the landlord here is renowned for his high charges."

Brindle folded his arms. "But surely your Sovereign will recompense your costs, if I am as intriguing to Her as you suggest."

"Of course," Herrick replied, his face trembling with agitation. "I did but think the children would prefer to remain on board. They did seem to take such pretty delight in it."

"Bog cheese!" Henry called, pushing by Brindle and staggering to the quayside. "I need land 'neath me, or I'll be shouting a rainbow."

Thomas Herrick tried to force himself to smile but the effort was beyond him. "So be it," he relented, tugging on his lace cuffs and steering well away from the ashen-faced Henry.

A genuine smile spread across the face of Richard Wutton. He knew full well how miserly the Queen was.

Thomas Herrick would never see his money again and he resolved to ensure that a prodigious reckoning would be his to pay in the morning.

At the end of the quay, a wide stair had been carved into the rock and the Queen's messenger guided them up to where a cool night breeze came pouring in. Soon they were standing under a stone arch beneath the protected heavens and a wide village street lay before them.

The apprentices had never seen so many buildings gathered together.

"Is this a city?" Henry asked.

Herrick laughed. "'Tis naught but a rural hamlet," he said. "But there is a royal palace several miles along this road and divers merchants and travelling folk make this a stopping point on their way to London. Come, let us partake of the Copper Cow's hospitality."

Across the street stood a half-timbered, three-storied building. High above the entrance to its yard, a post jutted from the whitewashed wall and hanging from this was an old broken cow. It might once have been made of copper but was now striped and streaked with lime and emerald verdigris. Passing beneath it, Adam thought the mechanical looked morose and miserable, and he wondered when it had last grazed in the fields.

"I could repair that," Henry boasted.

Herrick gave a ridiculing laugh.

"That would be most foolish," he scoffed. "For 'tis a

famed landmark hereabouts. The landlord here was kicked by that beast over seventy years ago and lamed as a consequence. Yet, Hobbling John Chester has had his revenge – he set the beast up there and so it has remained ever since. Once a swarm of bees made a hive in it and their golden yield did rain through the gaps to run oozing over the road. From that time, this thoroughfare has always been known as 'Honey Lane'."

The layout of the Copper Cow followed the usual pattern of wayside inns and was built around a central courtyard. This was a brightly lit space, with lamps hanging from the enclosing balconies and at the furthest end there were stables where the mechanical horses of guests were tethered.

In the centre of the yard stood a circular wooden fence, in full view of the balconies and Adam knew it to be where the cock fighting and dog baiting took place. Inspecting it more closely he saw that there were even some tin plumes and iron claws still lying in there.

The ground floor windows were all ablaze with light and behind them moved a press of figures whose voices streamed out in a happy, confused babble. Suddenly one of the inn's stout doors was flung open and the internal noise came spilling into the night as a man was pushed out.

"You've had your fill," warned a burly silhouette in the doorway. "Come not in here again this night, nor any other."

"I'll be back with the constable!" the ejected man threatened, grasping a jingling sack in one hand. "I'll not be cozened. Those birds were weighted against mine and the flicks in your ale house play with bristle dice and fullams."

"You and the constable? That's a tickler, that is."

"Watch your foul tongue, halt foot – or I'll maim your other leg."

"Be off, or I'll set the brass mastiffs on you."

The man spat and barged roughly past Adam and the others, his steely eyes trained upon the ground. It was not a pleasant face. Henry caught a glimpse of its sharp, mean features and was reminded of the rats he had made to torment Mistress Dritchly.

A chuckle came from the figure in the doorway. Then, with a start, he became aware of the group waiting in the yard. "Who's that there?" he called with a stern ring in his nasal voice. "'Tis long past ten of the clock and the baiting is over. If you've come to wager, then..."

Drawing his breath sharply, he recognised Thomas Herrick and his voice switched to that of a genial host.

"Why, my noble Sir," he greeted warmly. "I was expecting you and your party well before dusk and did begin to think you had passed us by. Come you in and sluice the dust from your throats. The rooms are prepared."

Herrick strode forward and slapped the man's paunching stomach with the back of his hand.

"Up to your old knavery, Chesters?" he asked. "A man's coin must ever be guarded in this establishment. How did you rob that poor fellow? Do the champions of the figging law still hole up here? They'd best not practise their trade on me or any of my company or I'll have their necks stretched."

The landlord of the Copper Cow gave a hasty laugh.

"I would you had not witnessed that sorry performance," he blustered. "Clink Kitson never did know how to lose with grace and this night's seen his pocket depleted more than usual. Came here with a real flimsy rattler of a fighting sparrow and is amazed when it falls to pieces by my prize rooster. Then he tries to win back his pence by gaming."

Herrick sneered. "No wise man he then; the dice of this house follow no natural law."

"Well, he's the fool for chancing," the landlord admitted, denying nothing. "But spare no charity for Clinker; he's a known padder and will cut some wretch's purse to quench his temper. Would have tried it in here if he'd stayed longer. I'm not sorry to have him ousted. I've half a dozen indoors who'd gladly sink a blade into him, the way he carries on."

With that he waggled his hands to usher them in, then gasped as he saw Brindle for the first time and could do nothing but stare at the Iribian's astonishing features.

"Lord in Heaven!" he cried. "Why, 'tis true, those

fanciful tales that have been buzzing around like wasps these past days. A more fearful face I ne'er did see. What a nose he has!"

The landlord of the Copper Cow was a large, clean-shaven man whose own nose bore witness to many past fights. It had been broken more times than he could remember and meandered down from his shaggy brows in a lazy zigzag of fleshy lumps. Tufts of grey hair sprouted from his flattened nostrils and ears, one of which gave further confirmation of a rough life for it was huge and gnarled like a piece of proudflesh that had bulged from its mould.

"A divine visitor is what they're saying," he jabbered, wiping his hands on his apron and taking hold of the Iribian's arm. "Fell out of Heaven, I heard. Why, you're well come, good master - it's the finest room you'll be having! I'm certain sure Master Herrick won't be minding as he normally resides there."

Limping into the inn, John Chester trawled Brindle after him.

"A shame about your room," Lord Richard goaded Herrick.

"I was going to surrender it anyway," came the unconvincing reply. "Who does that lame oaf think he is, laying his common hands upon His Excellency's person?"

Richard Wutton winked at the two apprentices then pushed into the tavern, licking his lips at the prospect of the costly wine which he would drink that night.

And so Henry and Adam entered the Copper Cow. By the time they stepped through the doorway, a deathly hush had already descended and it was like walking into a painting, for no one moved and every goggling eye was fixed on Brindle.

Adam had never seen so many people gathered in one place before. It was almost double the entire population of Malmes-Wutton. The patrons of the inn were a disparate brew: old and young mingled with the grave and merry. Many of them were local, downing ale after the sport of the cock pit, but others were travellers - merchants and sailors seeking diversion from the ships anchored down at the quay.

Every stool and standing space was taken. In one corner an area had been set aside for the playing of dice while, throughout the low-beamed room, games of cards were under way. Yet all motion was frozen and Adam nearly laughed at their half frightened expressions.

Brindle's nostrils quailed and shrank from the smell in the room. It was far more stuffy and airless than the latter part of the voyage had been. To make matters worse, few of the people gathered there ever bathed and others hardly washed. Puddles of spilt ale saturated the floor and someone had puked under a table. To the Iribian the crawling reek was appalling and he coughed at the unholy stench which battered his delicate senses.

But it was impossible for him to leave; the landlord had

him by the arm and a superior grin was plastered over his weathered face, divulging the absence of many teeth.

"See here!" Hobbling John proclaimed with consummate pride to his dumbstruck customers. "There's an angel in my tavern."

Immediately the talk broke out again. Most of them had heard the rumour of the Suffolk miracle and each had something to say about it. Someone crossed himself and dropped to his knees while another fell off a stool and tumbled against the table behind, scattering the players' cards.

"What ails its eye?" one of the braver souls at the back called out.

Thomas Herrick stepped forward, his costly clothes giving them no doubt that he was a nobleman and not to be disputed. It would be best to make certain that they were in awe of his authority.

"I am on an errand for Her Glorious Majesty, Elizabeth," he announced in his most imposing, haughty tone while placing his hand upon the hilt of his sword. "He that obstructs or hinders me shall suffer the severest penalty. I will not have His Excellency, Lord Brindle, plagued with foolish questions. There will be no pleas for healing and no heretical mutterings – is that understood?"

A sea of heads nodded dumbly and he turned back to Hobbling John. "Attend to our rooms," he instructed.

"This rabble is no company for such an exalted guest. But first bring us ale and wine. It has proven a most dry day in every meaning of the word."

The landlord released the Iribian's arm and hurried away. Brindle turned a concerned face to Lord Richard.

"Is that why your Queen has sent for me?" he whispered. "Can She truly think I am capable of healing? I am not the angel your people believe or wish me to be. If She truly expects it then She will be sorely disappointed."

Richard Wutton agreed. It was a disturbing thought and one even he had not anticipated.

"No," he muttered after consideration, making certain no one else could hear him. "Elizabeth is no fool. She will not think you are from the Almighty, yet what Her subjects suppose is another matter. How can She who was only anointed before God compare with one whom the populace believe hails from His very kingdom? She is a jealous monarch and will suffer no rivals, friend Brindle – again I say beware."

Since leaving the night barge, Henry Wattle's churning stomach had been gradually settling but, in that stifling room, it wormed and squelched within him once more. Fighting it in silence he was beginning to think he could win the battle when, suddenly, his eyes caught sight of the vomit beneath the table and the struggle was over.

"I have to go outside!" he balked, rushing to the door and hurling himself into the yard.

Stumbling against the cock pit, the apprentice took frantic, gulping breaths until, eventually, the burning in his throat abated and he let out a long dismal moan. For several minutes he stood there, gripping the circular fence. Then the urge to feel a cool breeze upon his face took possession of him, and he left the enclosed yard and strolled into the street.

Standing beneath the broken mechanical cow, he wiped his damp forehead and let the summer draughts refresh him. The unusual inn sign creaked on its chains and Henry regarded it with professional interest.

"An afternoon in the workshop and I'd have you booting landlords again," he said aloud. "There's no mechanical Henry Wattle can't mend, no matter how rusted they are."

"That crippled pirate kicked you out as well, has he?"

Henry jumped at the unexpected voice and, for a startled instant, thought it was the cow who had spoken.

"Who said that?" he demanded.

"Loaded dice and tainted cards, that's his sharp game," the bitter snarl continued.

Henry whipped around and peered into the darkness which shrouded the far side of the road. "I needed to take the air," was all he could think of in answer.

A movement stirred in the shadows. "The chit's ill, is he?"

From the concealing gloom a sinewy figure emerged, and the boy recognised it as belonging to Clink Kitson, the man the landlord had thrown out when they arrived.

"I'm feeling better now," Henry said, backing slowly into the yard.

"Don't you be going yet," Clinker cried, his long legs leaping quickly across the lane. "It's only a chat I be wanting. I was just sat over there on my lonesome, cursing my rotten fortune and wishing a judgement upon cheating folk who limp, when I hears your sparky words."

Henry affected a yawn and stretched his arms. "I'm really tired," he began, edging warily away.

"All I ask," Clinker begged, "is for you to run your expert eye over Jackspur, my fighting cockerel. Them brutes of Hobble John's have done for him good and proper, and I don't know how to fix the sorry wreckage. Folk say that squash-nose tops up their red temper with humour taken from his mad dogs and I'll believe it now."

"Jack?" Henry murmured.

"Jackspur, that's right."

The apprentice stared up at the man's pinched and hungry face. "Too much red ichor..." he whispered, as his thoughts travelled back to the woods of Malmes-Wutton and the clearing where Jack Flye had been killed.

"Dishonest, that is, and downright deadly."

Henry found himself agreeing. "Where is your mechanical?" he said readily. "I'll see what I can do to repair him."

Clink Kitson laughed and clapped the boy on the back.

"Over there, young master," he said, flitting back across

the street. "I bagged up all the bits I could find. A real piteous state he's in. How you've raised my spirits; if you can only get little Jackspur up and pecking again I'll swear you're the best tin doctor I've ever heard of."

Kitson capered like a giant daddy long legs to the entrance of a shadow-drowned alleyway that sneaked between two stone buildings. His caution forgotten, Henry followed.

"Here he is," Clinker said, crouching to pick a bag from the ground. "Poor Jackspur's in there."

Henry took the tinkling bundle but, before he could even open it, the man threw a wiry arm around his throat and dragged him into the darkness. His heels scraping along the alley floor, the apprentice kicked and struggled. He tried to call out but Kitson's arm was crushing against his windpipe and he could barely breathe. Then a point of cold steel pressed into his neck and the man sniggered menacingly in his ear.

"Just like a little coney," he growled. "Now, this poacher's going to see what's in that travel bag the little rabbit's got strapped so tight to his shoulder. Fine company he keeps. I saw that trussed up gentry you came with. Must have plenty of yellow money, that one."

Keeping his arm tight about the boy's throat, he cut through the bag strap and tore the pack open. "There'd best be some shillings in here or the rabbit'll lose its skin," he swore.

With his face turning purple, Henry gagged and choked. There was nothing of value in his bag.

"What's this?" Clinker snapped, squelching his fingers through the uneaten food. "What is it?" Enraged, he pushed the apprentice against the wall and smacked his fist across Henry's face, then snatched hold of his hair.

"M... mutton pasties," the boy sobbed hoarsely.

"Then it's the end for you," he spat. "Seven men I've sent galloping to Hell. Two I throttled, four I punctured and the last I battered till his head could pour into a jar. The Justices ain't nabbed me for them and they won't for you neither."

"I... I don't have any... any money."

A hideous leer crawled across Kitson's gaunt features. "You ever heard what happened in one of the Spanish isles nigh on forty years ago? Grew tired of eating false flesh, they did, so what do you reckon they ended up doing instead? After a while no travellers dared set foot there, 'cos none ever came back. Always seemed like a good notion to me, that did. You keep your mutton pasties, my little morsel – I always was partial to a rabbit pie."

Clink Kitson raised the knife and, with a final taunting cackle, hissed, "Poor little coney, shouldn't have popped his head out of the burrow."

The blade gleamed in the darkness and Henry gave a terrified shriek.

CHAPTER 2

Gog and Magog

✦

"Let the child go!" a fierce voice boomed.

Clinker whisked around and saw a towering figure rushing up the narrow alley. Quick as a snake, he pulled Henry in front of him and made sure that the knife blade was plain to see.

"Halt right there!" he yelled. "One step nearer and I'll carve a door to let out the lad's soul."

Only yards away, the tall shape stumbled to a standstill and a weird flicker of blue light shone beneath its chin.

315

‡

"Henry!" Brindle called anxiously. "Are you unhurt?"

Clinker pulled the apprentice's head back and the boy yelped in pain.

"He's just taking the night air," Clinker laughed. "Shall I cut him another mouth to let in a bit more?"

Brindle's shadowy outline drew itself up and his right hand went reaching for his hip. "If you dare put your mark on him," he warned, the spectral light gleaming coldly in his uncovered eye, "you shall taste an Iribian's fury. Release him whilst you still have a chance."

The cut-throat gave a deriding snort. "Who are you to make demands?" he taunted. "Yours is an empty hand to bluff with. No, Clinker holds the trumps this time. Now you stand back there – else I deal him a big juicy heart."

But Brindle remained where he was and, in the cloaking darkness, his fingers unclasped the scabbard hanging from his belt.

"You deaf, clod?" Kitson snapped. "I'm warning you."

"And I have warned you," came the assured reply. "For my hand is far from empty, as you can see." In one swift movement he drew the deadly, twin-bladed knife from its sheath and let it glitter in the blue light.

Clinker smothered a rasping cry. "What devil's weapon is that?" he croaked.

"'Tis only my reaping hook," Brindle answered, "yet 'twill serve to fillet your corrupt bones." And, with a careless confirming thrust, he drove the double blades into the wall, raking up a shower of sparks and scribing a deep wound into the stone with the barb at his elbow.

Henry felt Clinker's heart beat faster and the dagger at the boy's throat was quivering.

"That don't fright me," the man lied. "Doesn't take a knife sharp as yours to plough a bloody ditch in this tender field of flesh – so back off!"

Brindle lifted the blades in readiness and continued to speak with unnerving confidence. "I promise you that I can move with more speed than your eyes are able to bear witness. Your death will come before there is time to even register surprise."

At that moment they heard Lord Richard's voice call out in Honey Lane, quickly joined by Adam and Hobbling John Chester.

"Seems we'll never learn the truth of that!" Clinker cursed, his rat-like eyes shining, and he gave Henry a mighty shove which sent the boy lurching at the Iribian's feet. Hooting his contempt, Clink Kitson pelted up the alley and disappeared into the night.

Brindle lifted the apprentice off the floor and Henry threw his arms about him. "Thank you," he wept, clinging to him desperately. "I was so stupid – how did you find me?"

"I perceived that you had wandered from the yard and that villain's scent was still heavy in the air. Then I sensed your fear."

Henry buried his face in Brindle's shoulder and sobbed.

The Iribian glared into the distant darkness, his nostrils gaping and exploring. Then, in grim silence, he carried Henry from the alleyway.

That night Henry Wattle slept deeper than ever before in all of his twelve short years. The terror of Clink Kitson had faded rapidly under the concerned attention of Lord Richard and Cog Adam's friendship. Besides, with Brindle at his side he knew there was nothing more to fear. The landlord of the Copper Cow also made much of the boy and vowed that the Justice would be informed of the vile felon's actions at first light.

Hearing this, Thomas Herrick had uttered a lazy, unsympathetic laugh. Havering was riddled with low dens where Kitson could duck the noose. He was certainly beyond the law already.

It was a discouraging thought and, when he was certain that Henry had suffered no other hurt, Lord Richard retired to his bed with a bottle of the finest wine from Hobbling John's excellent cellar.

Henry and Adam had been given a sparse room in one of the attics, but the straw mattresses were clean and they threw themselves down, completely exhausted. By the time Thomas Herrick's report to the Queen left Havering aboard a night boat with one of his men, the two apprentices were sound asleep.

The hushed hours of darkness shifted slowly towards the dawn. A faint cry, howling in the remote distance, travelled unheard to the still emptiness of Honey Lane and Adam rolled on to his side. Dappled sunlight shone into his dreams and he was back in the woodland, watching Old Scratch charge at Jack.

The older boy's screams blistered his ears once more and Adam's eyes snapped open as he sprang from the pillow and stared, disorientated, about the darkened room. Dribbles of sweat trickled cold down his face and the boy reached for the comforting, keg-shaped form of Suet at his side.

But the bed was empty.

On the other mattress Henry was still slumbering, his steady breath rising and falling, and Adam wondered what the hour was. From the street outside, he suddenly heard the sound of footsteps. Hugging his knees, he listened keenly as the walker approached the inn until, eventually, the stealthy tread turned into the courtyard below.

With a creasing forehead, Adam wondered who could possibly be abroad in this inky night. The even footfalls ruled out Hobble John, and the boy's curiosity smouldered. Creeping from his bed, he tiptoed to the door and looked discreetly over the balcony.

Down in the courtyard a solitary lantern still burned but, by its light, he could see that the place was deserted. Whoever had come in from Honey Lane had either entered the empty tavern, was hiding in the stables or had gone swiftly to his room. Stepping closer to the railed edge in order to peer a little further, a loose board squeaked under Adam's bare feet and the boy flinched in alarm. He did not want to be discovered prying into this nocturnal business and he fled back into the attic.

The remaining night entombed the Copper Cow in silence.

When Adam awoke the second time, the sun was nudging into the room and the hooves of mechanical horses were clopping up the street. Henry was already out of bed and pulling on his breeches.

"Wish I still had them pasties," the boy chattered when he saw Adam blinking and running a hand through his fair hair.

"I've two in my pack," Adam mumbled groggily. "But won't there be a breakfast?"

Henry shrugged and rooted inside the other apprentice's bag. "That Herrick's prob'ly too mean to prise his purse open," he said, spitting pastry crumbs as he chomped between words. "All he cares about is getting our Brindle to the Queen."

Henry finished the hasty breakfast and wiped the debris from his lips, wincing as he accidentally brushed the ugly purple bruise dealt by Clink Kitson.

"That's twice Brindle's saved my life now," he murmured, adopting an uncharacteristic, serious tone. "Was there ever anyone like him? He deserves to be called

'Excellency' – I might start doing that myself. A guardian angel, that's what he is. Bum boils, Coggy – how lucky were we when he foundered in our sky?"

Still yawning, Adam said nothing and hunted for his clothes. Soon both boys were dressed and they left the room in search of the rest of their party.

Lord Richard was already downstairs, seated at one of the tables staring glumly at a trencher of bread and cold beef. The master of Malmes-Wutton was clearly suffering the effects of the landlord's wine, as he had finished the whole bottle before going to bed. His eyes were ringed with dark circles and he held his head as if it were an egg of the old world that was about to hatch.

With a flick of his eyes he bade the boys sit with him and delicately called for their breakfasts.

"Compliments of friend Herrick," he told them. "So eat as much as you can, though I fear that Hobble John's kitchen has forgot the true flavour of beef, if this sorry fare is aught to judge by."

Henry rubbed his hands together with renewed greed; his stomach had certainly recovered from the previous night.

"Where's Brindle?" he asked. "What a day this will be. The great isle of London, a royal palace and Her Majesty."

Richard Wutton's face clouded even more. "Aye, we've that trial still to come."

A kitchen boy, no older than the apprentices, came bearing two trenchers laden with more cuts of beef.

Henry fell upon his like a cormorant, then spat the barely chewed mouthful out. "Witch grease!" he cried. "Do they poison us? The meat tastes of mud."

Adam gave the unappealing grey slices a wary sniff and pushed the trencher away. "Least I still have one pasty left," he muttered.

"Never thought I'd miss anything about Widow Dritchly," Henry grumbled.

"And little did I think to find milk so strong within a cow," Lord Richard said, his head sinking into his hands.

"Good day," a clear voice proclaimed behind them.

The boys spun around and Henry leapt from his stool to give Brindle a welcoming hug. Then fell back, pointing to his face in amazement. Even Lord Richard blinked in disbelief and rose from his seat.

"What happened?" Henry breathed. "It's a wonder."

The Iribian chortled quietly. Every last scar had faded from his skin, and now his left eye was free from bandages and its emerald iris was as bright and clear as the other.

"But the injury..." Lord Richard said doubtfully.

Brindle brushed their surprise aside. "I have received the best possible care," he said lightly. "I owe you and Mistress Dritchly much."

"Nay, I saw how deep was the damage. No cure was possible; how was it done?"

"I am from Iribia. Our fibres are tough and do not yield easily."

Richard Wutton sat down again. "Even so," he murmured. "I am half tempted to believe this heavenly visitor foolishness. If the Queen asks if you are capable of miracle healing, how then am I to answer?"

"I am no angel," Brindle reminded him.

Lord Richard shook his head and looked at him. That day Brindle had put on the richest clothes from Edwin Dritchly's amended wardrobe: a jerkin of the darkest blue velvet, trimmed with picadils and shining brass buttons, over a marigold-coloured doublet, embroidered with symbols appropriate to a master of motive science.

"Well you're certainly an arresting spectacle, my friend. All eyes shall be upon you when we arrive at court."

The Iribian fidgeted and ran a finger around his ruff. "The attire is not fitting to meet your sovereign?" he asked. "I am ignorant of such matters. I do not wish to bring shame upon you."

"Forgive me," Lord Richard laughed. "I was but teasing. You'll pass muster sure enough. Indeed, this day you'll be giving Thomas Herrick competition."

Brindle did not answer and Adam observed him closely. There was no trace of where the wounds had been, not even any discolouration or bruising around the eye. He appeared flushed with health and vigour.

"Have you broken your fast?" Lord Richard asked. "Is there aught in the morning air of Havering to tantalise your senses?"

An enigmatic glint sparkled in the Iribian's large eyes. "I have found it to be most enlivening," he replied. "There is in these lands much to commend them. 'Tis a grievous pity I have not a second torc to bring my people hither – they would take great enjoyment in the delights you have to offer."

Adam wondered if there was more in those words than Brindle meant them to understand.

"But what of Master Wattle?" the Iribian demanded. "How does he fare after last night's evil happenings?"

"Ready to take on an army," Henry replied and he meant it.

"You slept without disturbance? Of dark dreams or aught else troubling you?"

"'Twas as if I had a stilling crest that had been firmly pushed."

"And Cog Adam, did he rest peacefully?"

Surprised by the question, Adam merely nodded, but Brindle's bright, lemon eyes seemed to pierce him.

"Are we to join Master Herrick aboard his night barge?" the Iribian inquired with an abrupt change of subject.

Lord Richard chuckled and tapped his hands together lightly. "Aye, the popinjay is down in the quay at this moment. But your nose is more tender than I guessed if you can sniff him out from here."

"His is an individual scent. This inn groans of his

attendance and will never truly be free of it, but the stronger trail leads out to the entrance of the quayside and fills that place like a lavender fog."

"Excellency!" Henry whistled. "You're a hound and a magician and a knight all fluxed into one."

"I am a balm trader only," Brindle disagreed, with a glance at Adam.

Henry nodded to the reaping hook sheathed at the Iribian's hip. "That's not just for cutting flowers," he insisted. "You should have seen it gouge into stone, Coggy – easy as if it were curd."

"To harvest the purest scents," Brindle began. "There are times when you needs must cut through the strongest stems. Young Adam, do you feel a chill? You are shivering."

"No," the boy said quickly. "I'm just impatient to be off, that's all."

"We have no reason to loiter here," Lord Richard decided. "The food is less palatable than the wooden trencher 'tis served upon. If we each have our bags then let us bid farewell to the Copper Cow."

"But where is Hobble John?" Adam asked.

"Went to inform the Justice in person of that foul brigand Kitson," Lord Richard told them. "He's been gone this past hour and will be another I fancy. We can't be waiting on him, the tidal breath won't permit it."

Out into the courtyard they traipsed, then under the

hanging mechanical cow. Henry looked across the road, at the alleyway where he nearly lost his life.

"Let's hurry," he said with a shudder.

Along Honey Lane they made their way and were about to pass into the entrance that led down to the quayside, when Adam heard the sound of hooves and turned to look up the street.

A mechanical horse was cantering towards the inn but carried on by when the rider saw them. It was the burly figure of John Chester and he hailed them with a wave of his hands and a ripe shout. "Hold a moment, good masters!" he called. "Hold a moment."

Hobbling John's steed was a hefty beast wrought of blackened steel and the apprentices admired the craftsmanship that had gone into its making. It was not the usual clunking horse a man of his station might be expected to own, but then the Copper Cow afforded its landlord a very agreeable living.

Reining the creation to a snorting halt, he wiped his glistening forehead and made a bow to them while remaining in the saddle.

"Why this is a fortuitous chance," he exclaimed. "I might have missed you and then you would be robbed of the tale. A happy day this is, for all of us who live in Havering."

"Did you speak to the Justice?" Lord Richard asked. "Will he seek out that cut-throat?"

The landlord gave a substantial laugh that shook his horse and set its head wagging. "Why no, he'll not be doing that," he guffawed. "I ne'er even crossed the distance to his hall."

"You did not tell him?" Lord Richard pressed, with bemused irritation creeping into his voice. "By the stars, man, why not?"

Hobbling John eased his mirth and wiped his eyes. "Clink Kitson don't need no finding," he claimed, "for he's found already."

"Then the Justice will need the lad here as witness," Lord Richard said. "But that must wait 'till we return from London and Her Majesty."

Henry imagined Clinker's wiry figure dangling from a rope and he grunted in satisfaction, hoping he would get a chance to dance around the gallows.

The landlord's shaggy brows pulled together and he leaned over in the saddle. "There'll be no assize for Kitson," he promised. "Why, none save the judgement we're all to face one day and he'll catch it hotter than most."

Lord Richard shielded his eyes from the sunlight as he stared up at Hobbling John. "He's dead then?"

"Like none other I ever saw," the big man drawled with morbid relish. "Tim Nocks, the herdsman, did find him a little after dawn, lying out in his field. He's a bold brute when all's done is Tim, yet he had the colour knocked from him this day. 'Twere him and Abel Linton, our constable this year, who I met on my way to the Justice and they shewed me what was left of Clinker."

"What was left?" Adam repeated.

"Why yes," John Chester affirmed. "In the days that are gone, in the world that was, there were butchers and slaughterers, and what I eyeballed not half an hour ago put me in mind of their crimson trade."

Lord Richard tutted and put his hand on Henry's shoulder. "An apt demise," he muttered thoughtfully. "Who did this murder?"

"I have a list of twenty would secretly sing and brag to it," the landlord replied, "and I might be one of them. Kitson was not a favourite son of these environs. But no, 'tis a worse fiend than he who has done this and Abel Linton has gone on to the Justice to set the wheels of law in motion."

"I pray you find him," Lord Richard said.

"I'm glad I could tell the tale in time before you departed," he answered with a toothless grin. "Why, the lad will rest the easier now, I'll be bound."

Henry only stared at him.

"And what of our angel?" John Chester cried. "Has he no word to say on this? If this is not a divine judgement and retribution then I know not what is. I believe your presence amongst us has brought this about."

Brindle seemed at a loss for what to say and it was then

that Henry finally found his voice. "Don't you speak to His Excellency like that!" he stormed. "You've as good as accused him of committing this murder."

John Chester's throaty laughter drowned out the rest of Henry's outraged defence. "No, no," he rumbled. "I'd not shipwreck my chance of Heaven by slandering one of its generals. 'Twas a frame of speech only, young master. Take it not so."

The boy glowered up at him but Lord Richard announced that it was time to leave and, with a final wave, Hobbling John Chester rode his horse under the sign of the Copper Cow.

"The isle of London awaits," Richard Wutton told them and they descended the rocky stairs to the quayside.

Adam o'the Cogs trailed behind, his mind filled with doubt and misgivings. Had he heard Clink Kitson's killer returning to the inn last night? The landlord's words chimed within him – who else could have sought out that villain in the dead darkness?

His suspicions festered, yet how could he think such things of the Iribian? Brindle had proven himself a hero on more than one occasion, but did that pardon murder? The boy was not certain. Clinker deserved to die, but not in the way Hobbling John described. Torn by these conflicting concerns, Adam grew silent but resolved to watch Brindle more closely than ever.

Thomas Herrick was combing his swallow-tailed beard

in his cabin when informed of their arrival and he appeared on deck greatly pleased to see them approach. Dressed that day in the pale colours of whey and watchet, he reminded Henry of a pint of cream that had soured in the sun.

"Earlier than I had expected!" he called. "My congratulations. I did think the young apprentice's foray into the darkling world of the cut-purse might have delayed you this morning. Or if not he, then Lord Wutton's partaking of Chester's costly cellar."

Then, with an eye on Brindle's midnight blue velvet, Herrick added, "And how is His Excellency? So intriguing, to array yourself in bygone fashions. I see that your eye is free of bandages. That is well – for deformity is repulsive to Her Majesty."

Boarding the vessel, Lord Richard's group watched as the canvas canopy was cranked over their heads again and the night barge's oars dipped into the water. Caught in the tidal breath, the craft was exhaled from the isle of Havering and went coursing through the Outer Darkness.

Henry's initial enthusiasm for the day ahead soon flattened as the prospect of another unrelenting voyage unfolded, but at least he did not feel ill this time. Lord Richard became ever more pensive as each land roved by. His dread of meeting the Queen once more occupied his thoughts to such an extent that he hardly heard the muted conversations around him.

Again Thomas Herrick attempted to engage Brindle in

a lively discourse, firing questions and doing his best with saccharine flattery. But, to his annoyance and consternation, the Iribian preferred to speak with the apprentices and the Queen's envoy was forced to stand idly by, excluded.

At one point, Brindle tried to rouse Lord Richard from his despondency and they talked on many different subjects. Adam endeavoured to overhear as much as possible, but Henry kept interrupting and so he only caught snatches of conversation.

"Tell me," Brindle asked. "This Uplifting you call the Beatification – how were you changed by it?"

Lord Richard regarded him with some surprise. "Changed?" he replied. "I don't know that I was changed. Days went by as before and although the mechanicals took a little getting used to, I think I remained pretty much the same."

"There must have been some difference," Brindle persisted. "Perhaps you did not feel it straightaway but it was there."

"I don't believe so. Of course it was a long time ago now. I cannot be expected to recall everything."

The Iribian stared at him encouragingly. "A long time?" he said. "Why do you say that with such emphasis?"

"Because in the old world I would have died, oh, a hundred and fifty years ago."

Brindle's face brightened. "Then you live longer here than in your former sphere," he stated. "Of course, now I understand. It resolves everything. I knew there was a reason."

"You have the answer to some riddling puzzle?" Lord Richard asked. "May I know of it?"

The Iribian took a vacillating breath, then decided against divulging what he had unravelled.

"Your pardon," he excused himself. "Not yet."

By the afternoon, everyone was subdued until, standing on the forecastle, Herrick announced that the journey was almost at its end.

Brindle and the boys gathered at the leaded window and gazed out. The edge of a modest island could just be glimpsed sliding out of view to the left while, ahead, another small land was moving towards them.

"Is that it?" Henry asked, disappointed. "I thought London was supposed to be grand and huge. Yon place is no bigger than Malmes-Wutton."

Thomas Herrick cleared his throat in mild agitation.

"We have just rounded the palace of Eltham," he said, "and that country now in our path contains the Queen's favourite estate of Greenwich. The isle of London is beyond."

Aware of the spectacle that was about to strike their eyes, Herrick stood back to allow them more room at the window and waited. Gradually, the oarsmen propelled the night barge around the leaded sky of Greenwich and all expression fell from the apprentices' faces.

"Behold the city of cities," Thomas Herrick half sang under his breath. "Fair London, the great seductress – is she not a ravishing beauty? Tempted and destroyed far too many men, she has, and will ever continue to do so."

As the protective panes of Greenwich scrolled beneath the ascending night boat, the greatest isle in the whole of Englandia appeared in the distance. Brindle murmured in disbelief.

"We never dreamed..." the blue stone whispered. "A supreme masterpiece hidden in the backwater of a region thought desolate."

Here was where the immense web of isle-linking chains converged, each connected to the inverted range of peaks which London was built upon. This was the centrepiece, the jewel of the uplifted realm, and the apprentices found themselves questioning their eyes.

Resplendent in the eternal night, the enormous country eclipsed all others they had seen in the two days of their journey. Over twenty miles it stretched in length, curving in a gradual, majestic sweep which was another five miles across.

The firmament itself was spectacular and fabulous to gaze upon. Pinnacles of elaborately chiselled masonry speared upward, echoing the spires of the churches below while, in the vaulted glass, images of clouds travelled over the diamond-shaped panes.

It was a bewitching illusion and Henry squashed his

face against the window, utterly captivated. "Only God could have done this," he whispered.

"What say you to that, Excellency?" Thomas Herrick asked of Brindle.

The Iribian ignored him, drinking in the enchantment of the uplifted isle.

Richard Wutton had not gone to the window. It had been fourteen years since he had looked on that wondrous scene and now he did not have the courage to view it again.

As the night barge floated closer the apprentices began to take notice of the other vessels sailing to and from the vast island.

"Balingers, galleons and carracks," Adam observed in fascination. "So many craft streaming about, like bees round a hive."

"'Tis a pity night has not yet fallen," Henry complained. "I wish I could see through the firmament. I'd dearly love to look down on the city as a bird would."

Hearing his words, Herrick gave a faint chuckle. "That desire is most easily granted," he said mysteriously.

Henry did not know what he meant but wasted no time trying to decipher it, there were far too many other delights to lure and command his attention. The night barge was rowed nearer, until the window was filled with London's immense splendour and the bouncing glare of the glittering sky played over the canvas canopy, splashing it with daggers of light.

Looking out at the countless, crowning towers, Adam noticed one that was greater than the rest. Two finer chains were anchored to its mighty pillars and rose up, climbing far into the blackness above where the underneath of a small fragment of jagged rock was bleakly delineated by the sun.

"What's up there?" he asked. "It's too small to be a proper island."

Thomas Herrick avoided the question and tried to direct the boy's eyes elsewhere. "The warden of the gate will soon be in sight," he chirped hastily. "His Excellency is sure to be impressed."

It was Lord Richard who answered Adam's inquiry. Finally stepping on to the forecastle, he peered through the window and, in a grim voice, said, "'Tis the Tower. Upon that barren crag stands the solitary fortress to which only the most politically dangerous prisoners are sent."

"I don't think His Excellency needs to know this painful detail," the Queen's envoy broke in. "Undesirables blemish every society; this can be of no interest to him."

"It is to me," Henry declared. "Are they manacled in irons and sent there on a galley to be tortured?"

Richard Wutton's eyes narrowed and his tone became even more solemn. "No night boat makes the journey to the Tower," he stated. "It can only be reached by those chains along which the smallest of cabins is hoisted. To be sent there means there can be no pardon, for no one ever returns. But yes – there is torture."

Disquieted by the edge in his voice, Brindle looked at Lord Richard and saw that his usually gentle features had grown hard and unforgiving.

"That is where your friend was sent?" the Iribian asked, recalling what Mistress Dritchly had told them.

Thomas Herrick clapped his hands over his ears and stared at them both, aghast and outraged. "Mention not that arch traitor's name," he cried. "I will not have it spoken aboard my night barge."

"Robert Dudley, Earl of Leicester," Lord Richard proclaimed in defiance. "I've not forgotten and if She has, I'll remind Her."

Divorcing himself from this treasonous talk, Herrick ran to the helmsman and ordered him to reach the gates as soon as possible. The view of the lonely rock disappeared as the night barge came about and sank towards the London horizon. But, instead of continuing down, it reached a certain height and remained level.

"Why aren't we heading for the entrance?" Adam asked Lord Richard.

"We are, but the threshold of London is not some underground cave, Cog Adam," he replied.

At long last, the gateway to the city rolled into sight and Henry squealed. "Pickle the Pope! It can't be true, Coggy, tell me that isn't there!"

Staring out of the window, Adam spluttered and stammered but could not answer.

‡

A monstrous, black-bearded face was glaring in at them. It was a startlingly gigantic countenance, painted in brave and brash colours. The head alone was the size of Wutton Old Place and each fierce eye was greater in length than Herrick's night barge.

"What is it?" Brindle asked Lord Richard. "A representation of your God?"

"Nay," the man replied. "That fearsome fellow is Magog, one of the two giants of the guildhall, legendary champions of London. In the old world they were not as large as this, since the Beatification they have become the porters of the entire island and have grown in stature."

Standing upon an outcrop of rock, the colossus loomed in front of London's leaded sky, wearing the helm and armour of antiquity. In one of the tremendous hands he wielded a sword, while in the other he carried a mighty set of keys.

Twice a day the mammoth keys were raised and lowered to allow entry, and now they were hoisted high. Exposed below was a huge opening in the vaulted sky and, through that, Henry and Adam espied enticing glimpses of the city beyond.

Steadily, the night boat veered about until the great entrance was directly ahead and the oars were lifted. Then, to the apprentices' great wonder, the titanic Roman face turned to follow their craft's approach and, from the open mouth, there galed the tidal breath.

Buffeted by the whirling squall, the vessel journeyed in

through the monumental gateway and immediately the golden rays of a summer evening flared through the window.

The city of London spread out before and beneath them and, when the canopy ceased to quake, Thomas Herrick commanded that the canvas be lifted.

With almost unbearable slowness, the two halves of the awning parted and fresh air and light flooded over the deck.

Racing to the sides, Henry and Adam did not know where to look first. They whisked their heads left and right, until Lord Richard pointed behind them. With a shock, they found themselves staring straight into a second enormous face.

Here was Gog, the second of the London giants. The same staggering size as the one who stood guard outside, this effigy portrayed a barbarian, wearing only a coat of leaves and crowned with a wreath of woven twigs. In his massive hand he clutched an axe and, on this side of the firmament, it was that which lowered every twelve hours to govern the departure of ships.

Henry cheered at him then stared over the side.

The aperture in the vaulted sky was situated twenty fathoms above the ground and the night barge gently descended past Gog's raised arm and his carved raiment of leaves.

Far below, the statue's legs straddled the banks of a

wide, crowded river and Lord Richard informed the apprentices that they were looking at the Thames.

Down through the balmy airs the vessel glided and the boys gazed at the surrounding city, breathless and awestruck. The lowering sun gilded every building and the church spires turned to golden needles pricking through a shimmering cloth. Dominating the skyline, the medieval fastness of St Paul's transcended all, proclaiming the power and magnificence of the Almighty to rich and poor alike.

Henry whistled through his teeth at the scale and grandeur of this strange landscape. "Makes our home look like an ant hill," he marvelled. "I never want to leave – not ever. What goes on in all those streets and lanes? Who lives in the hundreds of houses? I want to explore every last corner."

Leaning on the deck rail, Adam rested his chin on his hands. "I wish Jack could have witnessed this," he sighed.

Brindle closed his eyes and inhaled deeply. Out into those foreign quarters he set his sapient senses scouting and thrilled to the warm pulse of the life which teemed there. The myriad scents which greeted him were an overwhelming, chaotic tumult of delight and squalor. Delicious sweet fragrances wafted from the private gardens of the wealthy but, carried on the same breeze, was the foetid stench of open drains.

"How many dwell in this land?" he asked Lord Richard. The master of Malmes-Wutton tapped his fingertips together. "Oh, I should think at least thirty thousand souls," he said. "There were many more in the old world and countless here have died since the Uplifting. The plague and various sicknesses are frequent visitors to the greater isles."

"Thirty thousand," Brindle murmured and only Adam noticed that the Iribian's hand strayed unconsciously to the reaping hook attached to his belt and his long fingers were trembling.

Effecting a stately, balanced arc, the night barge floated downward to a spot where the river foamed and boiled and the gold of the scarlet vessel's decorative scrollwork burned like fiery serpents in the rays of the setting sun. With the slightest of yawing jolts, it touched the water and the oars were lowered.

They had finally arrived in the celebrated isle of London. Yet, of the four who had set out from Malmes-Wutton, only two would return.

CHAPTER 3

Gloriana

The River Thames was crowded with many other craft; from great, swollen-bellied galleons with a pageant of banners and pennants fluttering from their masts, to the small, island-confined boats of the ferrying watermen. Thomas Herrick's scarlet and gold night barge navigated between them, resembling a vain bird with exotic plumage pushing through a crowd of drab river fowl.

Returning to the forecastle, the Queen's envoy

commanded that his horse be brought up from below. Then, holding the mechanical's reins with one hand, he struck an heroic pose and lifted his head high, the cream and blue feathers ruffling in the band of his hat.

"And so returns the valiant conqueror of the Wutton philistines," Lord Richard said in an audible aside to Brindle and the apprentices. "One might be forgiven for thinking he is a caesar of Rome returning in triumph from the Punic Wars."

The heroic stance sagged a little when Herrick overheard but he recovered quickly. Everyone watching must be certain he had achieved his mission and he called for the Iribian to stand at his side. "Come, Excellency," he cried. "The bridge will soon be in view."

"Give him his moment," Lord Richard advised.

"What shall I do when I meet your Sovereign?" Brindle asked. "How should I be?"

"Be true to yourself, friend. No one could ask for more than that."

"True to myself?" the Iribian echoed and for an instant his face looked wretched and desperate. "No, that is what I must never be." Stepping up beside Thomas Herrick, Brindle's tall, distinct appearance immediately robbed him of any feigned glamour. The balm merchant's powerful presence was infinitely more aristocratic, and Richard Wutton was amused to see that his natural, noble bearing was almost princely by comparison.

"See, Excellency," Herrick prattled. "The bridge."

Behind the moving forest of masts, Brindle beheld a great stone structure spanning the river, upon which a hotchpotch of timbered buildings were crammed in an untidy line. Many projected precariously over the water, supported and braced only by stout wooden beams. In front of the most ornate edifice was a length of railing where many people had gathered to look down at the newly arrived night boat.

Thomas Herrick gave them an appreciative wave but the subsequent cries of "'Tis the angel!" left him in no doubt as to whom they were looking at.

"They do you much honour," he told Brindle with an indulgent smile. "The denizens of London hate all foreigners with a heated passion; already you seem to have won their hearts."

Overhearing, Lord Richard was sure that this was a matter Herrick would certainly repeat to the Queen's jealous ears.

The conceited man pointed to the huge wooden piers that the bridge was founded upon, around which the river raced in violent torrents. "Now we must shoot yonder rapids," he told Brindle. "Many faint hearts choose to alight here and await their craft on the other side, but we shall have no fear and the mob will love you the more for it."

Into the shadow of one of the arches the night barge went and the swift current rocked it from side to side until

Henry began to feel ill again. Staring up at the dark underside of the bridge, Adam enjoyed every instant of the rushing ride and revelled in the roar of the echoing waters.

Then they were through, to the sound of cheers from above. Brindle gazed up at the onlookers, his easy dignity extracting shouts of praise and bursts of bawdy song.

If they had only known the thoughts which festered within this visitor, they would have sung a different tune. Inside the Iribian a dreadful conflict had begun and when he saw their happy faces his mind flooded with the blackest cravings. How much longer could he contain and suppress these impulses? How he yearned to abandon his higher reason and submit to that overpowering instinct.

Once more his hand went reaching for the hilt of his reaping hook but, with a tremendous effort, he dragged it away and fixed his eyes upon the deck, where his stare collided with that of Adam. The boy pretended not to have noticed and turned quickly away.

Thomas Herrick watched the crowds with curdling interest, then observed with even more irritation the large number of other vessels sailing this stretch of the Thames at such a late hour of the day. The rumour of the Suffolk Miracle had spread throughout the island and, although he was pleased that everyone would know it was he who had brought in the celestial visitor, he also knew that the Queen would be furious.

The cathedral of Southwarke reared to the left, followed

by open fields and the theatres of Bankside. On the right,
the lofty height of St Paul's was succeeded by the mouth of
the Fleet River and the mansions of the wealthy until at
last, around the river bend, opposite the Lambeth Marsh,
the largest palace in Europe came into sight. A rambling
collection of imposing buildings, streaming with standards,
the royal residence of Whitehall was intended to impress
and its grandeur was not squandered on Brindle. Reaching
into the Thames there jutted a wide stone terrace and,
gathered there, beneath a kaleidoscope of bunting, was a
great assemblage of guards, pages, heralds, courtiers and
councillors. At the first glimpse of the scarlet night barge,
forty mechanical trumpeters stationed along the river stairs
blared a resounding welcome and Richard Wutton wiped
his sweating palms. The moment he dreaded had arrived.

As Herrick's night barge advanced, every other craft
pulled out of its path, clearing a direct course to the
terrace. The Queen's envoy puffed out his chest, adjusted
his creamy dollop of a hat and the vessel drew alongside the
stairs.

"Excellency," he said to Brindle. "Her Grace awaits."

Again the trumpeters let loose a joyful blast and the
gangway was slid across to the steps which were covered in
a sky blue cloth.

Leaving his horse on the deck, Thomas Herrick was the
first to disembark, then he turned and executed a practised
bow to invite the Iribian to follow.

Brindle stared over at the hundreds of people gathered upon the terrace and suppressed the urge which swelled unbidden within his soul. Only the mechanicals were silent now, for the gathering was whispering or exclaiming at his remarkable appearance – even the Yeomen of the Crown were murmuring to one another.

Behind Brindle the sun was setting over the marsh. Its rays glinted in his chestnut-coloured hair and glowed in the yellow metal of his torc, forming a bright halo around his head. The gasps from the attendant crowd increased.

With a cautious glance at Lord Richard, Brindle left the night barge but, before he could set foot upon the stairs, a tremendous, deafening roar came raging over the topmost step. There, prowling into view, came a fabulous golden lion.

"Nutmeg pudding!" Henry mouthed in wonderment.

It was the most sumptuous creation the apprentices had ever seen. Almost the size of a small pony, the beast was an heraldic interpretation yet it remained a fantastic feat of motive science.

The most proud and regal of visages had been wrought into shape from the precious, glittering metal, over which a complex intertwining relief of curling fur had been painstakingly chased. Beneath the ferocious-looking brows, two large rubies were set and, framing this mighty, kingly head, was a luxuriant mane made from coiled ribbons of flame-coloured velvet which rippled and churned like a rolling sea as the massive shoulders propelled the creature forward.

Yet, incredibly, a rider sat high upon the lion's back. Clinging to the lush mane as the mechanical padded powerfully down the stairs was a little, wide-eyed child. She could not have been more than seven years old and was dressed in a miniature green gown. She wore a garland of flowers about her neck and more blooms were woven into her white-blonde hair.

With a marvellously fluid gait, the lion approached the gangway. Adam's mind reeled as he tried to calculate how many pendulums were swinging within that gorgeous casing. Raising its right paw and swishing its jointed tail, the resplendent creature assumed the *passant guardant* posture of the three lions depicted upon the royal standards hoisted overhead and gave a thundering roar.

Blushing deeply, the girl looked across at Brindle and it was plain that she was more scared of him than the fearsome mechanical beneath her. Yet, taking a deep breath, she smiled prettily and recited the welcoming oration she had been bidden to say.

"Most honoured attendant from the abode of bliss,
Enter thou this land which God hath filled with beauty.
Behold our isle, hallowed by the Almighty's kiss.
Where Gloriana reigns, our Queen in Majesty."

Having ended her rhyme, the child tugged at the lion's mane and the creature returned with her to the terrace where it lay down, dangling its wide paws over the topmost step.

Taking note of this pomp and show, Lord Richard understood that Elizabeth of Englandia meant for the Iribian to know precisely who was monarch here. Even if he had hailed from Heaven, she was taking no chances and was forcefully asserting her right of sovereignty.

Again the trumpets blew. From behind the halberdiers, maidens dressed in white stepped forward on to the blue cloth, bearing shallow baskets filled with rose petals. Into the air they cast the delicate contents and a roseate blizzard swirled about the terrace while ten mechanical drummers pounded a steady rhythm.

A sudden applause broke out, but the noise was the beating of many wings as a hundred silver doves were let loose into the gentle storm of falling petals. The dazzle from their burnished feathers was blinding; the reflected sun flashed and sparked and everyone upon the night barge was compelled to cover their eyes from the intense glare.

Then, through this dancing brilliancy, to the accompanying music of ringing hooves, emerged a tall and radiant shape. Adam and Henry fell to their knees but Lord Richard remained standing and, similarly uncowed, Brindle returned the newcomer's appraising inspection.

A past mistress of orchestrating her perceived image,

Elizabeth, the Queen, had calculated every aspect of her appearance. Perched upon a sublimely crafted silver unicorn, she was a compelling vision of purity and power. Arrayed from head to foot in white silks and taffeta, she seemed almost to have stemmed from the realm of Heaven herself. Pearls shimmered like milky dew over her bodice and surcote, and even her skin was pale as a spring cloud. The only hint of colour came from a gold headdress fashioned in the shape of a rayed sun, and the deep, reddish-yellow of her hair which tumbled between the spearing points was as generous light spilling from the wan sky.

Looking no older than she had that night one hundred and seventy-five years ago, when she lay close to death with the smallpox, the daughter of Henry the Eighth and Anne Boleyn was a handsome woman of noble proportion. In all the uplifted world, and the old that had been left behind, there had never been anyone like her. Her long, oval face with its high forehead, aquiline nose and thin, firm mouth displayed the Tudor qualities of strength and determination, but the subtle intelligence which schemed and smouldered in her large dark eyes she had inherited solely from her mother.

Brindle beheld her and his senses swam. In his travels to remote spheres he had not encountered anyone in whom such eminence or immortal majesty was so naturally invested. For the first time since his night boat had crashed its way into Malmes-Wutton, he felt inferior and plebeian.

Unable to endure her arch scrutiny any longer, he bowed his head. Behind, Lord Richard ground his teeth together, saddened to see him fall under her enchantment as so many others had done before.

Encased in a frosty aloofness, the Queen stirred, the taffeta of her gown rustling in the fallen silence as she raised a slender hand to greet them. Then she spoke. Her voice was crisp and clear, tempered with a highborn confidence that was both adamantine and beyond disputing.

"You are well come to Our humble realm, Excellency," she declared. "We are most honoured to have you in Our midst. It was an unhappy misfortune which cast you to so distant an isle, for We could have enjoyed your company earlier had you been sent to a place closer to Our royal person."

The Iribian detected a criticism of Lord Richard and the spell dissipated.

"Gracious Madam," he said, lifting his head and knotting his brows. "I have been shown only courtesy and kindness. If it were not for the mercy and benevolent charity of Lord Richard Wutton, I would have perished."

The Queen's composure was nettled and for the first time she cast her eyes over the figures still aboard the night barge. "Glad am I to hear it," she announced gravely. "No subject of Mine would dare show offence to so important a visitor to these shores as yourself, Excellency. No matter who they be or whom they have known."

For a moment her face grew scornful, then the mood melted and she beckoned to Thomas Herrick to assist her from the exquisite unicorn. A mechanical ermine, covered in snowy fur, sat dutifully upon her lap and she passed it to one of her attendant ladies as Herrick took her hand.

"You have done exceeding well, Sirrah," she commended him when her satin-slippered foot touched the blue cloth in a swirl of embroidered petticoats. "Your Prince shall not forget it."

Herrick pointed his toe and made his expert bow. "I exist only to serve," he said.

"Would there were others who loved their Sovereign the same," she answered in a loud voice, with a darting glance at Lord Richard. Then, turning to Brindle once more, she summoned him to join her.

The Iribian left the gangway and ascended the stairs to stand at her side.

Elizabeth bestowed a cordial smile upon him. "In honour of your arrival, Excellency, a banquet has been prepared. Let us repair thither and you shall sit with Me. I would know the reason of your coming and why you did choose My realm above all others. Was it because the Almighty is not a Catholic?"

She laughed and the rest of the court fell in with her mirth, but Brindle stood apart.

"I am from Iribia," he informed her. "Whatever you may..."

Her raised hand silenced him. "Speak of it at table," she said firmly. "The tale will be the sweeter accompanied by sugared dainties."

Brindle understood that she did not want anything further to be said before so many people.

"As you wish," he agreed. "And Lord Richard and the children?"

The Queen's smile faded and she lifted her hand dismissively. "A place will be found for him, yet I would not weary your young companions any more. They look as pale and drawn as evening shadows." The hem of her gown swept over the steps as she spun around and lured Brindle after her. "To the banqueting house then," she proclaimed. "There is much I desire to learn."

With a brisk, purposeful stride she led him through the sea of people and Lord Richard and the apprentices crossed the gangway, only to see the crowd surge away from them, pulled in the Queen's magnetic wake. The trumpeters were dismissed and both the unicorn and the lion were taken to the treasure house, where they were stilled and locked away securely.

"Did you ever see anyone as beautiful as She?" Henry breathed, but Adam made no answer. His suspicions of Brindle were uppermost in his mind. Was the Iribian as noble and heroic as he appeared? What if there was a hidden, sinister side to his nature?

Richard Wutton grumbled into his beard, then

observed that the Queen's privy councillors were waiting for them at the top of the steps. At the forefront of that stern-looking group stood Sir Francis Walsingham and Sir William Cecil, and the master of Malmes-Wutton resigned himself to a tiresome confrontation.

Among that intimidating gathering, Adam recognised a white-bearded man and, standing at his side, was a squat figure made of copper.

"Doctor Dee and Lantern!" he cried, running up the steps to meet them. "I hoped I would see you here."

The old astrologer bowed solemnly and his mechanical secretary did the same. "Did I not foretell that providence would throw us together again?" the Doctor said, the corners of his snowy moustache lifting. "I must confess, even I did not expect it to be so soon."

"If time permits," the boy suggested, "perhaps I could see your library."

"Nothing would please me more," Doctor Dee told him, "if, as you say, time permits for a visit to Mortlake."

"Praise be," Henry groaned as he joined them. "What a joyful treat that will prove."

Hearing his flat, unenthusiastic tone, the astrologer regarded him darkly. "A sceptical star guides your destiny, Master Wattle," he said. "Perhaps I will cast your horoscope and see to what grisly demise your insolent young life shall come to."

That silenced Henry and Doctor Dee returned his

attention to Adam. "Alas, there is no time for such pleasantries," he lamented. "Her Grace is no lover of children and so you must be denied attendance at the feast this night. Lodging has been prepared for you in the palace. Lantern will usher you thence, if you would care to follow him."

The apprentices looked uncertainly at Lord Richard, who gave his assent with the briefest of nods. So Adam and Henry left the terrace, guided by the tubby copper secretary who proceeded in front of them, hopping and skipping under a covered walkway to demonstrate how well the repair to his knee was holding up.

When the children were out of earshot, Lord Richard approached the councillors. Dressed in his habitual, stark black, Sir Francis Walsingham greeted him with a predatory glint in his eyes. "A singular visitation," he said, brushing aside the courtesies. "You will tell me all you know of this strange emissary."

Lord Richard had been stealing himself for a quarrel with Her Majesty. One of her minions, albeit the notorious head of her secret service, held no fear for him now. "You mean to say you have not already been told?" he asked with mock surprise. "Dear me, Walsingham – your web is not so tight as I believed. Pray enlighten me – have you caused the death of any worthy masters of motive science in the two weeks since last we met?"

Walsingham's hooded eyes glowered at him but, before he

354

‡

could retaliate, the anxious William Cecil intervened. "My Lords," he said, "lay past conflict aside. Recriminations must needs wait. This visitor, Richard – where does he come from? Why is he here? Will he side with us against France and Spain?"

Lord Richard pulled away from them in disgust. "Death and war!" he snapped. "Why are your minds so hot for the shedding of blood? Have we learnt nothing?"

"You are polluted with the ideals of the weak and naïve," Walsingham said with cold disdain. "Did you not hear me at our last meeting? Never have relations with the Catholic powers been so hostile. We are teetering upon the brink of war, Lord Richard. The ambassadors are denied entry to court and they were forbidden to attend this gathering. Yet they, like the common people, know of it and have heard the rumours of your outlandish guest. The agents of our enemies will balk at nothing to deprive Englandia of any advantage this 'heavenly messenger' might give."

Lord Richard shook his head as if the Queen's councillors were infants. "Brindle is no more an angel than I am," he scoffed. "I'm mightily saddened at your credulity, Sir Francis."

"I speak not of angels!" Walsingham snarled back. "Do not paint me with the ignorance of the mob. Yet I do know that his night boat is unlike any within this uplifted world; perhaps he possesses other devices that would be new to us and to our enemies."

"What devices?" Lord Richard demanded.

"Weapons!" came the stinging reply. "He will have weapons."

"Then you don't know Brindle," Lord Richard returned. "He is a dealer in fragrance, not a soldier. A reaping hook is all he bears."

Doctor Dee interposed between them. "Her Grace must not be kept waiting," the old astrologer said. "Let us to the banqueting house. You may continue your squabbling there."

Richard Wutton marched away from them and the councillors hurried behind him – except for Walsingham. Alone at the top of the steps, the face of the Queen's spymaster grew even more austere and unyielding.

"Nevertheless," he muttered to himself in a voice of silken menace, "though Wutton's guest be a seller of daffydils, he will still have knowledge of weapons. Knowledge that he must reveal unto me, or verily I shall have it wrung from him."

And with that he strode after the others, leaving the terrace deserted, save for the petals which drifted over the blue cloth in the cooling summer airs.

Across the crowded Thames, reclining in a chair covered with velvet cushions, upon the deck of an elegant night barge, the Count de Feria, Don Gomez, lowered his spyglass and considered what he had seen.

"Ho, Lizabeth," he chortled to himself. "So, You play at the virgin again. What a drearsome performance that is, no? Again with the unicorn, again with the stupid ermine and all that white...! Holy Mother of God! Too many symbols – why She always dress in allegory and metaphor? Of the hat, is best I say nothing."

The Spanish ambassador was an impish-looking man, swarthy and saturnine in appearance. His hair and neat, pointed beard were dark and the clothes he wore were of the richest black, leavened only by the jet beads known as bugles, which glittered over his doublet like a thousand miniature versions of his own twinkling eyes.

"What did you make of their celestial visitor?" the figure standing behind his chair asked.

De Feria looked up at him and, with a ready wink, said breezily, "Is a great ape of the Indus, shorn of hair and tamed to wear hosen."

Alvaro de Quadra, the grey-haired Bishop of Aquila, despised the ambassador's levity and stared through the bustling river traffic to survey the sprawling palace. "Do you not rage to be banished from court at this momentous hour?" he demanded. "Who can tell what sinister and injurious intelligence these English will gain from this person?"

De Feria continued to smile, but all frivolity was quenched – deposed by a chilling stillness. "No," he stated suavely. "I not rage. I have learn not to let fury rule my head and shut out reason. He who rages, loses. My anger, he seethe and simmer and I stay strong. Oh, Alvaro, if you knew how I am detesting of this ignoble heretic and Her repulsing subjects. Yet the chief hate I brew for Her – illegitimate daughter of a despotic king and his lewd courtesan. Soon She taste the stew of my loathing, then it will scald and roast Her."

The Bishop nodded in heartfelt agreement at this damning condemnation. "What of the visitor?" he asked.

"No profit must She gain from this," de Feria vowed. "I will do all in my power to thwart Her. I will plot and conspire – already a pretty idea I have."

Sucking the air through his grinning teeth, the Spanish ambassador grimaced sharply and pressed his fingertips to his cheek. "Saints defend me," he moaned. "The hole in my tooth, he no like the stabbings of this cold air. We go make ready."

"Ready?" repeated Alvaro. "What do you propose, Don Gomez?"

The Count de Feria stretched out his legs and settled into the cushions as he gingerly probed his teeth with his tongue.

"Lizabeth's 'angel'," he said eventually. "He either depart with us this night for Spain – or he die here."

CHAPTER 4

The Queen's Salamander

The banqueting house of Whitehall Palace was a huge timber building, boasting two hundred and ninety-two windows and covered in canvas that had been cunningly painted to resemble stone.

With the Queen at his side Brindle entered, and his keen senses devoured the feast of vapours which wrapped themselves about him.

Thomas Herrick's long letter to Elizabeth had spared no detail. From the moment she received it that very morning, she had been at pains to ensure her mysterious guest would find much to delight him. A frenzy of preparation had ensued. The banqueting house had been swept clean and rosemary-scented water sprinkled over the floor, while perfumed bellows had blown juniper smoke into every corner. Great quantities of pansies – her favourite flower – had been culled from the palace gardens and brought in to keep the air sweet, and garlands of greenery festooned the walls.

The Queen herself was wearing a silver pomander, hanging from her waist upon a slender chain, and when she studied Brindle's savouring features, she knew it was well done. "Come sit beside Me," her usually forthright voice invited with coquettish glee. "You will tell Me of your Iribia and the balms that you trade."

Brindle allowed himself to be drawn deeper into the great room.

Countless candles had already been lit and the bright arrowheads of their flames sought out the gold plate displayed to impress visiting dignitaries and gleamed in the field of stars painted on the ceiling. Tiers of benches ran along the walls while, at the farthest end, upon a low stage, a table stood at right angles to them. At the centre of this elevated board, beneath a cloth of gold, was a velvet-covered throne and it was to this that the Queen took Brindle.

As the favoured courtiers, including Thomas Herrick, came streaming in behind them, Elizabeth seated herself and bade the Iribian to occupy the chair on her right.

"You no longer believe I am a herald of your God," Brindle stated.

The Queen's large eyes appraised him, weighing up how best to deal with this remarkable guest. "I have forbidden the archbishop to attend," she said candidly. "That alone should tell you. I perform the role My subjects expect of Me. It is they who, for the present, hold you divine. Your presence amongst Us was impossible to cloak and keep secret, Excellency. Out there on the terrace, I did what was expected. I am My people's anointed Prince – as head of their church, I must not be seen to grudge your arrival."

"And yet?"

Elizabeth gave an evasive smile. "I have not decided the 'yet'," she answered. "It may be you are a French spy and this an elaborate deception."

"I am no spy."

"No?" she teased. "I fear that the tally of things you are not will be o'erlong before the evening is done. But now I am concerned lest you think My welcome was wholly false. I would you know that I am highly pleased to receive you into My land – from wherever you hail."

Richard Wutton and the Queen's privy councillors were the last to enter the banqueting house. Lord Richard had been hard-pressed by many questions and was feeling in need of a strong drink. By the time they assumed their seats at the raised table, Brindle had told Her Majesty the tale of how his night boat had burst into the Malmes-Wutton firmament.

"And are We to expect any more of your kind thundering into Our skies?" she asked. "I like not that prospect, however gallant and pleasing your society might be. Our protective heavens are not wasp traps; We cannot have them littered with shipwrecks."

The Iribian assured her that no others would be arriving. "These islands are unknown to my race," he said. "Chance alone carried me hither and left me marooned, without hope of rescue."

"A tragic plight," the Queen concurred. "To be isolated and beyond aid. I too have known times of black despair. You must pray, Excellency. The Lord God delivered Me from a prison unto a palace – He may do the same for you."

Brindle's brows slid together. "Perhaps it is best if Your God leaves me here," he murmured.

"You sink into melancholy too easily," she berated him. "I could furnish you with a vessel to seek out your home and open trade links with your kind."

"Your night boats are not made for such long journeys," he answered gravely. "Besides, I do not think You would find the arrangement either beneficial or to Your liking."

Elizabeth's head reared. "Surely there are sufficient fragrances of note in My kingdom worthy of exchange," she protested.

The Iribian wavered before making a reply. "Oh, indeed,"

he said. "The scent of the bloom you call the rose would be most highly revered. I did hope to reward Lord Richard by giving him the monopoly with my people. He would have become the wealthiest and most important man in this uplifted world."

This answer did not please the Queen at all and beneath the table her foot began tapping irritably. Wearing a frosty expression, she avoided the impudent grin which had fixed itself to Richard Wutton's face and continued. "Does no other scent please you?"

Brindle let his eyes wander the crowded room and his nostrils trembled hungrily. "Oh, yes," he admitted carelessly. "I have discovered another, a thousand times more rare."

"May I know of it?"

The balm trader closed his eyes and when he replied it was as if he were speaking from a fair dream.

"It is a most subtle yet enticing aroma," he murmured, the blue stone of his torc glowing pale at his throat. "Outside the range of any perceptions save those of an Iribian. It is an unparagoned scent and one I never thought to find again. The original source was exhausted many years ago when I was young and now, in the sphere of my home, the smallest measure of the stuff is valued beyond price."

"Yet you have discovered a new supply, here – in My realm?"

"Oh, yes, Majesty," Brindle breathed. "There is an abundance here. A whole new vein to quarry."

"This is the most splendid of tidings," she cried. "And you believe your kind would be interested in this fragrance?"

The nostrils in her guest's unusual face began to glisten with moisture. "If they knew of its existence," he whispered, "no power living could keep them away. Of all the bouquets scattered throughout the great garden of the immeasurable darkness, there is but one peerless scent. To me and my kind it is sacred."

"You fascinate me. Why does this nonsuch odour have this hold over you?"

"Plants and beasts have odours," Brindle said. "This is a hallowed distillation of essence. It is everything to us: restorative, heal all, heart's ease, renewer of strength, repairer of wounds, anodynous mender of hurts. Once savoured, its virtue can never be forgotten and the soul weeps in torture to revel in it again. For an Iribian there can be no truer euphoria, no higher state of being, and too long now has my life trudged the melancholic mist without it."

The Queen listened with mounting astonishment. "All that eloquence for a smell," she uttered, waving the pomander under her long nose.

"Battles and wars have been fought for the merest catch of that scent," Brindle told her. "Our history is burdened and stained with terrible, demented campaigns."

"Do you hear that, Walsingham?" Elizabeth said with a glance loaded with meaning. "Battles and wars."

"I am glad that our visitor is not a gardener only," her spymaster answered with a sideways look at Richard Wutton.

"Yes, well, leave that for the present," she commanded before turning back to Brindle. "You must assist and guide Us in the construction of new ships, Excellency. Vessels capable of traversing the great distance to your home. I am already a tanner and tinsmith, weaver and shepherd – a dealer in perfume is a situation I would add to the list most gladly. Consider it a bargain then, should you contact your folk; the Sovereign Prince of this realm will be the One to benefit by the new commerce. Such a contract is only deserved and honourable."

Brindle stared at her aghast. "You do not want this covenant," he warned. "This is a thing best left in shadow."

"Do not presume to know My wants, Excellency," she retorted. "I do not think Philip of Spain would make so generous an offer. He and his cardinals would have had you burned for a snouting devil if you had suffered the misfortune of foundering in his realm."

The Iribian wrenched his eyes away and drove his senses to seek out the innocent scent of the cut flowers. "Your pardon, Majesty," he said thickly. "Within my heart a war is raging. You cannot know how tempted I am by Your offer, but my conscience grapples with itself. If I yield to my desire then I am lost and damned forever."

The Queen's foot tapped more rapidly. "Let your heart

not rage over long, Excellency," she told him, before raising her voice above the buzz of the general chatter and calling out, "Bid the Tizzys serve. Our glasses are empty and the plates are bare."

In the royal household, among the various mechanical musicians and fanciful beasts, there were many constructed servants who performed the menial tasks. To show the measure of her wealth and prestige, however, Elizabeth the Queen also owned a number of more sophisticated mannequins. To honour her, they were modelled upon her image. The most common type, of which she had twenty, were the Tizzys. These wooden figures executed the mundane duties of serving at meals and fetching food from the kitchens. The second form of mechanical was that of the brass Besses. There were five of these, and it was their responsibility to tend Her Majesty's extensive wardrobe, caring for the hundreds of fabulous gowns in her possession. Lastly, there were the two jewelled Elizas which remained always in the Queen's bedchamber as trusted ladies in waiting, under the supervision of Katherine Ashley.

From the corners of the banqueting house where they had been standing motionless, a dozen Tizzys stepped forward bearing jars of wine.

Carved into the likeness of Elizabeth as a young girl, the Tizzys were dressed in the green and white livery of the Tudors. In the centre of each high forehead the emblem of the double rose formed their stilling crests. They moved silently about the room, filling up the empty vessels and bringing out the comfits and elaborate sugar sculptures known as subtleties.

"Tell me, Excellency," the Queen resumed, "what think you of this palace? 'Tis the largest in the whole of Europe. It was greatly altered and augmented by my father; there is a splendid, full-length portrait of him in the mural of the privy chamber which you must see."

Lord Richard had downed his first goblet of wine and was wiggling a finger at one of the Tizzys when he overheard Elizabeth's words. "Friend Brindle cannot interpret flat likenesses," he piped up. "No matter who they're of."

The members of the council hissed at him and Doctor Dee placed a warning hand upon his arm.

Before the Queen could remonstrate, Brindle tried to appease her. "And what of Your mother?" he asked. "Are there paintings of her also?"

He could hardly have said anything worse and Lord Richard spluttered into his newly poured wine.

"No," she said in a voice of whetted steel. "There are none of her."

"No full-length ones at any rate," Lord Richard burbled into his goblet. "Perhaps just the head."

Fortunately, Doctor Dee had coughed over this last remark and the Queen did not hear it.

"Now, Excellency," she said, "I have steered the talk

too long. My good advisors greatly crave speech with you."

One of the Tizzys stepped on to the platform, bearing a dish of sugared spices and fruit preserved in syrup, and began serving these dainty sweets to the guests.

"You spoke of war, Excellency," Walsingham began with interest. "Doubtless your armaments are as exceptional as your night boat."

"My craft bore no arms," Brindle answered. "We are forbidden to do so."

Walsingham pressed his fingertips together and his interrogating stare jabbed from beneath his hooded eyelids. "Yet you have knowledge of weapons and engines of destruction?" he urged.

Brindle nodded reluctantly. "I am versed in their making."

"How efficacious and devastating would they be?"

"How devastating do you wish? I know of fire globes which could raze this palace to the ground in moments."

The other councillors murmured in disbelief but Walsingham squirmed with pleasure. "You will share this knowledge?" he demanded.

"And damn my conscience further?"

"This is a holy war. If you help rid us of this Catholic infection, the Almighty would smile upon you."

Brindle shifted uncomfortably. He did not want to involve himself in the petty politics of this realm, yet how could he avoid it now he was compelled to remain here?

Over the rim of his cup, Richard Wutton beheld his unease and saved him from Walsingham's rapier gaze by musing aloud, "What I never could understand is this. If the Almighty despises the Catholics as much as you insist He does, why did He include them in the Beatification?"

The Queen's spymaster turned a face on him that made Lord Richard return to his wine. Seeing his cup drained, the Tizzy took up the jar and, with a slightly trembling arm, replenished him.

"A globe of flame," Elizabeth marvelled. "You seem very much acquainted with that element, Excellency. Your night boat descends and you fall from its fiery interior, and now you talk of these destroying heats. Ah, I have it – you shall be my Salamander. That is what I name you."

From the look on Brindle's face it was clear he did not understand and he turned to Lord Richard.

"Doctor Dee!" The Queen called, brusquely cutting through her guest's confusion. "Explain."

The old astrologer cleared his throat and leaned across to Brindle, impeding any comment from Lord Richard. "The Salamander," he began, "is a creature of the old world which was believed to thrive in the domain of fire. Her Grace is wont to bestow upon Her favoured ministers and courtiers names best suited to their natures or position."

Elizabeth slapped the table. "Just so!" she exclaimed. "Sir William Cecil is my 'Spirit', Walsingham, my 'Moor'..."

"And what of your 'Eyes'?" Lord Richard's voice broke in.

There was an awful silence and everyone shot frightened glances at the Queen. This time he had gone too far. Robert Dudley had been Elizabeth's Eyes. No one had so much as mentioned him in front of her for fourteen years and all held their breath, dreading the imminent wrathful reaction. Her Majesty's face was a vision of white-lipped fury as she glared at the master of Malmes-Wutton. For an instant, Brindle believed she would explode with wrath and strike the man.

But Lord Richard's words had stripped away those fourteen years and in her mind she was sitting in a pavilion on the bank of a lake within the isle of Kenilworth. An artificial moon was climbing into the night sky and she was in the embrace of the one true love of her life. It was her own voice which spoke the affectionate name.

"My Eyes," she heard herself whispering. "Oh, my sweet Eyes."

The arms of her memory clasped her tightly and she cast back her head as his remembered lips caressed her throat.

As swiftly as it was summoned, the past vanished and the Queen crushed the old emotions she had kept hidden these many years. Lord Richard's brows were raised in censure and her temper came scalding to the surface.

"God's death!" her voice rumbled like a gathering storm. "I will stomach no more! Get out, Sirrah – go away from me before I do that which I should have done fourteen years ago and separate a traitor's head from its shoulders. Go – be off. I am sick of your sour puling."

Draining his third goblet, Richard Wutton rose from the table. "It is my great joy to leave, Your Grace," he announced. "The sooner I quit this place the happier I shall be."

Brindle showed signs that he would join him, but Lord Richard bade him stay. "You have not been given leave, friend," he said with a genial smile. "You must remain at the Queen's pleasure, till She has done with your company."

With that he left the banqueting house.

Watching him depart, composed and dignified, it took all of Elizabeth's formidable will to keep her temper under control.

"The man is an imbecile," Walsingham commented.

"But a righteous and honourable one," Doctor Dee added.

"The most dangerous kind," the spymaster returned tartly.

Her hands clenched, the Queen dragged her attention away from the open door. Now she could deal with the Iribian freely, without interruption from that stupid, stubborn man.

"You have not drunk of your wine nor touched the comfits," she observed. "Do they not please you?"

Still gazing at the entrance, Brindle could sense Richard Wutton moving through the palace.

"We are not accustomed to ask a question twice," Elizabeth rapped sharply.

Brindle started. "Your pardon," he said. "My thoughts were with Lord Richard – he commands much respect from me."

"And My fare does not?" she persisted. "Have you seen the subtleties? There is one in the shape of Paul's Church, and another is of the unicorn upon which I rode to greet you."

She signalled the attendant Tizzy. The mannequin walked unsteadily to fetch one of the sculptures.

"I do not find nourishment in the same way as You," Brindle stated to the Queen. "I meant no offence."

"What an extraordinary people you are!" she exclaimed. "To thrive upon scent alone. Perhaps I should make you my head gardener."

"Perhaps You should," he answered.

Laughing, she turned to Doctor Dee and demanded, "What do you make of my Salamander? Have you consulted the stars on this matter?"

The astrologer fingered his white beard. "Yes, Majesty," he said. "They are full of portent and signs of great battles to come. They have shown a great burning in the heavens; a Spanish ship will soon be blazing – above this very isle."

"Listen to that, Walsingham!" she cried in delight. "Your fears are over. Ah, here comes one of the subtleties. See, my Salamander, it is cunningly crafted into the shape of a dragon, another dweller in the flames."

Carrying the heavy dish upon which the sugar paste dragon was mounted, the Tizzy ascended the platform and tottered towards the throne. The plate shook in her wooden hands and the sculpture began to shudder and crack. The mechanical's erratic walk declined into a drunken lurch, then before anyone could stop it, the Tizzy flung the large dish straight at the Queen's head.

Leaping from his seat, Brindle threw his hands forward and caught the plate, just inches away from Her Majesty's face. Fragments of shattered sugar paste exploded across Elizabeth's pearl-encrusted gown and every voice in the room was stilled.

The Tizzy was shaking violently now, the mahogany sections of its body juddering and shivering with wild, uncontrolled convulsions.

"Jesu!" the Queen bawled. "I will have no shaking sickness in my household!"

Rising from the throne in her fury, she strode up to the quaking mannequin and brought her fist thumping down upon the Tudor rose set into its forehead. The smiting blow was so powerful that the Tizzy was knocked off its feet and went crashing backwards, falling to the floor with a clatter of limp, motionless limbs.

"Take that palsied doll away and burn it!" she commanded. Turning to Brindle, she added, "My thanks, Salamander. If it was not for your quick action, more than My gown would be ruined."

"It was nothing," Brindle assured her.

"The saving of the Queen's person must never be considered 'nothing'," she countered. Then with a light laugh she dispelled the tension and cried, "Look, My Lords – your Queen has a new favourite. Master Herrick, look not so crestfallen. Tell Me, My fire dweller, do your people know aught of dancing?"

"Your Grace?"

The Queen clapped her hands and called for the mechanical musicians to play. "Before this night has ended," she vowed to the Iribian, "you shall be well versed in all steps."

The music began and Elizabeth of Englandia led Brindle into the centre of the room to commence his first lesson.

Behind them on the platform, two more Tizzys silently lifted the stilled mannequin in their arms to carry it outside. Before they could perform the task, however, Walsingham stopped them and summoned Doctor Dee to his side.

"There is too much coincidence in the timing of this

shaking sickness for my liking," the spymaster said.

The Doctor agreed and carefully removed the mechanical's face to inspect the internals. "Nothing appears amiss," he muttered.

"What of the ichors?"

The astrologer ordered the other Tizzys to turn the figure over, then he unlaced its green and white bodice and removed a wooden plate from the mechanical's back.

"The red and yellow humours are balanced," he said, peering inside. "The green and black seem..." his voice dropped and he sucked the air in sharply. "See what we have here," the astrologer whispered as he removed a small spherical phial filled with an indigo liquid.

Walsingham's face darkened. "It is the same venom that Tewkes used in Belladonna, my horse," he said.

"That which turned it into an unstoppable killer," the Doctor nodded. "We have been most fortunate, Sir Francis. This evil juice did not have chance to complete its assassin's work – hardly any of the fluid has been spent. If the Queen had not stilled this Tizzy when She did then it would surely have murdered Her. Weapons more effective than a mere plate would have been used."

"Undoubtedly," Walsingham murmured. "Either on Her, or the Iribian. I find myself wondering just who was the intended victim."

Doctor Dee cast his bristling gaze about the banqueting house, glancing suspiciously at the gathered courtiers who were watching the Queen instruct her visitor in the art of dance.

"Verily," he said softly. "We are beset by enemies. Who knows where the next blow shall fall?"

Lantern had shown Henry and Adam to a poky little room at the far end of the palace. Glumly, the boys peered into the cramped darkness that was lit only by a single rush light. The chamber was dirty and unswept, containing just two wooden stools and a heap of filthy straw for them to sleep on. Over the walls and ceiling, the crumbling plaster was speckled with black mould. There was not even a window.

"Witch spit!" Henry cried in disgust.

Doctor Dee's copper secretary looked abashed.

"There are prisons and dungeons that could put this place to shame," Henry continued. "Are there no other rooms?"

Lantern shook his head in apology.

"It's not his fault," Adam told Henry. "I don't think we're supposed to feel comfortable – we're not wanted here."

"Well I can't sleep on that straw," the boy objected. "It looks as though it's jumping."

Adam turned to the mechanical secretary. "Will we be getting anything to eat?" he asked. "We haven't had very much today."

Lantern's round green eyes shone brightly and he made

a quick bow before trundling into the corridor, miming that he would return as soon as possible with their supper.

Grimacing, Henry sat on the stool and propped his head in his hands.

"Not fair," he complained. "We're missing everything. Brindle and Lord Richard will be with Her Majesty now and look at us. I didn't come all the way to London to be caged in a grubby hole."

"I wish I was back in Malmes-Wutton," Adam sighed.

"Well I'm not going back there till I've seen something of this island," Henry insisted. Leaping up, he kicked the stool into a corner and strode to the doorway.

"Where are you going?" Adam asked.

"Exploring," came the determined reply. "You stay here if you want to, Coggy, but I'll not. There's a city out there and I want to see it."

Into the corridor Master Wattle went marching and, giving a dejected glance about the cheerless room, Adam o'the Cogs immediately decided to go with him.

That region of the palace was shockingly run down and neglected. It was a long straggle of shabby, red-bricked buildings connected by a narrow passage. These mean apartments housed the lowest servants and, since the Uplifting of the lands, the rooms had grown ever more dilapidated – even dangerous. Ceilings had fallen in, there were holes in the roof and weeds grew up through the flagged floors.

"My rats wouldn't loiter in this muck heap," Henry said with disgust.

Leaving that slovenly den, the apprentices stepped out into the night, crossing a drab courtyard beyond which the irregular roofscape of the main part of the rambling palace rose and dipped under the firmament. The royal residence of Whitehall was so vast and sprawling that it covered twenty-three acres and was divided by King's Street, the main route from Westminster to the city. Adam and Henry had seen the road when Lantern guided them to their meagre lodging and it was towards that highway they headed now.

Passing through a walled rose garden where carved wooden animals sat atop tall, painted columns, Adam halted. He broke off a spray of eglantine which he put to his nose and recalled that afternoon with Brindle in Lord Richard's rose garden.

"Purity and absolution," he murmured to himself.

"What are you jabbering about?" Henry asked impatiently. "This is no time for gardening, Coggy."

Adam tucked the small white flowers into his tunic and they stealthily hastened towards the buildings which joined the Holbein Gate. "From there we can leave the palace grounds," Henry assured him. "Then we'll get to see what London's really like."

Adam had started to have serious doubts about this nocturnal venture. "Remember what happened last night when you went off," he hissed. "There's probably gangs of rogues out there, each one worse than Clink Kitson."

"I've learned my lesson," Henry promised. "We'll stick to the main streets and not go down any dark alleyways."

"I don't know..."

"Come on, Coggy! Show some guts for once – you can't be a worm all your life. Have some backbone; we won't be gone for long."

Stung by his words, Adam relented and they pressed on until a wide, timber-framed building reared before them. Warily, they hurried inside.

Finding themselves within a long, deserted gallery, the two boys crept along it as silently as they could. This was the way Lantern had brought them. It connected the two halves of the palace and was hung with tapestries and portraits. Adam wanted to linger and study them more closely but Henry dragged him on.

"No time for that," he growled. "You can gawk at them in the daylight tomorrow. Bum boils!"

At the end of the gallery, two Yeomen of the Crown were standing on guard. The apprentices were stricken with a fearful paralysis, until they realised that the guards were facing each other and had as yet not spotted them. Henry pulled Adam over to a well of shadow, just beyond the reach of candlelight.

"There were no sentries there before," Adam whispered. "What are we to do?"

Henry licked his lips as a bold and daring scheme fruited in his head. "Brazen it out," he replied. "Say we're on important business for the Queen and walk right by them."

"You're mad!"

"Oh? What can they do to us?"

Adam glanced down the gallery to the frightening spear and axe blades of the halberds which the guards gripped in their hands. "I can think of plenty of horrible things," he answered.

But Henry was not listening and stepped from the shadows, dredging Adam with him. Assuming an enforced casual air, he strolled forwards and began a tuneless whistle.

At once the Yeomen of the Crown turned. "Halt and declare yourself," one of them called.

"Henry Wattle – on the bidding of Her Majesty," came the insolent reply.

An amused leer twitched across one of the men's faces, revealing a row of blackened teeth. "Oh, are you now?" he asked archly.

"Indeed I am," Henry retorted, although his faith in this plan was fading rapidly.

"And who might your friend be?"

"Adam o'the Cogs," Henry told him.

"Can't he talk for hisself?"

"Let us by," Henry demanded with ever dwindling

confidence. "We are companions of the heavenly messenger. We arrived with him and Lord Richard Wutton not an hour since."

The guards looked at one another, then stood back to let the boys pass.

Neither Adam or Henry could believe that the bold and simple strategy had worked. Thanking their stars, they strode down the gallery and were about to march straight by the sentries when strong hands grabbed each of them by the arm.

"That's spared us a weary chase," cackled the guard who had spoken. "Now, it's to our Captain you'll be taken. Arrogant little dog – be whipped and put in the stocks to be pelted with stones, that's what you'll be."

"Unhand me!" Henry yelled, clinging to his woeful ploy. "I'll not go anywhere with a ruffian like you. I am a friend of Brindle's!"

"And I know Doctor Dee!" Adam shouted.

"Oho!" the second guard laughed. "Angels and devils – what diverse company this lying pair keep." Seizing hold of Henry's other arm, he said to his confederate, "You go fetch the Captain. I'll hold these two till you return."

"Aye, I'll seek him swiftly."

The first sentry hastened from the gallery. The second guard waited till he heard the running footsteps recede, then turned to his prisoners and grinned at them.

"Now then," he began. "I've no wish to spoil my

chances in Heaven or in Hell, so I'll loose you before black mouth Davey returns."

To the boys' surprise he released them.

"Thank you," Adam said.

Resting on the shaft of his halberd, the guard scowled at them. "But where was you two impudent fellows headed at this hour of the clock?" he asked.

"We wanted to get outside the palace and look on the city," Henry told him.

The man chuckled at their foolishness. "Did you think there'd be no one posted at the gate? Prize Toms of Bedlam, that's what you two be."

"Don't split your tunic," Henry said dryly as the sentry continued to laugh. "If you've done with us we'll away, back to our lodging."

"Won't you get into trouble for letting us go?" Adam asked.

"I'll say you were both too strong for me to keep captive," came the jovial answer. "I was no match for two such burly giants as you."

Henry managed a weak smile and started to retrace his steps up the gallery. "'Tis a good thing he became a guard," the boy breathed to Adam. "The oaf would never have made it as jester."

They had only gone a few yards when the man came running up behind them.

"Hold!" he said with new urgency in his voice.

"What have we done now?" Henry moaned. "Or have you thought of some other ribald mockery?"

"Are you still wishing to see the city?"

"Not if we have to steal past a hundred guards to do it." The sentry clicked his tongue then tapped a forefinger against his nose and winked. "I reckon I know a way," he declared. "A nice easy path for you to slip in and out without notice."

Henry folded his arms. "A way in and out of the palace that isn't guarded?" the boy said. "You'd best stop up your ears, friend – before any more brains leak out."

"'Tis a secret way I speak of," the man reassured them. "Harking back to when old King Harry would visit his lady friends without the Boleyn getting to hear of it. 'Tain't far and does lead straight to the road."

Henry looked questioningly at Adam.

"If it's so secret," the apprentice muttered, "how does he know of it?"

"Us Yeomen have to know every hidden track," came the proud and ready answer. "'Tis unknown to every other soul though."

"Very well," Henry decided for both of them. "Lead us there."

"You must be quick, before Davey returns with our captain. This way, my titchy Gogmagogs." Propping his halberd against the panelling, the Yeoman took up a candle and led them into one of the empty rooms which opened off the gallery. Down a small stair they followed him, to a stone antechamber where a faded tapestry was draped across the far wall and before that stood a tall oak cupboard.

Passing the guttering candle to Henry, the guard heaved the cupboard forward and drew the tapestry aside.

A waft of cooler air came pushing into the room as a dark entrance was revealed in the stone wall and the sentry chuckled at the apprentices.

"Now, nip you in sharply," he instructed. "This secret way will take you clean down to the King's Street."

Holding the candle before him, Henry stepped into the dark doorway and the wildly leaping flame revealed a dank passage and another set of stairs.

Before joining him, Adam thanked the guard again.

"No matter," the man said. "Just you have a care outside these walls. There's many a footpad and foist in yonder city."

"You'll keep the way open, won't you?" Adam asked nervously.

"'Course. You come back whenever you feel as how you've seen enough."

The boy smiled awkwardly, then ducked under the tapestry and the two apprentices set off, the bobbing glare of the candle flame shrinking down the passage.

Letting the tapestry fall back into place, the guard chuckled again, but this time it was not a pleasant sound and he pushed the great wooden cupboard back before the entrance. Leaning against it, he pulled from his belt a small leather purse and took out a shining gold coin.

"That were earned easy enough," he snorted. "This – and two more pieces waiting on delivery. I didn't even have to go looking for the poxy young coves. A fine night's work this has been."

Sniggering to himself, he left the antechamber and returned upstairs to his post, confident that those two boys would never be seen or heard of again.

Descending a spiral stair, Adam and Henry were unaware of the danger they were heading into. By the time they reached the bottommost step, the twisting journey had stolen their sense of direction and they assumed that the new passage which confronted them would lead to a concealed entrance near the road.

The cool night air was blowing more strongly through this dank way and Henry had difficulty shielding the candle from its buffeting influence. The arched walls of the tunnel were unusually damp, some places dripped with water and their feet splashed through many dirty pools.

"We must have gone down deep," Adam murmured. "I reckon we're underground, under the foundations of the palace. This is the river seeping in."

"There'll be more stairs then," Henry said. "To take us back up level with the road. Look, there's a bend ahead. The steps'll prob'ly be just around that. Bum breath! 'Tis a good thing Brindle is not here to whiff this spot. 'Tis foul as Satan's privy."

As they followed the wet path around the corner, the breeze unexpectedly grew in strength and rushed about Henry's protecting hand. The candle flame quailed briefly, then perished and the boys were suddenly lost in the dark.

"Coffin maggots!" Henry cried, throwing the useless candle away. "We'll have to stumble along now."

Putting their hands to the slime-running walls they blindly groped their way forward until at last they realised that the pitch gloom was lifting. Ahead of them a shimmering grey light illuminated the end of the tunnel and they went hurrying towards it, grateful to be getting out of the stinking murk.

As they drew near to the exit, the sound of rippling water came echoing to greet them and serpents of soft silver light went wiggling over the arched stonework.

Finally, the apprentices emerged into the night and they blinked in astonishment at where their journey had brought them.

"We must have made a wrong turning," Henry muttered.

Staring at the unexpected sight in front, Adam was only just beginning to understand. Glimmering sombrely below, reflecting the bright stars far beyond the firmament, flowed the broad midnight ribbon of the Thames.

Instead of reaching King's Street, they had gone in completely the opposite direction. The tunnel they had blundered along had led straight to a narrow flight of stairs leading down to the river. The tide was turning and a desolate, muddy bank had been exposed either side of the steps but there, pulled out on to the miry shore, was a rowing boat.

Adam peered into the darkness. The river's edge was devoid of any movement and stretched in both directions without a sign of any presence but their own. The boat appeared to have been abandoned.

"Why don't we take it?" Henry whispered. "The oars are there and this way will be even better than going by the road."

"You're quite happy stealing, aren't you?" Adam tutted.

"What's wrong with that?"

Eagerly, Henry negotiated the slippery stairs and Adam was obliged to follow him. When they reached the bottom, they were thankful to discover that the mud was not too thick and squelched quickly to the forsaken boat.

Suddenly a fierce shout rang behind them and both boys spun around to see three cloaked figures come leaping from the concealing shadows where they had lain in wait.

"Get them!" A harsh voice called. "Hold them!"

With the river on one side and the towering walls of the palace rising on the other, there was nowhere for Adam or Henry to run. There was no time to jump into the boat and row to safety, and when they tried to cry for help, cruel fists punched the breath from them.

Against their powerful assailants, any struggle was futile and the attack was over in seconds. Callused hands snatched them, twisting the apprentices' arms behind their backs, gags were pulled painfully tight across their mouths and their eyes blindfolded.

Screaming noiselessly into the filthy restraint, Adam felt iron bands clasp around his wrists, pinching his skin as they snapped shut. A similar pain bit into his ankles as his feet were locked together and, like game poached from the old world, he was lifted high and dropped into a great sack.

A grunt of exertion sounded through the coarse cloth when the man hoisted the boy higher and cast him into the boat. But the villain's vicious strength had hurled Adam a mite too far and the apprentice's head struck the wooden side. A white flower of agony exploded behind his crushed eyes and, as the boat was hauled out into the water, Adam o'the Cogs lost consciousness and lay as still as death.

CHAPTER 5

With the Count de Feria

E ven as the Queen led Brindle into the centre of the banqueting house to teach him the steps of La Volta, the sack containing Cog Adam was dumped unceremoniously on to a creaking wooden floor.

A second squeaking 'thud' proclaimed the unloading of Henry next to him, accompanied by the Wattle boy's stifled yells.

Adam had known nothing of the journey to this place. When the craft finally came to a bumping rest, he had not felt those same unmerciful hands haul him up and carry him ungently through darkened streets. Now the fall from his captor's shoulder had jolted him out of that oblivion and his thoughts gradually came drifting back. Distorted voices filtered into his slowly returning senses and with them came a terrible pounding which crashed against his bruised temple like a hammer.

"I am much grateful," thanked one of the speakers in a thick, garbled accent. "So high pleased with this and what swift work it was, you clever fellows."

"Haw!" crowed a different, more brutish voice. "Thems took no difficult catchin'. We bagged 'em just like two pigeons."

"Yes, yes, you is deserved of your wage and there, she is an extra shilling for each of you – so prompt."

"That's what we likes to see, a gentleman with loose purse strings."

"Well, is closed now. Go, spend coin on drink, gambling or in pretty arms, if you can find a pretty woman in this country. They all are looking like milking maids to me, no? With faces like the dairy pudding."

"Any more little tasks you want doin', you know where to find us."

"In gutter and low den of vice – I know."

"Always happy to be of service, ain't we?"

There was a murmur of agreement then three voices called, "Goodnight to you, Master."

"Yes, hurry out - slink back to scum and worthless lives."

Heavy footsteps shuffled away from the bound apprentices, a door closed, then a lighter tread returned, halting beside the squirming bundle that was Henry.

"Where my pinking dagger? Ah, there she is."

Henry felt a firm tug on the sacking, immediately followed by a ripping noise and the thick cloth was torn aside.

"Ho, one little bird to the cage. I hope he have good voice to sing. Don Gomez want to hear lot of tunes tonight."

A sharp jab in his shoulder told Adam that the owner of the voice had turned his attention to him and had pushed the knife a trifle too deeply through the sacking.

"Pardonny - is always lacking the patience."

The sack containing Adam was ripped open.

"Oh, ugly mark on this one. Those clumsy fellows, they think only with knuckles. Prithee Our Lady, no damage have they done."

Adam felt a cool hand pat the throbbing side of his head and the sudden pain caused him to sit upright as the blindfold was pulled from his eyes.

A flesh-coloured shape shimmered before him and it was only when his mind started to clear and his vision rolled into focus that he realised he was looking at a face. It belonged to an olive-skinned man with a neatly trimmed black beard and intense, sparkling eyes. "There," the richly dressed stranger said with a flashing smile. "You are well, no? Is good, is very good."

The man's forehead crinkled for a moment as he put a hand to his cheek. "Such discomfort the teeth is having this day," he moaned. "Holy Child of God, I no like this suffering. Englandia, it have no surgeons worthy of my mouth, is trusting none of them."

The face moved out of view as the man stepped around Adam to untie his gag and the apprentice stared groggily about the room.

It was a fine, panelled chamber, with a sumptuously woven Turkish carpet covering half the floor. Colourful tapestries ornamented two walls, a large latticed window filled another with glass while on the fourth, in the bare space next to the closed door, was an object he had never seen before but had read about in Lord Richard's library – a crucifix. The significance of that papist symbol had hardly registered when Adam remembered Henry, and he glanced quickly at the boy crouched nearby. He too was bound, but apart from a few minor cuts and scratches, he appeared none the worse.

Cursing under his bad breath, the Count de Feria complained about the tightness of the knot which kept Adam's gag in place. Then the gag was whipped away and Adam licked his parched lips while the Spanish ambassador set about removing Henry's blindfold.

"Where are we?" Adam demanded. "How dare you hold us to ransom? When our master finds out he will have the Queen send Her army to find us. Unfasten my hands and feet."

The Count paused and stared at him in bemusement, then chuckled and shook his head. "Ransom? Oh no, Don Gomez he no want money. You talk, that is all he wish. Little birdies must sing."

Having uncovered Henry's eyes he concentrated his efforts upon the gag and suddenly the boy's newly released voice yelled out, piercing every room in the building.

"Stinking sweat rag! I do not want to know where that had been. A sewage wallower's breeches would be like honey in comparison – ack!"

Having untied all that he intended, the Spanish ambassador drew up a cushion-laden chair and settled himself into it. On a low table at his side there was a delicate glass of sweet wine and he sipped at it appreciatively.

"Don't sit there tippling!" Henry snapped, struggling in his fetters. "What about these?"

Lounging on the cushions, the man wagged a warning finger. "No undo hands," he said. "This way best for talk."

"You've got the wrong people," Adam protested in furious indignation. "We're not important, we're just apprentices. We don't even live on this island."

The ambassador shrugged. "I does not blame you," he

said. "Too much the hive of common rabble. As for the climate, in winter she so damp and chill is a miracle I not die, and in summer it stink. After this night, howsoever, Don Gomez Suarez de Figueroa – he leave for his home."

"You're a foreigner!" Henry exclaimed with belated realisation. "Pope's peaches – you're one of them dirty Spaniards!"

The Count leaned forward and the gleam in his eyes was enough to make Henry recoil. "Hear me, noisome child," he threatened. "I not care for your insults but should you be speaking of his Holy Eminence again, I no wait for my new friend to join us – I kill you now."

"Go sit on a nun!" Henry retorted. "You don't scare us, for all your weird ways. Coggy an' me won't be here long – we'll be rescued."

De Feria raised his eyebrows. "Poor mad boy," he sighed. "You is far from aid. This house, she away from road and there are being many guards here. Scream, please – nobodies are hearing this."

"We don't have to shout," Henry rallied. "Brindle will find us; if we were locked in a box and buried in the ground, he'd sniff and find where we were."

The Count's eyes twinkled with keen interest. "Ah, yes, your angel messenger," he drawled. "How good you make mention of he. Is why I inviting you here. You will be telling me every things you know."

"Me?" Henry roared in defiance. "Tell a filthy

Spaniard about our fabulous Brindle. You can take a running jump out through the tidal breath – the plum of your head's lost its stone."

"Good!" the ambassador beamed with pleasure. "You try to make the difficulties and bite your tongue – I like, I like."

Adam found their gaoler's suave calm frightening. "But we don't really know much about Brindle," he said. "We can't tell you anything."

"I be judging of that," de Feria promised. "How many are to follow? What their shot and cannon like? Does he fight for Lizabeth?"

Kneeling on the floor, Henry raised himself up as high as he could manage and threw his head back with insolent pride. "Brindle has hundreds of night boats," he lied, "crowded with thousands like him, and they're rushing towards your greasy countries already. Have your king polishing his own palace steps by the end of the week, they will. So you let us go now and we'll not tell our angel what you done to us."

Pressing his lips together, the ambassador rose from his chair. Then, with the back of his hand, struck Henry across the face. The Count's jewelled rings cut the boy's cheek and Henry glared up at him murderously.

"Is most serious," de Feria warned. "You be learning manners and tell what I want knowing."

"All you need to know is where they're going to bury you."

The Count made a faint chuckling sound and directed

his gaze upon Adam as he took another sip of wine. "And you, you of the fair head. Will you be singing song I want hear?"

In spite of his fear and the throbbing of his temple, the apprentice returned the stare and in a level voice said, "I've already told you – we don't know anything about Brindle."

"Except that he's from Heaven and will kick you into Satan's pit!" Henry added.

De Feria peered at them over the rim of his glass, turning the finely twisted stem in his fingers.

"But you think he come to save you, no? You give me very good idea, yes is very good plan. You helping me a lot."

"I'd die first, you foul beggar," Henry shouted.

De Feria put the glass down and raised his hands in apologetic surrender. "I did do the trying," he cried to the ceiling as if calling God as witness. "Was been very kind, very charityful. But no, they not polite – birds won't sing. No choice is left."

Leaving the chair, he made for the door and crossed himself before the crucifix.

"What are you going to do now?" Adam asked.

"Do I not say?" the Count laughed in surprise at his forgetfulness. "I get new friend. He make tongues of birds trill with many pretty tunes. Oh yes, they always sing loud and lovely for him."

Again the ambassador chuckled, then he pulled open the

door to reveal a small landing outside. It was the first clue the apprentices had as to where they might be. Adam glanced at the window and wondered how high it was from the ground, but all speculation was futile while their hands and feet were shackled together.

Leaning upon the banisters, de Feria called down in Spanish, then half closed the door behind him when he returned to the room. "My men, they send new friend up to join us. What a happy group we is being then. Such music we will be having, no?"

"Are all Spaniards as feeble-brained as you?" Henry asked. "Or did you have to toil at it?"

De Feria returned to his chair. "Ho," he grinned. "So soon you be sorry for that. I pity, I really do."

Henry opened his mouth to answer, but the impudent words never left his lips for an ominous, lumbering noise sounded abruptly beneath the room and he looked across at Adam.

"What was that?" he murmured.

The other boy shook his head as the alarming din moved through the chambers below. It was a heavy clanking and, in his mind's eye, he pictured some ungainly contraption walking towards the foot of the unseen stairs.

"Is my new friend," the ambassador informed them. "He very modern, very impressing – cost many ducats. I like very much."

"This friend," Adam muttered. "It's a mechanical?"

The Count clapped his hands. "Yes!" he cried. "Is much special. Ah – he come to greet you!"

A tremendous, rattling crash resounded beyond the door as a great hulking weight heaved itself on to the first wooden step. Another pounding clang erupted, then another and another as the unknown creation climbed ever closer. With every clamorous tread, the floorboards trembled and the half-closed door shuddered on its hinges. Unable to tear his eyes away from the shivering gap between it and the frame, Adam could feel his horror mounting.

"What sort of mechanical is it?" he asked.

De Feria sipped at his sweet wine, swirling it noisily around his mouth before replying. Returning the fragile glass to the table, he raised his brows and his coal black eyes glittered with malice.

"Is Torture Master," he hissed.

With that, the landing reverberated under a juddering thud and a giant silhouette reared up behind the doorway.

"Enter, my friend," the ambassador called. "Come in and view these taciturn birdies."

The door flew open, shoved with a horrendous force that sent the timbers quivering, and the shape that was revealed behind made both boys cringe. There, framed in the doorway, was the most terrifying mechanical they had ever seen. Even the grotesque memory of Old Scratch withered before it. The wild boar of Malmes-Wutton had grown hideous over the years, but this evil creation was deliberately designed to instil fear and panic. Looking on it, Adam forgot all about the pain of his bruised temple.

Made almost entirely of iron, the Torture Master was a crude parody of a man. Resembling a nightmarish, skeletal suit of armour, the huge mechanical was forged from many metal bands. With a clink of chains, it stooped under the lintel and came stomping into the room where it towered above everyone.

The apprentices stared upward in awful disbelief.

Thick bars, joined together by metal hoops, created each section of the legs and were connected to the lower body by great spiked wheels. Within the monster's stomach, hot coals burned in a brazier which could be stoked and inflamed by a pair of iron bellows. Directly above this, the ichor vessels were protected behind a grilled chest plate and three pendulums maintained the monster's balance.

From the massive, spoked shoulders, long arms hung at its sides, but instead of hands and fingers, horrific-looking implements thrust down from the elbows.

It was a walking cage of despair. Clamped on to a broad collar was a fiendish-looking head. More spikes formed a jagged crest upon the topmost band, but two curved spurs jutted out at the sides like horns, reinforcing the malevolent, diabolic aspect.

Yet perhaps the most sinister element was its face. Hammered from two sheets of iron, it was fashioned into a primitive mask, the sort that occasionally embellished a scold's bridle. Two narrow slits made the eyes and, beneath the ridged nose, a vulgar, leering mouth had been clumsily painted. Whatever ghastly crimes the Torture Master committed, it would always wear that same fixed smile – the last sight its victims would ever see.

Shrinking as far from it as his manacled feet would allow, Henry could not look away.

"Is fine, no?" the Count de Feria boasted. "So clever, the crafted makers of Spain. Is torture chamber on legs."

With a flourish of his hand, he indicated the deadly-looking devices built into the framework. "He lack nothing. Few castle dungeons are equipping better. Is most splendid, and so convenient for manoeuvring. I really not knowing what they think of next. I am wonders if it can also be doing the tooth extraction."

Excited by his degenerate toy, he sprang from the chair and pointed out his favourite tortures.

"Pincers for the tearing of flesh," he extolled. "Eye gougers, thumb screw in place of thumb – is funny, no? But see, put foot here and foot there – hand there and there – Torture Master raise arms and he is rack. Can stretch up a whole other yard, no spine survive. I specially mirthed by that. Oh, there is the foldaway scavenger's daughter, and these are drawing hooks. What a pity is so hard to clean."

Stepping away from it, he tilted his head to one side as though viewing a work of art and murmured with adoring enthusiasm, "Altogether, is forty-seven different torments. This style very adept at prolong the agony but keep blessed release of death at bay."

Turning back to the terrified apprentices, the Spanish ambassador laughed impishly. "Every diplomat should have one."

Then he snapped his fingers. A rush of air issued from the bellows and the coals in the brazier glowed a fierce red as the mechanical took a clunking step forward. Henry and Adam cried out and the Count de Feria drained his glass.

"Stop it!" Henry yelled as the Torture Master advanced, its gruesome instruments waving menacingly before him. "Call it off!"

"No can stop him," the ambassador replied. "Is no – oh, how you say? Is no stilling badge," He looked on proudly as his merciless toy clumped towards them to begin its vicious work. There was another whoosh of air and the coals burned yellow. Adam and Henry wriggled to the corner, but the armoured horror reared over them.

"I'll tell you!" Henry bawled. "Whatever you want to know about Brindle – I'll tell."

De Feria smiled indulgently. "I know," he said. "Always they do. Now you regretting such nasty impolititude."

The cruel arms came reaching down and Henry screamed as great iron pincers clamped about his shoulders.

"Get it off him!" Adam begged. "He said we'd tell you.

Anything you want – just don't let that thing hurt him."

The Count put a finger to his lips. "Not like to interrupt Torture Master now," he said, scandalised. "Is rude, he must continue. He so artful, is joy to watch and I always learn – so ingenious. Anywise, your angel – he come seek you out whether you dead or living, no?"

Shrieking, the Wattle boy was plucked off the ground and the mechanical plunged a long poker into the heart of its brazier.

"No!" Adam wept. "Please don't let it do that, please!"

"Hot needles and brandings," the ambassador cooed. "I am loving this. Skin, it scorch so easy, but what a smoke and smell it make."

Hanging by his shoulders, his shackled feet dangling above the floor, Henry could feel the intense heat blasting from the Torture Master's stomach. The grip of the pincers was almost unbearable, but not too painful to make him pass out. The mechanical knew its job too well to permit that and the painted leer seemed to relish the boy's terror. There was a rattle of metal and the poker withdrew from the coals, its tapered tip glowing brightly as it danced in front of Henry's eyes.

Lying helpless at the monster's spurred feet, Adam tugged and wrestled with his restraints until the manacles grazed and scraped deep into his wrists. Turning his face away, he heard his friend cry out.

"Brindle – save me!"

But the Iribian was far off in Whitehall Palace, dancing with the Queen, and the reek of the apprentices' intense terror never reached his refined senses.

"Brindle!" Henry shrieked again.

"Ho, your angel no answer," de Feria scoffed. "Maybe you next see him in Heaven."

With taunting slowness, the poker moved closer to the boy's face, scribing a burning circle in the hot, shimmering air as if trying to decide where to strike. Then it darted forward. The fiery point licked briefly across his brows and Henry felt his forehead boil and scorch. A noise like frying bacon filled the room. The ensuing screech was ghastly to hear.

"Why are you doing this?" Adam cried. "It's obscene – stop it!"

The Count was too engrossed to answer. The Torture Master moved the smouldering poker clockwise before its victim's face a second time. Unable to cover his ears to drown out his friend's screams, Adam threw back his own head and shrieked with him.

Suddenly, a different sound thundered inside those panelled walls and both voices were lost in an almighty blast of flying glass. Spangling shards exploded across the room in every direction. Yelping in Spanish, the Count de Feria protected his face with his hands and ducked behind the chair as shooting splinters clattered like hail against the Torture Master's frame.

Showered in broken fragments, Adam stared past the horrific mechanical and spluttered in amazement. Suspended in the pincers' grasp and still sobbing from the pain of his burn, Henry flicked his eyes downward and hope instantly soared in his breast.

The large window was utterly destroyed. Severed ribbons of lead curled inwards and, stripped of their panes, they looked like wintry twigs. Through this jagged opening the evening airs rushed in to swirl the eddying dust and sparkling powdered glass around the short, rotund figure which was now standing in the centre of the room.

With a candle burning brightly in his hat and his round green eyes blazing with avenging anger, Doctor Dee's secretary was an unlikely saviour, but the apprentices were overjoyed to see him.

"Lantern!" Adam called.

The copper mannequin came crunching through the shattered debris.

Without relinquishing its hold on Henry, the Torture Master rotated its great head and looked down on the comical figure for the briefest moment before returning its macabre attention to its young victim.

Marching right up behind the Spanish monster, Lantern gave one of its legs a hefty kick.

A faint tremor travelled up the Torture Master's iron frame and the large head swivelled about once more. Clenching his gauntleted hands, Lantern threw up his fists and pummelled the air with them while dancing on his toes, inviting the terrible creation to mechanical combat.

The chains within his massive opponent clinked in mockery and its bellows blew with contempt. As Lantern delivered another puny blow, the Spanish ambassador rose from behind the chair and regarded the copper secretary fearfully.

"Is the wizard's imp!" he exclaimed, crossing himself. "It see too much. No let it escape. I order you!"

Lowering Henry to the floor, the Torture Master rounded on Lantern, dwarfing him with its monumental size. The brazier glowed inside its metal ribs and it took a lumbering step nearer.

"Crumple and smash it!" de Feria commanded.

Lantern's head whisked about to glare at him and in that moment a powerful arm came sweeping from the side to knock him off his feet. The tubby secretary tumbled backwards and went bowling through the door on to the landing where his pedalling legs were thrust either side of a banister post. The Torture Master went lurching, crashing over the wooden floor in ponderous, splintering paces.

Behind it, Adam squirmed to Henry's side and stared at the awful burn which striped his forehead.

"Are you all right?" he asked.

The Wattle boy nodded, but his face was wrung with pain and he was shivering from shock.

"We're going to get out of here," Adam promised. "Don't worry."

On the landing, Lantern pulled his boots from the banister, flipped himself upright and went charging back into the room, impatient to rejoin the fray. His adversary planted its great spurred heels wide apart in an assured, aggressive stance. Spreading its arms, it spanned the room and when the secretary came capering through the door, the Torture Master reached out to seize him.

The mannequin ducked and leapt aside, valiantly dodging the tools of torment as they came hacking and lashing for him. But the craftsmen of Spain had endowed their vile creation with many infernal instruments and, as Lantern hopped to avoid the row of four savage claws which rushed towards his feet, a spiked club swooped in from the other direction and drove into his back.

There was a battering of copper as the spikes pushed ugly dints into the polished surface and Lantern was hurled to the ground, clattering like an empty kettle.

"Come on, Lantern!" Adam yelled desperately. "Get up – you must!"

But Doctor Dee's assistant seemed incapable of lifting himself from the carpet and his round eyes could only watch hopelessly as the Torture Master raised one of its heavy iron feet, swinging it directly over his head. From the grille in Lantern's tall hat, the candle flame went licking up to cast its wavering light on to the large metal foot above. One forceful stamp and the secretary would be flattened beyond repair.

"Finish it!" the ambassador squawked, banging his fist on the cushions of his chair. "Crush him!"

The Torture Master whirled its head about in order to see the horror graven upon the apprentices' faces and gloated at what it saw there. Then the frightening mask spun around again, but Lantern was no longer lying on the floor – he had rolled swiftly out of danger and was already back on his feet and stooping to grab hold of the carpet's edge.

Too late the Torture Master understood what the dwarflike mannequin was about to do. Before it could lurch clear, Lantern heaved at the carpet with all his mechanical strength and the Spanish nightmare was sent toppling backwards. Like a felled tree it plummeted, a vision of collapsing might as the branching arms thrashed in vain. Its awful weight thundered down, the room shook as the floor splintered and snapped, and the frightening mechanical was on its back, the many spikes of its shoulders skewering the wooden boards.

Not wasting an instant, Lantern bounded forward, dragging the carpet with him to throw over the Torture Master's stricken form. Then he hopped on to the chair and began tearing down the tapestries while de Feria ran, wailing, away from him.

"Stand!" the Count commanded, darting to the carpet under which the Torture Master writhed, already ripping his spikes out of the floorboards.

Jumping from the chair, Lantern dragged the hangings with him. Even as the iron monstrosity started to lift itself up, he cast the tapestries over its head and, tearing a long strip from the bottom of one, he capered around the smothered mechanical and tied the hangings tightly.

Bound in the thick cloth, the Torture Master's bellows roared murderously. The ambassador hurried to release it, only to be hurled blindly aside. Shrieking in Spanish, the Count de Feria called to his men below. Lantern gave a little hop, picked up the chair and, holding it before him, charged straight for the ambassador, propelling him clean out of the room.

Twisting the chair around in the doorway, the secretary wedged it securely, trapping the Count on the landing. Then he scurried past the mountain of heaving tapestry to where the apprentices still crouched huddled in the corner. Briskly he reached behind the boys' backs and, with a twang of his strong fingers, snapped each set of manacles in two.

"Thank you, Lantern!" Adam cried, nursing his raw wrists as the mannequin proceeded to prise apart the locks which shackled their feet. Henry nodded gratefully, then stared past the secretary's shoulders and sobbed in fear.

Lantern whipped around and saw that the tapestries were beginning to smoulder. Threads of black smoke poured up from the charring cloth and tongues of flame suddenly leapt upwards as a white hot poker came ripping through the burning fabric.

Quickly, the copper mechanical pulled Henry to his feet then pushed both boys towards the window. They scrambled on to the sill and peered out through the broken leads. A pile of barrels had been stacked against the building, forming an easy stair for their escape, and the apprentices hastily lowered themselves down.

Within the room, Lantern waited a moment before joining them. Hungry fires were consuming the tapestries and, out of the searing heats, rose the hideous head of the Torture Master.

On the landing the ambassador was joined by his men who pushed past him and kicked the chair out of the door frame. Into the room they surged, but were driven back by the intense flames.

Dashing to the table, Lantern snatched up the wine bottle, hurled both it and the glass at de Feria's head, then dived for the window.

Silhouetted against the blazing fires, the blackened frame of the Torture Master lunged after him – but was too slow. Doctor Dee's secretary leaped from the room, somersaulting into the night.

"After them!" the wine-soaked Count raged, smacking the faces of his men while gingerly touching the place where the bottle had struck him. "I forbid you to let them escape. Despatch all guards. Seek them out, scour the streets – find them!"

His soldiers pounded down the stairs and the ambassador glanced furiously into the inferno-filled room.

"Out! Out!" he yelled to the Torture Master. "We have made this island too hot to hold us. We must hasten to my ship and be ready to leave at once."

From the swirling flames the towering mechanical came stomping. But the burning floorboards could no longer support its lumbering weight and, with a burst of showering sparks, they collapsed and the metal giant went crashing down into the room beneath.

"Holy Mother!" the ambassador muttered with a shake of his head. "Is useless as a rope of sand. Someone pack that thing in its chest and send it to the night boat. And be fetching many buckets to quench this unbearable hotness!"

Running for their lives, Adam and Henry fled the grounds of de Feria's isolated residence. The squat figure of Lantern quickly overtook them and he guided the apprentices along an unlit, hedge-lined lane. Behind them they heard the cries of the Count's men as they came rushing from the burning building, and the hope that had blazed just as brightly in their hearts died.

"I can't run any more," Henry panted, stumbling to a halt. "That devil's crushed my shoulders. I think the bones are broken." Lantern ran his gauntleted fingers gently over the boy's bruised skin.

"Is it serious?" Adam asked.

The secretary paused as he pressed Henry's shoulder. The apprentice winced and cursed loudly. Lantern appeared satisfied and beckoned them on.

"Seems you'll live," Adam said.

"Doesn't feel that way to me, Coggy," Henry answered through gritted teeth.

The shouts of the ambassador's men grew louder and the apprentices could hear their feet pounding over the gravel towards them.

"Henry!" Adam hissed. "Hurry!"

But the other boy knew it was impossible. "You go," he urged. "I'll hide. I really don't think I can..."

The agony of his experience engulfed him and Henry Wattle fell to the ground as Spanish voices called out close behind.

"Henry!" Adam cried.

At once Lantern crouched beside the unconscious boy. There was only one chance left and he slung the apprentice over his own copper shoulders, then up the lane he raced and Adam hastened after.

They did not have far to run, for the narrow road cut across an area known as Paris Garden which bordered the Thames. With Henry still upon his shoulders, Lantern tottered down the river stairs where his small rowing boat was waiting and carefully placed the boy inside. Holding the craft steady while Adam clambered aboard, the secretary jumped in and took up the oars just as de Feria's soldiers came rushing down to seize them.

But they were not quick enough. Lantern dipped the oars into the water and the little vessel shot out into the middle of the Thames, leaving the men stranded upon the stairs.

"You did it!" Adam shouted, throwing his arms about the mechanical's crimped copper collar. "You rescued us!"

Lantern's green eyes glimmered back at him and the boat journeyed upriver, back to the palace.

CHAPTER 6

Scrying the Shew Stone

"Witch widdle!" Henry's voice moaned as he came to. "I feel like Death has battered me with a stick and pinched me black and blue all over."

Adam had ripped a piece of cloth from his shirt sleeve and dipped it into the river to dab on Henry's blistered brow and the cold water had awakened the boy from his swoon.

"Where are we?" he asked in a scared voice as the

memory of their plight came crowding back. "What's happened?"

Adam reassured him that all was well. "We're nearly at the Whitehall steps," he said. "Then we'll be safe behind the palace walls."

"We have to tell Brindle," Henry added. "He has to know what that stinking Spaniard tried to do – the Queen must be told as well."

Pulling one last time on the oars, Lantern let the boat glide towards the palace stairs where it bumped to a stop and he hopped out to help the apprentices ashore.

Following the tubby secretary, the boys entered the rambling palace once more and every Yeoman of the Crown that they met let them pass without question. The imp of Doctor Dee was known to them all and they were too afraid of him to dare deny them entry.

Lantern led them through unfamiliar halls and courtyards and Adam became increasingly confused.

"You are taking us to Her Majesty?" he asked.

The mannequin gave a skip but offered no other answer. They travelled a little further until they arrived at a wall of ivy in which a stout, studded door was the only feature not to have been choked by the rampant, strangling growth. Lantern pushed the door open and the boys discovered a spiral of stone stairs winding up into a tower. Inside all was dark and silent, the only illumination coming from the candle within the secretary's tall hat. The many punctures

414

in its conical sides threw golden, dancing lights over the blank, curving walls.

Up and up the three ascended until at last they reached an arched entrance covered by a black cloth embroidered with silver stars. Here Lantern bowed low and, beyond the curtain, they heard a sombre voice.

"Enter, you credulous hotheads. What fevered malady of the wits drove you forth this night?"

When Adam and Henry pushed past the curtain, they found themselves standing in Doctor Dee's dimly-lit apartments. Sitting before a large, circular window and with a great book open upon his knee, the astrologer glared at the boys from beneath his snowy brows. The latticed glass behind him was painted with images of the sun and esoteric, magical symbols. Beyond the firmament the bright stars came glinting through in brilliant colours to glitter and gleam over his fine white hair. He looked every inch the dangerous wizard that many people considered him to be and even Adam was disconcerted by his appearance and solemn manner.

"Sit you down," he said sternly. "Here is food and drink. Satisfy your hunger, then tell us of your ludicrous doings."

Only then did the apprentices notice that another figure was sitting in the half shadow beyond the reach of the solitary candle flame which burned steadily at the Doctor's side. When Lantern stepped past them, his own cheerful light shone full into that person's face and the boys recognised it at once.

"Lord Richard!" Henry cried.

The master of Malmes-Wutton nodded a greeting. His hair was damp and his face pink as though he had recently plunged his head into cold water, and he eyed them with a bleak seriousness which they had rarely glimpsed in him before.

"Do as the Doctor instructs," he told them. "Pull up that bench and sit at this table. The ale is not worth the gulping but the cheese and manchet will fill you."

The boys obeyed gladly while the copper secretary set about putting flames to more candles. Gradually, the chamber swelled with light and Adam and Henry gazed about them, crumbs falling from their open mouths.

The lodging of Doctor Dee was crammed with the strange paraphernalia needed for his mysterious studies. Highly polished brass cylinders used to measure and map the constellations glowed and winked in the candle shine, as did elaborate astrolabes and sextants constructed to his own meticulous specifications. Mathematical charts shared the walls with drawings of the new zodiac, bundles of dried herbs hung from the ceiling and glass lenses of various sizes magnified the warm light, casting trembling pools of radiance in every direction. Oddly-shaped bottles containing acids and chemicals lined a long shelf, while books filled every other spare space. Within an alcove, sitting on top of an ebony box, was a human skull and Henry swallowed nervously when he looked into the dark hollows of its eye sockets.

"We only wanted to have a look at the city," Adam told them. "We meant no harm. What happened after was not of our doing."

With interruptions from Henry he quickly recounted the events of the evening while Doctor Dee and their master listened intently.

When the tale ended, the astrologer closed the book on his lap and turned to his secretary. Passing a bony hand over the dents inflicted upon his copper casing the old man enquired if he was quite well. Lantern bowed and the doctor took a deep, considering breath.

Lord Richard examined Henry's wounds. The burn across his forehead would scar him for the rest of his life but although the bruises that blackened his shoulders were horrible to see, they were not serious.

"So," Doctor Dee said at length, "that sable jackanapes, the Spanish ambassador, is up to his usual mischief. I had not suspected he had smuggled one of their new Torture Masters into this realm. Walsingham will be most interested – but not yet. The Count de Feria's plots can wait – there are more pressing concerns."

Swallowing his last mouthful, Henry piped up, "We

must warn Brindle that the Spaniards are scheming to capture him. He'll soon send them running."

Doctor Dee placed his hands upon the table and looked at him grimly. "It is of your heavenly messenger that I wish to speak," he uttered.

"Where is he?" Henry asked, leaping from the low bench. "I'll go tell him."

"Patience," the old man commanded. "He is in no danger. When I left the banqueting house but a short while ago he was dancing with the Queen, to the chagrin of Thomas Herrick and those creatures like him. Nay, Her Grace will not tire of the Iribian so soon."

"But..."

The Doctor rapped the table, demanding that the boy return to his seat. Henry yielded and Adam looked from the astrologer's melancholy face to that of Lord Richard.

"What has happened?" the boy asked. "There is more to your moods than you are telling. Why did Lantern bring us here?"

"Lord Richard and I were discussing the science of mathematics," the old man began vaguely. "A problem has come to my notice which does not... add up. I do so like things to be ordered and quantified. When an enigma presents itself I cannot rest easy till it is solved and understood."

Richard Wutton twitched in discomfort and came bluntly to the point. "It would seem that John Dee has no liking for our friend Brindle. This dry old snake does not trust him and he shook me from my bed to plague my pickled mind with a volley of infernal questions. I've spoken up for our guest but still he is not satisfied. Never could comprehend the meaning of loyalty and friendship, could you, John?"

"There's nothing wrong with Brindle!" Henry cried hotly. "Don't you think you're better than him, for you're not – wizard or no wizard. Worth ten of you, he is, and I won't have a word spoke against him."

The astrologer raised a hand for silence but was not angry at the boy's impetuous outburst.

"Your devotion does you credit," he said kindly. "Yet you know more about this stranger than I. Pray, indulge my suspicions. They are not ill meant and I do not wish to persecute him. My one desire is to serve and protect the Queen and Her realm. If the Iribian presents no danger then I will beseech your forgiveness, but there can be no harm in prudence and caution. I would learn more of your unusual friend. Lord Richard has told me much but perhaps you two can enlighten me even further."

Appeased by his words, Henry calmed himself. "'Course," he said. "I'll help Brindle any way I can and prove that he's the grandest person you'll ever meet. Saved my life twice, he has. There's nothing I wouldn't do for him. He's the best, ain't he, Coggy?"

Adam had been listening, wrapped in quiet thought.

There was definitely something unsettling about Brindle which disturbed him and when Henry nudged him to speak in the Iribian's defence he was not sure what to say.

Doctor Dee noticed his reticence and seemed pleased by it.

"Coggy!" Henry insisted. "Tell him how splendid and good Brindle is."

Adam stared down at his hands. "Henry is right," he said carefully. "Brindle has saved us both."

"Toad's whiskers!" Henry cried in disbelief. "Can't you do better than that? Who rescued us from Old Scratch and tried to protect Jack? Who stopped Clink Kitson slitting my throat? What's the matter with you?"

Before his friend could reply, Doctor Dee's chair scraped over the floor and the old man left the table.

"We can learn nothing in this fashion," he declared, crossing the room to clear a stack of books and parchments from the lid of a large chest. "I shall consult a higher wisdom than our own and settle the matter once and for always. If there is aught to fear from the Iribian then we shall soon know."

Lord Richard shifted awkwardly. "No, John," he objected. "I will not witness this. I never believed in this folly of yours and refuse to begin now. Let the matter rest – Brindle is as noble a being as I've ever encountered."

"It is the only way," the astrologer responded with a

curt finality as he turned a silver key in the chest's ornate lock and reverently raised the lid. "Or are you afraid of what we may discover?"

Richard Wutton grumbled into his beard, wishing the Queen's astrologer was more liberal with refreshment.

"Whatever you say," he muttered. "Though if you persist then I demand the children be excused. They have no need to see a feeble-headed old man make himself appear even more foolish."

With infinite care, the Doctor removed from the chest a bundle of black velvet. "On the contrary," he announced, "I believe that they are the very ones who ought to observe this wonder. Adam o'the Cogs most specially so."

"What does he mean?" Adam asked. "What is he going to do? Why me?" Lord Richard gave a sorry shake of the head and shrugged.

"John Dee thinks he is going to confer with angels," he answered with weary scepticism. "For too many years he has professed to having been granted visions and hearing voices. Knowing his taste for watery ale I do doubt it most sincerely. 'Tis all polemic nonsense, but I don't see why you should be singled out for this pitiable display, Cog Adam."

Bearing the velvet bundle over to the table, the astrologer laid it down gently. "Do you not?" he asked pointedly, and the question made his former friend avoid the piercing gleam of his eyes. "Do not think you have deluded everyone, Richard. You never did set much value upon my Enochian researches. May this night remove the scales of unbelief from your eyes. Many secrets have been revealed unto me by communing with the discarnate beings. In any case, it is always rewarding to educate the ignorant."

In expectant silence, Adam and Henry watched him unwrap the folds of velvet and the hairs on their necks tingled with anticipation until the object hidden inside was finally revealed.

"Behold the shew stone!" the Doctor proclaimed. "The black mirror through which the celestial hosts hold converse with me. No one outside this chamber has ever set eyes upon it – you three are the first to be so honoured."

Lord Richard and the apprentices gasped in astonishment. The shew stone was a disc of highly polished black glass in which the reflection of every candle flame leaped and flared; yet it was not the unusual mirror which surprised the onlookers, but that which framed it.

Encircling that smooth darkness was a broad band of yellowish metal overlaid with intricate, serpentine designs in which many small, coloured stones were set. They had all seen its like before and stared, dumbfounded, until at last, Henry blurted, "Brindle's torc! 'Tis a perfect match."

His master looked up at Doctor Dee in bewilderment. "Whence got you this?" he murmured. "How did this thing come into your possession?"

"Now you understand a portion of my disquiet," the old man said. "This precious scrying glass was entrusted unto my keeping by the last of the special ambassadors, those many years ago. When I beheld your Iribian wearing a collar of the same devising, I was naturally curious."

"Brindle did say he knew of the special ambassadors," Adam broke in, "but he would tell me no more than that."

The astrologer rubbed his long fingers together. "Then let us commune with those who can furnish a solution to these riddles," he said, "and maybe allay our doubts. Lantern, pray attend to the candles and cover the window."

Obediently, the copper secretary extinguished each candle in turn. With every quenched flame the room shrank back into darkness and presently the only light emanated from the mannequin's hat and the pale glimmer of his green eyes. Ambling to the window, he pinned a blanket across it and the gloom closed in even more.

Doctor Dee cleared the shadow-engulfed table of everything save the black mirror and returned to his chair, bidding Lantern join them. "My copper companion is so much more than a mere secretary," he told them. "His assistance with my mathematical calculations is invaluable to me, yet he is more than a common mechanical and possesses many hidden and secret talents. Oh yes, there is a great deal more to my friend Lantern than his sums and parts. He is the most talented and successful medium I have ever had the privilege to work with."

"I don't like this," Henry breathed, his face splashed by the golden stars spilling from the conical hat as the mannequin sat beside him. "Is he going to do magic? I don't want to see no devils conjured out the dark."

"Henceforth you shall all remain silent," the Doctor instructed. "There must be no interruption."

"Get on with it," Lord Richard prompted.

The old man threw him a warning glance and Richard Wutton mouthed an apology.

"Lantern," the Doctor resumed, "take up the shew stone. Let us speak to the powers of the spiritual realm."

Lifting the black mirror, the mechanical set it down before him, then spread his gauntleted hands upon either side and tilted his head back to gaze at the shrouded ceiling.

Doctor Dee closed his eyes. "Hear me," he called in a voice charged with force and authority. "Ye immortals of the outer reaches. Harken to my prayer. Thou angels of the Creator's glory, beneath the government of Uriel, I – John Dee – summon you here. Leave your sombre habitation. Come, be amongst us. By the Call of the Thirty I command it."

Breathing shallowly in the semi-dark, Henry wiped his sweating palms on his breeches as fear swelled within him. It seemed as if the atmosphere in the room was becoming charged with a hidden, crackling energy. Beyond the range of Lantern's radiance, the raven murk began to churn and seethe, as though teeming with inky, squirming forms.

The boy's scalp crawled and gooseflesh prickled along his arms when Doctor Dee sang out a babble of Latin words. Henry turned to Adam to see how he was enduring this unnatural litany. His friend appeared mesmerised, yet when he became aware of Henry's questioning eyes, he gave only the faintest of nods.

Feeling estranged from the others, Henry's chest tightened as the dread mounted. In the corners of his vision he thought he caught sight of blurred shapes reeling behind him and he drove his fingernails into his palms in an attempt to ignore those imagined horrors.

Abruptly, Lantern's candle started to fizz and spit, and the unexpected sound made Henry jump. Then the light flickered and dimmed. The warm, slender beams which radiated from the secretary's hat changed hue until the four people around the table were flecked with pale silver speckles and the candle's tapering flame transformed into a wintry, argent spike.

"Enter this, the uplifted realm," Doctor Dee exulted. "Bosco-Uttwar, speak unto us."

Behind the round lenses of Lantern's eyes, the green glow diminished to a blank emptiness and the faint ticks and whirrs of his internals faded into silence. Henry edged away as the astrologer pointed at the shew stone and hissed, "See – the hosts of Uriel prepare the way."

Over the surface of the mirror, a milky, phosphorescent vapour was moving, leaking from the ether like whey straining through muslin. Above the smooth, black glass it coiled smokily upwards and Henry bit his lip to keep from crying out. In the encompassing frame, the coloured stones glimmered with light. Then, impossibly, the dark reflections shivered and rippling rings disturbed the surface as the mirror became like water.

Henry almost fell from the bench, scrunching his eyes to make certain they had not deceived him. Widening circles radiated out across the viscous glass but none of the mysterious liquid splashed on to the table or escaped the confines of the frame.

Adam's eyes bulged in wonder and even Lord Richard was impressed, although he cast doubtful glances at Doctor Dee, hoping to catch him out in some trickery. The molten shew stone surged and eddied as invisible forces whisked through the glistening fluid, spinning and turning until a vortex formed in its heart, sucking a winding funnel down into unknown depths.

To the apprentices' amazement the twisting whirlpool plunged beneath the level of the tabletop, sinking to an incredible, remote distance. For several moments the eerie phenomenon continued to swirl and then, far below in the darkest reaches, a dim spark twinkled into existence. From that spiralling abyss the distant star came streaking to the surface, imbuing the rippling edges with stark, frosty light. Out from the gyrating shaft it rose, floating noiselessly up into the shimmering vapour where it hung on the air, shining a cold, ghastly glare on to all their faces.

"I am here," intoned a bleak, echoing voice and

Henry whipped his head around in shock – for the disembodied words had emanated from Lantern. He was about to jump from his seat when Adam gripped his hand, compelling him to stay.

"Welcome," the Doctor murmured, his eyes shining.

The voice spoke again and the copper of Lantern's casing rang faintly, endowing it with a metallic resonance. "Why was the invocation made?" it demanded. "What sacred wisdom would you glean of me?"

"Forgive this summons," the old man addressed the glowing mist, "but there are weighty matters here which require your guidance. A stranger has come amongst us. We are in need of your counsel."

"A stranger?"

"One who has come from outside the uplifted isles. He calls himself Brindle – a merchant in balms and fragrance."

The pillar of smoke flared as the star blazed with white fire. "Fragrance!" the voice chimed and to Adam it sounded almost panic-stricken. "Tell me, from whence does this merchant hail? Know you the sphere of his kind?"

Lines of concern etched themselves on the astrologer's face as he too marked the note of alarm. "Yes," he replied uneasily. "The world is called Iribia."

The intense light faltered. "An Iribian..." rang the distressed cry. "Then all is lost."

"Explain," the Doctor called. "Why are you afraid?"

"Death shall sluice the streets," came the ominous, frightened answer. "None shall survive. The Iribian will see to that. Listen to me, I beg you. Heed this warning and heed it well. 'Ware this stranger. Do not allow him to remain amongst you; expel him at once – it is your only hope for salvation."

Shadows of doubt crept over Lord Richard's features and he listened gravely.

"In the name of all you hold dear, harken to me," the hollow voice urged. "The Iribian will slaughter each one of you. The carnage shall not end."

"No!" Henry spat, his temper boiling. "Brindle's not like that. I don't care what you are – Brindle's good and decent."

"He is an Iribian!" the voice shrieked back. "His race are hated throughout the great darkness; they are a byword of horror and repugnance."

Stunned, Lord Richard drew a hand over his face. "I cannot believe it," he murmured.

"Know then," the voice declaimed. "Learn the black secret of the perfume chasers and fill your hearts with terror. They are a pestilence, leaving only death and despair in their wake."

"But why?" Richard Wutton countered. "What have Brindle's people done? What is this heinous sin they have committed?"

The hanging mist pulsed angrily. "Across the Outer Darkness there bleeds a savage, ruthless trail. The teachers of the past, those who you called the special ambassadors – have you not wondered why they never returned to your islands? Why they abandoned you to this lonely night? Learn now the hellish truth and know the vile nature which lurks within your stranger's breast. Every one of your special ambassadors is dead. Mothers and infants, the aged and infirm – the Iribian hordes butchered them all. Nothing could stop them, they were possessed and insane. The wise race who taught and guided you in the early years of the Beatification were slaughtered to extinction and their world is now a vast, desolate grave."

The spirit's awful words pealed about the chamber and everyone caught their breath. It was too hideous to imagine.

"I don't understand," Lord Richard uttered. "Why would they commit such a foul outrage?"

The star burned fiercely. "For the deathscent!" the answer came ringing back. "A whole race massacred, simply for the elusive scent released at the moment of death. *That* is what transformed the Iribians into the loathed abominations they are this day. Harvesting this subtle smell was all that they craved; to them it is above value. To inhale this most precious of essences, the Iribian will kill and kill again. He must – he cannot stop himself; he is a crazed, wild beast."

"But surely," Doctor Dee began, "there is no danger to

us. We are a race apart from the special ambassadors. There is no deathscent to be inhaled here."

"Vain, unhappy wretch!" the voice countered. "Unlearn your pride. Did you think your uplifted lives were prolonged simply by the grace of your God? Verily the children of mankind have been augmented, the tale of their years is stretched, because they too are in possession of this same secret gland. When you die, thou shalt surely excrete the accursed musk which only the Iribian wolves can detect. Once the merchant you have nurtured discovers this, he will slay each one of you and grow stronger with every merciless breath. Banish him whilst there is yet time. Purge your lands of this disease – shun him. At the peril of your souls, he must not unearth this concealed knowledge."

Adam's stomach twisted and clenched inside him as his confused suspicions finally became clear and he turned a drained, horrified face to Lord Richard. "He already has," he choked. "In the woodland – he was with Jack. It happened then – I saw it. Brindle *knows*!"

Richard Wutton returned his stricken stare. "That villain Kitson," he murmured. "Hobbling John said he had been cruelly butchered."

"And the next morning Brindle's eye was healed!" Adam cried.

The floating star flashed with icy light. "Then in truth it is too late!" the voice wailed inside Lantern. "He cannot deny his base, bestial instinct. The hunger will torment and burn in his blood. There is naught he can do to prevent it – his kind cannot control the killing madness. Even now he will be selecting his next victim. The deathscent enhances and invigorates his strength, and your weapons are too slow and primitive to halt him. If you love your lives then flee. Go from this reflected realm. It is doomed to death!"

Henry had listened to these ghastly words with increasing fury and anguish. Unable to bear any more, he leaped up and yelled at the top of his young voice as hot tears streamed down his face. "Stop! It's a lie! This is a demon you've conjured – you're a foul and filthy witch! Well, you'll not turn me against Brindle!"

"Henry..." Adam began.

But the Wattle boy would not listen and glared at him in revulsion. "All of you are lying!" he bawled. "And you, you dirty orphan, you disgust me the most. Brindle loves us! He would never hurt anyone, he would never harm me! I know he wouldn't. How dare you speak such squalid stories? He's better than you, he's better than all of you – he's better than Jesus!"

With that the enraged apprentice gave Lantern a brutal kick and the mechanical went tumbling from the bench. At once the link with the strange, ghostly voice was severed and the glimmering star was instantly extinguished. The black mirror ceased swirling.

Henry ran to where the secretary had fallen and blew into his hat before anyone could stop him. Immediately, the room was thrown into absolute darkness and Adam felt someone brush roughly past him.

"The window!" Doctor Dee called in the impenetrable night. "Tear down the cloth."

Confused noises blundered in the dark as Lord Richard fumbled his way to the wall. There was a clamour of rustling paper followed by heavy bumps as unseen books were knocked from their shelves, then Richard Wutton gave a grunt and the blanket was ripped clear.

The light of the sparkling heavens came filtering through the latticed panes and by their dim gleam they found Lantern still lying motionless upon the floor. Henry was no longer in the room.

"He's gone to Brindle," Adam realised. "We must stop him!"

"Her Majesty," Lord Richard uttered. "Brindle's still with Her."

They hurried to the curtained entrance, only to be called back.

"Wait!" the astrologer cried, running his hands over the tabletop. "The shew stone is not here! The crazed boy has taken it with him."

Adam stared at Lord Richard and each shared the same sickening thought.

"If Brindle gets hold of that," Adam whispered, "he'll be able to construct a beacon and call the rest of his people here."

Shouting Henry's name, they ran down the spiral stair, leaving Doctor Dee to stoop over Lantern. The eyes of the mechanical flickered and the old man staggered to the window, where he gazed up at the glittering heavens.

"Lord have mercy on us," he breathed.

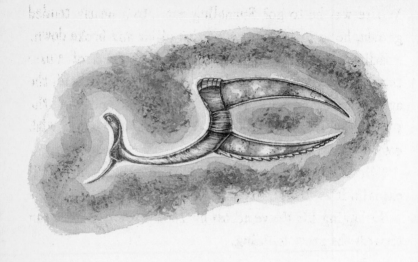

CHAPTER 7

The Deathscent

With tears stinging his eyes, and clutching the black mirror tightly, Henry Wattle charged through the palace. The guards who had seen him and Adam go by earlier, escorted by Lantern, let him pass. Shaking their heads at one another, they wondered what unholy terrors the astrologer had shown the boy and knew better than to interfere.

Down the panelled halls Henry fled, his mind a battleground of confusion and fear. What was he to do?

Where was he to go? Stumbling out into a neatly tended garden, he leaned against a wooden pillar and broke down.

Minutes trickled by and, gradually, strains of music entered his raw, pounding desolation. Lifting his head, the apprentice stared across the low hedges and saw the windows of the banqueting house scintillating with countless candles.

"Brindle," he sobbed. "He'll tell me it's not true. He'll explain. It's a dirty plot, that's what it is."

Dragging his sleeve across his face, Henry Wattle ran towards the great building.

Thomas Herrick's smile had congealed on his lips. Watching Her Majesty instruct the Iribian in the dancing had been a sore trial. For three years he had been the Queen's favourite partner and jealousy curdled inside him.

Brindle was an eager pupil. Already he had mastered La Volta and his strong arms had lifted Elizabeth higher than any man had ever done before. Herrick was incensed. Her loud laughter pierced him and when she saw his brooding face she laughed even more.

"Come, Sirrah!" she cried. "We will have no sullen wretches here. Grudge not My sweet Salamander. I am considering the bestowal of lands upon him – sulk any more and I shall give him yours."

Master Herrick forced a grin on to his lips. "But this is

unfair, Your Grace," he entreated, "for the sun to shine upon a single bloom. What are the rest of us to do? We shall wither in the shade."

"I would not have you pine without Me," she said judiciously. "Let the musicians commence a new tune. I must bring warmth to My garden of pretty courtiers. The Tinternel then."

The music was instantly replaced by a different melody and the Queen turned a sorrowful expression to Brindle.

"Alas, good Salamander. I must obey the will of My subjects. I am always theirs, such is the unhappy lot of a monarch. Stand aside and when this dance is over I promise to instruct you in its movements."

The Iribian bowed and drew away to the tiered benches. A spiteful thrust jabbed from Thomas Herrick's eyes as he took the Queen's hand and led her into this new dance.

Brindle let his senses drift over the merry assembly. The richly-coloured costumes did indeed put him in mind of a garden. Thomas Herrick was not the only gentleman who vied for the Queen's attention with costly clothing. The Iribian understood perfectly why this race had appealed to those his kind had hunted to extinction. He could appreciate what had attracted them and knew why they had been chosen to occupy these islands in the deserted regions of the darkness. They had an exuberant flair and imagination and their attention to the smallest detail was unlike any he had ever encountered. It was all most impressive and Brindle marvelled at the monumental achievement of bringing them here. Yet they were ignorant of their true purpose in these isolated isles and, beneath the luxuriant display of velvets and silks, he could smell the earthy sweat and dirt of this uninformed people.

Without thinking, his hand slid to the hilt of his reaping hook. It would be childishly easy to kill everyone in this room. One swipe of the blades would release that sacred essence and set his blood on fire, inspiring him with a tireless vigour. Absently, he counted the heads of the dancers and his mouth watered. Watching them weave in and out of one another, he pictured himself among them, leaping, and lunging with the twin knives. A divine providence had sent him here, a paradise where he was a tiger among the doves.

The emerald horseshoes of his eyes sparkled; if he relinquished control and abandoned himself to those primitive instincts his mind would never know a melancholy moment. The guilt and sorrow of the intervening years would vanish as the exquisite joy of the deathscent would uplift him to an unassailable rapture.

A loathsome chuckling broke into his black thoughts and he was shocked and sickened to discover that the laughter was his own. In that moment he despised himself. He must never again succumb to the awful lust which had damned his people and made them the scourge of other societies. There were other nobler joys and, for the first time since Jack Flye had perished, he found himself thinking of his family and wondered what his children were doing without him.

A glad and grateful smile tugged at the corners of his wide mouth. The choice was made. There would be no more killing. If the Queen permitted, he would retire to a lonely isle, away from temptation.

Sir Francis Walsingham was still huddled with the other privy councillors upon the raised platform, viewing the proceedings with hawklike concentration. Brindle glanced at him. He would never divulge the secrets of Iribia's infernal weaponry to Her Majesty's spymaster. They were not ready to wield such destruction – no one ever was.

Turning his attention back to the dancers, he gave himself to the merry tune and quickly memorised the movements. Then, dodging past the outlying figures, he made his way to the Queen and offered her his hand. It was a breaking of etiquette but Elizabeth was charmed by the impulsive gesture and readily assented. Glowering, Thomas Herrick was dismissed to the side of the hall where he gritted his teeth, almost wishing he had never brought the Iribian to London.

Now that the terrible burden was lifted from his conscience, Brindle danced more expertly than ever and the Queen was delighted.

"If you are as accomplished in the saddle," she said,

"you must ride with Me on the morrow. My horses are the finest in the realm."

The balm trader accepted and, overhearing the invitation, Thomas Herrick's displeasure was complete.

Another melody commenced. Around the spacious hall the courtiers processed in line, with the Queen and her new favourite at their head. Then, abruptly, Brindle faltered. Instead of leading Her Majesty through the aisle of expectant dancers, he turned and stared at the entrance.

"Salamander?" Elizabeth began. "Why do you hesitate? The steps of this are simple enough."

The pigmented flames around Brindle's eyes bunched together as he frowned. "Fear flies this way," he muttered, his nostrils trembling. "Henry – he is confused and afraid. Something has happened."

To the Queen's astonishment, he left her side and strode toward the doors. Her surprise inflamed to anger and she stormed after him. "How dare you leave Me!" she cried. "God's death, I will not brook such impertinence and want of courtesy."

The music died but her indignant shouts were joined by a second commotion outside the entrance. "The heavenly messenger!" Henry Wattle's voice was shrieking. "I must see him!"

Having run to the banqueting house, the apprentice had been stopped by the guards posted outside. No matter how hard he kicked and yelled, they would not let him enter.

"Brindle!" he shouted. "Brindle!" Within the great building, the Iribian bellowed for them to let him pass and the startled sentries put aside their halberds.

Henry pelted between them and came barging in. The sumptuous sea of courtiers parted before him, clearing a direct path to Elizabeth and the Iribian.

Clasping the shew stone to his chest, Henry blundered to a standstill.

"Who is this ragged urchin?" the Queen demanded, glaring down the divided gulf. "You have not the right to permit his entry. Explain this intrusion."

Brindle did not hear her. He was staring at Henry's tormented face, horrified at the burn which marred his forehead.

"Who has done this?" he thundered. "What has befallen you?"

Reaching out, he stepped forward but the boy gave a pitiful screech and pulled away. "Tell me it isn't true!" he pleaded. "Tell me!"

"The boy is mad," Elizabeth declared. "Remove him."

"No!" Brindle protested. "Henry, what have you heard? Why are you afraid?"

"They said you were a murderer," the boy snivelled. "A killer who'd gut us all, butcher us for the smell of our death. They said you were evil."

The Iribian's jaw tightened as he flinched from those terrible, condemning words and a murmur of shock rippled around the room.

"Do you believe that?" he asked.

Henry shook his head. "But Lord Richard and Coggy did," he gulped. "It were that blasted doctor's fault, him and his haunted secretary. The things they said about you. Oh, Brindle..."

All eyes were fixed upon the Iribian, regarding him with distrust and suspicion, but he was oblivious to them. The only thing that mattered was to soothe the boy's distress.

"Let me see your wound," Brindle said tenderly. "It needs dressing and you must rest."

There could be no mistaking the genuine concern and compassion in that voice and Henry broke down again. Any grain of doubt he may have had was banished and he rushed forward. The Iribian wrapped his arms about him and the apprentice wept, his body shaking with uncontrollable sobs.

"Do not fear," Brindle said gently. "The danger is over. I won't let any harm come to you. As a son to me, you are."

Moved by Henry's grief and the Iribian's earnest affection, the Queen forgave his interruption and called two Tizzys over. "Take the child to a bedchamber and feed him well," she commanded. "He is overwrought."

Henry reared his head. "I won't go," he swore defiantly.

"They'll be here soon. Here to accuse Brindle. I'll not leave him."

"You are mistaken, child," she chided. "Doctor Dee would not charge my Salamander of any wrongdoing. He has assured me the stars augur favourably. Your betters have played a game with you, that is all."

"Do as you are bidden," Thomas Herrick's voice rallied to the Queen's aid.

"I won't!" the boy insisted.

"God's blood!" Elizabeth cried at his obdurate insolence.

"Bum boils!" Henry retorted.

Brindle placed his hands upon the apprentice's shoulders, unaware of the bruises dealt to him by the Torture Master. Grimacing, Henry winced. Only then did the Iribian notice the object he had been grasping to his chest.

"What is that?" he asked.

Henry held out the shew stone and Brindle drew a sharp breath when he recognised the design of its frame.

"I... I took it from the Doctor's tower," the apprentice stammered. "I wanted to give it to you. I knew you needed it."

Brindle sank to his knees. He could scarcely believe it. Running his eyes over the twisting yellow metal, a faint cry of jubilation burst from his lips. "All the elements are in place," he whispered, touching the blue stone of his torc. "I can construct a beacon. I am no longer cut off from my home. I can return to Iribia." An entirely different future was opening before him. "I can see my family again. Henry, I owe you my deepest thanks."

The Queen roared in exultation. "That is excellent news," she announced. "The prosperous trade we spoke of can begin. Your people will be most welcome in My kingdom."

Still kneeling, Brindle looked up at her – aghast. "No," he murmured. "That must never be." But his voice went unheard as Lord Richard Wutton and Adam o'the Cogs burst into the banqueting house.

"Don't give it to him!" Adam yelled, dashing forward to wrench the mirror from Henry's hands.

"Your Grace!" Lord Richard panted, out of breath. "This fellow has deceived us all. He is not who he pretends to be."

The Queen looked from one to the other in consternation as Walsingham and the rest of the council made their way forward.

"Lord Richard, hear me," Brindle begged. "You must allow me to explain. Whatever you have been told, be not hasty in your judgement. You are my friend and I yours; listen to me – please."

"Hear him!" Henry yelled as Adam wrested the shew stone out of his fingers.

The master of Malmes-Wutton listened to them both and, away from the fervid cries of the disembodied voice in the tower, he felt the anger cool inside him and his usual level-headed reason returned. "I did not want to believe you would betray me," he said. "It is only fair that you be permitted to deliver your version of what we have been told."

"I agree with you, Richard," Walsingham added. "This is a tale we must all hear."

"He's a black-hearted killer!" Adam shouted, dismayed at Lord Richard's wavering resolve. "You don't understand! You don't know what he's done!"

"But I intend to," the spymaster promised. "Although not here in full show. This is a matter for Her Grace and the Privy Council."

Elizabeth concurred. "Take the Iribian to the council chamber," she instructed. "We will uncover the truth of these singular indictments there."

"My thanks," Brindle said. If he could only make them understand that he was no longer any danger to them. If they could only be made to know a fraction of his people's shame at what they had done. If he confessed to everything then maybe he could begin again with a less burdened heart. If this primitive race could forgive him, then it might be possible to forgive himself.

Walsingham summoned the guards from the entrance but, before they could reach the balm merchant, Thomas Herrick intervened. The charges against Elizabeth's Salamander had pleased him greatly. He felt only hostility and resentment towards the usurping stranger and was delighted that his own position in the Queen's affections now looked to be restored. Always pushing himself forward, he could not resist doing so at that fateful moment.

"Your pardon, Your Grace," he toadied. "Innocent or no, this dubious personage must be disarmed. Permit me to remove the curious knife he bears."

Without waiting for an answer, he leaned across and pulled the reaping hook from its sheath at Brindle's side. At once the Iribian sprang to his feet and seized hold of the man's wrist.

"That is an heirloom of my house," Brindle growled. "It was to pass on to my eldest son. I will not suffer you to so much as touch it. Release it from your sullying clutches."

Herrick spluttered and tried to drag himself free. "Unhand me, you uncouth knave!" he cried. "I am doing Her Majesty's bidding – do not obstruct me."

"I will not quarrel with you," Brindle warned, his iron grip squeezing the vain man's wrist even more tightly. "If I have to surrender the weapon then so be it, but never unto you. You have done naught but show discourtesy and contempt for those I hold in esteem. Give the knife to one of the boys. They have in them more nobility than you can ever pretend."

Struggling to liberate his hand, Thomas Herrick's face had turned crimson with the strain. Between him and the Iribian the two blades of the reaping hook flashed and glinted as they shivered in his quivering grasp.

"Let it go," Brindle ordered.

"Get away from me, you snorting beast!"

Exasperated by this public brawling, the Queen could stomach it no longer. "Enough!" she roared. "Herrick! Do not think you can hurl your insults in My name. Until this affair is decided the Iribian will continue to enjoy his status as the emissary of a foreign power. Do as he bids – give the weapon to one of the children."

The dismayed man turned his head toward her in surprise and, considering the matter settled, Brindle released him. Yet the distracted Herrick was not expecting his sudden action. The muscles in his arm were still pulling and straining. Before he could stop himself, the fist which gripped the razor sharp blades jerked violently towards his own face.

Every voice cried in horror. The Queen covered her eyes and Adam turned away as Thomas Herrick fell, twitching, to the ground, the pale silks of his expensive garments darkening with his own blood.

"Fetch the physician!" Walsingham called. "Quickly! Staunch the flow, someone."

Brindle staggered backwards, overwhelmed with a terrible fear. He threw his hands to his forehead where the long slit of his cranial nostril began to quiver, opening like a flower with fleshy petals as it quested the air.

"No!" he howled. "Help me – take me from this place. I beg you!"

"What ails him?" Walsingham shouted.

Richard Wutton rushed forward and tried to drag the Iribian away, but Brindle reeled back, falling into the crowd. The courtiers stumbled away from him as he toppled to the floor, calling out in a desperate, beseeching cry, "The man is *dying!*" he yelled. "HELP ME!"

It was no use. As Thomas Herrick's final feeble movements ceased, Brindle began to shake. An excruciating, dolorous roar erupted from his lungs.

"Look at his skin," the courtiers exclaimed. "What is happening?"

"Lord of hosts!" the Queen whispered.

Within the Iribian's flesh, a luminous, spectral sheen was creeping, flowing through his veins until he glowed with a ghastly light. The battle had been decided against his will. His futile struggle against the base forces of his nature was ended – and he had lost.

"It's what I glimpsed when Jack died," Adam breathed. "It's what the deathscent does to him."

There was a heart-thumping pause. Then Brindle raised himself from the floor and the transformation that had disfigured his noble countenance was terrible to witness.

The Iribian was almost unrecognisable. His lemon and green eyes were wild and staring and shot with silver, threading veins. His many nostrils were gaping and his features shone with a livid, streaking light which moved beneath the surface of his flesh like sheets of cold flame.

Yet it was Brindle's expression which alarmed and frightened the apprentices. He now resembled a feral, hungry beast and even Henry shrank away from him in terror.

With swaggering, powerful strides, Brindle pushed through the frightened people until he stood beside the body of Thomas Herrick once more and sniggered cruelly. Then he pulled the reaping hook out of the dead man and rounded on Adam.

"Give me that device," he ordered in a gargling, bestial voice that was not his own. "Bring it to me!"

Grasping the shew stone in trembling hands, Adam shook his head. "You can't have it," he answered. "I'll break it before you can call more of your kind here."

A vicious snarl gurgled in Brindle's throat and he raised the bloodstained reaping hook as if to lash out at him. Then he spat and in one swift movement dragged the Queen to his side, pressing the blades to her neck.

Elizabeth of Englandia was too afraid to utter a sound. The gleam of the bright knives threw her into a panic and her eyes rolled pitifully in her ashen face.

A woeful hush had fallen in the great room and no one dared move.

"Give me the device," Brindle's repulsive voice repeated. "Or your Sovereign goes the way of Herrick."

Adam wavered but Walsingham hissed in impotent wrath, "Obey him. Do whatever he says."

"You must," Lord Richard urged.

Adam took a pace forward but Brindle barked for him to stay where he was. "Slide it along the floor to me," he snapped, edging towards the wall.

The apprentice lowered the mirror to the ground, then sent it skimming towards the Iribian's feet.

Brindle stepped on it, and dragged the shew stone with him as he drew the Queen over to one of the banqueting house's many large windows.

"You'll never escape," Walsingham spoke up. "You won't leave this palace alive. Let Her Majesty go, unharmed, and we will be merciful."

A guttural laugh crowed from Brindle's mouth and he brandished the reaping hook menacingly in front of the Queen's face. "Oh, I shall get out of here," he vowed, the blood vessels pulsing in his temples. "Never doubt that. You cannot hurt me, not now."

The twin blades swung back. Elizabeth saw them poised to come slicing down and she steeled herself to meet Death as had her mother before her.

"Don't!" Henry yelled.

The knives sang through the air but the sight of the apprentice's tortured face stayed the Iribian's hand. Raging, he spared the Queen's life. Shrieking insanely, he threw her from him, snatched up the black mirror then flung himself through the glass window.

As the panes shattered and crashed, Walsingham and

the others rushed to Elizabeth's aid. "Leave Me!" she bellowed, spurning their hands and rising in thunderous wrath. "Get after that creature. Get after it and bring Me its ugly head!"

Through the grounds Brindle ran, his long legs carrying him swiftly towards the palace gates. The unearthly light still shone in his flesh and when the alarm was sounded the guards who came running could see him glimmering like a phantom in the darkness.

Mortally afraid, they were driven to pursue him by their captains but each one was slaughtered by the Iribian and his strength increased. By the time he reached the Holbein Gate he had killed five men and the four sentries guarding the way to the King's Street were cruelly cut down. Pausing only to inhale the last of them, he left the palace of Whitehall behind him.

Along that shadowy road Brindle bolted, the shew stone in one hand and the reaping hook in the other. He was terrible to behold. As some harrowing apparition loosed from the underworld he rampaged, bolting by the Charing Cross and the royal mews, his great leaping strides taking him into the Strand.

In the distance, at the edge of the isle of London, the vast effigy of Gog reared above the spires and rooftops. The massive silhouette of the barbarian's statue found a resonance deep inside the Iribian and he rushed up the wide, dirty road, keeping the towering figure in his sights.

Behind him the sound of a warning bell began to toll across the sprawling estate of the palace and he knew that soon the entire city would be roused. Throwing back his head, he let out a grim, demented laugh and the folk who dwelt in the nearby houses came running to their windows. Screams and shouts cut the air when they saw him but the spectre was away before they could hasten to bolt their doors. Over the Fleet Bridge he sprang, then down towards Thames Street, and the few people abroad that night fled before that grotesque, shimmering nightmare.

Without any trace of fatigue, Brindle headed for London Bridge. He could smell the distance he had put between him and his pursuers and was pleased. At Whitehall the Queen's men were all astir and the mechanical horses were brought from the mews as they prepared to hunt the deranged monster down. The reeking cloud of their fear made his tainted mind rejoice and he reached the north gate of the old bridge with an obscene grin twisting his flickering features.

"Hey there!" A stern voice called as a portly night-watchman caught sight of his loping figure. "Where might you be...?"

The question was left unasked. All at once the man saw the luminous glare of the Iribian's skin and the gouts of blood glistening on the knives he wielded in his hand.

"Save us!" the nightwatchman yowled, and he ran for his life. "The graves are emptying. The dead are waking!

Lanky corpses are here to drink our blood!"

Growling, Brindle let the stupid human go. On to the great bridge he stepped, passing between the shops and dwellings which lined it. From the spikes set high above the gates, the reek of the rotting human limbs impaled there stung his nostrils and his malformed face sneered. These barbarous creatures were no better than his own kind – worse perhaps, for they slew each other with a revolting readiness.

Approaching the southern bank, he hastened across the bridge and paused at one of the gaps between the buildings. In front of the old drawbridge gate, he strode over to the railings and lifted his eyes to the colossal figure of Gog which straddled the Thames.

The effigy's momentous axe was lowered halfway, but there was enough clearance beneath it for a night boat to escape through the massive aperture in that vaulted firmament. Glancing down at the black waters of the Thames, Brindle saw many vessels just waiting to be taken and he thrilled to think of the crews he could butcher in capturing one.

In the distance he heard the clattering hooves of mechanical horses and behind them the uproar of running foot soldiers. Yet there was still time to accomplish his most important task.

Removing the torc from around his neck, Brindle unfastened one of the entwining pieces of decoration, revealing a cavity filled with connected filaments and gleaming strands. From this he pulled out a slender rod of yellow metal, tipped with a tiny round gem set within a domed surround. Then he examined the shew stone and, with a deft twist of his fingers, detached a small, tadpole-shaped segment of its frame.

Clasping the collar about his throat once more and laying the black mirror against the railings, the Iribian held up the two pieces between his fingers and murmured softly to himself. The power to destroy this absurd collection of islands was now his to wield. Once the two elements were joined, a compelling plea for deliverance would commence the journey through the Outer Darkness to Iribia.

"Come, my kindred," he whispered, half closing his eyes to savour the critical, doom-laden moment. "Follow my beacon. This forsaken realm wherein the delicious deathscent flourishes will be hidden from our sphere no longer."

It was the work of an instant to slot the jewelled rod into the side of the larger piece. At once the gem began to crackle with an inner light and a greater stone set in the other segment flickered with a regular, winking radiance.

"So, 'tis done," Brindle remarked without a trace of remorse – he was beyond that now. "The call goes forth, reaching beyond the firmament. They will come and I will greet them from across a sea of slain."

Staring at the device a little longer, he slipped it into a velvet pouch fastened to his belt, then moved away from the railing. A group of men were approaching. His senses detected their sordid, unwashed garments and their unclean bodies. Yet at the forefront of that gang was, a fragrant personage who smelled strongly of sweet wine.

They were not a part of the force storming through the city in his pursuit; this foetid gang were advancing from the Southwarke side of the bridge. Gripping his reaping hook firmly, the Iribian turned to face the shadows which smothered the southern shore, then heard a gleeful laugh drift out from the murk.

"Most happy luck I is having this night," a voice chuckled. "Is seeking two naughty runaway youths, only to be finding their very own precious angel. Oh yes, Mistress Fortune she smile down on top of me. Don Gomez, he full of the joy at this unlooked meeting. Thanking you, Our Blessed Lady."

Out of the gloom and on to the bridge stepped the elegant, saturnine figure of the Spanish ambassador. Prowling behind, drawing their swords and daggers, came thirty-seven of the vicious cut-throats in his service.

"You is travelling with us this night," the Count de Feria beamed. "To Spain."

CHAPTER 8

The Breath of Innocence

Brindle's keen glance alighted upon each of the villainous brutes in the ambassador's employ. They were all desperate, cruel-looking men with coarse, scarred faces and were undaunted by his unearthly, glowing appearance. "I go where I will," he snorted, "and my path lies not with you."

The Count de Feria tutted at this foolish obstinacy. "His Highness, King Philip, He most eager to make acquaintance," he said. "Is most rude to decline His

Majesty, indeed I cannot be allowing this. Have night boat ready, is moored close by to take us from this uncouthing city."

"You'll need better persuasion than that," the Iribian jeered and he brandished his reaping hook threateningly.

The ambassador sighed, then clicked his fingers. At once the rough gang surged forward, yelling and shouting. Brindle merely laughed at them and leaped into the centre of the thoroughfare to give his arm room to swing, unhampered by the bordering walls.

With one darting lunge he thrust the twin blades into the chest of the first man, then tore it free and drove the barb at his elbow through the throat of a second. Both men collapsed lifeless at his feet and his skin shone more brightly than ever as the hallowed aroma of their death roared through his nervous system.

Invigorated, Brindle fought on, with a ferocious glare in his hellish eyes. Cursing, the Spanish ambassador's thugs rushed around him, encompassing the Iribian with their slashing steel. But the balm merchant whirled in a tight circle, shearing the menacing swords in two with screeches of sparking metal, lopping the hand off one who dared press too close.

"Don't be harming him!" the Count de Feria called out behind them. "Is needed alive. No kill the angel."

But his men were too busy struggling to keep their own lives to pay any attention to his ludicrous commands. Six of their number now lay dead and their spectral opponent was crowing with every fresh kill.

Agile and lithe, meeting their blows with lethal grace, Brindle moved with almost supernatural speed. Rapidly, the corpses mounted around him, impeding his attackers. A particularly repugnant member of that murderous crew, with rat-like eyes and a sewn-up nose, tripped over one of the fallen. When he came blundering forward, Brindle's glittering knives sent his head spinning into the gutter. Out over the river the clamour of the battle went ringing and those who dwelt upon the bridge, above the many shops, were terrified when they peered out of their windows at the carnage below.

As one possessed by a host of devils the Iribian fought. Lashing and cutting with unbridled zest, he jumped and struck, ducked and pounced and no one could withstand him. He was an unstoppable, inexhaustible force. Then, when he gulped down the eleventh glorious deathscent, a new noise was added to the turbulent sounds of combat.

From the northern shore the mounted forces of the Queen came galloping and Brindle eyed them grimly. Even in his enraged state, his bestial mind doubted that he would be able to repel all of them and the contest with de Feria's men doubled in savagery in an effort to cut a passage through them. Immediately, a twelfth villain had his arm scythed through at the shoulder before the legs were hewn from under him, then another was slain and the Iribian sprang on to a heap of carcasses to deal out two more bloody deaths.

"Leave him!" the ambassador's voice called when he too saw the horses charge on to the bridge. "Stop the riders; they must not capture the angel. Go – halt them!"

The remaining survivors of his men were only too glad to flee from that berserking monster. Hollering, they streamed past him to confront the oncoming horsemen in that narrow stretch – leaving the Count de Feria unprotected, with no one between him and Brindle.

Standing upon that island of corpses which rose from a scarlet sea, the fiend with the bitter, dripping blades turned his luminous face towards him and cackled malevolently. "Do you still wish me for a travelling companion?" he asked.

The Count shook his head. "No," he spluttered, backing slowly away. "You can be doing what you wish, go anywheres. Oh, what a tiring night. Is thinking I go lie down."

Brindle leaped from the heaped bodies of his victims and landed with a splash in the stream of their blood. "No need to leave for that," he growled. "You can lie down here, amongst your friends."

"Pardonny!" the ambassador entreated, making a tip-toeing retreat. "Is very sorry. Was big mistaking."

The Iribian advanced and the petrified Spaniard fumbled at his side for the rapier he carried. But his hands were trembling and, before he could remove it from the scabbard, Brindle was standing over him. The harrowing spectacle of those pitiless knives, as they came close to his face, burned itself into the Count's brain. Cowering, he closed his eyes and crossed himself.

Brindle bared his teeth and tensed his arm for the kill. But, before he dealt the butchering blow, one of the Queen's horses came storming through the human blockade. There was no time to linger and ingurgitate this cowardly Spaniard's death. Spitting with defiance, the Iribian ran the remaining distance along the bridge to the Southwarke shore and went glimmering into the shadows.

Still timidly waiting for the slaughtering stroke to fall, the Count heard the hooves thunder closer. Swallowing nervously, he ventured to open one eye. The heavenly messenger was nowhere to be seen and he cried out in relief, while checking his body frantically to make sure he had not been wounded.

Yet his plight was far from over. Even as he praised and thanked the Lord, his men were driven back by the mechanical horses and the ensuing rout came sweeping towards him. Before he could dash to safety, the Spanish ambassador found himself caught up in the thick of the fray.

In that cramped space, the conflict was a confused scramble of pushing bodies and clanking forms. The metal chargers stamped and trounced as their riders struck out

from the saddle with spear and sword. Heartened to be free
of Brindle's lethal knives, the Count's men fought back
with a new and determined ferocity. Horsemen were
dragged from their mounts, a side section was prised off a
stallion's casing. As its bellows sent up a frightful,
whinnying shriek, its internals were hacked and punched
until the pendulums were torn free and the beast fell
against one of the buildings, smashing through the
shuttered windows.

The discordant din was deafening. Hemmed in by this
jostling, clanging skirmish, the beleaguered Spanish
ambassador wheeled about, anxiously seeking an escape.
One of his own men staggered into him and the Count was
sent teetering deeper into the struggle, narrowly avoiding
the downward thrust of a rider's spear.

Fearing for his life, he hopped back from a stumbling
horse and shoved his way past another of his hired villains,
only for the man to cry out and collapse, felled by a slicing
sword. "Mother of God!" de Feria squealed, turning wildly
in terror and despair.

From the northern approach to the bridge the palace
guards finally caught up with the Queen's horsemen and
the confusion trebled as they piled into the rear of the
crowded thoroughfare. Trapped in the midst of that
confined and heaving scuffle, the Spanish ambassador
lurched from one peril to another as he wove clumsily
through the riot, cringing from stabbing blades and

crunching hooves. His sole thought was to reach one of the buildings. If he could gain the relative safety of one of those walls there was a chance he could batter his way in through a window or edge himself along until clear of this horrendous, deadly crush.

Squeamishly stepping over a trampled corpse, he elbowed a meandering path towards the side. His goal was almost within reach when two riders and three of his men went lumbering in front of him, barring the way. Exasperated, he squawked in fury. Alarmed at that sudden shrill noise, one of the felons swung blindly around and smashed a hammering fist into de Feria's jaw.

Emitting a startled squeak, the ambassador was knocked to the ground, falling headlong across the body he had previously managed to avoid so daintily. Nauseated, he tried to stand, but at that moment one of the horses veered to the side and he found himself crouching beneath it, woefully afraid in case its hooves kicked or crushed him.

"Holy Mother!" he whimpered, compelled to scurry along on his hands and knees like a cur as the mechanical plunged back into the mob. "Be saving me from this madness."

Into this chaos a breathless Adam and Henry came running. Disobeying Lord Richard's orders to stay behind, they had pursued the Queen's guards through the city. There was still a tension between them but the shock of Brindle's foul deeds had brought about a temporary truce.

Now they viewed the disordered tumult on the bridge and looked at one another fearfully.

"Do you think Brindle's in the middle of that?" Henry panted.

Holding his cramped sides, Adam fought to regain his breath. "If... if he is," he wheezed, "he's done for, and good riddance."

"Stop it!" Henry cried fiercely. "It wasn't his fault. Brindle couldn't help it – you saw what happened."

"Oh, I saw," the other boy retorted. "I saw him threaten the Queen and run off with Doctor Dee's shew stone. Didn't you hear them back at Whitehall? They said he'd murdered nine men getting to the gate."

Henry's face scrunched with wretched creases and he hurried on to the bridge. "I heard them!" he shouted. "But that wasn't our Brindle."

"Where are you going?" Adam yelled. "Get back here, you idiot!"

"I can't," came the dismal response. "I have to know. I have to see him."

For an uncertain instant, Adam watched Henry Wattle hurry towards that brutal engagement. Then he groaned and sprang after him.

To the rear of the pushing mass of guards Henry ran, yelling Brindle's name at the top of his voice. But the clamour of the confrontation drowned out every other noise and he wished he could see what was happening in the centre of it all. "Wait!" Adam called, racing up and seizing hold of his arm in case he tried to shove his way into that lethal scrum. "You're insane."

Henry could hardly hear him, but he was not listening anyway. A sudden surge drove the clashing forces further across the bridge and the railed gap between the buildings was suddenly revealed behind them.

"Look!" Henry shrieked. "The black mirror."

Lying where Brindle had left it, the astrologer's shew stone had miraculously escaped any damage from the rampaging feet and hooves. Only when the apprentices darted over to snatch it up did Adam notice the missing segment.

"What if he's already made his beacon?" he said gravely as he ran his hands over the yellow metal frame. "His people will come in their thousands to kill us. We'll be hunted to extinction, just like the special ambassadors were."

Henry did not answer; his attention was captured by something happening below them on the river. Pushing his face between the railings, the boy stared down and sobbed.

"There he is."

Leaping down the Southwarke river stairs, an apparition-like figure was jumping the steps four at a time, heading straight for a three-masted night boat – a small caravel which was moored at the edge of the Thames.

Adam glanced up at the giant, dark outline of Gog –

there was still room beneath his massive axe for a vessel such as that to pass through and escape. "He's going to get away," he said.

Henry shook his head vehemently. "No, he's not. I'm going to stop him."

"Don't talk stupid," Adam muttered. "Even if you could get to him, there's nothing you can do now. He's evil."

Kicking the railings, Henry rounded on Adam. "Not deep down he isn't!" he cried. "I know it. If I could just talk to him, I know I could call the real Brindle back."

"There is no real Brindle. He was always like this inside. He'd kill you the minute he saw you!"

"No, he wasn't and he wouldn't. He didn't kill the Queen because I stopped him. It's true, Coggy – why won't you believe me?"

Adam stared down at the caravel and watched the Iribian creep on to her deck. A startled shout came from the crewman on watch but one swipe of the reaping hook stilled that voice forever. Both apprentices witnessed the lambent light flare over the balm merchant's features as he inhaled the invigorating deathscent.

"That's why," Adam snapped. "How many men are aboard that craft? How many more is he going to kill?"

On London Bridge, the din of the fighting had abated. All of the Count de Feria's men were dead and Henry looked quickly at the assembled guards and horsemen who were pressing through that narrow way. He could never squeeze through them to reach those river stairs in time, so he gritted his teeth and did the only thing left to him. He clambered on to the railings.

"What are you doing?" Adam cried.

"I can't desert Brindle now," the boy answered. "I have to help him."

"You're as mad as he is!" Adam yelled. "If the fall doesn't kill you, you'll be drowned and if, by God's grace, that doesn't happen, then that devil down there will rip you apart."

"If there's a chance I can save him, I have to try," Henry insisted as he lifted his leg over the spike-tipped railings, wincing from the pain in his bruised shoulders. "Whatever you say, I know that he was different before. He needs me and I owe him; we both do – you know that."

Staring at the drop, the apprentice sought for ways of easing his descent. Directly beneath him one of the great buttressing beams drove down into the wide shoulder of a huge stone support that rose up from a wooden pier. The angle of the timber brace appeared gentle enough to scramble down – then if he could lower himself from the sloping corner of the great stone column and jump the remaining distance...

Henry's eyes were drawn to the dark, churning water and his fingers locked suddenly about the rails as he froze. "I can't do it," he gasped. "Oh, Coggy, I can't do it."

Adam reached to help him back down. "Glad to hear it,"

he scolded. "What were you thinking...?"

The expression of abject dismay and self-hatred which contorted Henry's face pierced his heart. This was the second time he had failed the Iribian: first in the residence of the Spanish ambassador he would have betrayed him to protect his own skin from the Torture Master; now he could not face the perilous drop into those violent rapids.

"I wanted to save him," the Wattle boy snivelled. "Oh, Brindle, forgive me – I'm too scared." And he hung his face in shame.

Adam stared in stunned surprise. He had never seen the cynical Henry so affected by anything before and a peculiar tingling began to creep up inside his chest. "You really thought his redemption was worth risking your own life for," he murmured. "It really meant that much to you?"

Henry nodded wretchedly. "But I couldn't do it!" he wept. "I'm too much of a coward."

"Yes, you are," Adam answered grimly, fixing him with a bitter glare. "But you also have a family at home to go back to. As you so regularly point out, I have nobody. If Brindle's going to murder one of us, it ought to be me."

Before he realised what he was doing, Adam o'the Cogs placed the shew stone on the ground and climbed over the railing. "You always were full of big talk, Henry Wattle," he exclaimed. And with that, he swung himself down on to the stout timber strut below.

"Coggy!" Henry cried, watching in amazement when he

saw what his friend had done. "Be careful!"

The massive beam was wet and Adam made a slithering descent to the sloping shoulder of the stone pillar. There was no going back now. Craning his head up, he could see Henry's face squeezed between the rails, while below the turbulent water continued to rage and foam. Gingerly, he inched his way to the edge of the angled stone, estimating that the fall to the pier beneath was nigh on twenty feet.

"I'm going to break my neck," he muttered, cautiously manoeuvring himself as close to the brink as possible.

The cool air rising from the Thames streamed through his straw coloured hair. He knew that the longer he waited, the worse his fears would grow; so, taking a great, determined breath, he dangled his legs over the side and pushed himself clear.

"COGGY!" Henry's voice sang in his ears as he fell. "I didn't mean those horrible things I said before – I'm sorry!"

Adam's knees buckled and pushed into his chest when he hit the pier with a jarring thud that knocked the wind from him. Falling on his face, he lay spluttering and coughing as he retched the air back into his lungs.

Across the river, hideous screeches proclaimed the Iribian's slaughterous progress on board the night boat and those dreadful sounds brought Adam shakily to his feet. One more leap and he would plunge into the swashing torrent of the Thames which came shooting under the bridge. Even experienced watermen drowned attempting to navigate those wild, frothing rapids in their rowing boats; how could a boy who had only ever swum in the village pond possibly survive? But it was too late to turn back and, with a grim resolve, he dived off the mighty pier and disappeared into the white-capped fury of the river.

High above on the bridge, Henry Wattle squeezed his eyes shut and prayed.

As the last of the crew collapsed at Brindle's feet, the Iribian jerked the twin blades of his reaping hook from the man's chest and laughed faintly. His cranial nostril was shivering with relish as the power of the deathscent coursed through his tall frame, renewing his energies and lapping his pale flesh with that macabre, frosty light.

He had never known such a glut of sensation – this surfeit of bliss was glorious. In his youth he had only been involved at the very end of those deranged wars against the special ambassadors. The scents he had culled in those massacres he had been forced to share with the others in his brigade. Now this ravishing heal-all was purely for him. Throwing back his head, he shook the ponytail of his hair and brayed in exultation.

Brindle knew that soon his people would follow the trail of his beacon, yet until they came it was not wise to remain in this island. Hurling the slaughtered crewmen over the

side, he set about casting the vessel adrift. Chopping
through the heavy ropes which tethered the night boat to
the shore, he glanced up at the enormous figure of Gog then
made a hurried inspection of the caravel as the current
teased it slowly out into the middle of the river.

Such craft were common on the Thames. They were used
as fishing boats in the coastal isles but, out in the perpetual
void, they were swifter than the larger galleons and could
travel at speeds of up to eight knots.

The lateen sails of this commandeered night boat were
already set and, in his possessed and primal state, Brindle
thought nothing unusual in that. Once away from shore, the
three large triangles of canvas quickly filled with the
breeze which gusted through the arches of London Bridge
and the caravel began to cut sharply through the water
towards the effigy standing guard at the entrance in the
firmament.

Hurriedly, Brindle searched for the mechanism which
operated the protecting canopy. There was no sign of it on
deck, so he kicked his way into the steerage hold at the
aftcastle where the tiller was housed. In that low, lantern-
lit space the smell of the pitch and tar was almost
intolerable to him, but at last he found what he had been
seeking – a sturdy metal wheel linked to chains and gears.

Gripping it in both strong hands, the Iribian cranked
the wheel around and chains went rattling through the ship,
setting in motion the raising of the deck canopy.

Presently, a sonorous clang proclaimed that the awnings were sealed. Brindle prepared to return to the deck, but halted when he noticed the door of a cabin. Curious, he investigated and discovered a tiny room which a single bunk and large wooden chest amply filled.

The chest served as a table and was laden with maps and charts of the uplifted isles. But there were also several prayer books, jewel boxes, a silver crucifix and a small casket covered in blue velvet which contained four phials filled with an indigo liquid and the empty impressions where two other glass vessels had been.

A contemptuous snort issued from Brindle's throat as he realised that he was on board the Spanish ambassador's ship after all. This anonymous, commonplace vessel was how the Count de Feria had planned to smuggle the Iribian out of Englandia. Growling, Brindle swept the objects to the floor and was about to lift the lid of the chest when his nostrils quivered and his eyes gleamed. A rumbling snarl left his lips, then he spun around and marched briskly out.

Encased in the canopy's canvas cave, the deck of the caravel was swamped in a sombre gloom which the two lanterns hung on the main and mizzen masts failed to lift. But the balm merchant had no need of illumination. The figure he found there, staring in revulsion at the blood-soaked deck, was hidden in shadow. Even though his signature scent was obliterated by dirty Thames water, Brindle knew him at once.

"Adam o'the Cogs," he hissed. "What supreme madness has brought you hither, into the jaws of the Iribian jackal?"

Soaked and shivering, the scrawny apprentice raised his eyes and returned Brindle's unfriendly glare. His struggles in the river had left him spent and he had only just managed to clamber on board the night boat before the canopy had sealed behind him. Already the air was stale in here, made foul by the grisly stench of hacked flesh and spilled blood, and the exhausted boy felt sick.

"Are you not afraid to be in the presence of this ravening beast?" Brindle demanded. "I have slain many of your kind this night and will continue to do so."

"That's why I came," Adam told him. "To stop you."

Brindle laughed and the cold colours which rippled through his skin shimmered bleakly.

"A little late for that, Cog Adam," he scoffed. "I am stronger now than at any time in my life. There is no turning back for me. The weak, compliant creature you knew has departed and can never be recalled. Those impurities have been burned away in the crucible of this ludicrous realm. You should have acted on your early suspicions. Oh yes, I saw your gimlet eyes dogging my movements. I knew you had caught a glimpse of the deathscent's power that day when Master Flye died. Then, in the Copper Cow, when I returned after paying my call on Clink Kitson – did you think I could not smell you spying upon the courtyard?"

471

"I hoped I was mistaken," Adam said. "I liked you, we all did, but now you disgust me."

"I care not," Brindle replied, unmoved. "Your shallow, stammering mind cannot comprehend the beauteous rapture an Iribian experiences at the ending of a human life. If you could but perceive a thousandth of that overwhelming ecstasy, you would not condemn me."

Appalled, the apprentice backed away. "I knew Henry was wrong!" he shouted. "He thought there was a chance that you weren't wholly evil – even had me half believing it. But you're worse than Satan himself. To murder someone merely for the reek of their death is the most disgusting, loathsome wrong I could ever imagine."

Brindle took a step towards him. "Surely any murder is wrong," he said with a malicious sneer curling his thin lip. "Can there be any deed more base? Yet with my kind we have good reason: we kill to refresh ourselves or repair our hurts and enjoy a tantalising sip of what you might call Heaven. Oh yes, child, your deaths mean so much more to us than they ever could to you. Your lives are never wasted – we value them far too highly."

"You're a monster!" Adam yelled, stumbling back. "I wish we'd let you die when we found you. We all trusted you."

The Iribian prowled closer. "Is it wisdom to befriend the beast?" he growled. "You must not trust that which you cannot tame."

Furious and afraid, Adam edged away. "Are you going to butcher me now?" he spat defiantly.

A shudder gripped the caravel as the vessel reached that part of the Thames which boiled and bubbled. Tremendous forces seized the night boat and it began to lift from the water. Within the Count de Feria's cramped cabin, the lid of the wooden chest started to open, pushed up by an iron claw.

On the deck, Brindle ran to the prow and stared through the window set into the timbers. Up out of the river they rose, in perfect alignment with the aperture high above in the starlit heavens.

Adam was holding on to the heavy ropes which trailed down the mainmast, to keep his balance as the craft continued to rise. "You didn't answer," he snapped. "Are you going to kill me?"

"All things are possible," came the callous reply. "'Twould be a blessed release for you if I did – a kindness even."

"Before your degenerate race comes to turn these islands into abattoirs, you mean!" Adam yelled.

Brindle's fingers played about the hilt of his reaping hook. "Not really," he said. "You still don't see, do you? Mankind was never meant to dwell out in the deserted void. You have no right to be here, but then how can I expect you to believe that? You still cling to the absurd conviction that your God raised these islands and set them in the great darkness so you might be closer to Him. I marvel at the credulity of you ignorant people, I truly do."

Returning along the deck, he purred with amusement and casually drew the twin knives from their sheath. "There can be no future for you out here," he announced. "Your keepers are dead."

The dim glow of the lanterns glanced over the blood-stained blades as they moved towards the apprentice but Adam stood his ground and looked Brindle steadily in the eye. "What do you mean?" he demanded.

"Do you still not perceive the truth of it?" the Iribian taunted. "Those benign tutors you're so in awe of, the ones you named the special ambassadors..."

"That kind people you hunted out of existence!" the boy countered.

"They weren't teachers," Brindle sniggered. "They were collectors! They visited your old world and discovered the wildlife with all its dogma and peculiarities much to their liking. But, oh, how quickly your species perished compared to their own protracted lifespan. That is why you were brought here and amended. Ha! Cog Adam, your precious Englandia with its haughty, conceited monarch is no more than a series of elaborate cages, a playground to be visited and enjoyed at their leisure and you are the exhibits. This uplifted world of yours is a pleasure garden – there was never anything sacred or holy about it."

"You're lying!"

Brindle brought the knives of the reaping hook close to his own face and viewed the boy through the slender gap between the blades.

"It astounds me how you have managed to survive for so long without your caring patrons," he remarked. "Perhaps in that you were indeed blessed, but it cannot continue forever. Structures fail, untended devices falter. My chance arrival amongst you was the real blessing. I shall bring an end to this unnatural menagerie, populated by its mongrel aberrations – verily 'tis the most merciful thing to do."

Adam's head reeled at the Iribian's words; he wanted to deny them and scream but the caravel gave an abrupt lurch and the apprentice thrust all other doubts and fears to the back of his aching mind.

"Don't do this," he begged. "Whatever you think of us, you can't let everyone be murdered. Don't we deserve better than that? Please don't set up the beacon – don't bring your people here."

Brindle pushed the tip of one blade carelessly into the stout mast and carved a snaking line down its length. Beneath his malignant features the luminous sheen pulsed starkly as he regarded Adam and, in a chilling whisper, announced, "'Tis done."

The apprentice shook his head in disbelief. "It can't be," he murmured. "Your torc, it's still working."

"Oh, Cog Adam," the Iribian scoffed, "you know only the rudimentary science of spindle shafts and pendulums.

Even now a summoning call is journeying through the furthest reaches of the desolate night. My homeland will hear it, they will be coming."

Adam's anger scalded inside him and he cried out in rage. "You're obscene!" he shrieked, springing forward to strike Brindle's face with his small fist. "Stop it! You must – stop it!"

The Iribian pushed him away and the boy was flung across the deck, careering into a heap of coiled ropes.

Moving to the prow once more, Brindle gazed out of the window. The massive torso of Gog was scrolling by outside. Up over the darkened city the caravel floated, soaring steadily over the spires and chimneys, into the lofty airs which coursed beneath the leaded firmament.

"Soon the tidal breath will have us," Brindle declared, "and this island will be left behind."

Staggering to his feet, Adam dragged a hand over his eyes, determined not to shed any tears. "So that's it!" he spat. "You run away and hide, waiting for reinforcements. You're as full of big talk as Henry. Not only are you an abhorrence, but you're a craven one at that!"

Brindle whipped around and stormed towards him, cutting the air with his blades. "Be silent!" he thundered, the blue stone in his torc flaring to a dazzling brilliance. "Else I will trim your tongue."

"You're going to butcher me anyway," the boy breathed, undaunted as the knives swept in front of his face. "I'll say what I like. Your deathscent's turned you into a braying coward, far worse than Clink Kitson ever was. It's true: the Brindle you were before was more courageous than you. He was noble and excellent. Mistress Dritchly knew it, that's why she nursed him back to health. That's why he saved Henry and me from Old Scratch. What happened when that better part of you died – did you enjoy the smell of *that* as well?"

"Enough!" Brindle roared and the spectral glare danced beneath his skin as he gripped the reaping hook with trembling hands. "One more insolent word and I harvest your scent now!"

Adam screwed his face into a fierce snarl of hate. "Go on!" he bawled. "Cut me down; I'm the same age as your youngest son. Do you think he'll be proud of what you've done here? When you and your kind have slaughtered us all, I hope your guilt hounds you to everlasting torment. That remorse you spoke of in Lord Richard's garden – I pray it haunts and harries you until the end of your days."

The Iribian towered over him and raised the vicious weapon, ready to strike, but Adam was not finished. A sudden remembrance blazed in his thoughts and he reached inside his tunic, bringing out a broken, thorny stem from which a bedraggled spray of white petals dropped to the floor.

"Here!" the apprentice cried, his voice blaring with condemnation. "There's the only absolution you'll ever receive. Damn you to the eternal fires!" And he violently thrust the eglantine he had plucked from the palace garden straight into Brindle's face.

Incensed, the Iribian snatched the bloom from him and crushed it in his fist.

Holding his breath, Adam waited for the reaping hook to come razoring for his throat but Brindle made no other move. He stood there, transfixed, with his pale, luminous hand shaking and outstretched, his eyes locked on the pathetic, scattered rose petals which had fallen to the deck. Even though the filthy Thames had sullied them, his delicate senses captured the faintest echo of their former perfume. Abruptly, his savage mind flooded with the memory of that sunlit afternoon in Malmes-Wutton.

"The treasure beyond rejoicing – the breath of innocence." The words came croaking from his trembling lips. The battle he had thought was over erupted within him once more and his face distorted grotesquely with unbearable pain and suffering.

Tightly, he squeezed the broken stem until the thorns pierced his palms and glimmering blood trickled between his fingers. Confusion and madness fulminated in his eyes and he blundered back, casting the reaping hook to the floor as a terrible, despairing screech left his lungs.

Adam watched in amazement. The Iribian's flesh throbbed with that deathly light more fiercely than ever and the veins in his temples shone like jags of frozen lightning. Howling, he fell against the canopy and slid down the canvas, writhing in anguish as the two opposing sides of his nature strove for supremacy.

In the gloom of the steerage hold, a stooping skeletal shape left the cabin and prowled forward.

The apprentice thought quickly. He ought to run to the tiller and return the caravel to the river. He didn't want to spend another minute sealed in this cramped space with that deranged monster. Then, watching Brindle squirm helplessly on the floor, an insane impulse urged Adam to go to his aid.

"Don't be a fool!" he upbraided himself. "This is your chance: take up his knives and slay him – kill him now. He was going to murder you – do it, Coggy. It's you or him."

Slowly, the boy reached for the abandoned reaping hook, all the while keeping his eyes trained on the Iribian. Brindle was shrieking in pain, his features contorted in terrible spasms as his pale flesh rippled and quivered with jolts of light. At that moment he was as vulnerable as an infant; ridding the uplifted isles of his terror would be the simple work of a moment.

Adam's fingers closed about the hilt of the reaping hook. It was wet and sticky with blood and, with a yell of disgust, the boy flung it away. Staring at his palm which was now stained crimson, he was appalled at what he had been about to do. Yet the boy was also angry with himself – what other solution was there? Brindle had to die.

"But I can't do it!" he cried wretchedly. "I can't kill him."

While he shivered and wiped his palm, he failed to see a tall, sinister figure emerging from the shadows behind. The Iribian's screeches were deafening now and Adam did not hear the clink of chains as a towering framework advanced with lumbering steps.

Brindle's torment increased, while the slit in his forehead flared and pulsed, gulping at the air with frantic movements like a cruel mouth choking for breath.

Stunned and bewildered, Adam watched as the Iribian's howls reached a crescendo.

"No more!" Brindle screeched suddenly. "No more!" Raising a quivering fist, he drove the rose's thorny stem deep into his gaping nostril. The ensuing scream was hideous. Bright, shining blood flowed down over his face and coursed through his hair as the thorns gouged and tore into the flesh.

"Brindle!" the boy shouted. "What are you—?" With no thought for his own safety, Adam moved nearer. Before he could reach the Iribian, the deck juddered under them both and at last he heard the clang of stomping metal. Recognising that terrible, baneful sound, he whirled around in horror.

Rearing into the canopy's high shadows, the Torture Master loomed over him once more and the boy whimpered with fear as that leering mask swivelled from side to side, gloating at the prospect of finally fulfilling its earlier task.

Terrified, Adam staggered away and went reaching for the discarded reaping hook, but the Spanish mechanical came lumbering after him, its iron claws and implements of torment thrashing through the air.

Just as the apprentice's fingertips brushed against the bloodsoaked hilt for the second time, the terrible pincers clamped sharply about his shoulders and drove into his muscles. Adam yelled, but still he strained and struggled until his hand closed about the weapon. Then he was hauled off the deck and hoisted high.

Oblivious to the nightmare that had come among them, Brindle lay on the floor, staring at his open, bleeding palm, his forehead a tattered mass of torn flesh. The phosphorescent flames which blushed his skin were failing and the blood that streamed down his face was darkening to a putrid orange.

A blast from the Torture Master's bellows fired the coals in its brazier and a long poker was thrust into their centre. Hanging by his shoulders, Adam kicked against the broad, grilled chest, causing the chains within that awful frame to clank wildly. Another whoosh from the bellows made the coals glow an intense yellow and a moment later the poker was withdrawn.

"Not this time, you rickety scrap of dungeon rust!" the boy cried and he lashed out with the twin knives, smiting them against the poker's hinged rod with all his strength.

There was a scream of metal and a spurt of flame as the bar was sliced in two and the length of severed iron clattered to the floor. The bellows roared in fury and the stump of the mutilated rod flicked uselessly on the mechanical's powerful arm. Adam felt the vicelike pincers tighten round his shoulders and he yowled in pain. Extending its limbs with a shrill squeak, the Torture Master lifted the apprentice even higher and shook him violently.

Adam cried out. An iron claw shot towards his hand and the reaping hook was dashed from his grasp. Through the air the blades went spinning, glittering a deadly wheel of reflected light through the shadows until they flew through the canopy, shredding a gaping rent in the canvas. Down through the dark night, the Iribian's weapon spiralled, plummeting eighteen fathoms to the Thames where it sliced into the water and vanished in the polluted depths.

High overhead, silhouetted against the titanic figure of Gog, the ascending caravel looked like a child's toy. The night airs tugged and pulled at the ripped, billowing canvas, tearing an even larger hole in the awning. When those chill winds blew upon Adam's face, he knew that as soon as the tidal breath propelled the night boat beyond the aperture, the airless void would kill both he and Brindle. Through the fluttering gash in the canopy he saw the massive head of the statue come into view; at any moment the barbarian's painted face would turn and catapult them to their deaths.

Yet there was nothing he could do. Manacles snapped about his wrists and the pincers released his shoulders, only for his ankles to be snared in tight iron bands. The boy's hands were thrust above his head and, in measured, ratcheted degrees, the Torture Master began to increase its height, transforming into one of the most agonising instruments – the rack.

Adam felt his back stretch and his vertebrae click. "No!" he beseeched. "You're ripping me in two!"

On the deck, Brindle was quivering. Goose-flesh crawled over every inch of his form as the livid light ebbed from his veins. Drenched in cold sweat and oozing blood, he continued to stare at the thorns in his palm until the boy's shrieks penetrated his jumbled thoughts and he lifted his head in a daze.

The scene before him was horrible. Adam was screaming, his spine pulled to an impossible tautness. With his head thrown back, he saw the Iribian gazing at him and screeched for help. "Please!" he cried. "Brindle!"

But the balm merchant remained on the deck, the dying flickers of the ghostly sheen dissipating through his skin and, with his last breath, Adam cursed him. "You demon!" he choked. "I hope you rejoice in the stink of my death as much as you did the others. Hades take you!"

The boy's hoarse voice rose to a squeal as his back cracked and the repugnant grin on the Torture Master's mask filled his vision. A reverberating jangle of gears and grinding wheels suddenly boomed from inside the great image of Gog and its huge head began to rotate, turning towards the night boat.

Adam's bitter words blistered into Brindle's mind, burning themselves on his conscience. At last the final, lingering traces of the deathscent were expurgated from his veins and his true self gained mastery of his soul. A barrage of emotions exploded in the Iribian's mind, but fury and horror overrode all else when he realised what was happening and the noble Brindle who had valiantly fought against Old Scratch sprang to his feet in a righteous fury.

"Release him!" he commanded fiercely.

The mechanical ignored the demand.

"Put the boy down!"

But the Torture Master obeyed only the Count de Feria and his instructions earlier that evening had been clear – the children were to suffer and die.

Enraged, Brindle rushed forward and seized hold of the vile automaton, pulling on the upraised arms. With a shudder the mighty limbs began to yield to his formidable strength, bending in his straining grasp, and an agonised cry of relief burst from Adam's lips.

Mirroring the movement of the massive effigy outside, the Torture Master's mask slid around to face this unwelcome, powerful assailant and its internals clanged discordantly.

"I said put the child down," Brindle repeated, heaving

the iron limbs out of shape to ease the boy's torment.

In defiance, a spiked club swung out from the mechanical's thigh, striking the Iribian in the side. He crumpled to the deck, relinquishing his hold on the mechanical's arms which redressed the distortion and bounced back into position, forcing Adam to screech with renewed agonies.

Brindle's brows creased in wrath and he threw himself against that infernal creation, avoiding the sadistic implements which flashed out to hit him.

"The ichors!" Adam wept. "Smash them."

Shielded behind the iron lattice of the Torture Master's armoured chest, the phials containing the cordials were out of Brindle's reach. Bawling in thwarted rage, he leaped away but returned an instant later brandishing one of the murdered crewmen's rapiers.

"I will not tell you again!" he thundered and, raising the sword over his head, he plunged it deep into the nightmare's internal workings. There was a shattering of glass and yellow bile squirted into the Iribian's face, but he held on grimly and tried to wrench the foil free for a second destroying thrust. But it would not budge; iron-toothed cogs bit into the steel and chains screeched on their gears, mangling the rapier in a tenacious grip.

A blast of outrage whistled from the bellows as the sudden imbalance of humours inflamed the fury of the Torture Master to a fearful intensity. The manacles holding Adam flew apart and the vengeful device rounded on Brindle.

Yelping, the apprentice slumped to the deck – and at that moment the night boat shook. The tidal breath came galing from the mouth of Gog and tremendous forces began to wind about the vessel's timbers. The ruined canopy was torn asunder and a ragged length ripped free of its framework, to fly twisting into the funnel of air. For a brief moment it whirled in the howling cyclone. Then, with a tremendous rush, it was sucked out into the void.

Around the caravel those squalling forces twined and the din from the canopy's flapping shreds was deafening.

Staring up at the space beneath the giant's axe, Adam looked at the empty darkness beyond. Already he was finding it difficult to breathe. From the deck those objects not fixed down were snatched by the wind and sent shooting through the aperture, while torn rigging lashed perilously like whips overhead.

His long hair streaming wildly in the tempest, Brindle ran to the aftcastle and burst into the steerage hold. But the Torture Master was at his heels and the doorway splintered around its demented, invincible bulk as it came pounding in pursuit, every instrument of torment bristling with malign intent. The low ceiling buckled and smashed before its unstoppable might and the terrible arms demolished the remaining planks, flinging them up into the screaming storm.

Racing to the tiller, the Iribian slammed his body into it and the night boat pitched in the sky, swinging sharply starboard. Flailing its harrowing devices, the mechanical was hurled off balance and went crashing through the wall of de Feria's cabin. The spiked iron head rammed into the hull, bursting through the timbers and, from the brazier in its stomach, the glowing coals exploded. Many went showering down to hiss in the Thames far below, but others shot across the floor where they scorched and smouldered, igniting instant fires.

Brindle's action had jolted the caravel out of the vortex and it dropped alarmingly. The keel collided with Gog's enormous shoulder and an almighty tremor shivered up the three masts. With a crackling groan, the mizzen yard broke free and toppled from the heavens, its sail fluttering after it. Foundering in the air, the night boat twirled downward, scraping against the giant figure as it sank.

Still holding the tiller, Brindle tried to steady her. The caravel veered unsteadily around in a yawing arc and pulled away from the statue, meandering away from the river and over the rooftops. Only then did the Iribian notice, with dismay, bright flames licking up from the wreckage of de Feria's cabin.

Running on deck, he found Adam still lying on the floor, weak and aching.

"The ship is burning, Cog Adam," Brindle told him urgently. "It cannot remain aloft much longer. I'm going to return her to the water as quickly as I can but you must be prepared to jump clear, lest she breaks up too soon."

Fearfully, the apprentice stared up into his mutilated face and was relieved to see that no trace of that brutish primitive remained. The dignity which had once seemed divine and had won the affection of Mistress Dritchly had returned to the Iribian's countenance and the boy smiled. "Brindle," he said warmly. "It's really you, you're back. Henry was right – I should not have doubted."

Taking Adam in his arms, Brindle lifted him gently to his feet. "I deserve no glad greeting," the balm trader uttered gravely. "The guilt is still mine. Many perished at my hands this night. There can be no escaping that. I must submit to your justice and suffer the consequence."

"The Queen will have you executed."

"Then so be it. If it brings an end to this evil I will gladly welcome..."

His words died as he remembered the device he had made to summon the rest of his kind and he reached for the velvet pouch hanging at his waist. But the cord which tied it to his belt had been cut and he turned a horrified expression on Adam.

"The beacon!" he cried. "I have lost it! The call must be silenced – my people must never find this realm."

As the leaping flames spread to the rigging, both of them searched the deck, but the pouch was nowhere to be found.

"It isn't here!" Adam called. "The tidal breath must have hurled it out into the void."

Fiery shreds rained down as the triangular sails began to blaze. Sheltering the boy from them, Brindle led him back to the shattered ruin of the steerage hold.

"Will the beacon still guide your kind here?" Adam demanded.

"Not if it journeys far from this forsaken region," he muttered, stumbling through plumes of thick black smoke and avoiding the fierce heats to return to the tiller. "We must set hope against despair and pray that my race never discover this—"

A horrendous shriek burst from his lips as a long iron needle shot out of the smoke, stabbing him through the arm. Rising from the burning cabin, looking like a mechanical forged in the smithies of Hell, the Torture Master came lumbering for the final confrontation.

"The tiller!" Brindle yelled at Adam. "Take us down."

The boy hesitated, but the balm trader pushed him out of the mechanical's path, yanking the sharp spike from his flesh. Surrounded by flames, the Torture Master lumbered towards them and Brindle staggered away, luring it as far from Adam as possible. The apprentice could only watch in fear as the monstrous invention struck out with its iron claws, slashing mercilessly at the Iribian.

Grappling with the tiller, Adam steered a course back to the river, dipping the prow as low as he dared. Then, braving the searing temperatures, he ran from the refuge of the steerage hold to help Brindle battle the Torture Master.

Into the inferno that the night boat had become he bolted. The remaining masts were now pillars of livid flame and tattered fragments of canvas flowed out like banners of fire. Behind the caravel there streamed a wake of glimmering ash that scintillated in the darkness and, down on London Bridge, the Queen's soldiers and Henry Wattle witnessed that terrifying spectacle in awed silence.

Over Gog's great contours, the infernal glare of the terrible burning flared and flickered as the ship descended, looking like a floating bonfire. Henry bit his lip until it bled.

In the heart of that furnace, Brindle and the mechanical were locked in a desperate combat. Yet the Catholic invention was almost invulnerable and the Iribian could not hope to stop it. Countless cuts and gashes raked his flesh. His garments were torn and quantities of dark orange blood sizzled over the Torture Master's torrefied frame. Pitted against this indomitable foe the Iribian continued to strive, his fists punching into unyielding iron. Blow after blow he struck but it was all in vain - against the Spanish ambassador's sadistic toy there was nothing he could do.

When Adam came running to find him, Brindle was trapped behind a curtain of fire with the fiendish creation standing in its centre, letting the ruddy blaze shoot up through its metal framework.

It was a portrait of evil which the boy would never forget.

Wreathed in dazzling sheets, the mechanical raised its arms, splaying the heinous implements as the painted leer on its mask caught alight. Wearing this diabolic, incandescent grin, the Torture Master brought a heavy mace hammering through the smoke and Brindle was beaten to the floor.

Battered and burned, unable to escape, the Iribian waited for the death blow. But even as the mace plunged down to split his head, Adam o'the Cogs came charging through the fire and rammed his shoulder against the mechanical's mighty casing.

Boosted by the rolling motion of the night boat, the boy's valiant lunge was enough to send the devilish device toppling. In a scorching blast of heat it went crashing through the deck and fell into the hold beneath.

His hair singed and steaming, Adam somehow dragged Brindle to the side. The caravel was beginning to break up. Charred and glowing timbers flaked from the hull; soon the entire ship would disintegrate and he stared over the deck rail. The Thames was still many fathoms below, but there was no other chance left to them.

"We have to make a leap for it!" he yelled.

The Iribian nodded feebly. He had lost a lot of blood and was weakened and shaken but, leaning briefly on the rail, his confidence rekindled and the emerald horseshoes of his eyes gleamed at Adam through the smoke.

"I am ready," he declared. "You and I, together."

Quickly they swung their legs over the side and prepared to jump. Behind them the fires roared more furiously than ever and, as the planks of the deck began to collapse and the foremast ruptured and split into forks of flame, they threw themselves from the ravaged ship.

Yet in that same instant a skeletal figure punched its way from the hold and an iron manacle snapped around Brindle's wrist.

Through the night Adam plummeted alone, a tiny, wriggling shape tumbling from the heavens. By the time he splashed into the river, the Iribian had already been hoisted back on to the night boat to continue the deadly contest.

Into the deep, cold Thames the apprentice fell, submerging beneath the surface for what seemed like an eternity. Then up he came, spluttering and gasping, shocked at the sudden change from roasting to freezing. Churning his arms through the water, he whisked about and sought for Brindle. Then, hearing shouts high aloft, he realised what had happened.

"No," he whispered. "NO!"

On board the caravel the fight was almost finished. Surrounded by flames, the Torture Master crushed the Iribian to its horrendous frame. Shackles and bonds lashed tightly about Brindle's limbs until he could barely move. Then cruel spikes came pushing from the grilled chest to impale him.

Gritting his teeth, Brindle seized hold of the breast-plate and, with the last ounce of his dying strength, twisted and prised one of the iron bands out of shape, exposing the remaining ichor bottles within.

The blank mask switched feverishly from side to side as the Torture Master tried to stop him, but it was too late. The Iribian's fists reached into the meagre opening and ripped the phials from their pipes.

"Your ambassador is going to have to find himself a new plaything!" he shouted and he smashed the ichors against the blank metal mask.

A whining squeal of metal signalled the end. The Torture Master's internals ground to a halt and the pendulums were stilled. Inside the head the chains ceased clanking and the harrowing contraption was merely a distorted parody of a human shape – inert, grotesque and lifeless.

The traps and shackles which held Brindle captive sprang apart and he rolled from its spikes, the front of his body punctured by horrible wounds. Clutching his stomach, he staggered to his feet. The night boat was almost totally consumed. The flames scorched and blistered him but he threw himself towards the side in a last effort to escape.

Before he reached the edge, the main mast collapsed, crashing down into the stern and the violence of its ruin tipped the caravel almost vertical. Brindle was thrown back, into the burning steerage hold and the unwieldy framework of the stilled Torture Master was sent rolling through the choking smoke after him.

Having swum to the shore, Adam crawled from the river and cast himself on to the muddy bank, staring fearfully up at the final minutes of the fire ship.

"Come on," he prayed. "Get out of there." Yet, even as he voiced those words, he knew that if the Iribian managed to survive that furnace he would be killed for his crimes.

"He's dead either way," the boy murmured.

His upturned face dripping with slime from the river, Adam watched the final, spectacular moments unfold. Pitched in that near upright tilt, the blazing night boat was rising again, heading straight for the aperture in the firmament once more.

In the burning aftcastle, the Iribian's legs were pinned under the mechanical's crushing weight and he was now too weak to lift it. Beyond the fume and the glare, he beheld the massive head of Gog begin to turn towards that incinerated vessel and he laughed bleakly. Although his many nostrils burned, the hair shrivelled on his head and the garments given to him by Mistress Dritchly burst into devouring flame, he knew that his life was not destined to be claimed by the fires.

From the mouth of the giant barbarian the tidal breath came whirling. The fire-enveloped craft was seized in those supreme forces and shining tongues went streaking through the twisting airs – out into the airless void. Caught in the swirling vortex, the cindered timbers of the night boat cracked and splintered. Flaming sections detached, to be shot through the aperture and, at once, the intense crackling fires were quenched.

In the heart of that bright, seething maelstrom Brindle grinned as he sang out the names of his wife and children.

Far below, Adam watched aghast as the burning speck above was drawn ever closer to the entrance in the firmament and his scorched, muddy face ran with tears.

"Brindle," he breathed.

Suddenly, from that remote inferno, a familiar, laughing voice called out, "Purity and absolution."

And the apprentice knew that the words were meant for him to hear. Brindle had forgiven himself and found his peace at last.

With a roaring whoosh, the remains of the night boat were catapulted through the aperture. Immediately the flames were extinguished and so was the laughter.

Floating through the Outer Darkness a fragile, blackened hulk began a silent, endless journey. On the shore of the Thames, Adam o'the Cogs bowed his head.

A New Apprenticeship

Concentrating on the task he had set himself, Adam squinted down the length of brass pipe in his hands. Poking a long, thin brush into the slender tube, he twirled it fiercely until he was satisfied that all was clean within.

Lying upon the table in front of him were the disassembled pieces of a wooden mannequin – the Tizzy that the Queen had stilled on that fateful night. Adam returned the pipe to its correct position inside the workings. Two weeks had passed since that terrible time. Restoring the mannequin had been a consummate challenge but now the task was nearing completion.

Every feeder tube had been painstakingly washed and checked, and those parts that had been corroded by the Count de Feria's malignant indigo ichor had been replaced.

Perched on a stool at his side sat Lantern. The copper secretary observed all that the boy did and nodded approvingly.

Holding up a small burnished wheel so that the light flashed over its surface, Adam was reminded of the blazing night boat which had been catapulted through the tidal breath. Hardly a moment passed without him thinking of it and the boy shook himself, endeavouring to dislodge that painful memory.

Much had happened in the intervening weeks. It had taken a whole six days for Her Majesty to calm down. At first she had unfairly blamed Lord Richard for daring to bring the Iribian to court and threatened him with all manner of dire punishments, including banishment to the Tower. Eventually, however, Walsingham and Doctor Dee persuaded her that it was no one's fault but Brindle's.

Since then she had been sullen and yesterday had capriciously removed herself to the palace at Richmond, compelling the astonished court to follow her. Only Doctor Dee remained behind at Whitehall, for there were still matters which needed his attention.

Throughout this time Lord Richard and the apprentices

had been the guests of the old astrologer and it was in his apartments that Adam discovered the discarded Tizzy and busied himself with its repairs.

Now, staring at his work, he inspected the three pendulums in the mannequin's back and looked abstractly at the replenished ichor bottles.

"You waste your time with that," a voice broke into his thoughts.

Doctor Dee was standing in front of the circular window, peering out through the coloured panes, absently twirling a finger through the ends of his long, white beard.

"Her Majesty will not want the Tizzy back in her service, even if you have remedied the harm done by the Spanish ambassador. She still believes it had the shaking sickness and would rather open the palace to lepers than be seen to own so tainted an automaton."

Adam shrugged. Now more than ever he needed to keep himself busy. Only that morning Lord Richard and Henry Wattle had left the isle of London and commenced the journey back to Malmes-Wutton without him.

"This really is the best arrangement," the old man said gently. "Richard Wutton has many debts. I have paid him most handsomely for your apprenticeship. How else was he to replace all those costly mechanicals destroyed by that wild boar of his? I have been more than generous, young Adam. There might even be enough left over to restock his wine cellar."

The boy was only half listening. Three short hours ago he had bade farewell to Henry and his former master. It had been an emotional parting and even Henry had snivelled into his sleeve, rashly promising to undo the mischief he had made with the rats by creating a mechanical cat for Mistress Dritchly. Then their night boat had pulled away from the river stairs and journeyed under the bridge before rising up and passing beneath the great axe of Gog. Standing on the steps, Adam was left with a dreadful sense of loss and felt completely alone. He had never wanted to leave Malmes-Wutton and now here he was beginning a new life in the city of London as apprentice to the Queen's astrologer.

Momentarily lifting his gaze, he found that Doctor Dee was staring at him and a benign smile lifted the corners of that silvery white beard.

"Trust me, Adam," the Doctor said. "This existence will commend itself to you in time. There is far too much skill in your fingers and your brains to squander them in the backwater of Richard's petty estate. Your mind is hungry for knowledge; with myself as your tutor, that famine will be appeased."

The boy lowered his eyes. Part of the reason he felt so miserable was because he was actually looking forward to working for the astrologer and could not help feeling guilty and disloyal to Lord Richard.

Lifting the Tizzy so that it sat stiffly up on the table,

he made the final adjustments and prepared to press the Tudor rose set into its forehead.

"There's no guarantee you have eradicated the problem," Doctor Dee told him. "We know too little about the fatal Spanish ichor. If, when you hit that stilling crest, the Tizzy continues to shudder and reaches for something to hurl at us, then all your work will have been in vain."

Adam glanced at the carved wooden face of the serving maid. He was confident he had removed every trace of the insidious blue ichor and that it was now perfectly harmless.

"I know my trade," he said firmly.

"Then prove it, Adam o'the Cogs," the astrologer chuckled. "Why do you waver?"

Before his fingers touched the carved rose, the boy frowned as a sudden idea seized him.

"I'll show you how much I trust my own abilities," he announced and he reached into the pocket of his jerkin to take out a small glass phial. It contained the black cordial of Suet – the only part of the little piglet that remained – and Adam gazed at it thoughtfully.

Beside him, the green lenses of Lantern's eyes glimmered with understanding as, with expert hands, Adam quickly fitted Suet's ichor into the Tizzy. Then he closed its back plate and deftly pushed the stilling crest.

At once the mannequin jerked into life, the ichors rushed through its pipes and the pretty carved head switched from side to side as it took in the unfamiliar surroundings. Holding his breath, Adam took a step back and watched intently, but the Tizzy showed no sign of any trembling and merely waited for its first command.

Rising from the stool, Lantern began to applaud and the boy laughed, but Doctor Dee tutted into his beard.

"Once more I admire your skill, young Adam, but again I tell you, no one will want this creation. You will never be able to rid yourself of it."

"I don't know," Adam answered. "It might be useful."

The astrologer shook his head. "As firewood only, I fear," he sighed. Then he called the boy over to the window and gestured to the haze of buildings jostling beyond the curve of the river.

"Look at that great city," he muttered, his tone becoming serious. "Is it not wondrous fair? I pray that it remains so, yet I have foreseen dangerous times ahead. Englandia will have need of fighting machines, not housemaids. Walsingham has intercepted new intelligences: the war with Spain is fast approaching." A piercing glint shone from beneath the Doctor's brows and he whispered darkly under his breath, "When the Catholic storm breaks, we must be ready."

Ambling after them, Lantern slid his gauntleted hand into Adam's and gave it a squeeze of friendship. Doctor Dee's face had clouded with the grave futures he predicted and they all stared out at the spires and rooftops of London.

Behind them, the Tizzy's attention was attracted by its own discarded workings which were scattered over the tabletop and began playing with them. Picking up a brass pipe, it gazed at the corroded holes and tilted its head on one side.

"There is much to be done," Doctor Dee declared darkly. "We can no longer fritter away time and resources. Deadly work lies before us and we had best begin at once. The safety of the realm is in our hands; perilous adventures await each one of us."

Adam opened his mouth to speak, then gasped as an unexpected sound startled him and they all whirled swiftly around.

Still sitting upon the table, the Tizzy had raised the pipe to its wooden lips. As its internal bellows blew and the jointed fingers danced over the holes, Edwin Dritchly's favourite tune floated up into the air.

"*O Mistress Mine...*" Adam smiled.

In his cabin, on board a night galleon bound for the isles of Spain, the Count de Feria read through his correspondence and set quill to parchment to write a letter of his own. With a flourishing hand, he addressed it to King Philip himself and, in cypher, set down all that he knew concerning the heavenly messenger.

A momentary chill passed through him when he recalled

that fearful night upon London Bridge. He had barely escaped with his life and he made certain that the King was fully cognisant of the valiant part he had played in the whole, mysterious affair.

Don Gomez de Feria had never before experienced such extreme terror but now the trauma was past he complimented himself on his courage, reflecting that the night had not been a complete failure. Pushing the tip of his tongue into the gap where his rotten tooth had ached so bitterly, he thanked the fist that had punched him in the jaw. The offending molar had shot from his mouth in what was the most painless extraction he had ever experienced.

There was, of course, another bonus gleaned from that frightful time scrabbling beneath the royal guard's mechanical horse and he lifted a velvet pouch from a small jewel box. Wearing a delighted grin, he foraged inside and took out the souvenir he had brought back from the bridge that night.

Now, holding it between his fingers, he marvelled at the precious thing. Resembling a golden tadpole, set with a wondrous blue stone that blinked and pulsed with an inner light, it was a curious device and the Spanish ambassador was captivated by its strange beauty.

"Is so fair," he cooed. "I have it set into brooch – oh yes, most pleasing. It bring Don Gomez much luck he thinks."